Ridiculous

by D.L. Carter

Cover Design by Amber Scott
ebook: ISBN- 9781794241183

D.L. Carter LLC

Dedication

Although she is no longer with us, I would like to thank Mrs. Fuller, my high school English teacher. Believe it or not, I have a variety of learning disabilities which makes it difficult for me to spell words correctly or consistently. This issue got me placed, briefly, in the Special Learning track at school. It was Mrs. Fuller who noticed that I was carrying Lord of the Rings around with me one day and asked why I was carrying a book for someone else. Obviously, someone as disabled as me could not possibly be reading it herself. Ha! When I demonstrated I was able to READ even if I couldn't write she had me bounced back to the regular classes. Even though the rules of English Lit. required her to mark me down for each and every grammatical error and spelling mistake she would write, in some amazement I remember, how impressed she was with the breadth and comprehensive nature of my imagination.

Many years later I still remember her telling me to put the story down on paper somehow. The publishers will hire someone to fix the little things. It was the story that counted.

So, Hi to Mrs Fuller and all her ilk. Thank you from a C+ student.

Chapter One

"Dear Heavenly Father, protect us!" came a shout from the master bedroom. "He is dead!"

Millicent Boarder raised her eyes to heaven, sighed, then gathered the clean bed linens more tightly to her chest and ran the last few steps to the upper landing. A loud and sincere wailing followed the shout, but even without that guide, Millicent knew where to go. There was, after all, but one "he" in this household – her second cousin, Mr. Anthony North, now apparently deceased.

Also summoned by the shouting, Mildred emerged from the doorway to the servant's staircase.

"Whatever is the matter?" whispered Mildred. "I have but this moment soothed Maude to sleep."

Millicent continued down the corridor, glancing back at her middle sister.

"It would appear that Mr. North has had the bad taste to die."

"Oh, Lord," cried Mildred, turning deathly pale and stumbling to a halt, one hand clutched to her chest. "Whatever shall we do?"

"Have the grace to control yourself." Millicent pushed the oak door open with her shoulder. "I cannot be calming both you and Mother. One of you will have to wait."

With a shrug Mildred considered this comment, composed herself, and trailed along behind Millicent. Inside the bedchamber their mother, the widow Felicity Boarder, sat on the floor beside the master's great bed, her face buried in her skirts. Millicent left it to Mildred to rush to their mother's side to try to stop the wailing.

Instead, with a firm and steady step, Millicent moved to the bedside. The chest of the man who lay there did not rise and fall. His pinched and reddened nose did not flare and the hands so often raised to strike, pinch, or grope lay limp and curled on the counterpane.

"Shake him. Oh, shake him, Millicent," cried Felicity. "He may be sleeping only."

"Through this caterwauling?" Millicent cast a disdainful glance at her mother. "I very much doubt it."

Instead of releasing a fresh wave of tears, Felicity raised her reddened face to her daughter.

"What are we to do?" she asked in a helpless, childlike voice. "Where are we to go? If it were not for Mr. North taking us in..."

"Yes. Yes," said Millicent briskly, most of her attention directed toward straightening the cooling limbs. "Surely, he was the most generous man in Christendom to take in a widowed cousin and her three daughters and put them to work as unpaid maids, cooks, and housekeepers. If we are very, *very* lucky, we shall never see his like again."

"He may have been unkind..." began Felicity.

"And cruel and spiteful and heartless," added Mildred.

"But he gave us shelter when even his brother would not." Felicity twisted her apron between shaking fingers. "Perhaps ... perhaps if I write and say how
useful we were to his brother, Perceval would take us in now."

"I beg you would not," said Mildred with a shudder. "I do not want to volunteer my labors in yet another miserly relative's home for no wages and even less consideration."

"But what else can we do?" Felicity's voice rose; and she sobbed into her apron.

Millicent and Mildred exchanged tired glances. A dull thump came from above their heads.

"Maude must be awake," said Mildred. "The fever is broken, but she is weak yet. What shall I tell her?"

"Tell her everything will be well," replied Millicent.

"You cannot lie to her," cried Felicity.

"Mother, please. If you cannot be composed, at least be silent. I am trying to think."

Millicent stared down at the vessel which had once contained her cousin's soul.

Strange, she thought, how small he seemed now. No longer the monster of her day-to-day life since they had come three years ago. No, not now. Instead, he was a withered thing, pitiable and fragile. Millicent stretched her long-fingered hand out beside his.

How odd that she had not realized that the man had been much the same height as she. His hair, the same sandy color. Surely, she had been given ample opportunity for study. As she wrote with the neatest script and possessed the best mind for numbers of her family, her near-blind cousin had dictated all his business letters to Millicent. She was the one who had spent hours in his study, bent over ledgers and documents while he had stood only inches from her chair.

He claimed to be blind, but Millicent suspected he was merely nearsighted and too much a pinchpenny to invest in proper eyeglasses. And after glancing up one morning to see the man smirking at her bosom from a distance of only a few inches, Millicent took to wearing shapeless dresses with necklines up to her ears.

"Perhaps if we summoned the doctor?" suggested Felicity.

"That drunk? To do what?" demanded Mildred. "His visit yesterday did no good. He wanted to bleed all of us, including the healthy. 'Tis his answer for all ills. The last time I checked, bleeding was not the cure for death!"

Millicent's attention wandered back to her cousin's hair and she ran her fingers over her own tightly braided bun as she thought. The idea teasing in the back of her mind was so strange, so audacious that she could not put it to words.

And yet, it could be the only thing that would save her mother and sisters from a return to the workhouse and years of degradation and poverty.

"Mildred, dear," said Millicent in a soft and absent tone. "Be so kind as to run down to the sewing room and fetch the shears. On the way back, go to our room and fetch my brown gown."

Their mother's head came up in an instant.

"Millicent? Mildred? What are you about?"

Millicent yanked down the sweat stained and soiled sheets that covered her cousin and began removing his nightshirt as Mildred fled the room.

"Millicent! Stop!" Felicity climbed to her feet. "This is unseemly."

"He's dead, Mother," said Millicent. "He cannot be shocked."

"But ... but, what are you doing? I insist you tell me at once."

Millicent fetched a bowl of cold water and a cloth from the nearby table and began washing the body.

"Millicent!"

"Mother," said Millicent, as Mildred returned, breathless and burdened. "You best begin referring to me as Mr. North."

"What?" cried Mildred and Felicity together.

"We will send one of the gardeners down to the village, to the vicar, with the message that Millicent Boarder has just died and Mr. North, concerned about further contagion, wants her out of the house and buried immediately. The vicar, of course, will protest that the grave cannot be dug until tomorrow, what with the freezing rain. He will call to offer condolences and bring his brother the undertaker. By the time they arrive, we will have Mr. North dressed in my gown, wrapped up, and ready for encoffining."

"Millicent, you cannot be serious," said Felicity, her shocked voice barely louder than a mouse's whisper. "This is obscene. You cannot do that to Mr. North's body. God will never forgive you."

"And being homeless and penniless is not obscene?" demanded Millicent. "Did Mr. North ever, in life, spend one moment's thought on our care or future? No, he did not. And I will not worry one moment about the damage to my soul, what little there might be, if we bury him under my name while I take on his. God has other business more important than me to occupy his time."

"But you cannot. You are a woman." Felicity gestured towards Millicent's bosom.

"How kind of you to notice."

"Millicent? What about the chemise and stays?" asked Mildred.

"Mildred, you cannot be thinking of aiding Millicent in this mad venture!" cried Felicity.

Millicent glanced back at her sister with a frown. "You would want to wear stays once you are dead?"

That thought caused Mildred some confusion, as if the rest of the conversation were entirely normal and ordinary, and the subject of stays the most astonishing thought to cross her mind today.

"Well, I should feel undressed without my chemise at the very least. Besides, the more layers of fabric we dress him in the less likely anyone is to notice he is not a she."

"Good point," said Millicent.

"Girls, you cannot do this. It is the most ridiculous thing I have ever heard. Millicent, you cannot impersonate him. Mr. North is known in the neighborhood. Worse, you would have to wear breeches. People will see your lower limbs. You will be found out in an instant and we shall be shunned. Far better to throw ourselves on the mercy of your cousin Perceval. He will have both Anthony's and his own estates now. He can afford to be charitable."

"*Worse* I shall have to wear breeches? *Worse?*" Millicent came to her full height and glared down at her mother.

She never in her life had been so angry. Not when she had learned that her father had made no plan, had written no will for the protection of his wife and children and what little he had possessed had gone to male relatives. Not when she had been turned out of her home, forced to endure months of degradation and uncertainty in the workhouse then forced to fetch and carry for an abusive and unfeeling cousin. Never.

Until this moment she had not realized it was possible to tower in her own rage.

"Do you believe, Mother, that it is better for us to be penniless dependents? To be servants? To be slaves to the whims of miserly men? That it necessary we permit everything we own to be taken from us, as when Father died? Heaven forbid we protest. Heaven forbid we take action to protect ourselves." Millicent fairly vibrated in her anger. "Do you believe it better that we starve in the street rather than I should wear men's trousers? We may die of starvation, but at least we will have maintained the proprieties; that is the most important thing! By God, Mother, are you so lost to simple sense that propriety is more important to you than life itself?"

"Yes. No. Oh, Millicent. Do not shout at me. I am so afraid."

"Then let me take care of you. Please, Mother, I can do this."

"Think of your sisters. Think of the disgrace when you are found out. You cannot shame them like this."

"Oh, really, Mother," said Mildred. "I agree with Millicent. Indeed, we are lucky that she can attempt this. I am too short for such a thing, with too much bosom. No one would be deceived for a moment. But Millicent is tall; everyone will believe she is a man."

Millicent grinned down at her sister. That was the simple, honest truth. Though there was only one year difference in their ages, Millicent towered over her middle sister. She was, in fact, taller than most of their acquaintances. Her sisters and mother were all tiny pocket Venuses with thick golden curls, as opposed to Millicent's straight sandy hair that resisted the most tightly knotted curling papers – back when they had time to bother with such things. Their petite forms were graced with generous curves and tiny waists. Compared to them, Millicent frequently felt like a hulking giantess. A skinny, flat-chested giantess. Well, to be honest she did have bosoms, but she anticipated no particular difficulties concealing them. The only thing the women had in common were eyes of golden brown that glowed catlike when strong emotion moved them.

"I will fetch a chemise and stays … well, no, not the stays," said Mildred thoughtfully. "You are right, of course. We deserve to be comfortable in our graves, if nowhere else."

"But it will not work," repeated Felicity.

"Mother!" Millicent stopped, sighed, and continued in a softer tone. "Let us at least try and see what we can make of him. Consider the alternatives."

Mildred returned with chemise, stockings, and shoes and the two women set to work dressing the body.

"We have to work quickly while the body is still soft," said Millicent.

"His hair is a problem. 'Tis too short," said Mildred.

"I told you it would not work," murmured Felicity and was ignored.

"We have to cut my hair, anyway," said Millicent. "Fortunately, he and I are of much the same shade. If we cut my hair while it is still in braids and wrap them around his head…?"

"It will fall off or come undone." Mildred finished her task of tying frayed ribbons to hold up Mr. North's stockings. "Wait. I have an idea."

Shortly thereafter, they were finished. Millicent's hair was shorn, shorter than Uncle North's and loops of her carefully braided hair were sewn to a frilly cap Mildred had found and tied onto the dead man's head. It took all three women working together to carry the heavy body out of the master bedroom and down the corridor to an empty guest room. The body was dressed in Millicent's oldest brown dress, arms folded over the flat bosom, masculine hands hidden beneath a bouquet of dried flowers from the still room and the whole wrapped tightly in old, patched but clean sheets, awaiting the arrival of the undertaker.

As soon as the body was prepared, Millicent and Mildred set to work on Millicent's transformation. Her face was whitened with flour and her nose reddened with rouge. Her recently trimmed hair was hidden under a sleeping cap. Dressed in her cousin's thick powdering gown and with the room curtains closed tight, the two women hoped that their trick would succeed. Sitting up in the recently vacated master's bed, Millicent huddled under the quilts just as a heavy cart rumbled into the forecourt.

It was decided that Mildred should handle the vicar and his brother since Felicity could not yet be relied upon. Instead Felicity was banished to the servant rooms in the attic where Mr. North insisted the women should live, to sit with Maude.

Three years ago, after the death of her husband had left them alone and penniless, Felicity wrote politely to all her acquaintances and relatives explaining her plight and that of her three daughters. The first round of letters was met with universal rejection. A second set of letters, desperate and begging, went out. That time Felicity received but one positive reply, from Mr. Anthony North.

Relieved, the women had traveled to Mr. North's principal estate in north Yorkshire to be met with the news that Mr. North had dismissed all his female servants in anticipation of the Boarder family arrival. It was his expectation that those positions would be filled, unpaid, by the bereaved ladies. Without other recourse, the ladies had done so for three long years.

Everyone in the neighborhood knew about Mr. North's nip-farthing ways; therefore, the vicar was not surprised when Mildred answered the door instead of a footman, butler, or housekeeper, and led the way upstairs to where the body rested. Mildred's fingers were tight crossed behind her back all the time the vicar and undertaker stood beside the bed. At any moment she expected an outcry. To her relief and astonishment, neither man protested – "surely this is no woman." Indeed, the undertaker barely glanced at the body, spending more time staring about the room at the furnishings.

"My mother is upstairs with Maude," said Mildred, after Mr. Abram, the vicar, said a short prayer over the deceased. "We are still concerned about the health of my youngest sister. Fortunately, Mr. North's fever has broken. He is still weak and would prefer no visitors."

"The neighborhood has been much afflicted by this fever," said Mr. Abram. "This is hardly my first visit to a house today for this same sad reason. We must pray for Mr. North's and Miss Maude's continued improvement."

"I must speak to Mr. North, at least," rumbled the undertaker. "I must have instructions regarding the coffin."

Mildred blinked, then realized what the man meant. He wanted to know how much Mr. North, known skinflint, was prepared to pay for the burial of a woman who had been, for all intents and purposes, his maid.

"And I must speak to him regarding the eulogy," added Mr. Abram.

Another petition for money.

With a nod Mildred led them to the master bedroom. After a soft knock, she opened the door and permitted the two men to precede her. If this subterfuge were going to fail, it was best they know it now when they could still pass it off as Millicent's miraculous recovery.

"Mr. North," said Mr. Abram with a cough to clear his throat. "Please accept my condolences on your loss."

"Keep away from me," rasped Millicent and covering her face, went into a spasm of sneezing and coughing. "I have barely survived one foul pestilence; I do not need yours."

"My apologies." The vicar retreated a few steps.

"And close the door. You are letting in drafts."

With the light from the corridor blocked by the door, the bedchamber was plunged into a deep gloom, making it impossible to tell if the figure in the bed were male or female. Even so, Millicent took no chance. Covering her face with a large handkerchief, she sank further back under the many coverlets and quilts.

"What do you want?" she demanded in a hoarse whisper.

"I only wish to know about the funeral…"

"Take the body away and put it in the ground," snarled Millicent. "Do you not know your own business?"

"Ah." The vicar blushed and glanced across at Mildred, who put a suitably distressed expression on her face.

"Mother would appreciate it if the body could rest here tonight," said Mildred hesitantly, "so we may take leave of our sister."

"There is no need for that," muttered Millicent around another faked sneeze.

"Please, sir." Mildred did a fair job of pretending to be meek and grieving. "I will never see my sister again."

"All right, damn you. Just keep it far from me," said Millicent.

"Do you have a particular preference for her placement in the cemetery?" pressed the vicar.

"I shall not pay to have that worthless chit buried under the nave if that is what you are getting at," growled Millicent. "Bury her with the paupers; it matters not at all to me, but she must be out of the house at first light."

Both Mr. Abram and the undertaker paled at that cruel dismissal. Mildred managed a choked sob that she covered when the figure in the bed turned to glare in her direction.

"About the coffin. I have a fine…" began the undertaker.

"Wrap her in newspaper. Put her in a sack like a drowned cat. I will give you one pound between you. Do what you will with her."

Wisely, neither man asked about grave markers.

"Fetch my purse," commanded Millicent, pointing to where it rested on a dressing table.

Weeping softly, Mildred carried it, unopened, to the bed. Millicent muttered and grumbled as she searched vaguely through the contents. She knew Mr. North's habits better than anyone. She made sure to caress each coin, rubbing it between thumb and finger before returning rejected coins to the purse. Eventually, she drew forth ten tarnished shillings that she counted one by one into Mildred's hand to be carried to the vicar.

"I shall not be well enough to attend the internment," said Millicent, as the men retreated from the room, "and her sisters and mother, well, rather than allow them to cause a scene, I shall keep them home, as is proper; there will be no need for church prayers."

The two men bowed their way out of the

bedchamber without meeting Mildred's eyes. With the aid of the gardener, and with Mildred watching from the shadows to be sure no one closely examined the body, Mr. North was encoffined in a thin pine box and carried down to the drawing room.

"I will be back first thing tomorrow to collect her," said the undertaker with a professional pretense of sympathy.

"Thank you for your kindness," said Mildred.

As soon as the men departed, Millicent descended from where she had kept watch from the top of the stairs.

"We did it," cried Millicent. "They did not suspect a thing."

"You were everything that was miserly, mean, and unfeeling," said Mildred, hugging her sister. "Of course they believed you were Mr. North."

"It will not work, you know," said their mother, emerging from the servant's stairs. "You cannot go into local society. Mr. North may not have gone about much, but he was well enough known hereabouts. One day, two at the most, is all we have. We should pack our bags, take as much as we can carry that can be sold, and leave tonight."

"Mother, you underestimate me," said Millicent. "I have been giving the matter some thought while we waited and I know exactly what to do. Mr. North may have gone about in *local* society, but since he inherited he has not ventured further from this estate than twenty miles." She paused and grinned at her sister.

"In a few days, we are going to put the story about that Mr. North has recovered somewhat from his
fever and he has decided to go to Bath, where no one knows him, to take the waters for his health."

"And taking us with him?" asked Mildred. "Why would he?"

"But of course. Otherwise, he would have to hire servants in Bath, and you know how expensive city servants are. Far better to have us since we cost him no more than food and lodging. We will hire local people to clean and maintain this house, to scrub it from top to bottom, and drive out the disease while he is away."

"That is all very well to say," said Felicity. "But we have no money to live in Bath."

Millicent rolled her eyes and glanced across at her grinning sister. "Mother, you forget. I shall be traveling as Mr. North. We have his money!"

Felicity waved a hand around the gloomy hallway. "Look at the way he lived. He had little. We must be careful to husband every penny."

"He may have given you and everyone hereabouts the impression that was the case, but it is not true. I have been managing Mr. North's accounts and correspondence for three years, Mother. He has an annual income of nearly twenty thousand pounds. He lived like this because he was a mean, unimaginative miser."

"Why did you not say?" demanded Felicity.

"Would it make any difference? He made it clear to me he had no intention of paying us a salary no matter what his income was. I did not want to torment you with the knowledge."

"We are rich! Rich!" Mildred laughed and clapped her hands. "Excellent. Then we can afford to
hire staff. I so look forward to having a bath I have not had to heat and haul the water for myself. Dresses. Hats. Oh, I do long to wear gloves without holes again. My hands are so cold!"

"And so you shall," Millicent assured her.

"But, you are not looking to the future," Felicity's teeth worried at her lower lip. "This masquerade cannot hope to succeed."

"That is because you have only seen me in my night cap and powdering gown. Come, Mildred. Let us garb Mr. North in his Sunday best, such as it is." Holding hands, the two women ran upstairs to plunder Mr. North's dressing room.

The late Mr. North was so much a miser that most of his clothes had been obtained secondhand, and, therefore, not tailored to his form. Likewise, he was not much concerned with fashion and content for his clothing to hang loosely on his skinny body; he did not bother with the expense of a valet, or fancy cravats and such.

It felt quite peculiar, Millicent found, to put off her chemise and stays and wrap layer upon layer of Mr. North's cravats about her torso to bind down her breasts. None of his collars were particularly high, but the cravat Mildred tied was good enough to conceal Millicent's lack of an Adam's apple. Millicent was quite shocked to discover how close in size and form she and her cousin were. Even his shoes fit, after a fashion, once she had layered on two pairs of knitted stockings. Mr. North's one and only walking stick and hat were fetched from the hall closet to complete the ensemble.

At last Mildred led the way downstairs and halted just inside the drawing room where Felicity waited with the closed coffin.

"May I present Mr. North of Yorkshire," declared Mildred waving her hand toward the door; Millicent entered, swinging Mr. North's cane, then made an elegant leg toward her mother.

Felicity came to her feet with an astonished cry.

"Dear God," cried Felicity. "I never realized how masculine your features are, Millicent!"

"Why, thank you, Mother," replied Millicent dryly, straightening up from her bow.

"No, my dearest." Felicity fluttered her hands in the air. "I do not mean to say that you are not handsome as a girl, but you quite surprise me as a man."

Felicity cast her eyes over Millicent's form as the girl bowed her acknowledgment of the compliment, then turned to bow to her sister.

"Millicent, you should be more careful. Do not bow so deeply," cried Felicity. "It pulls the fabric too tight across your ... sitting area. Perhaps you would do better in knee breeches. Or with a longer frock coat."

"With knee breeches she would have only silk stockings from knee to ankles," replied Mildred with a laugh.

"Something must be done." Felicity blushed for her daughter. "No. No, I cannot permit it, Millicent. You must go upstairs and dress properly at once. We shall write and take our chances with Cousin Perceval."

"Mother." Millicent paused, coughed, and continued in a lower tone. Only she of her sisters did not possess a soprano voice and had been content with contralto. Now she concentrated on speaking from the
bottom of her vocal range. "Cousin Felicity. This will
never work if you are forever fussing about my limbs being exposed, or my way of walking and talking. You should begin now, and forever after, to address me as Mr. North."

"Millicent..." began Felicity.

"Cousin Felicity, please remember your daughter Millicent died today. There is her coffin," said Millicent, pointing at the sad pine box. "I am Mr. North."

"This will never work," moaned Felicity.

"Say it," cried Millicent. "Say 'Good morning, Mr. North.'"

"Oh, dear. I cannot."

"Say it," shouted both her daughters.

"Millicent…"

"Millicent is dead," cried Mildred. "I grieve for her, but it is for the best. Mother, I do not wish to go to the work house. I do not wish to get a job as a maid, or a governess or heaven spare us, sell myself on the street for bread. You saw it, did you not, while we were there in the workhouse. Those poor women giving themselves to strangers in the back alley for a few pennies. Is that what you want for yourself? For me?"

Felicity rocked back and forth with both hands pressed to her face.

"Say it," said Millicent in a gentler voice, resting one hand on her mother's bent shoulder. "Call me Mr. North and I promise you, you will have servants tending you for the rest of your life. Hot chocolate in bed. Beautiful clothes. You will never have to worry again. I shall put Mr. North's wealth to work providing you with a good and safe home!"

After a long pause, Felicity raised a pale face and regarded her daughters. She glanced upstairs toward the place where her youngest lay sleeping off a fever, her body weakened by the ravages of three years of hard work and privation. Then she looked Millicent directly in the eye, rose to her feet, and gave a curtsy worthy of the Queen's drawing room.

"Mr. North, how good to see you looking so well."

Later as the women took supper at the kitchen table, Felicity returned, reluctantly, to practical matters.

"I suppose if you stay indoors and avoid society no one will see you and find you out," said Felicity, staring at her eldest daughter as if she had never seen her before. "Be honest, Millicent. You are tall for a woman, but you are not manly. Your form is thin, not muscular. You have no aggression in your features. No one who meets you will believe you are any sort of man at all!"

"Muscles would matter if I were doing manual labor," said Millicent, "but I'm not replacing the blacksmith. I am a man of property. Of leisure. Of money. I may be as weak as I wish."

Felicity shook her head. "If you were attempting to be a lad of sixteen or so, perhaps. But Mr. North is what? Thirty?"

"Mother, please," said Mildred. "There are as many types of men as there are flowers in the garden. Only compare in your mind the figure of the vicar to that of Father, for example. Or that fellow we saw in church last summer who was on repairing lease visiting his family. You know, the one who wore green pantaloons, a red and blue-striped waistcoat, and those silly buttons! Stockings with padded calves? Would you say he was the same type of man as Mr. North? What do you think, Millicent? Perhaps you should dress like him."

"Good God, no," said Millicent. "I do not think I could be that sort of man. Can you truly see me as a fop?"

"You will make mistakes; I know you will," cried Felicity.

"Your faith in my acting abilities is touching," said Millicent dryly. "The more I think on it the easier I expect it to be.'"

"What do you mean?" asked Felicity.

"I mean that trying to be a Corinthian would be a waste of time and I could never carry it off. Neither could I mince about like that fop! Mildred's point is a good one. There are many types of men in society. If I set out to be deliberately silly, inconsequential, and foolish, then if I should do something odd, people will say, 'Oh, that is just that odd Mr. North. Think nothing of it.'"

"But not a fop?" Mildred frowned. "That sounds like a fop."

"No, dear. A fop dresses in the extreme of fashion. I shall be a fribble! A rattle. A fool."

Felicity groaned and dropped her face into her hands. Over her head her daughters continued the debate.

"Even if we stay in Bath for a year's mourning, it will not be long enough for people hereabouts to forget what Mr. North looks like," said Mildred.

"Yes, exactly," said Felicity.

"Why would we return?" asked Millicent. "Are you so very fond of this county? This house? Personally, I find both rather dull. You forget, both of you, that this is not Mr. North's only property. It is merely the one in which he chose to live. While we are in Bath, I shall write to all his, that is to say *my* tenants and look over the list of available properties. Then we shall choose someplace where Mr. N … where I am not previously known. I believe you will be surprised by the range of choice available to us. Or we could stay in Bath. I have read that a respectable number of the Ton visit there and the entertainment is on par with London."

Mildred rose and spooned broth into a dish and arranged it on a tea tray.

"We shall have to wait for Maude to be well enough to travel," she said.

"Agreed," said Millicent. "Although, we shall tell everyone that it is Mr. North's comfort we wait upon. If anyone calls before we leave we shall tell them that Mr. North is still indisposed and unwilling to leave his room while contagion is about in the neighborhood. Tomorrow, Mildred will follow the coffin to make sure it is buried without incident."

"You told the vicar you would keep her at home," said Felicity.

"Would anyone be surprised that the girl disobeyed me and slipped out, since she loved her sister so much?" asked Millicent. "You may be assured I shall punish her appropriately upon her return. After the internment she can visit the baker's and such and start spreading the story that we will need servants to watch the house while we are in Bath. We will give the impression that Mr. N … that I will be coming back. But, so what if I chose to go elsewhere? I am the master of the house, after all. I may go where I will."

"Where shall we go?" asked Felicity. "Where will we live?"

"Cousin Felicity, we shall have the whole winter to decide."

It took three weeks for the removal to Bath to be arranged. Felicity spent every waking moment of those weeks expecting the next knock on the door, the next letter delivered would be the one that revealed the deception, but all went well.

Mildred followed the cart containing Mr. North's earthly remains to the cemetery. Felicity went back every morning for the next week to put flowers on the grave. This far from London there were no grave robbers so the body was permitted to rest undisturbed. Since it also gave the impression that a mother was grieving deeply for a lost daughter, no one attempted to prevent Felicity's visits.

The servants who had been supplanted by the arrival of the Boarder family were contacted and persuaded to return. The old housekeeper expressed relief that Mr. North would be absent "for some time."

Mr. North's old carriage was hauled out and cleaned, horses rented, driver and outriders hired, and on the arranged day, an ailing Mr. North cursed and grumbled his way downstairs – a blanket over his head as shelter from the elements. A still weak Maude was aided into the carriage by her devoted mother and remaining sister and all four quit the neighborhood.

Chapter Two

Millicent did not even glance up from her luncheon when the knock came on the door of their rented Bath house. There was a shuffle of footsteps as their housekeeper, Mrs. Hall, emerged from the rear of the building to answer the door. Their residence in Bath, so far of three months duration, had been an inspired idea. At Maude's suggestion, they put around the story that they had already spent six months mourning their departed sister back in Yorkshire, which permitted them to appear in public in half mourning and participate in some social events.

Aside from joking once how sad she was at being so quickly forgotten, Millicent made no other comment since she was delighted to see how well her family had settled into their new lives. Back in Yorkshire, under the influence of the late Mr. North, all four of them had withered. Not so much in their physical forms, since Maude had grown inches and gained curves and now was a well-favored girl of eighteen. No, it was a starvation of the mind and spirit they had suffered from most. Mr. North had permitted no calls to be paid upon him, and as they were used as servants in his house, the women were reluctant to encourage the ladies of Yorkshire society to visit.

But once they had settled into a rented house on a good, fashionable street in Bath and Millicent had arranged for subscriptions to the local assemblies, memberships to lending libraries, and had sent the others out shopping for new, fashionable clothing, she had the pleasure of seeing the light return to her sisters' and mother's eyes. Instead of creeping around a dull and empty house in fear of Mr. North's blows and shouts, they walked, heads held high, confident and happy.

No one questioned her appearance as Mr. North, either. Although she made a thin figure of a young man, Millicent successfully appeared at public locations in masculine clothing and introduced herself about as Mr. North without raising a single eyebrow. She presented herself at the local branch of the Mercantile Bank, and as she was in possession of the account numbers and evidences she had taken from the late Mr. North's lockbox, money was issued to her and notes of hand honored without the slightest comment.

Everything went so well and so easily that she was not worried when the housekeeper brought a bundle of mail to the table. As the "man" of the house, it fell to Millicent to review all correspondence before passing it on to the ladies.

"An invitation to an evening of dinner and cards," read Felicity, opening the first letter Millicent passed to her. "From a Lady Whenthistle. Do we know her?"

"We met at the assembly," replied Mildred. "The widow of Sir Richard Whenthistle with the purple turban and astonishingly black hair for her age."

"And six flounces at the hem," added Maude with a shudder.

"We shall go," declared Felicity.

A discussion of who would be there occupied the ladies while Millicent opened and set aside mail from her various tenants. One letter written in haste and in a clumsy hand had Millicent putting down her knife and fork to read it a second time with greater attention. Maude noticed Millicent's frown first.

"Is it bad news?" asked Maude.

"From Yorkshire?" added Felicity in panicked tones.

Millicent shook her head as Mildred rolled her eyes and grinned.

"As it happens, the letter is from Wales," said Millicent. "I have interests in several farms there. The tenant of the largest, a Mr. Prichart, informs me that this year's spring floods are worse than usual and several of his fields have been inundated by rising waters. He wishes to discuss the situation with me as he suspects that it will reduce the amount of acreage he can bring under cultivation this year. There have also been drownings amongst his stock."

"Are any people hurt?" asked Mildred.

"Strangely, there is nothing in this letter about people." Millicent dropped the letter beside her plate. "Perhaps he believes Mr. North is not interested. He shall discover otherwise. Mildred, dear, please ring for Mrs. Hall. I need her to find out the mail coach schedule while I pack."

"Pack?" demanded Felicity, as Mildred complied. "Why? Where are you going?"

"I want to meet with Mr. Prichart. I find it curious that he can already calculate the amount of acreage he can plow this early in the spring."

"But you cannot!" cried Felicity. "To travel alone, so very far. My dear Millicent, it is impossible."

"She's dead!" hissed Mildred as she rose and shut the dining room door. "As you well remember, Mother. Millicent is dead!"

"But. But." Felicity glanced back and forth helplessly between her two elder daughters.

Millicent sighed when she realized the problem. While they were living in Bath, there was no real difference from the lives they had lived with their father. Millicent continued to obey her mother in most things, leaving the ordering of the household to Felicity. Millicent's task, as her mother saw it, was to go to the bank and fetch money and if she insisted on doing so while wearing trousers, well, Felicity pretended not to see.

Millicent continued the correspondence with Mr. North's many tenants and business interests; Felicity was not involved in this activity and was unaware of the extent and amount of work it entailed. She was also unaware of the other masculine activities Millicent pursued.

To test her disguise Millicent went to coffee houses and public rooms to chat with other land owners about their responsibilities. She even rented a horse twice to gain some experience in riding with a gentleman's saddle.

Today was the first time Millicent truly planned to act as the male head of household in her mother's presence. For them to survive, for Millicent to truly become Mr. North, she must take advantage of the freedoms and responsibilities of being male. She arranged her features in a semblance of her father's when he had attempted to persuade her mother to some action and spoke firmly.

"My dear cousin Felicity, I do appreciate your concern for my choosing to travel in the early spring. I am certain the roads will be dreadful. I hear that Wales has rain every second day even at the best of times. However, given the concerns expressed by Mr. Prichart, I must go immediately and see to this issue. I regret, now, sending our carriage back to Yorkshire, but we had no need for it here and I wanted to spare myself the expense of a place on the mews."

"You cannot travel in such a way. Impossible! I will not permit it."

Before Millicent could reply, Mildred seized Felicity's hands.

"Mr. North, our cousin, can do what he chooses, Mother."

"But Millicent…"

"Millicent is dead," chorused her daughters.

There was a soft knock on the door and Mrs. Hall entered at Millicent's invitation.

"Mrs. Hall. It seems I must travel to Wales." She consulted her letter. "Merthyr Tydfil is the nearest major town. Please send a maid and find out from the mail coach office where I must go and what changes are necessary."

Mrs. Hall nodded and paused with her hand on the doorknob.

"Seems to me, begging your pardon, Mr. North, that you'd be better served with a post chaise. It's a fair way by mail coach to Wales. You'd be better off setting your own path. You can change drivers when you get to Wales and get a local man to take you about."

Millicent fiddled with her knife and nodded. "You may be right, Mrs. Hall. I do appreciate the suggestion."

"No. You cannot go. I absolutely forbid it," cried Felicity.

Millicent froze. Mildred rose to her feet and Maude remained seated, eyes wide and shocked. When Millicent had gathered her courage and risked a glance toward the waiting Mrs. Hall, she could almost feel the tension flooding out of her body, leaving her weak and a little light-headed. Instead of glaring at Millicent with suspicion, Mrs. Hall politely had cast her eyes down as it was unseemly for servants to notice arguments between their employers.

Whatever reason Felicity might have for objecting to Mr. North's travel plans, Mrs. Hall did not consider it her place to know.

Thank goodness!

"Mrs. Hall, if you would be so kind?" said Millicent, gesturing toward the door.

The housekeeper gave a brief curtsy and left the room, closing the door softly behind her. Millicent watched her leave, then gave Mildred a nod. Mildred went immediately to the door and rested her head against the wood.

"She's gone back to the kitchen," whispered Mildred, after a pause. "That woman has not a curious bone in her body."

"Bless her for it. Keep an ear out in case she comes back." Millicent walked the length of the table to crouch down beside her mother. "Cousin Felicity, compose yourself. There is no reason for me not to travel. Many men do the same every day and come to no harm."

"But you are not a man. What if you are found out?" Felicity produced a lace trimmed handkerchief from somewhere about her clothing and dabbed at her eyes. "You might become ill on the journey and need to call a physician. You will be revealed!"

Millicent rested her head against her mother's shoulder.

"Oh, my dear, I cannot live my life hidden in a deep, dark room, forever afraid of what might happen. I cannot and you cannot ask that of me. I am Mr. North! God willing, I shall continue to be Mr. North for many years to come. And as Mr. North, if I must travel, just as I must learn to ride astride, I will do so. I must because these are the sort of things a country gentleman such as myself does."

"But…"

"Hush!" cried Mildred. "Someone is coming!"

Mildred leapt away from the door and hurried across the room to her place. Millicent walked back to stand at the head of the table. A moment later there was a tap and the kitchen maid entered.

"I have come to clear away, ma'am," she said with a curtsy to Felicity.

"Oh, certainly." Felicity glanced across at Millicent. "I believe we should all appreciate a cup of tea in the drawing room."

The family proceeded to the airy chamber that overlooked the busy thoroughfare outside their home. Felicity settled herself in the largest chair, immediately beside the fireplace, her back straight, and folded her hands in her lap. Millicent settled on a couch and relaxed against the cushions ignoring her mother's disapproving look.

Once the door closed, Felicity opened her mouth to continue her protests. Millicent did not permit her to utter a single sound.

"Before I depart I shall make arrangements to pay the rent for the next six months and I will arrange for funds to be available to you at the Mercantile. What do you think, Mildred? Will four hundred pounds be sufficient for household expenses for the spring and summer?"

Mildred's eyes widened at the amount.

"Oh, of a certainty, Mr. North. Much more than we would need."

Millicent gave a deep, husky laugh. "Oh, I know that. I just want to be certain that, should some emergency arise or my return is delayed, you need not wait to hear from me before dealing with the problem."

"Thank you. That is comforting," replied Mildred.

Felicity leaned forward and prepared again to speak.

"And I shall ensure you have my directions," said Millicent. "I think, since I am taking the time to travel all the way to Wales, that I shall visit all my interests there. If I remember correctly there is a coal mine as well as sheep farming. When I go from one to another, I will be certain to let you know."

"Yes, that is a good idea," said Mildred. "To go and see just one tenant would be a waste of your time."

"Girls!" cried Felicity and Maude giggled. "I will not be ignored," added Felicity.

"We are not ignoring you, Mother," said Mildred.

"Yes, we are," Millicent corrected her. "There is nothing she can say that will change my mind." Millicent lowered her voice, glancing toward the closed door. "Were I the man of the family in truth, Felicity might protest some action of mine all she wished, but in the end I would do what I thought was right. Therefore, my dear cousins, I will leave you to your tea and your embroidery. I have much to do before I depart."

And she escaped leaving Felicity spluttering behind her.

Two Weeks Later

Millicent, wrapped in three heavy blankets and fast asleep, landed hard on the carriage floor, her head a scant inch from the heated foot rest. She struggled to free herself from the tangle of blankets as she slid across the floor. Outside she heard the shouts of her driver and the screams of horses. The carriage tilted to one side, but to her infinite relief, did not fall. Instead it swayed and came to a crooked stop with Millicent pressed against the boxes tucked under her seat. She freed herself as quickly as she could, threw open the carriage door, extending her bare head out into the torrential rain.

Somehow her driver had managed to stop the horses a bare finger's width from a recently overturned vehicle. The damaged carriage's wheels were still turning uselessly and the trapped horses screamed and thrashed in their traces as they struggled to regain their feet. The outriders attached to that carriage tried to calm their own mounts or sat staring open-mouthed at the wreck.

When Millicent ventured out that morning, the rain had been little more than mist in the air and the road already wet and slick. In the current downpour the unpaved country road was little better than thick soup, and when navigating the sharp turn, the unfortunate carriage wheels either had caught in the mud or found themselves unsupported, resulting in the dreadful crash.

Millicent dragged on her many-layered greatcoat, left her crushed hat on the floor, and leapt down from her carriage to land ankle deep in the mud.

"Rogers," she shouted to her lead outrider. "No, do not dismount. Go! We are only a few miles from Trenton Manor. Tell Mr. Prichart we need carts and men. Tell him to send for a physician and bring help back as quickly as you can."

With a touch of his mittened hand to his cap, the rider was off and Millicent turned her attention to the overturned vehicle.

"Jacob. Ben. See to the horses before they injure themselves. Mike, find the driver and footmen." Now that someone was in charge the other outriders shook off their confusion and aided Millicent's men. Orders given, Millicent slogged through the mud toward the carriage.

"The driver's here under the horses," shouted Ben. "He's dead, sir."

"Ah," was all Millicent said, putting aside grief for a stranger as she climbed up the axle to the highly polished, slippery side of the carriage.

It was necessary for her to grip the length of fabric that covered the heraldic device on the door to remain stable on the thin wood wall. Kneeling on the mahogany, she wrested the door up and open and let out a breath of relief. Inside three people, one man and two women, were attempting to untangle themselves from their belongings.

Bruised, shaken, but alive.

"Ahoy," cried Millicent, knocking briskly on the open door. "Well met by moonlight. Permission to come aboard, Captain?"

The carriage rocked as a liveried footman joined Millicent beside the door.

"Stay out," shouted the man within. "'Tis bad enough in here without a fool cluttering up the place."

Millicent blushed, but stayed where she was. A young woman in such a situation would weep and faint. A young man, despite insults, would remain to be gentlemanly and useful.

"Are there any injuries?" she asked in a more formal tone.

"I fear I have broken my wrist," said the older woman, whose frilly lace cap had come askew and now the ribbons were over her left ear instead of under her chin.

"I am well," said the young girl, currently huddling against the far window.

The man struggled to position himself under the open door and took the small girl by the hand.

"I shall boost my sister up first," he declared. "Are you ready?"

Millicent glanced across to the footman, who nodded.

"Boost away," said Millicent.

The gentleman put his hands under the girl's arms and lifted. She, however, struggled and protested when he shifted his grip to her behind. Millicent and the footman leaned in to seize her hands, but their wet leather gloves would not grip.

Muttering imprecations against the weather, Millicent seized the tips of her gloves with her teeth, pulled them off, and leaned in again, gripping the girl's hand in one hand and wrapped an arm about her waist with the other. At her cry of shock, Millicent grinned.

"May I have this waltz, my lady?"

With the footman gripping the back of Millicent's coat they raised the girl to the level of the door. Lacking any better leverage Millicent threw herself backwards onto the carriage. With a cry the girl popped out of the door and landed hard on Millicent's lap. The watching footman winced.

"Ah, I realize we have not been properly introduced," said Millicent to the dark haired creature who sat shivering on her lap. "But I fear you have hopelessly compromised me. We shall have to be wed."

"Here is her cloak," shouted the gentleman in the carriage and tossed it up. Millicent wrapped it around the girl and before she could react, Millicent sat up and slid them both to the edge of the carriage.

"Ho there, Benjamin. Be a good fellow and carry this little girl across the mud. It will not do to have her boots ruined. Tuck her away in my carriage."

Ben, a tall, broad-shouldered creature that Felicity would have regarded as the figure of a true man, caught the girl and stomped off across the mud with her in his arms. Dismissing the girl from her mind, Millicent returned to the door and gazed down into the most magnificent blue eyes she had ever seen. Heat ran through her sending a tingle burning under the skin of her cheeks and catching her breath in her throat. The gentleman below paused in his tending of a woman who could only be the girl's chaperone, to stare up at Millicent. The rain pelted down upon dark curly hair granting his locks a brilliant sheen. When Millicent's head returned to block his light, he glanced up at her with such force of personality that she felt the shock through her bones and down to her chilled toes.

He was amazing. His hands were graceful as they moved over the chaperone's limbs. His voice, deep and gravelly, spoke soothing words and Millicent longed to be the recipient of that soothing, that comfort.

Millicent fell into lust without regret. If her foolish, hidden female heart must bestow itself on someone, why not on a man with the body of a Greek god? So beautiful. She sighed and gazed at him, open-mouthed.

"She is not badly hurt," said the Greek god. "Merely, her wrist. I suspect a sprain, rather than a break, but we should be careful, nevertheless. Mrs. Fleming, I shall boost you up, as before. This gentleman shall catch you."

"I cannot do it," wailed the woman, huddling against the Greek god's chest. "I cannot."

The gentleman and Millicent exchanged a glance of fully male accord at this display and Millicent reluctantly shook herself out of dreams of kisses and moonlit walks in darkened gardens to consider solutions to the impasse.

"Pass up a couple of those boxes," she ordered. "'Twill clear the floor and give you better footing."

He nodded and started shifting the debris.

"And you," said Millicent to the footman on the other side of the door. "As soon as the floor is clear, go down. Sir, I suggest you take up that pretty scarf over there and use it to wrap the injured limb against the lady's chest. Leave the good arm free."

He considered for a moment, then nodded his concurrence.

"Whatever for?" asked the chaperone.

"To protect your arm and ensure you will not be tempted to use it," said Millicent. "We will need that strong blanket I see there as well. We shall make a sling of it and raise you up."

The carriage rocked as yet another footman climbed up to sit opposite Millicent. The rescue went as Millicent planned right up until the moment that the chaperone emerged from the carriage. Mrs. Fleming did not know how to climb out of the sling without revealing her lower limbs.

"For God's sake," growled Millicent as her arms ached and chest burned from the effort. Surely now she would be revealed as a weak woman just because another, damned female was too proper to show an inch of ankle! "Swing your legs, your limbs, rather, across that way. Slide off the blanket."

The chaperone did so, shrieking when the footman seized her ankle to assist her. The resultant wrestling match, the footman trying to hold her and the lady attempting to keep her skirt covering her limbs, nearly had them all falling back inside.

When the lady was finally assisted to the drenched ground, an exhausted Millicent glanced back down to the trapped gentleman.

"I hope," she said with feeling, "that you will be less trouble."

He flashed her a grin full of mischief and brilliant white teeth, leapt up, seized the edge of the wood, and hauled himself out all in one motion. The rain moistened his buckskin unmentionables and they clung to the muscles of his thighs and displayed for Millicent's view a superior posterior.

"May you burn in hell for such strength," muttered Millicent as color flooded her face.

The Greek god laughed briefly and offered his hand. Millicent accepted it in her own bare, chilled hand and gasped as heat rushed up her arm and fogged her brain. Never in her life had so simple a touch stirred her blood and mind completely. Her confusion was to such a degree that she nearly missed his next words.

"Thank you for your timely assistance. Have we totted up the damage?"

Millicent nodded, swallowed, and tried to work her dry mouth enough to speak.

"You have lost your driver and one of the footmen," she said. "It appears they both fell and broke their necks when the carriage went over."

"Ah," an expression of genuine sorrow crossed his face.

"Your horses are all well. Merely shaken a bit with one or two scratches. However, I fear it will be necessary to shoot your carriage to put it out of its misery."

He glanced around at the shattered axle and sprung wheelbraces and nodded his agreement.

"You there," cried Millicent, noting that one of the outriders was beginning to unpack the trunk of the damaged vehicle. "Do not put the trunks in the mud. Put them on the roof of my carriage or on the side of this one until a cart arrives. And put the bodies on the wayside. I know you want to wrap them in blankets, to be civilized Christian men, but keep the blankets for yourselves for the moment. Heaven spare us if you all catch cold. Your departed friends will understand."

"Yes, sir," came the grateful answer.

The gentleman slid on his arse across the wet, polished wood, dropped down with a splash, and stalked off across the mud to where the small girl was leaning out of Millicent's carriage.

"Mrs. Fleming says she needs brandy, Timothy," she called.

"Of course. You there. I am sorry, I do not know your name. There's a picnic basket on the floor. Have the footman fetch it up to you."

Millicent pretended to doff the hat that was crushed on the floor of her carriage.

"Mr. Anthony North of Yorkshire. At your service." Then she smiled down at the footman. "Can you fetch yourself out of there, my friend?"

"Yes, sir, Mr. North."

The picnic basket was located and tossed up. Millicent left the servants to finish the unpacking and slogged through the deep mud across to her rented carriage. Inside both the Greek god and the small girl were dancing attendance upon Mrs. Fleming. Now that she had a better view, Millicent could see what she had thought was a child was actually a young woman, most likely the same age as Maude.

"There you are," said Millicent, passing the basket to the young lady. "All the comforts of home."

"You must live in a very strange home," replied the lady.

"I have been accused of that many times," murmured Millicent with a smile.

To her surprise the smile was answered with a giggle and blush. Inside the carriage efforts were in hand for the injured chaperone's comfort. All of Millicent's blankets were tucked tight around her body. Brandy was even now being pressed to her lips and a rain soaked handkerchief lay across her forehead

Standing out in the rain, with her feet ankle deep in freezing mud, yet more water pouring out of the sky and down the neck of her shirt, Millicent realized that there were advantages to being female.

"Mr. North, please come in out of the cold," ordered the gentleman.

Millicent did not bother to point out the cheek of inviting her into her own carriage.

"In a moment. I must see to the moving of your carriage off the road and the setting of watchmen in both directions. I do not want anyone else coming round that curve and landing in this pig's wallow with us."

To her surprise the nobleman did not close the door, but climbed out to join her.

"You are quite correct. I fear my wits are rattled."

A flick of his wrist was enough to communicate with his outriders and two men ahorseback headed in opposite directions to look out for other traffic. The remainder of the men gathered around, and with much pushing and swearing, with all the luggage removed, the damaged carriage was pushed the rest of the way into the ditch.

"'Tis good for nothing more than kindling, now," he said with a sigh.

"I'm sure that local families will come out and scavenge what is useful. The squabs at least will make fine chairs." Millicent halted and glanced across at the gentleman, expecting him to order the removal of his soft leather seating to where the rest of his luggage waited. Instead the man nodded.

"Well, then, some little good may come of this." he waved to a footman who leapt up and shut the carriage door the better to preserve the interior.

"Cart approaching," shouted one of the watching men.

Within a few minutes three men on horseback accompanied by a farm cart slid to a stop beside them. The lead rider scanned the men afoot.

"Mr. North?" cried the florid faced man glancing back and forth between the two well-dressed men standing in the mud.

"That is I," said Millicent, stepping forward. "Mr. Prichart, I assume."

"Indeed, sir. At your service. Is this your carriage that's come a'cropper?"

"Not I, 'tis this gentleman's."

"Shoffer," said the gentleman with a bow. "Thank you for coming to our assistance."

"Where were you heading, Mr. Shoffer?" asked Millicent.

"Merthyr Tydfil and then on to Shropshire. The carriage with my valet and servants travelled ahead of us. It is likely they have not noticed we no longer follow."

"With the road this much a slurry it would be difficult to send a messenger to them and fetch them back," said Millicent. "I suspect it would be best if you came with us to Mr. Prichart's and await a change in weather."

A very worried expression crossed Prichart's weathered face.

"I dunno about that, Mr. North. My wife only prepared one room for a visitor. She will be fit to be tied if I turn up with more than she's expecting."

"Do you have outbuildings, Mr. Prichart?" demanded Millicent, her voice deepening with fatigue and cold. "Hayricks? Stables? Buildings with roofs to keep off the rain? Do you have more than one drawing room?"

"Well, yes. Yes, we do."

"Then we shall do very well for a short time and not mind the inconvenience. The ladies within my carriage shall have the room you set aside for my use and Mr. Shoffer and I shall make do with beds on the floor of the second drawing room. As I have no wish to leave any of the servants out in this dreadful weather, may I hope you can accommodate them in the servant hall and outbuildings, with blankets and food?"

"Of course, sir."

"And some provision needs to be made for my servants who have died," said Mr. Shoffer. "Can you offer them proper respect until their burial?"

"Yes, sir." With a sigh, Mr. Prichart touched his whip to his dripping hat and directed his servants to gather the dead and the luggage and place everything on the cart.

"In a few days, I will be able to take you to Merthyr Tydfil myself," offered Millicent. "Will that serve?"

"That will do very well, Mr. North," said Shoffer.

Millicent gestured toward her carriage and slogged along behind Mr. Shoffer. Climbing inside last, she sighed and rested her head briefly against the stiff squabs before shaking herself to wakefulness.

"Well, now, Mr. Shoffer, I must appeal to you for an introduction to these ladies. I fear I have been beforehand as we have shared a lovely waltz and I am yet to know their names."

The chaperone gave Millicent what was intended to be a quelling glance as the younger girl blushed and giggled. When the chaperone gave her a sharp jab in the ribs she looked away and shrank down into the shelter of her cloak.

"This is my sister, the Lady Elizabeth Shoffer and her chaperone, Mrs. Fleming."

Lady Elizabeth gave a quick nod of the head, but Mrs. Fleming examined Millicent from her bedraggled hair and mud splattered great coat to her missing gloves and sodden boots and sniffed her disapproval.

"You are in a significant state of dishabille, Mr. North."

"I do apologize, Mrs. Fleming. I was engaged in sea bathing when you happened upon me. I shall repair myself as soon as possible."

There was a sound suspiciously like another giggle from within Lady Elizabeth's cloak.

"Fool," said Mrs. Fleming and closed her eyes, dismissing Mr. North.

Millicent only grinned.

Lady Elizabeth settled her head against the nearest wall, then sat upright again with a small cry.

"Oh, no, I have broken the brim of my hat." She snatched the remains of her pretty befrilled bonnet off her head and ran small fingers along to where it was bent at an odd angle. "And it's soaked. I cannot appear in this before strangers. What will I do?"

There was a groan from her brother at this purely feminine distress. Millicent considered informing the young girl about the dead men outside, but changed her mind. Why add that grief to the stresses of the day? It was likely that no one had mentioned the deaths to her. Instead Millicent sat forward and smiled.

"But Lady Beth, why do you worry? You look so dazzling in it that I am certain within a week every fashionable lady from London, to Bath and Edinburgh, will be wearing broken brimmed and wilted hats. Why, you have only to appear once in it and all the ladies will run crying to their haberdashers demanding just the same thing."

"What nonsense," sniffed Mrs. Fleming, her eyes still shut.

"I am surprised to hear you say so," said Millicent. "Surely, the brilliant and charming Lady Beth is London's leading light of fashion. How can it be otherwise?"

"I am not, you know," whispered Lady Elizabeth. "No one pays any attention to me."

"But you are a lovely young lady of style and..."

"Do not foist yourself upon the lady," interrupted the chaperone. "Just because you happen to have made the acquaintance of..."

"Mrs. Fleming," growled Mr. Shoffer.

"Well." The woman glanced at the gentleman seated beside Millicent, then reading a message there, flushed and looked away. Speaking in softer tones, she continued. "Because we must accept your assistance does not mean you may make a play for Lady Elizabeth. Mind yourself."

Millicent looked first toward the gentleman and seeing no offense, rather an expression of curiosity, she returned her attention to the girl.

"Lady Beth, you do surprise me. Why, just the slightest of your smiles and my heart beats so hard that I am surprised you cannot hear it."

Beth shifted on her bench and lowered her eyes to her gloved hands.

"You cannot put yourself forward as an arbiter of fashion and style," said Mrs. Fleming. "Look at you."

Millicent glanced down at her sodden, loose fitting woolen trews, caked with mud to the knees, her unbleached linen shirt collar wilted from the rain and hanging over a simply knotted cotton cravat.

Fortunately, despite her soaking, there was nothing showing that would hint that under all the wet fabric was a young woman. Millicent pulled her overcoat tighter around her body, just to be safe. The chaperone's disapproval was clear, and frankly, well earned, but that did not mean that Millicent would act ashamed before such a judgmental woman.

"I see nothing wrong," said Millicent spreading her hands. "I am myself, most sincerely."

"What in the world does that mean?" demanded Mrs. Fleming.

Inspiration struck Millicent with the force of lightning. She had not considered how she would respond to direct curiosity should she ever be questioned regarding an action or error of her appearance and now she had the most brilliant idea. A piece of nonsense that she had made up to amuse her younger sisters years ago would serve very well.

"It means, I decided long ago to live as if I were a cat. After all, as the old saying goes, a cat may look at a king."

"Fool," said Mrs. Fleming.

Lady Beth sat up and for the first time met Millicent's eyes.

"I do not understand. What does that mean?"

"It means that of all God's creatures a cat is at all times himself. When in the presence of a king, mere mortal man must bow and lady, curtsy. A dog, well trained, will grovel and beg. Horses wait patiently in the rain upon his pleasure. But a cat cares but for himself. He will walk into any room and stare you in the eye, be you king or clown and he will hold his own opinion of you. He will turn his back on you if you displease him, stand, sit, or walk away as is his will. And a king will tolerate this from a cat, but from no one else, since to protest would be the veriest waste of time."

"How very odd," said Lady Beth with a giggle. "I have never thought of that."

"And so I model myself on a cat, disdaining fashion to dress comfortably and pleasing myself with my manners."

"Of which you have none," came the slurred voice of the chaperone.

"How much brandy did you give her?" whispered Millicent.

"Just enough," Lady Beth whispered back and a faint smile turned the corners of her mouth.

"Excellent," said Millicent, as a snore arose from the blankets covering Mrs. Fleming. "Lady Beth, pray tell me, what sort of cat would you like to be?"

"I hardly know," said the girl uncertainly, glancing toward her brother.

The man shifted on the seat and his soaking wet thigh came into burning contact with Millicent's leg. She was so shocked by her own body's melting reaction that it took her fully five seconds to pull herself away. She stared at the floor as she tried to bring her breathing back under control. How could it be that such a casual touch could so disconcert her? She had ridden in post carriages with men on both sides, even while dressed as a woman, and felt nothing – except fatigue, but the slightest touch of this man's flesh and she was afire.

She concentrated on his rumbling voice to try and gather her scattered wits, but it so warmed her flesh she was surprised steam did not rise from her clothing.

"Now I think on it," said Shoffer, entirely unaware of her discomfort. "I should like to be the big black bully of a tomcat who, back in my father's time when guests visited, would appear in the front hall to examine them. It really was quite amazing how he would sniff their boots, walking around each and every person and growling deep in his throat if they should move away before he completed his examination. It was as if he thought our house his. In good weather, he would position himself on the very top of the statue of a lion that guards the main steps and gaze out over his domain. I was quite in awe of him as a child. That cat was the only being my father treated as an equal. That tom would seat himself on a bookshelf in my father's study and my father would greet him with respect each morning."

Both Millicent and Beth laughed, Millicent being careful to keep her voice deep and laugh with her mouth open instead of giggling.

"Now you, my dear Beth," continued Shoffer.

"Well, I do remember on a charity visit I saw an old woman sitting beside the fire. The cat in her lap was a tiny golden kitten so curled up that I could not see her ears or her tail, but just a little bundle of fur. When the old woman stroked her, the purr was so loud the house shook with it." Lady Beth smiled at her brother. "I should like to be that safe and happy."

"And so you shall," replied her brother.

"But is that the only cat you wish to be?" pressed Millicent.

Seeming startled at the thought she could be two, the girl considered.

"Well, I did see a cat once that I admired riding a horse."

"Do you tell me so? I cannot believe it," cried Millicent. "A cat? Riding a horse?"

"Oh, yes." Now animation came to Lady Beth's face and color to her pinched white lips and cheeks. She leaned forward to punctuate her tale with waving hands. "The horses were out in the field when a tiger-striped cat jumped onto the back of the lead stallion and dug in her claws. Well, he was so surprised he reared up and I was most certain that the cat would be tossed off and killed. But no, she dug her claws in and when the stallion took off across the field as fast as he could; she rode him all the way. And when she passed me, I swear, I saw such a grin on the cat's face as I have never seen before."

"She was having fun?" inquired Millicent.

"Oh, yes. I should like to have fun."

"I am certain you shall, if you wish it," said Millicent.

The animation faded from the girl's face. "I think not."

"Why ever not?" asked Millicent, glancing across at Shoffer. "Is your brother so unkind as not to let you ride?"

"Oh, no, I am certain Timothy is everything that is kind."

That comment caused Millicent to raise her eyebrows and turn her face toward the dark visaged giant at her side.

"My sister and I have not been much in each other's company," he said by way of explanation. "Since the death of our parents she has lived with our grandmother. It has been decided it would benefit Beth to spend time at my estate before attending a few summer house parties, in the hope it will give her confidence to face another season."

Lady Beth shrank back against the squabs and hid her face in the folds of her cloak's hood.

"You have had a London season?" asked Millicent in her softest voice.

The answer was the barest nod.

"And it did not go well?"

An even smaller shake was her answer.

"Whatever is wrong with London?" demanded Millicent.

Lady Beth gave a tiny giggle, but did not answer. Millicent was about to question further, but a touch on her sleeve stopped her. She glanced over to the man beside her and saw him shake his head. Millicent nodded and sat back trying to ignore the discomfort of her soaked and chilled clothing. Obviously, the London season was a forbidden subject.

So be it, for now.

Chapter Three

Their arrival at Mr. Prichart's home was exactly as that worthy man had warned. No sooner did Millicent, Shoffer, Lady Beth, and Mrs. Fleming cross the threshold than Mrs. Prichart collapsed on the staircase leading to the upper house weeping and wailing that the whole world would know about her failed housekeeping. She was not prepared for the arrival of four guests instead of one; therefore, she had failed as a wife, a mother, and a hostess.

Millicent was shocked by the clamor the woman produced and wished she could take herself far from this embarrassing scene. Mr. Prichart, his hat caught in both hands, knelt at his wife's side begging her to calm herself and tend to their guests. For a moment, remembering how Felicity disliked surprises and how distressed her poor mother became when there was a disturbance to her housekeeping, Millicent felt some pity for Mrs. Prichart. But then she saw the woman's eyes scanning her audience, gauging their reactions to her performance. Those were not the eyes of a distressed woman, but a manipulative old fox. Millicent, with chill water making her clothing cling to her skin and her woolen trews chaffing her thighs found no patience with this production.

"Mrs. Prichart," began Millicent. "Surely you are not saying that you should have foreseen unexpected guests being blown in by a storm."

"Oh! Oh! Oh!" cried the lady, mighty bosom heaving as maids ran around for handkerchiefs and hartshorn, the housekeeper stood wringing her apron and the cook stood watching from the servant's staircase. "What is to be done?"

It was clear to Millicent in a moment that Mrs. Prichart's moods, high or low, ruled this household and nothing would or could be done except at her will.

Pushing past the frozen servants, Millicent took Mrs. Prichart by the hand, hauled her to feet, and hustled the woman into the front parlor. When Mr. Prichart moved to follow Millicent seized the door and pulled it half shut.

"Please, Mr. Prichart. I feel it is my duty as the person who has brought this chaos to your door to attempt to calm your wife. Please see to the comfort of my friends."

And with that Millicent shut the door and crossed to where Mrs. Prichart lay slumped on the sofa, her cries increasing in volume when she saw the door was shut.

Millicent sat on the footstool and took one of the large woman's hands in hers, patting it gently to gain her attention.

"Mrs. Prichart," said Millicent, "I know your type. I have seen it before. You learned early in your marriage that if you wept your husband would do anything to calm you."

Millicent frowned. The woman's eyes narrowed showing she was attending to every word despite her noise.

"Now," continued Millicent, "I am not your husband. I am, however, *his landlord*. Mr. Prichart has summoned me to show me the reasons he should not have his proper rents levied. Under these circumstances, if I do not like his excuses I am fully entitled to turn him and all his family out to make way for someone who will pay the rent."

Mrs. Prichart's cries ceased in an instant. Millicent continued in an even softer voice.

"I do not like loud noises, Mrs. Prichart. I do not like them at all. If you make a sound louder than a mouse's whisper in all the time I'm here, then I will turn your family out. Do we understand each other?"

The woman opened her mouth, but thought better of it and nodded instead.

"Excellent. Now, you are going to go out there and escort Lady Elizabeth and her chaperone up to the room you set aside for me. Mr. Shoffer and I will use this parlor and you will permit the housekeeper and cook to use their best judgment to take care of our servants. Now, get up and do your duty for your household, family, and husband. And Mrs. Prichart? No word of this to your husband. That would not be wise."

Mrs. Prichart leapt to her feet and fled the room. Millicent remained where she was. She did not hear the orders given so soft a voice did Mrs. Prichart use, but within a few minutes she heard many footfalls hurrying through the house.

Mr. Prichart, hat still in hand and with Mr. Shoffer on his heels, wandered into the parlor looking back over his shoulder appearing slightly awed.

"You are a miracle worker, that you are, Mr. North. I have never seen anyone calm m'wife so fast. I hope you will teach me your secret."

"It's a gift I regret I cannot share with you," murmured Millicent with a wry grin. "I wonder if you might have some towels or blankets fetched as I have no wish to drip mud over your carpets. And my green valise from the carriage. It has my shaving kit and a set of dry clothing. Everything else can wait until the weather is better."

"Oh, yes. And for you, Mr. Shoffer?"

Shoffer described his own small trunk.

"I will have it brought in right away," Mr. Prichart assured them. "And you will be wanting some brandy, too, I will be bound."

"Tea for me," said Millicent.

"Myself as well," said Shoffer.

Mr. Prichart bowed himself out of the room.

Millicent sat back on the footstool and started working to remove her soaked boots. The parlor was narrow and wide, with furniture of different styles, ages, and conditions crowding it. Despite the variety of furniture, it contained nothing big enough for her to hide behind. She had just put herself into the strangest of situations. She had been pretending to be a gentleman long enough that deferring to a lady's need was now automatic. But that left her having to share a sleeping chamber with a man, to have to remove her clothing in the presence of a real man! Now that she could think Millicent cursed herself for not suggesting she should have one parlor while Shoffer the other – although that might have increased the inconvenience to the family; it was better that she had not.

Felicity was right. She was risking being revealed as a fraud – worse, a thief – at any moment with her bold behavior. While she sat, one ruined boot in her hands, a boy who looked so like Mr. Prichart with his broad, weathered face, and gap-toothed grin that he could only be a son, ran in with blankets and towels in both arms followed by a taller son with the requested valise and trunk.

"Ma says as how she will send in some hot water for washing as soon as the ladies are settled upstairs," cried the younger boy before fleeing the room.

Millicent stood in the middle of the room, her hand on her soaking cravat and wondering what to do next even as her face warmed with a blush. Did gentlemen ask each other to turn their backs when they undressed? Or could she ask for a dressing screen to be brought in?

She remembered a tale her father used to tell about a time

when he was tutor to a rather well-to-do family where the boys of the family had gone swimming in a river together, naked. She considered turning her back and hoping Shoffer would not notice or comment on the cravats around her chest when she heard Shoffer go to the door to call the young boys back into the room.

"Tell me, lad," he said. "Does this house have a withdrawing room, or do you have commodes about the place?"

"No commodes," was the reply. "We have an outhouse just out past the kitchen garden. Just follow the stone path."

Shoffer groaned and the boys giggled. When Shoffer left the room, Millicent let out the breath she had been holding and rushed to wedge a chair under the doorknob. Once done she stripped naked faster than she had done in all her life, and had fresh clothing on and a new cravat hiding her throat before the next knock on the door.

By the time Shoffer returned from the outhouse, the chair was back in its place, Millicent was dry, her hair combed and she was settled on a couch sipping tea and flipping through a book on farming she had discovered on a shelf.

"Tea, for the love of God," cried Shoffer, ripping the cravat from his throat and dropping it in a sloppy pile at his feet. "I am frozen half to death."

He loosened the top few buttons before pulling his shirt over his head and adding it to the pile on the floor. He bent over to pick up a dry blanket which pulled his breeches tight across his buttocks. Millicent stood and turned her back to the sight, a blush flooding her face and busied herself at the tea tray.

"Cream, no sugar," added Shoffer.

"To drink or to wear?" shot back Millicent, glad her tongue had finally separated from the roof of her mouth where it had lodged at the sight of a man's solid, hair-sprinkled chest.

When she had undressed the dead Mr. North she had kept her eyes closed most of the time. What glimpses she had taken of his form had been disappointing since Mr. North was a narrow-chested, wasted individual who had taken no exercise, not even horseriding, due to his poor eyes. It occurred to her as she concentrated on stirring her tea that this was a good opportunity to discover what a healthy male's body looked like. There might be some part of her disguise that could improve with that knowledge. Drawing a deep breath she flashed a glance toward the half-dressed gentleman.

Mr. Shoffer's body was appropriately impressive to carry around his brilliant smile and fine eyes. His shoulders were wide and well muscled, as were his arms. A testament, she supposed, to years of riding and curricle driving. His abdomen was hard and rippled with muscle and the vee of dark hair that marked his chest narrowed to a line that descended down to his trousers. For a moment her fingers itched to follow that line and explore his body. To discover the mysteries the falls of his trousers concealed. Shocked at the path her thoughts followed, she forced her gaze away and concentrated on the tea pot.

"Dear God, you are a silly rattle," said Shoffer, rubbing his hair briskly. "But, you have a point. At this moment I'd pay a hundred pounds to sink into a tub of warm tea to my chin."

"I expect the house does contain a bathtub," said Millicent.

"It does. I have just seen it being carried up to my sister's room."

"Ah, well," sighed Millicent, wishing for that long ago time when she had quarreled with her sisters as to who would be first to take a bath – and won. "A gentleman waits upon the comforts of a lady."

"Exactly so," said Shoffer coming bare-chested to sit beside the fireplace – full square in front of her – to towel his hair dry. "Speaking of my sister…"

"You need not fear, sir," interrupted Millicent, turning her gaze away from his nakedness. On the other side of the room he had been much easier to take. This close, her insides turned to melted wax and her brain insisted removing her own clothing was the only appropriate response. "I only teased her to distract her from the accident. I know my place and will maintain the proper distance in future. I am not so ignorant that I cannot tell that *Mister* Shoffer could not be your only title."

"You are correct," said Shoffer, with a smile that showed the damned man possessed a dimple in his cheek! How was she to maintain her composure? "Shoffer is the name used by my intimates. I am, in fact, Timothy Shoffer, the Duke of Trolenfield."

"I beg you, Your Grace," cried Millicent. "Do not tell Mrs. Prichart."

Shoffer laughed. "I do understand you, but then, perhaps you should not call me 'Your Grace.'"

"My lord, perhaps. I'm certain you have some minor title

that would be less intimidating. Sir? Vicar? Indian Chief?"

"You are the least encroaching gentleman I have ever met," Shoffer dropped his towel on his lap and turned to face Millicent.

She kept her eyes firmly locked on his and refused to glance downward at the carved torso or the broad column of his throat.

"Indeed," continued Shoffer. "I am amazed at your calm. There is no bowing or scraping in your manner at all. Were I the King indeed, I believe you would be little changed, oh, Master Cat. You have managed a disaster on the road, my servants, your tenants, and my sister with such alacrity and humor I cannot be less than impressed."

And if he had known I was a woman, thought Millicent, he would have dismissed my orders, ignored my aid, and banished me to the corner to get on with fainting and weeping as is appropriate to my gender.

"Perhaps I should hire myself out?" Millicent wondered aloud. "I would, if I could but think of a name for the service."

"Court Jester?"

They both laughed.

Shoffer resumed drying his hair and chest. For a moment Millicent wondered what it would be like to be the one moving the towel across that skin, or better yet, having *him* dry her. She blinked realizing she had missed some comment by the duke.

"I beg your pardon?"

"I said, I would like you to give Elizabeth, or Beth, rather, since she seems to approve of the diminutive, conversation lessons."

Millicent stared at him for a long moment, then realized her jaw was dropped open and shut her mouth with a snap.

"I'm sorry; I do not have the pleasure of understanding you. I cannot think of anything a duke's sister could learn from me."

Shoffer crossed the room to drag a fresh shirt out of his case. He grimaced at the creases, but pulled the thing on to Millicent's mixed grief and relief and buttoned it up.

"My sister told you that she had an unhappy season this last winter in London. Indeed, that conversation in your carriage is the most words I have heard from her in all my life."

"She seemed chatty. Well, not chatty, but she responded quite well to my conversational gambits."

"She did with you. But last winter she stood so quietly beside my grandmother, so unresponsive, that it began to be bruited about that she possessed no wits at all! My sister, an idiot! It is not to be borne!"

"I cannot believe it. She is a little shy, I admit, but with a little encouragement I am certain she was charming."

"No, North, you do not understand. She said nothing! Made no movement unless ordered. Did not meet the eye of any of her suitors. Stared at the floor from arrival to departure. A stiff wooden doll has more life than she. I admit I became quite frightened for her. My grandmother, when I asked her, could not give a reason for the odd behavior. When I called upon them for morning visits Beth gave me quite the same treatment. Her reticence gave me concern and I would know the reason for it and have it corrected before next season."

"Is she still grieving for her parents?"

"I hardly know, since she does not answer my questions. Besides, they have been dead for many years. That can hardly be the explanation."

"How very odd," said Millicent, running her hand through her hair and pulling the strands forward. It was getting long and shaggy again. She should have cut it before she left Bath. Long hair might give her away to an observant person. She must exercise more care!

"That is a dreadful haircut, by the way," said Shoffer. "When we catch up with my valet, I shall have him do a better job."

"I thank you, no; I permit only one person to cut it," said Millicent frowning. "Your sister seems everything charming and quite bright. Only think of that story she told about the horse and the cat."

"You are the only one to think so. And I must admit, despite my many efforts I have never been able to draw her out as effectively as you. That is why I ask, since we will be here a few days at least waiting for the roads to dry, that you would talk with her. Teach her conversation. For a woman to be a chatterbox is more acceptable than one who is completely silent. Men like a woman to listen once in a while, but this is ridiculous."

With that comment the duke rose and pulled down his mud splattered trousers. Millicent averted her eyes lest the sight of his thighs clad only in damp smallclothes strike her blind or witless. Then she realized that he had discarded his smallclothes as well and was as naked as the day he was born!

She winced and bit her lip lest a moan escape.

By the gods – thank goodness men could swear; nothing less than profanity could relieve her agitation – he was perfect. Not for him withered buttocks and hocks. Smooth firm globes of flesh, a perfect peach paraded before her. Millicent set down her cup with a rattle and clutched at her constricting neckcloth as Shoffer walked across the room and bent over his valise.

When he lifted fresh clothing out and turned toward her, his masculine parts came into view directly at a level she could not ignore. Her years of study of ancient Greek and Roman statues were not enough to prepare her for the sight. God had not seen fit to provide the Duke of Trolenfield with a natural fig leaf. Indeed, such a leaf would not have been enough.

His member fortunately was at rest, nestling in a small mass of dark curls. She gulped and looked away. At least now she had an idea of why gentlemen occasionally seemed to have some mass behind the falls of their trousers. She wondered briefly if having such a thing made walking uncomfortable. Shoffer turned and bent again as he put one foot then another into buff inexpressables. When his private places were covered Millicent could finally draw air into her lungs and reach for her tea cup with trembling hands. Keeping her face turned from Shoffer, she could only pray that the disorder of her thoughts was not visible on her face.

Standing up and moving away, she decided, would be too obvious. Gentlemen of Shoffer's rank were accustomed to undressing before their valets. Instead she concentrated on sipping tea until the man was clothed again. When the torture was over she shot to her feet.

"I must see those boys about the withdrawing room," she said and ran from the room.

The withdrawing room, she was reminded by the housekeeper, was a privy, which turned out to be a chilly hut standing alone and proud, buffeted by wind and rain at the end of a stone path. Millicent shivered at the thought of using such a thing in midwinter. Indeed, it was moderately horrible to use it during a cold spring rainstorm, but the chill air and odiferous hut was enough to calm her agitation. By the time she was back in the warm house, she was calm and under control – but determined not to go back to the parlor until she could not avoid it. As she walked back through the corridors she saw two maids descending the steps carrying covered chamber pots. Yet another example, Millicent thought, of the advantages of being female.

Trenton Manor was a decent-sized, two-story building in the shape of a horseshoe, with narrow enclosed passageways running to the stables and other outbuildings. No doubt, given the winter weather in Wales, such a thing was necessary. Millicent's wanderings took her to the stables where she found her hired driver and outriders had been given the hayrick for their beds. Looking at the soft fragrant straw Millicent suspected they would have a better bed of it than she, trying to sleep on a short lumpy couch or the carpeted floor of the parlor.

She accepted their assurances that they'd been promised a good meal and were warm and well tended, and returned to the main house leaving them to small beer and a dice game.

From the uproar she walked in on it seemed that Shoffer's status as a titled gentleman had been revealed. Millicent followed the noise to the kitchen.

"A duke! A duke!" shrieked Mrs. Prichart. Her position in the center of the kitchen ensured that no work could be done around her. "Oh, what are we to…"

The woman froze seeing Millicent enter, then fell silent and pale into the nearest chair. Everyone in the room, gathered to witness her histrionics, turned to stare.

"Yes, he is a duke," said Millicent softly.

"But what are we to feed him?" demanded Mrs. Prichart.

"Food, I imagine," said Millicent, "since it is only a rumor that they live on moonbeams and starlight."

"We cannot have him sleep in the parlor!"

"You have already moved all the boys into the same room to clear a room for Mr. North," said her husband, "and the ladies have taken that one. The girls already share a room. We have none other to offer beyond our own bed."

"Oh. Oh. Oh." whimpered his lady. "What are we to do?"

This time Millicent was convinced Mrs. Prichart's distress was real. Stalking down the corridor, Millicent flung open the door into the front parlor to find Shoffer stretched out on a couch, his arm flung over his eyes, asleep. Leaving the door open Millicent tiptoed back to where Mrs. Prichart sat and pulled her to her feet. Millicent pressed a shushing finger to the woman's lips and led the way to the parlor.

"See," whispered Millicent, pointing toward the sleeping peer. "All is well. All the scones gone from the tea tray and he is fast asleep. Your hospitality can be judged a success. Keep your bed. His Grace and I shall sleep here quite happily."

Then she turned the woman over into her husband's keeping.

"When shall we gather for supper?" asked Millicent.

"In an hour, Mr. North, in the other parlor," replied the housekeeper. "The ladies have requested trays in their room."

Millicent nodded and tiptoed into the parlor, closing the door softly behind her. The next hour she spent trying to read and not to watch the steady rise and fall of the duke's linen covered chest. When the hour was almost up she woke the duke with the simple expedience of kicking his couch. The man came awake in an instant and blinked at her.

"Good God, I did not expect to sleep."

"It is well that you did to fortify you for what is to come." At Shoffer's questioning look, she continued. "Someone told Mrs. Prichart your rank."

"Dear God. But it was not me."

"Quite likely one of the ladies," said Millicent, pointing to the ceiling. "Though to be honest, I think she would still be in a taking if you were a mere baronet."

"True." Shoffer rose and retied his cravat. "Well, since it is too late for me to be a vicar, shall we go and face the mob?"

"Be careful of the food. Mrs. Prichart was trying to think of a dish worthy of your eminence."

Shoffer pulled himself up and regarded her with stony ducal dignity.

"My dear sir, I survived the food at Eton. I can survive anything."

Dinner itself went fairly well with the younger children of the house fed early and it being too late for any strange dish to be added to the menu. There was at table only Millicent, Shoffer, Mr. and Mrs. Prichart and two daughters of marriageable age – Eilowen and Gweneth. Since from their manners and features Millicent could tell the girls would age to resemble their mother, she felt some pity for Shoffer when the girls fluttered and giggled at every word he uttered – until she realized that she too was under siege.

Millicent found her pose as a foolish rattle served her well for deflecting the flirtation directed toward her by the second eldest daughter. Millicent was on her best form directing outrageous remarks to everyone at the table be they male or female. By the end of the evening everyone declared they could not remember laughing so much in their lives, and neither of the girls behaved as if they were in expectation of an offer.

When Millicent shut the door behind her hosts leaving just herself and Shoffer and a pile of bedding in the parlor, she rested her head against the wooden panels and gave a heartfelt groan. Shoffer laughed.

"Oh, come now, dear fellow. You were excellent and you know it. The ladies of the household are entirely yours to command." Shoffer struggled for a moment with his fashionably tight jacket then surrendered. "Come over and help me with this damnable jacket."

Millicent walked slowly across the room and took hold of the collar as Shoffer wiggled this way and that. Her fingers brushed against the warmth of his neck and the fine, soft hairs and she could feel the tingle all the way to her toes. Shoffer, of course, did not notice her blush or any fumbling in her assistance. In a few minutes, he was freed and the jacket hung on the back of a chair.

"So fine a line to walk," continued Shoffer, unwrapping his cravat, "between flirtation and interest. I have never seen so direct a look between a man and a woman as you gave Gweneth mean nothing more than intelligent attention. If I were to try to imitate you I would find myself facing a demand for a betrothal."

"I may yet," said Millicent. "I must take care. No doubt that calculating look on Mrs. Prichart's face was meant for both you and me."

"And yet you diverted it. My admiration, sir. Of course, it increases my determination that you should try to work with my sister."

"I am supposed to be here to work with my tenant, Your Grace. Mr. Prichart intends to take me over the property tomorrow, rain or not."

"There are still the evening hours."

"When we will be obliged to spend time with our hosts."

The duke, it appeared, could be stubborn.

"Beth shall see you in conversation with others which will aid her immeasurably, I am certain."

"Perhaps."

Millicent doused the candles, leaving firelight only to light the room and shrugged out of her own loosely fitted jacket. She shifted her pile of blankets to the other side of the room and sat on the floor with the back of her chair between herself and Shoffer before stripping off her shirt and loosening the band of cravats around her breasts. Tugging her nightshirt over her head she climbed under the blankets before removing her trousers. The carpet under her pallet smelt of years of heavy boots, dogs, and dust but, after the strenuous events of the day, an exhausted Millicent was asleep within minutes.

They knew morning had arrived when heavy footsteps echoed through the house. Millicent opened one eye, grunted, and stared at the ceiling as feet crossed back and forth over her head. She lifted herself enough to peer through the nearest shuttered window. It was still pitch dark outside. She fell back onto her pallet with a groan.

"Farmers," came a muffled voice on the other side of the room, "have no respect for sleep."

Millicent grinned to herself and rubbed sleep from her eyes. There was a hard knocking on the door; one of the younger sons entered bearing a pitcher of steaming water, a bowl, and two rough towels.

"Pa says how he will be taking yourself around the property this morning, Mr. North," said the boy in a voice that he probably intended as a whisper. "Breakfast in the kitchen, if you do not mind, soon as you are ready."

"If I must, I must," groaned Millicent, testing the air outside her cocoon of blankets and finding it not at all to her liking. "And His Grace?"

"Oh, toffs like him sleep 'til noon. Ma will find something for him and the ladies will keep him company 'til you and Pa are finished."

There was a thud from the other side of the room. Millicent rose to her knees to see over the couch she had chosen as her protection, blankets still wrapped around her torso. Wearing only his smallclothes, the duke tossed his blanket aside and strode across the room to where the boy had placed the shaving water.

"Be damned to that," swore Shoffer as goose pimples spread over his bare skin. "Be a good lad and tell my groom to saddle my horse. I will view the property with Mr. North."

"Language," said Millicent mildly, settling her blankets tent-like about her body and climbing from the floor to collapse into a sagging armchair.

Shoffer snorted as he bathed his face in the steaming water and began working up lather in his shaving cup. Millicent watched the efficient movements, a slow heat climbing in her belly. While he applied a brush load of foam to his face, Shoffer shot a glance toward Millicent.

Millicent flinched and ducked back down to her hiding place. It took a few minutes of struggling to tighten her breast bands without drawing attention to her activities or removing her nightshirt. Finally, she was able to pull on her clothing and wrap her cravat loosely around her neck before rising to her feet.

"You are a lucky fellow," said Shoffer, as he scraped lather from his face. "Your hair is so pale your night's growth barely shows. Or are you younger than I have guessed?"

Millicent halted in her tracks, confused for a moment, then she raised her hand to her hairless cheeks. Fortunately, aside from the candle next to Shoffer's shaving mirror and the glow from the banked fireplace, there was little enough light in the room for her to be seen.

"Well, sir?" said Shoffer. "Are you twenty at least?"

"Really, such a thought," said Millicent, as her heart began to beat again. "I am four and twenty and have been shaving for a decade. I shall tend to my whiskers once you have cleared the field."

Shoffer blinked at her, then down at the jug of hot water.

"Oh. I do apologize. This was sent for you."

"Rank hath its privileges, Your Grace," she said with a wave and hurried from the room.

By the time Millicent returned from the privy, Shoffer was gone. Even though she did not shave, she kept a kit in her travel bag. Using the left over water from Shoffer's shave, she ran the shaving brush over her soap and left enough foam in the cup to create the illusion of having shaved. After a quick breakfast in the kitchen, Millicent found herself in the forecourt shivering in her greatcoat as the sun struggled to make itself visible through a thick mist.

"Wet Wales," muttered Shoffer, as he wound a scarf over his face and pulled his hat down securely against the wind. He glanced toward the sky. "It will rain again within the hour."

"Not today," said Mr. Prichart. "The wind is picking up. The clouds will stay, but there will be nothing more than water in the air."

"In other counties we call that 'rain,' Mr. Prichart," quipped Shoffer, settling himself on a magnificent grey mare.

Millicent, offered her choice of one of Shoffer's outriders' mounts or one of Mr. Prichart's farm horses, requested the most placid mount available. The gathered men smirked at each other when an aged pony was brought out.

"Will this do?" inquired Mr. Prichart innocently.

Millicent examined the creature closely. "Have you nothing smaller?"

"Oh, do get up, Mr. North," said Shoffer, as the farmer and his workers chuckled. "The sooner we have viewed the property the sooner we can return to the fireside."

"Truly, I am not skilled with riding," said Millicent, as she hauled herself into the masculine saddle. "I hope we do not have far to go."

"Unfortunately, no," said Mr. Prichart.

And so it proved. It was not necessary to ride more than a mile to find the reason Mr. Prichart had written to his landlord. Winter snow and rain, worse than any in living memory, had caused a nearby stream to break its banks, spilling freezing water over the low lying fields. Mr. Prichart, Shoffer, and Millicent sat their horses on a hill overlooking the flooded area while still more precipitation fell to cling to clothing, skin, and hair.

"How much land is affected?" inquired Shoffer.

"All told, sixty acres."

"Truly?" asked Millicent, rising up in her stirrups and pointing. "I thought I could see grassy land over there."

"Aye, you can see the top of the grass, but there be two or three inches of water underneath. Cannot graze sheep on such lands."

Uncertain as to the truth of it, Millicent said nothing.

"He is right, you know," said Shoffer in a soft voice. "Sheep are funny things. They eat grass down to the nub in dry weather. They eat wet grass with no ill. But if you put them out on pasturage like this, and do it too soon after the water has retreated, they get a cough from it and become poor goers. Their feet will rot. Some will die of it."

"You have seen this before?" asked Mr. Prichart.

"I have an interest in sheep farming in Scotland," replied the duke.

"How much of your land do you expect to be able to farm this year?" Millicent asked Pritchart.

"Depends how long it takes for the water to retreat. It's not stopped raining yet so we might have half our usual pasturage for a good part of the year. I do not want to go replacing drowned stock if I got nowhere to put 'em. They will overgraze the land and starve."

"Can you do anything to direct the water back to its previous path?"

One of the farm workers snorted at that, but Mr. Prichart answered Millicent's question in a serious manner.

"We do not know, lad. See over yonder? The stream bed itself is under all that water. And with the lower lands flooded, the water has nowhere to go."

"Oh." Feeling very foolish Millicent rode alongside the men as they traveled. Shoffer and Mr. Prichart discussed various breeds of sheep, alternative feeds, and other such matters while Millicent stared into the distance and tried to think of some intelligent seeming comment she could put into the conversation. It was not until near luncheon when they had turned and headed toward the manor that Millicent again spoke.

"It seems to me that I am limited in the aid I can give you, Mr. Prichart, since I must expect other farmers to whom I rent in the neighborhood will be making similar requests. We must take the long view in the matter. If I recall your letter correctly, you request the rent be reduced by a third. I think I can accommodate you. You will contact me if your other interests cannot be encouraged to make up the shortfall. Next year, the first two quarters will be reduced again on the understanding that you will use the money to purchase new stock. From what His Grace is saying, you might consider speaking to his man in Scotland and seeing if you can improve your stock with an infusion of his sheep."

Mr. Prichart and the duke regarded her with matching shocked expressions.

"Well, well. That be generous of you, Mr. North. Thank you," said Mr. Prichart.

Millicent flushed, worried that she had yielded too fast or reduced the rent too far. Behind the farmer's back Shoffer dropped a wink to Millicent which confused her further.

She waited until he guided his mount to ride alongside her.

"Was it too much? Too little?" she whispered. "I cannot calculate his income from an acre of land. I could but guess."

"I must say, from the state of the roads and fields hereabouts, your offer is a good one. It is a difficult balance to maintain — your needs for your rents versus the needs of your tenants."

Mr. Prichart paused to speak to one of his workers who stood watching the waters with a sour look on his face. Shoffer nudged his horse a little closer.

"If you had but waited until we could have spoken privately, I would have advised you thusly..." he paused, then smiled, "to do exactly as you have done."

Without thinking, Millicent slapped him across the back of his arm. Then flushed and withdrew her hand. That move, in an assembly room with fan in hand, would have been judged flirtatious. Man to man, she was uncertain if the gesture was acceptable. Truly, she should pay more attention to her manners. She cast her eyes down as Shoffer roared with laughter and slapped her hard across the back, nearly knocking her from her saddle.

"My dear Mr. North, you are too uncertain of your own skills. Have you but recently come into your responsibilities?"

It took a few moments of searching her memory for Millicent to find the answer. It would not do for some chance remark of Mr. Prichart's to reveal an inconsistency.

"Ah, it has been some six years since my father's death. But this is the first serious matter to come to my attention since then."

"In that case you have been much blessed. I find I must deal with a disaster somewhere at least once in every year."

"Rather, perhaps, you have been cursed."

"Or you have been negligent."

Millicent paused, blushed, and looked away. Shoffer leaned closer still.

"I am sorry, my friend. Please do not take offense. I am not as skilled a rattle as you and only wished to match your humor."

"No, Your Grace, you have not offended. Instead, you have reminded me of my indolence. Once granted my inheritance, I retreated to one of the smaller estates to the north and did not venture out again for several years. My only excuse…" she paused and considered believable lies to explain the years the real Mr. North spent closeted up in his Yorkshire estates. Saying she had been a practicing miser and misogynist would not do.

"Lack of preparation?" suggested Shoffer. "You are young for your responsibilities and could have been no more than eighteen when your father died. Your father could hardly have expected you to inherit so soon. My father trained me from boyhood for my estates. I imagine if the training were not completed, I would have found it difficult, nay, impossible. Even a small estate has its particulars and problems. If I may be so impolite as to inquire, how large an estate weighs on your mind?"

Millicent closed her eyes and rattled off the list of Mr. North's properties she had memorized. She opened her eyes and peered up at Shoffer sitting tall on his much larger horse, with a rather stunned expression on his face.

"That is a considerable estate," he said, after a pause.

"I know." By this time they were back within sight of the manor buildings. Despite the weather, Mrs. Prichart and her daughters were out and about in the kitchen garden. One of the girls caught sight of Millicent and Shoffer and her shout immediately set off a round of handkerchief fluttering waves and curtsies. Exchanging a glance with Shoffer, Millicent straightened her spine. "The sad thing is, so do they."

Chapter Four

Dinner, set at country hours, was not bad. Millicent concentrated on being the fribble and rattle that everyone seemed to accept so well and distracted the women of the family for most of the meal with humorous stories of Bath society. The eldest daughter, Eilowen, positioned between Shoffer and Millicent, practiced what coquetry she knew to no avail. Millicent pretended not to notice and left Shoffer to suffer and deal with the situation as best he could. As with every social event both good and bad, dinner came to an end and Mrs. Prichart, determined to demonstrate the superiority of her household, summoned the ladies to accompany her to who knew where since the other parlor was currently a bedroom.

A bottle of port was brought to the table and Shoffer offered around his own selection of cigars. Millicent declined both.

"I must say," said Mr. Prichart to Millicent as the door closed behind the ladies. "That you are not the man your father's letter led me to believe you were."

Millicent's hand trembled on her wineglass. Letter? Whatever had the old man written? That Mr. North was as blind as a bat? Had it given his age? His interests? What item of description had revealed Millicent's deception?

Her breath caught and she could barely bring herself to raise her eyes to her hosts.

"Why, I expected someone, well … I'm not sure what I expected," continued Mr. Prichart. "You are a rattle, that's for sure, but not stupid or ignorant. You listened to me, to his Grace here, and took time to think about my problems. I have to say, I never expected to respect you."

"You do surprise me," said Millicent, forcing herself to unclench her death grip on the glass stem before she shattered it. "Firstly, because I was not aware of any letter."

"Oh, it arrived a few months before your father died. It was supposed to reassure me that you would not be my landlord for long. Gave me the impression you were ill."

Millicent said nothing, but sat contemplating her wine while her mind raced. Obviously, Mr. Prichart brought this subject up for a reason, but she did not know what to do. It was not as if the late Mr. North had taken her into his confidence regarding his relationship with his parent, nor even on the subject of his health.

"Mr. Prichart, I suspect you have performed a miracle," said Shoffer. "You have rendered Mr. North speechless."

Millicent cast a faint smile in his direction. "I am merely contemplating the contents of such a letter. Until this moment, I was unaware of communication between my father and Mr. Prichart and I was wondering why Mr. Prichart should be my father's confidant. Did you know him so well?"

"Never met him. All matters between us were dealt with by letter with his man of business. But you misunderstand me, Mr. North; I was not the only one who received it. It was my impression that a similar letter was sent to all those who would become your tenants. I do remember discussing the matter with Mr. Owens on market day. You will be calling upon him next, I imagine, since his property is nearest, near thirty miles from here."

After some hesitation Millicent ventured a soft, "I wonder what he wrote."

"I have the letter still, Mr. North, if you wish to see it?"

When Millicent did not answer Shoffer stood, glass of port in hand.

"Of a certainty, he would. If you would be so kind, Mr. Prichart?"

"It's in my office." Mr. Prichart heaved his bulk out of his chair and led the way from the room.

"Where are you going?" cried Mrs. Prichart as they passed the open door of the kitchen.

"Just a few items of business, my dear. We shall have you back to sit with us in a moment."

Mrs. Prichart appeared to be about to protest, but with a worried glance toward Millicent, she fell silent and let them pass.

Mr. Prichart settled himself comfortably in his tiny estate office. The lack of decoration and layers of dust told that this was one area of the house that Mrs. Prichart did not enter. Probably, Millicent mused, because she would not fit between the stacked boxes of papers. Mr. Prichart appeared to want to be a literate man. His private retreat was filled with pamphlets on various farming techniques and years of scandal sheet papers from London piled on every flat surface and shelf.

Shoffer picked up one yellowed sheet of newsprint and raised an eyebrow.

"Aye, I have heard your name before," said Mr. Prichart. "You need not worry we will write to the gossip sheets about your visit, although nothing will stop my wife from crowing over the other families in the district. It is her greatest woe at this moment that the roads are too bad for any dinner invitations to be sent out."

"I am thankful for the rain for that blessing," murmured Shoffer, "if for nothing else."

"If you stay long enough nothing will save you," added Mr. Prichart, emerging from under his desk with a heavy lock box. "She's been at me and at me about hosting some entertainment before you escape."

"If the wind continues as it is all night," said Shoffer, indicating the trembling shutters with his glass, "then the roads will improved enough for a messenger to go in the morning. I have written to my man of business to send our older traveling coach and have it meet us. I expect it will take Mr. North a few more days to complete his business with you, then we can impose on him for assistance in reaching Merthyr Tydfil to await the coach's arrival."

"Mrs. Prichart may never forgive me for letting you go before she can show you off to all the neighborhood."

"My apologies for the ear bashing you shall suffer after our departure," said Millicent. "But, in this season of the year, if you have two days good weather together you cannot waste them."

"Spoken as a true country gentleman," said Mr. Prichart reaching into his box. "And here it is. I keep the rental documents together with your correspondence, Mr. North. Here is the last letter from your father. The next to arrive was from the lawyer informing me that I should continue depositing the rent at the Mercantile, but under a different name."

Millicent accepted the bundle and read the letter. The first time she read through quickly seeking such a line as "my true born son has a mole shaped like a rabbit on the back of his thigh, if he should call on you, demand to see it!" but there was no such statement. The second time she read through, Millicent could not hold in her gasp.

"Mr. North," said Shoffer. "You have gone quite pale."

For the first time, Millicent felt a small stirring of pity for the departed Mr. North. Holding the thin sheet of paper to the light she read:

Mr. Prichart,

I write to inform you that death will soon require me to divide my properties between my sons, Perceval and Anthony. I would prefer that all go to Perceval, but my father's will requires I equally share the estate. Your misfortune, sir, is to be counted amongst those properties that will come under the control of my younger son, Anthony North. Do not despair, as I have so created my will that Anthony cannot sell nor gamble away his inheritance. We can only hope that his degenerate lifestyle will result in his speedy death and you will not be long burdened with him. When the day comes that Anthony descends to receive his eternal judgment everything that he owns will devolve upon his brother, and you shall come under the better husbandry and management of my son Perceval.

Until that time, hold fast and endure.
Respectfully, etc.

"My God," said Shoffer. "Why would he do such a thing?"

"But your reading is very fine, Mr. North," added Mr. Prichart, seeking to offer some comfort. "And you have a splendid voice. Perfect diction."

"Titled estates are wrapped in entails all the time, Your Grace," said Millicent. "You hardly can be surprised when your lessers begin to imitate the practice."

"But to write such a note, to people with whom you must work. Disgraceful! No matter what his opinion of you, that was unjust!"

Millicent did not answer for her mind was racing and she read and reread the line "sell nor gamble away" as her mouth dried and hands shook.

"North?" Shoffer left his perch and crossed to tower over Millicent. "Pray, do not be overset by this. Just because the man did not understand your humorous nature..."

"It is not that, or if it is, it hardly matters." Millicent folded the note and glanced across at Mr. Prichart. "I hope you do not mind that I keep this, and the letter from the lawyer?"

"Why ever for?"

"Because if I was given this information at the time of my father's death, I do not remember it. I must ask to see a copy of the will to know if any provision has been made for me to bequeath something to *my* heirs."

Shoffer's head came up and he frowned, but Mr. Prichart's face continued to display his lack of comprehension.

"This letter says everything will devolve upon Perceval," continued Millicent. "Everything! I must know if there is any flexibility. If I acquire dependents, may I provide for them?"

"My God, you are right," said Mr. Prichart, as understanding dawned. "If you wed and have children, will they, with your money and property, go to your brother?"

"I would not throw a dog onto Perceval's charity," said Millicent. "He has none."

"Then you certainly must speak to the lawyer who probated the will," said Shoffer. "I am surprised that you were not fully informed."

Millicent said nothing. It was entirely possible that the late Mr. North had known the full terms of the will, which might have explained why he had never married. No doubt the provisions had been discussed at length prior to the old man's death, probably at volumes that shattered the window glass. But she needed to know the full extent of the entail. In the back of her mind over the last few months, had been the confident thought that she could provide very well for her sisters' futures. She had Mr. North's full estate to bestow upon them as dowries, as well as making provision for her mother – an annuity or some such – so that she would never be helpless, penniless, or again, afraid.

But now? Perceval North fully and legally expected to receive all of it upon Anthony North's death.

With no dowry at all, what sort of marriages could Mildred and Maude make?

And if anyone ever discovered Millicent's deception would she be merely deported or hanged?

"We should rejoin the ladies," suggested Mr. Prichart.

"It will not be taken amiss, given the news, if you choose not to," said Shoffer.

Millicent shook herself out of her distraction.

"Gentlemen, the old Mr. North has been dead for years. Any evil he has set in motion will wait. You will find I am not easily or long cast down." She stood and waved for Shoffer to precede her through the door. "Besides," she whispered as Shoffer drew near. "I am not so unkind as to leave you to these ladies without some protection."

"The full legions of Rome would not be enough, I suspect," shot back Shoffer.

The evening was not so bad as Shoffer had feared. Millicent was back in good form by the time they entered the best parlor. She cajoled the girls of the household into presenting their party pieces. The house possessed no piano, but there was one lap harp and both girls were blessed with surprisingly good voices. Millicent even dragged Shoffer to his feet and persuaded him to sing the male part of a sad Italian love song they both knew. Millicent, singing the lady's part in a false and brittle soprano, effected to be so overcome with tears that by the end she was sobbing into a handkerchief and Shoffer laughed himself into a chair.

"It is ever so," said Millicent, returning the borrowed handkerchief to the eldest daughter. "Men cannot endure tears."

Mrs. Prichart blushed.

"Not so," said Shoffer. "I do just require that each emotion should be offered at the appropriate time."

"And when, pray, are tears appropriate?"

"When I am not in the room," replied Shoffer, to universal laughter.

"There, ladies, you have it," said Millicent. "When we have departed you have His Grace's permission to weep, but I think he would prefer the return of his cravats and handkerchiefs."

Both girls blushed, confirming Millicent's suspicion that some pilfering of the ducal linens as souvenirs had occurred.

"Well, now, I must say, 'tis time for those who must rise with the sun to seek their beds," said Mr. Prichart.

Everyone else came to their feet.

"I do hope your sister will be recovered enough from her ordeal to join us tomorrow," said Mrs. Prichart to the duke.

Shoffer shot a puzzled look at the ceiling as if he had just that moment noticed the girl's absence. "I am certain she shall."

Later, when Millicent was hidden again behind the back of her chair and had pulled on her nightshirt, Shoffer returned to the parlor, came around the couch, and sat on the floor beside her.

"I went upstairs to speak to my sister while you were in the privy," he said.

Millicent seized the nearest blanket and pulled it up and around her shoulders, and holding it tight across her chest, dragged another blanket across her legs. Fortunately, Shoffer was distracted enough not to pay any attention to her excessive modesty, but stared off into the distance.

"Mrs. Fleming was asleep already so we could speak. It seems that the reason Beth has not been seen today is Mrs. Fleming will not let her leave the room. They took all their meals on trays in their room at her command."

Grateful that he had not cried out "Fraud!" or "Female!" Millicent's heart settled back into its proper beat.

"Did she give a reason?"

"Not that I understood. We could only converse in whispers and not for long, lest Mrs. Fleming awake."

"Perhaps, if the weather is good by Welsh standards, we can invite her to ride out with us tomorrow. Mrs. Fleming can hardly accompany us with her wounded hand. And riding with her brother's protection would be eminently suitable. You may converse then."

Shoffer slapped her across the back with enough force to knock her sideways onto her pile of bedding. Laughing as if she had done it intentionally, Shoffer hauled her back upright by the arm.

"You are a good fellow, North. All I can think is your father was a narrow-minded idiot who did not appreciate your humor."

"You are kind to say so, Your Grace."

"Oh, stop with the 'Graces,' I beg you. Call me Shoffer and have done. I will tell you, North. I do not trust easily or often. I have few true friends as a consequence. Sycophants and pretenders without number follow me about and I tolerate them since I must. But, based on our short acquaintance, I know I can trust you and I ask you to call me friend."

He held out his hand to Millicent who felt like a complete fraud.

Sitting there beside him on the floor, the firelight flickering over the planes of his face and flashing highlights on his curly hair, Millicent almost cried.

Almost confessed.

Almost leaned forward to catch his hand and hold it to the breasts hidden beneath their bindings.

But, she did not.

If she did she would ruin her sisters' futures, her mother's security, and her own life, since the theft of such a large estate would be judged a capital crime.

No. Instead she gave a sharp masculine nod, and grasping Shoffer's hand in both of hers, gave it one hard squeeze and shake. Looked directly into his dark eyes and fell the rest of the way, helplessly, in love.

Later, wrapped in her blankets, unable to relieve her feelings with tears for fear he might hear, she held his offer of friendship in her heart and tried to convince herself that it was enough.

Would be enough.

Was not enough.

Thudding of farmer's feet on hard, bare wood floors woke Millicent and Shoffer the next morning before the sun even hinted at rising above the horizon.

Again they shaved in barely heated water, pulled on wrinkled shirts (by now Shoffer was borrowing linen and small clothes from Millicent's supply of men's clothing), and joined the parade to the kitchen for a hearty farm breakfast.

After speaking briefly to Mr. Prichart, and Eilowen, who was supervising breakfast, Shoffer ran upstairs to tap on his sister's door. The girl must have been awake and waiting for the knock since she emerged immediately and was taken to another room by the daughters of the household. Within half an hour she was down, dressed in an old-fashioned riding dress two sizes too large. After breakfast, Shoffer lifted his sister onto a pony bearing an equally ancient side saddle.

Lady Beth raised her face to the sky as a breeze brushed over her face.

"Is it raining or not?" she asked. "I cannot tell."

"'Tis what we Welsh call a bright day," said Mr. Prichart.

"That's not what we Irish call it," muttered one of Shoffer's grooms.

Millicent glanced up at the sky. At the moment the air was full of water from a mist that writhed and glowed over the fields.

"I think it will clear later," said Millicent. "We might even see the sun."

"If it does, then it will be what we Welsh call a blessed day," said Mr. Prichart.

"That's not what the Irish call it," muttered the groom and ducked his head down when he saw Millicent glance toward him.

"What do you call a bright and sunny day?" asked Beth. "This is useful for me to know since talking about the weather, apparently, is the only thing you can talk about at Tonnish events. You as well," she added to the groom.

"Well, it is the best day, since a bright and sunny day is a good day for getting work done," said the farmer.

They all turned to face the groom.

"Well?" prompted Shoffer.

"A blessed day is every day," said the groom, "since it's a blessing that anyone's alive. The best day is payday, which cannot come around often enough for any man."

They all laughed at that, even the groom after Millicent felt around inside her glove for a sixpence she kept there for just such occasions, and handed it to him with a bow.

"I must honor anyone who tells a better jest and gets a heartier laugh than I do," she said.

"You must remember the replies, Beth," said Shoffer, as Mr. Prichart took the lead and set his horse's head toward his distant orchards. "As you said, the weather is the only safe conversation with strangers."

Lady Beth's face immediately fell and she glanced away. Shoffer shot a helpless glance toward Millicent. Men, Millicent told herself, as she brought her little pony up alongside Beth, were helpless creatures in the face of a shy girl, even when she was a relative.

"We appreciate you taking the time out of your busy schedule to ride with us this morning, dear Lady Beth," said Millicent, managing a half bow in her saddle.

"Thank you for inviting me," was the polite reply.

"I hope you have taken no injury from being tossed around in your carriage the other day."

"I am quite well."

At the formality of her replies, Shoffer rolled his eyes and made a "get along" gesture toward Millicent.

Millicent reviewed a number of conversational gambits and decided that the truth would be a good start.

"Lady Beth, I hope you will forgive your brother for involving me, but he has expressed some concern about your happiness. Apparently, there was some problem with your coming out."

"Mr. North!" cried Shoffer sharply, then softened his voice. "That was not what I meant. Forgive me, Beth, I asked Mr. North to give you conversation lessons. Fool that he is, he did not realize that I wished him to do so in a way that would not embarrass you."

"Now, Shoffer, calm yourself. Lady Beth will take no offense at this. She has a better understanding of her problems than you or me; and there is no better way to solve them than with her help. I could chatter away for hours and all she would learn is that I am a twit."

Beth giggled and blushed. "I do not think that of you."

"She may think that your dress is provincial and your cravat a disgrace," said Shoffer. "But you are not a twit."

"But the purpose of your enrolling my help is your sister's happiness. She already knows how to listen and I am certain she was taught to dance. Now we must discover what makes her unhappy and that, only she knows."

Shoffer sat back in his saddle and they both waited for Beth to respond. Even though the silence stretched uncomfortably long Millicent said nothing. Beth, with her posture perfect despite the ancient side saddle and borrowed clothing, was a dazzling example of her class. Pretty, dignified, and silent.

Ah, thought Millicent, and wondered how much of her help would be accepted.

"My dear," began Shoffer.

"I am very sorry to be a disappointment to my family," whispered Beth.

"Never, dear Beth. You are not."

"I am," said Beth in a voice near tears. "I cannot think of how to be different. I follow all Grand'Mere's rules when we are out and about, and then when we are home again, she is so very cross with me for failing to dazzle."

"Beth…"

"Excuse me, Your Grace. Lady Beth, if you would be so kind, I have never been a lady of your rank and refinement; therefore, I do not know the rules. Please tell me one or two of them."

"I may not speak to anyone of lesser rank," said Beth immediately.

"Lady Beth, you are the daughter of a duke," said Millicent. "The only persons who outrank you are princes, kings, and queens. As they are rather few upon the ground, you must suffer from a serious lack of suitable people with whom to converse."

"Yes, exactly," cried Beth.

Shoffer and Millicent exchanged a glance.

"I am afraid it is not possible for me to create new people of proper rank for you to meet, Lady Beth," said Millicent.

"I wish you could, Mr. North. I do wish you could. I would like to have some friends of my own."

"Whose friends do you have?"

"My Grand'Mere's, I suppose. They are the only people she took me to see when we were in London."

"Who are they?"

"Oh, Dowager this and Lady that," said Beth with a dismissive wave of her hand. "They are all much of an age with my Grand'Mere, and look and act the same. They discuss their many relatives, their illnesses, and the importance of young women listening silently to the wisdom of their elders. When Grand'Mere leaves the room the other ladies tell me about their sons and nephews and how eager the gentlemen are to make my acquaintance. Then we go home and Grand'Mere tells me that to create an alliance with any of their families would be a disgrace because they are beneath me in consequence, so I am not to encourage the pretensions of their sons."

"I'm confused," said Millicent.

"So am I," cried Beth, her voice becoming shrill. "I do not know who I am to talk to. I wanted to come down when I heard you laughing and singing last night, but Mrs. Fleming said that it would not be proper for me to leave the room. That I must always remember to display the proper condescension."

Millicent almost fell off her horse at the news of Mrs. Fleming's snobbery. "The proper condescension when someone overturns their house to offer you hospitality and shelter from a storm is to say the most sincere thank you that you can!"

Beth glanced across to her brother, as if expecting a contradiction.

Shoffer, however, nodded. "I would hope, sister, that you would always remember to give thanks in such circumstances and to adjust your manners so that you do not discomfit your hosts."

"Mrs. Fleming said that the Pricharts are so very far below me that it would be a disgrace and degradation for me to eat at the same table as them. She said that efforts would have to be made to conceal the fact I was ever here or else I would be turned away from all good society."

"Mrs. Fleming is a snob." Millicent snorted. "I do not know that many of the Ton's gossips make a point of calling upon country farmers to find out who has taken shelter in their house."

"She said that Timothy would have to pay a great deal of money to them to stop the gossip."

"And I believe that the Pricharts' feelings would be desperately hurt if His Grace would attempt to render a bribe of that nature," said Millicent. "The Pricharts are of good country yeomen stock and have their own pride. There is no degradation in being here. Did Mrs. Fleming say that Shoffer would suffer?"

"No, but he is a man. A woman's reputation is much more fragile."

"Beth, I want you to know I would never suggest you do anything that will damage your reputation," said Shoffer. "With that in mind, I will inform our hosts that you will be taking dinner with them, with all of us this evening. If Mrs. Fleming protests, pray remind her that I pay her salary."

"Actually, Grand'Mere pays her salary."

Shoffer frowned at that. "I pay her every quarter."

"So does Grand'Mere."

Millicent snickered at that news. "Clever Mrs. Fleming."

"This is unconscionable," said Shoffer.

"Oh, for pity's sake, forgive her," said Millicent. "As she is in service, you can assume that there is not a Mr. Fleming to care for her and she does what she does from necessity."

"Well, she need not take such pleasure in it," said Beth. "If I try to do anything fun Mrs. Fleming informs me that she will include a report in her letter to Grand'Mere."

"How often does she write these letters?" asked Millicent.

"Every day, it seems. The only reason she has not written one here is her hand is too sore."

Millicent grinned at Beth. "It seems some good has come of this accident. We must arrange a way for her again to hurt her hand. In a kind and gentle way, as I have no wish to hurt a lady."

For the first time in their acquaintance, Lady Beth snorted, which seemed to surprise her as much as the gentlemen with her.

"I would hurt her," said Beth. "She had the nerve yesterday to suggest that she dictate her daily letter to me!"

Millicent almost fell off her horse laughing. Shoffer roared so loud that the farmers, now far ahead of the dawdling trio, turned to stare.

"Dear God," cried Millicent, when she recovered her breath. "We must take note of date and time, Shoffer. Today your sister made her first joke!"

Shoffer made a show of pretending to draw paper and pen out of his coat, sharpening the imaginary nib as he did, and miming writing.

"I begin to think," said Millicent, "that Lady Beth's problem arises from her grandmother's wish that she be quiet, biddable, reserved, condescending, and proud while also being the brilliant, dazzling, popular star of the season. She does not know that her own training and rules prevent Lady Beth being that success."

"I find I agree," said Shoffer, after a moment's thought.

"So do I." Beth shook her head. "It made no sense to me. I was taught to dance and expected to do so, even looked forward to it, but whenever anyone gathered their courage and appeared to be about to ask me Grand'Mere would whisper, his rank is too low, or his family's title too recent a creation, and I was required to refuse. I am commanded to speak, but there is no one to whom speaking would not be a degradation. What was I to do but stand still and be silent?"

"Toss your grandmother's rules out of the window and have some fun," suggested Millicent.

"But I live with Grand'Mere and she would be so cross with me. She would…" Beth stopped and stared at her hands. "She … I could not disobey her."

"I do not advocate the full rejection of the rules of good behavior," Shoffer mock scowled at Millicent. "But, there is fun to be had even so. I cannot think what my grandmother intends. If you do not speak to young women, you will have no friends. And if you speak with no men, how are you to marry?"

"There are other things to do in London beyond dancing, talking, and getting married, or so I am told," said Millicent.

"And I have never done any of them. I have never even been to a lending library, or to Gunther's for an ice. Or to see the fireworks or the museums."

"Then arrangements must be made," declared Shoffer. "Next season you shall most certainly go to Gunther's. I shall take you, since I am fond of ices myself."

Millicent shifted in her saddle. Yesterday's brief ride taught her an affection she had never thought to experience for the sidesaddle. The way gentlemen rode chafed her thighs and her bottom ached as if made from bruises. Obviously, she should have practiced more.

"Why do you live with your grandmother since her company makes you unhappy?" asked Millicent.

Beth glanced toward her brother and away. "There is nowhere else to go."

"What is he?" Millicent jerked a thumb toward the duke. "A fish? Does he not have a house, or a dozen?"

"He is busy with other important matters," recited Beth.

"Oh, my dear, I am so sorry," cried Shoffer, leaning out of his saddle to grasp the girl's hand. "If I had but known you were unhappy I would have taken some action."

"How, pray, was she to tell you?" demanded Millicent. "Write a letter? I have no doubt that nothing from her to you ever was mailed without the approval of the duchess."

"Yes," said Beth, in response to a questioning rise of the duke's eyebrow.

Millicent made a note to herself to try and acquire that skill. It was a particularly masculine gesture and quite powerful to judge from her own rapid heartbeat and eagerness to reply to it.

"Grand'Mere said I have no skill at letter writing and I was to learn by taking her dictation."

"Well, this situation is over," said the duke. "I want your letters to be in your own words and no other's."

"And to be certain, the two of you will agree on a phrase to put into Beth's letters whereby the duke shall always know that the letter was Beth's own creation," added Millicent.

"I pray you, cease behaving as if we dwell within a dreadful Gothic novel," said Shoffer.

"I have never read one," declared Beth to Millicent. "Can you make recommendations?"

"Certainly. I recommend you read as many as you can … particularly late at night by the light of a guttering candle."

"Mister North!" cried Shoffer. "What are you encouraging my sister to do? Dreadful novels are hardly proper for the development of her mind."

"Oh, come," laughed Millicent. "You may hold to that posture if you can put your hand on your Bible and swear to me you do not have a dreadful novel in your luggage. I shall bet half a crown that you do." She leaned toward the giggling Beth. "I can say that, you see, since I have seen a copy of *The Adventures at the Midnight Hour* next to his shaving brush."

"May I read it when you are done?" asked Beth.

"Certainly not. It is hardly the thing for a lady's sensibilities."

"Ah, by that you will know that it has frightened your brother," whispered Millicent.

"I am not frightened by the mere workings of an author's imagination," sneered the duke.

"Oh, please, tell me about it," begged Beth.

Millicent slowed her horse's pace and permitted Lady Beth to move closer so she might tease and mock her brother. By the time they had reached a bridge damaged by a mud slide, Beth had browbeaten her brother into promising to read the book aloud to her. Judging by Shoffer's brilliant smile, he was quite happy to have her chattering at him.

After examining the scene, Mr. Prichart suggested his visitors return to the warmth of the house while he took care of his other duties. Millicent debated with herself, then attached herself to the farmer and sent Beth and Shoffer back together. It was Millicent's view that Beth would benefit from a closer relationship with her confident brother, and she, Millicent, should spend less time with the duke. Even the slightest smile, the briefest contact eye to eye was enough to raise her heart rate and send a flush to her cheeks. Fortunately, the weather was chill enough that her high color could be dismissed.

Since she had only a day or two yet to spend in his company, she could hope that her strength and luck would hold and she would not reveal herself.

Chapter Five

The entertainment that night after dinner was a reading from Shoffer's book. He chose the most thrilling chapter and told the story with such voices and atmospheric noises that there was complete silence from his audience.

Shoffer chose to address them from beside the fireplace. The firelight was kind to him: highlighting the sculpted planes of his face, displaying the breadth of his shoulders and narrow waist, and particularly fine, in Millicent's opinion, legs and thighs spread dramatically wide as he braced himself for his reading.

He was an unexpectedly dramatic orator. With one hand he held the book raised before his face, the other gracefully inscribed arcs through the air, his long-fingered hand flickering back and forth, drawing his awestruck listeners into the tale.

If pressed Millicent would have been unable to say what the story was about. All of her attention was caught by the rise and fall of his voice, the swell of his chest as he breathed. For the full hour Millicent watched, entranced. She could imagine those graceful movements of his hands gliding over a woman's body, caressing and awakening her to passion. Her own skin prickled and warmed, and beneath the protection of her thick linen shirt and loose masculine jacket her breasts grew heavy and nipples tightened.

While all the other listeners gasped and shuddered at the dangers Shoffer related, Millicent focused on the beauty of his mouth, watched his well cut lips move, admired the firmness, the color. The pleased, smug smile that flickered and was gone when his audience shivered and sighed. At one point, he pursed his lips to imitate the moan of a ghost and heat filled Millicent's face and chest. She could easily imagine those lips pursed to deliver a kiss. That mouth would not be hard then, but warm and soft and smooth, claiming a lady's own with passion and power. Millicent had never experienced a true kiss, but knew through to her bones that Shoffer's would be incomparable.

When his tongue darted out at one point to soothe and moisten his lips, Millicent's heart clenched and heat pooled in her center. She had no idea why that movement should so affect her, but she watched intently lest he should do it again.

Shaken, inflamed, distracted – she came to herself with a start when Shoffer slammed the book shut. Indeed, she was not the only one to cry out in surprise. Glancing around the room she could only hope that they put her flushed face and flustered demeanor down to the terror of the story.

Both of the daughters of the house were huddled against their mother and the younger boys kneeled at their father's feet. Lady Beth held to her brother's feet, gazing up at him in open adoration. Millicent brushed one hand over her face, hoping to calm her blushes and grateful that she was not the only one to be red-faced and shivering in the aftermath of his reading.

"Well, now," said Mr. Prichart, rising. "I shall have no trouble waking anyone tomorrow morning since they will not have a wink of sleep tonight. Even so, up you go and off to bed."

Millicent bowed as the ladies left and grinned at the smaller boys. Leaning forward she whispered as they left. "When I was younger, I was glad I slept in my brother's bed when there was a bad storm." And the boys all agreed that was a good thing.

Once they were alone, Millicent bowed to Shoffer.

"You have an excellent speaking voice, Your Grace, and an entrancing manner. Should you ever tire of your responsibilities, I can predict a successful career upon the stage for you."

"And I for you. I shall do the dramatic parts and you, the comedy."

"And Lady Beth for Juliette."

"She is a trifle shy for that, but much better than I have seen before. I judge you have a good effect upon her."

Before Millicent could reply there was a light knock on their door. Shoffer nodded permission for Millicent to answer. She was halfway across the room before she realized she had responded to an order not even uttered. Wrinkling her nose she opened the door to reveal their host.

"Mr. Prichart?"

Their host stared straight over her shoulder as if she was not there. Millicent began to feel like a particularly clumsy and inconsequential butler.

"Ah, good. I caught you before you were abed, Your Grace. The rider you sent out earlier has returned. He said that the weather has changed and there will be a heavy freeze tonight."

"Oh?" Shoffer stopped loosening his cravat and paid more attention. "How long will the freeze last?"

"I know not, but my feeling is that you should plan on leaving early in the morning. If the frost holds hard you should be able to get to Merthyr Tydfil by luncheon. If the weather breaks, as I fear it will in a day or so, we shall have either sleet or snow. Either way the roads will be dreadful. It would be better we get you to Merthyr Tydfil, or you may end up caught with us here till summer."

"I agree. I shall go and so inform my sister and her chaperone. Mr. North, can you and Mr. Prichart be finished with your business by first light?"

"We have agreed in principle to the changes in his rents," said Millicent. "There is just the enscribing to be done."

"Then have at it, sir; then, we shall get what sleep we can. Mr. Prichart? If you could inform our staff of our departure?"

"I suspect your rider has already informed them of his observation. Well, Mr. North, shall we adjourn to my office?"

Sighing Millicent resigned herself to another hour tied inside her breast bindings and trailed along behind Mr. Prichart.

Mrs. Fleming was not a person who traveled well. Even in the best of weather, she kept her hartshorn close to her nose and a bowl between her feet. Having to travel in freezing weather was trial enough, but in bad company? Horrors! She was not pleased that Lady Beth had disobeyed her the previous day and socialized with her inferiors. And now, to be trapped inside a carriage with the fribble Mr. North for hours, it was not to be borne! It was that lady's full intent that Mr. North be brought to an understanding of his inferior position in relation to the great house of the Duke of Trolenfield, even if it took the whole journey to Merthyr Tydfil to do it.

The milieu was, therefore, not very comfortable inside the rented carriage the next morning. Millicent, never been fond of sitting with her back to the horses, endured as best she could, since manners required that ladies face forward. Mrs. Fleming had arranged things so that Shoffer sat opposite his sister and Millicent faced Mrs. Fleming's deepest and most speaking frown.

There was not a joke or frivolous remark Millicent made that could shake that lady's disapproval. Lady Beth and Shoffer, however, exclaimed themselves well pleased with their traveling companion and competed with each other to cap Millicent's jokes.

"What are your plans for the summer, Mr. North?" asked Beth as the carriage lurched and shuddered over frozen ruts in the road.

Since the girl's face was pale with a faint green tinge, Millicent was determined to be distracting.

"My habitual laziness has been undermined by Mr. Prichart's demand I should visit his farm. After meeting him, I find myself overwhelmed with curiosity about the rest of my holdings. I expect I shall spend the spring and summer going from farm to farm, dazzling the farmers' wives with my wit and…"

"And debauching the farmers' daughters?" accused Mrs. Fleming.

"I think I have more respect for my tenants than that," said Millicent in chill tones. "What I intended to say was, avoiding the parson's mousetrap."

"I could see that Mr. Prichart's daughters were very impressed with you," laughed Beth.

"Not me," said Millicent. "I could stand on my head when your brother is in the room and no one would glance at me."

"The very idea!" gasped Mrs. Fleming. "I hope you gave them a stern set down, Your Grace. Such presumption! That is why I insisted that Lady Elizabeth should hold herself distant from those people. The duchess will not be pleased to hear you permitted Lady Elizabeth to be approached by those of such low estate."

"I saw nothing wrong with Beth meeting examples of hard working people," said Shoffer. "Much of our wealth comes from the labor of such and she should know and respect them."

"She should pay charity calls in the company of a vicar's wife," declared Mrs. Fleming, "but by no means should she enter their houses or speak to them beyond the most condescending of greetings. To do more would be a degradation."

Beth flushed and Millicent remembered the girl describing a scene involving a cottage fireside and kitten. Obviously, Beth had done more than nod from her place in a barouche while doing community visitation.

"I do not believe speaking to another human being is in any way a degradation, Mrs. Fleming," said Beth, surprising that lady into dropping her hartshorn. "They have souls, as do I."

"Her Grace, your grandmother, would be shocked to hear you say so, Lady Elizabeth."

"Since she is not here, then she shall not know," said Shoffer, his direct gaze setting Mrs. Fleming to the blush.

Beth bounced on her seat as much from the uneven road as her own excitement at challenging the authority of her chaperone.

"I am looking forward to the summer house parties I shall be attending. I hope to dance more than I did during the season."

"Her Grace has already written to your hostesses informing them which persons it will be appropriate for you to dance with," said Mrs. Fleming.

"As I will be attending these gatherings as well, my sister may apply to me for guidance and I shall provide any introductions that are necessary. It is my intention that Beth should enjoy herself." Shoffer glared at Mrs. Fleming, awaiting her response with interest.

Millicent caught Beth's eye and grinned.

"Lady Elizabeth may enjoy herself, within reason," replied Mrs. Fleming.

"Within reason? I have often wondered what reasonable enjoyment looks like," said Millicent. "Is it one third of a picnic, or one quarter of being rowed about a lake?"

"An hour of horseback riding in bad weather," suggested Beth. "One half hour of whist with a deaf partner."

"You enjoy that? I am all astonishment," cried Millicent.

"Lady Elizabeth," cried Mrs. Fleming. "Mr. North, I do protest. You are overly familiar. His Grace's sister, should you presume to address yourself to her, is Lady Elizabeth!"

"Truly?" asked Millicent.

"Elizabeth Rose Edwina Genevieve Helene, actually," said Lady Beth.

"Good heavens. You should be six feet tall to bear the burden of so many names."

"It is the weight of them that keeps me short," joked Lady Beth.

"Of all the preposterous things!" The carriage bounced and swayed at that point and Mrs. Fleming went decidedly green. "Oh, why must we travel in this dreadful farm cart?"

"It is a rented vehicle, I do admit, Mrs. Fleming," said Millicent, "but travel tomorrow would be worse and if we stayed another day, then we might be trapped at the manor in a blizzard. Just imagine the degradation."

"Oh, yes," added Beth. "Why if I had another two conversations with Mrs. Prichart, I should lose all my good sense and my speech would be provincial beyond all repair."

"This is not a matter for humor," cried Mrs. Fleming. "Your Grace, I do not understand why you do not support me in this? Your sister's reputation, her very station, may be undermined by such bad associations."

"I do hope, Mrs. Fleming, that you are not suggesting that I am leading my sister astray?"

The chaperone gave a long suffering sigh. "Your Grace, you are a man..."

"Never say so," cried Beth. "Timothy, is this true? How long have you been a man? And what of Mr. North? Is he a man as well?"

Millicent's heart stopped, skittered, then Beth burst out laughing, soon joined by her brother. Mrs. Fleming scowled at them both.

"I would judge, Your Grace," said Millicent when her heart resumed a regular beat, "that your sister has improved somewhat in the matter of chatting."

"Never say this change has your approval?" demanded Mrs. Fleming.

"It has, although, Beth will need to practice the degree of speech appropriate for the company she is in. Such informality as today is appropriate for dear, close, and trusted friends such as Mr. North, but not for common acquaintance."

"I understand," said Beth, calming, but flashing Millicent a sparkling look from beneath her lashes.

"I do not agree," said Mrs. Fleming, "and Her Grace will not approve. Mr. North is exactly the type of encroaching person that she most dislikes. I shall write to her as soon as we arrive at the inn."

"No, you will not," said Shoffer. "My sister is currently in my care and if I approve her conduct there is no reason for you to communicate with my grandmother. In fact, I think I disapprove of the degree of familiarity between you and Her Grace. Are you not being presumptuous? Encroaching?"

The suggested hypocrisy set Mrs. Fleming to the blush.

"Her Grace has commissioned me to do so."

"And, I, since I pay your salary, say you should not!"

There was a heavy silence in the carriage as Mrs. Fleming digested this announcement. Millicent wondered how much the duchess gave the chaperone for her to be a tattle tale upon her granddaughter.

"I wonder why it is your grandmother has permitted you out of her sight?" said Millicent, when the silence lingered too long.

"Oh, she has been unwell since the season," said Lady Beth. "The London air is foul with smoke and she has retired to the countryside to recover."

"She would have kept Beth with her," added Shoffer, "but I suggested she come home with me. Her Grace's residence is too far from any company and I feared Beth would... Well, I wanted to encourage her to be more social and thought she could do so in my neighborhood. There are no people her own age near my grandmother's abode."

"Lady Elizabeth," repeated Mrs. Fleming.

"Are you suggesting that you may order me not to call *my* sister by an informal name?" asked Shoffer in chilling tones.

Mrs. Fleming faded from green to very white.

"Lady Elizabeth Rosemary Gertrude," said Millicent. "I'm sorry, I have forgotten the rest. In your kindness, may I be permitted to call you Lady Beth?"

"You may **not**, you encroaching mushroom," cried Mrs. Fleming.

"Yes, he may." Lady Beth scowled at her chaperone. "Mr. North is my brother's *particular* friend and I regard him highly as well. I should like it very much if he would call me Beth."

Mrs. Fleming retreated to the depths of her cloak to cope with her rage and nausea as best she could for the remainder of the journey.

"To stave off boredom, may I suggest we play Faro?" suggested Millicent.

"We will not be able to shuffle or lay out the cards the way the carriage bounces about," protested Lady Beth.

"Ah, but there is a special way to play in these circumstances," said Millicent. "You do not use cards at all."

Shoffer stared at Millicent until she felt surely he must see through her disguise; then he laughed and shook his head.

"Very well, I yield. Tell me, how do you play cards without cards?"

"It all depends on how convincing you are." Millicent's eyes were wide and innocent, for just an instant; then she grinned wickedly. "If you claim you have laid down the Queen of Hearts and I do not believe you, then, sir, you may not play that card. But if you can convince me you have it in your hand; then the card is played."

"How do I convince you?"

"How well do you remember what cards look like?"

"I understand," cried Beth, and indeed she proved most proficient at bluffing. By the time they reached Merthyr Tydfil she had bluffed and teased them both out of twenty pounds.

They spent three days in Merthyr Tydfil enjoying what few distractions and entertainments could be obtained in a market town during rain mixed with sleet. Beth located several maps of England and Wales in a local bookshop and the three amused themselves trying to locate the Shoffer family and North properties and planning out Millicent's summer journey. Shoffer's memory proved useful for Millicent, as he had traveled in the area before and could recall which were the best inns on any particular road; therefore, he could give sensible suggestions to Millicent upon her itinerary. On the third day, the Trolenfields' second best coach arrived. The next day, since the weather was dry, for that instant, the decision was made for Shoffer and his sister to depart immediately. Beth demanded a promise that "Mr. North" should write to her. Shoffer granted his permission for the communication with the proviso that he be permitted to write as well. Laughing, Millicent gave those promises and waved them off, fully expecting never to see or hear from them, him, again.

Despite her best efforts to put Shoffer out of her mind, she cried herself to sleep that night. Worse, she requested the innkeeper move her from the room she had previously occupied into the one used by Shoffer for those three nights; and she slept, curled up on the same mattress, hugging the pillow that was briefly his.

Idiot, she told herself, and yet her grief was irresistible. She had met the perfect man, young, strong, handsome, and humorous, who had listened to her nonsense, had laughed with her and teased her.

And not for a moment had he realized her true gender.

Not that it was surprising. Her breasts were barely noticeable even naked. Her hips were slender and her hair, shaggy, unkempt.

What sort of woman could she be under such circumstances? She must content herself to be a plain and inconsequential man.

Necessity demanded it.

It would have been best if she had never met him. Never known the pain of wanting. And yet, she gave thanks that she had met him and dreamed of him nightly.

A letter, redirected from the Pricharts' farm, found her the next day and recalled her to her responsibilities. Felicity, distressed and anxious for news, demanded to know when Mr. North was returning to Bath.

Millicent pulled out her traveling writing desk and the bundle of letters Mr. Prichart had given her. On rereading, the late Mr. North's letter was no less disturbing. The ladies living in Bath could not be told by letter of this complication, especially since Millicent could not answer any questions bound to arise from the news.

Taking her courage in both hands, and simulating Anthony North's scrawl as best she could, Millicent crafted a letter to the late Mr. North's lawyer requesting, if he be so kind, a copy of the draft of the will.

Knowing lawyers, she enclosed a sovereign under the seal as payment for his labor.

The answer to her request came within a month, while she was visiting her partially flooded coal mine, and was as bad as she had expected.

According to the will of the late Christopher North, his son Anthony was forbidden from selling or gambling away any part of his inheritance. On Anthony's death the listed items he had received from his father were to be passed to his brother, Perceval, just as he had received them. No provision was made for such things as wives or children. None at all.

Millicent put her copy away and brooded.

The property of Mr. Anthony North was her responsibility even if she could not use it to provide for her sisters' futures. For the moment the rents paid for their needs. She must continue as planned, visiting the tenants and collecting the rents. Dowries and annuities would wait for the future. With luck, inspiration might strike before Felicity was ready to marry off her remaining daughters.

The late afternoon sun beat down on the refuse scattered about the inn's forecourt, raising a foul stench. Millicent ducked gratefully into the shade of the inn's public room and permitted the maid who appeared from the shadows to take her valise. The innkeeper appeared almost immediately, filling the narrow hall with his bulk. Millicent hoped that boded well for the food in the place since the man was fully as wide as he was tall. The innkeeper bowed, running a hand over his red and sweaty bald head.

"Good evening," said Millicent in her deepest voice. "I am Mr. Anthony North. I wrote ahead to reserve a room."

This information was greeted with a broad smile.

"Mister North, indeed you did, sir. Welcome to the Hind and Fox. Jacob Fields, at your service. You are a prodigious popular gentleman, or so my wife informs me. We have several pieces of mail awaiting you. Two of them with fine and complicated crests on the seal. My wife has custody of them at the moment. I shall have them fetched up to your room with your baggage."

Millicent smiled at that information, hoping that her recently acquired tan would cover any blushes. Complicated heraldic devices could only be Trolenfields. It was not as if she had any reason to blush. Shoffer thought of her as an acquaintance only. A fribble. A useful man to know when one wanted a shy sister to chat. That was all.

And the thought stabbed through Millicent's heart.

It was not as if, even if she had met him as a young lady, things would have been any better. Indeed, it would be worse. As the penniless daughter of a tutor, she would never have been granted the honor of an introduction. Shaking herself out of the dismals, Millicent concentrated on Mr. Fields.

"Indeed, that is good news," said Millicent. "Please tell your good lady that if she waits until I have had a chance to wash off the dirt of the road and read my letters, I should be pleased to give her what gossip I have and I shall cut off the seals for her to keep. She will have to be content with on-dits from Bath, since I have no acquaintance in London."

"Thank you, Mr. North. That will please her mightily." Mr. Fields gestured the maid toward the narrow staircase. "Shall I send up a small beer or brandy with your wash water?"

"Tea will do," said Millicent.

The maid who brought up the tea tray was young and buxom. She made a point of jiggling her breasts in Millicent's direction when she bobbed her curtsy and accepted her tip. Millicent sighed and shook her head, politely declining the proffered companionship, endeavoring to give the impression of fatigue rather than disgust. The maid took the rejection in good spirit, no doubt expecting to have other opportunities to seduce Mr. North.

Millicent dismissed the girl from her mind as well as from the room and made good use of the jug of hot water to wash herself before pouring a cup of tea and settling down beside the window to read the five letters the maid had carried up with the tea. One, very thick, was from Bath, and likely from both her sisters as well as her mother. Two were from tenants and one each were from Shoffer and his sister.

It took a great deal of her willpower not to tear open the letter from Shoffer first. Indeed, she sat with it in her hand for several moments before putting it to one side. It was as if she had not received a letter every month from the man since parting from him in Wales. As Shoffer had assisted her in plotting out her summer tour, he knew approximately when she would be at various towns. Despite the fact the letters were full of advice on negotiating with tenants and comments about farming such as would be shared between gentlemen of similar age, wealth, and interests, Millicent kept them in her valise and read them until she knew every line, as if they were missives of a love-struck admirer.

Sighing, Millicent set the package aside and took up her mother's letter. Distance, it seemed, reconciled Felicity to her daughter's odd life. The letter was much the same as she would have sent to her husband, or to a son – demanding, petulant, and gossipy. Since Millicent sent an express telling them that a previous innkeeper's wife was in the habit of opening her guests' mail, the letter contained no references to Millicent's true gender.

Bath, it seemed, was pleasant in the summer time, with frequent entertainments and more visitors from London and outlying counties as gentry, bored with their own homes, sought distraction. London, everyone swore, was pestilential in the summer. Bath was blessed with clearer air, softer breezes, and was therefore to be preferred.

The downside to the new visitors, Felicity informed her, was that she was gradually coming to realize that the people with whom her daughters had danced and flirted the past winter, were the *impoverished* members of the Ton.

"I will not," wrote Felicity, "permit the girls to marry into poverty. They are pretty girls, with good address and talent. I am certain they can do very well for themselves if we were to just put them before the proper people. Maude, particularly, has sufficient beauty for her to deserve to have ambition. Therefore, Mr. North, I implore you, this winter the girls must have a season in London."

Millicent swore ripely – one of the advantages of being a man – and tossed the letter to one side. A London season? If Felicity imagined that the men of the Ton in London were in better funds than those in Bath, she deluded herself. Likewise, how could she imagine that two girls with no dowry at all could attract even a highly placed country gentlemen, let alone a titled one?

Of course, Felicity probably expected that Millicent would bestow some part of Mr. North's estate upon her sisters. Millicent, coward that she was, had not written to her mother and sisters about the exact nature of the elder Mr. North's will. She planned to disclose that information in person, rather than commit it to paper, and because she could imagine the histrionics that particular revelation would inspire, she happily delayed her return to Bath.

Taking a sip of cooling tea to fortify her, Millicent returned to the letter. It seemed that Felicity was advised by one of the visiting matrons that rental houses in the fashionable areas of London went early. Therefore, Mr. North must act immediately to obtain the proper house for the family for the season.

And how did she imagine Millicent would know how to do that? With no experience of the capitol herself how would Millicent know the proper streets, the proper rents? When they had removed to Bath, Millicent had set the family up in a good hotel for three weeks while she had hiked all over Bath examining houses and exploring neighborhoods. Now she was expected to choose from a distance, or did Felicity imagine Millicent would go to London now to find a house?

Lacking inspiration Millicent turned to her other letters. Determined to prove to herself, if no one else, that she was not preoccupied with the Duke of Trolenfield, Millicent read her tenants' letters first.

One wrote to thank Millicent for rapidly approving the repairs to various outbuildings and to tell her of the progress of the work. The other to confirm the appointment for Mr. North to visit. Both brief, to the point, and barely legible.

Finally, Millicent carefully lifted the seal from Shoffer's letter with her pocket knife and set it aside as a gift for the landlady.

My dear Mr. North, – ran the duke's bold script – *my sister informed me this morning of her intention to write to you. She has become most bold since making your acquaintance, but as before, I assure you I have no objections to the change. She is much more interesting than the wilting flower she was under the domination of our grandmother. As to her, and my, reason for writing. We have made a game of following your planned progress through England's fair fields, using maps and my old toy soldiers. We have come to the conclusion that in order to return to meet with your family in Bath you must pass near to my principal estates in Somerset.*

We have just returned from a house party in Dorset and Beth has declared it was a terrible bore. There was no one there, she says, who knew how to make conversation, or play cards in an interesting manner and she was not interested in dancing with any present. She is determined that this summer should not pass without some entertainment; therefore, she has announced, mind you without so much as a by your leave to her chaperone or to me, that she is going to invite you to visit. She also wants more training from you in the manner of conversation with strangers, a subject in which you are an acknowledged master, at least in this house. I admit to you that Beth had some trouble during the house parties. As each visit went on, she became quieter and more reserved. I believe she would benefit from more nonsense from you. Knowing that you have responsibilities elsewhere, the suggested visit should be for a fortnight's duration, before you return to hearth and home. I hope you will accept the invitation for I have found the summer to be dull myself. If you agree, Beth and I will return to Somerset for the remainder of the summer, the better to enjoy your company. Yrs, Timothy Shoffer.

It took Millicent a few moments to recover from the near informality of the invitation and signature. Timothy, indeed! Where was the "by the Grace of God and King" prior to "the Duke"? And the suggestion that the duke's family would move from one place to another for her convenience? Astonishing.

Millicent's chest tightened and she clutched the letter to her bosom before cursing herself as a fool. The duke regarded her as a friend, a male friend, nothing more. Never more.

Dropping the letter to the table, she pressed her hands to her face and blinked rapidly to hold back tears. As if Shoffer's opinion of Mister North did her any good. They could ride about the countryside together, undo their cravats, and relax with feet on furniture while smoking cigars and drinking brandy late at night – except that Millicent could not bring herself to either drink or smoke.

What good did that do Millicent Boarder, the late and barely lamented daughter of a country gentleman, to be friends with Timothy Shoffer?

What good did visiting at the request of his sister do for Millicent's heart?

Nothing, except tear a great hole in it.

In the terror of the moment, when her cousin had died, Millicent had not thought of anything beyond securing the safety and well-being of her mother and sisters. She had consigned her name and future to the grave and taken on the mantle of Mr. North willingly, but without considering the consequences for her feminine heart.

There might be, if she could think of a way to grant her sisters decent dowries, a chance of obtaining marriages for them. Husbands and homes and children for Mildred and Maude, but not for Millicent. For Mr. North? Nothing.

Even if there were not the terrible will of the elder Mr. North there was no way for Millicent, as Mr. North, to marry.

There could never be the love of a husband to warm her nights. Children to tease and torment and fill her days. No one to love her, to care for her. No warmth, no passion. No love.

She pressed the heels of her hands against her eyes.

No love. No intimacy. No kisses. No one to caress and hold in the dark of the night. No one to teach her the secrets of the marriage bed. Instead she would go virgin to her grave.

She might love Timothy Shoffer, the Duke of Trolenfield, but there were was no way for her to realize that love.

Tears fell despite her best intentions. Hastily, she put the letter aside lest her tears smear and smudge his words.

She loved him and he thought of her as merely a friend.

Horrible, unjust reality. How could she endure it?

For two days Millicent ignored the letters resting on the table back at the Hind and Fox. In fact, she did not open Beth's letter that whole time. Instead, she met several times with her tenant, visited the local shops, and avoided the matrimonial trap set for her by the tenant's wife. (A disheveled daughter was to jump from behind a hay rick with witnesses at hand to declare that North had interfered with the daughter. However, Millicent overheard the plot being hatched and took another path.)

She was packing for the next stage of her tour when she felt she could avoid answering the letters no longer.

Beth's letter was longer and chattier than her brother's, as was to be expected from a young lady. She included a fair amount of gossip about people Millicent could never hope to meet and included a reference to Mr. Simpson, the duke's much trusted and overworked man of business, solving another complicated problem.

Millicent's eyes narrowed as she thought. If anyone would know how to choose a house in London, Mr. Simpson would. In fact, Mr. Simpson would be so well informed that he would know within a whisker an address in London that would inform all callers that here lived a country gentleman of some means, with two distant relatives with no dowries to marry off.

However, writing to Mr. Simpson would not do. Such a request of someone else's man of business required a personal appeal. Mr. Simpson would require his employer's approval before undertaking such a task. Therefore, it was necessary for Millicent to accept the duke and his sister's kind invitation so she might seek the advice of his secretary.

At least, that was what Millicent told herself.

And while Millicent visited with the duke's sister, she would appeal to that young lady for assistance in firing off Mildred and Maude. An introduction or two from someone so high in rank would ensure the opening of doors and issuance of invitations.

It was only to advance her sisters' places in society that she would spend two weeks with Timothy Shoffer, by the Grace of God and King, Duke of Trolenfield.

And may God have mercy on her poor heart.

Chapter Six

Millicent's reception at the Duke of Trolenfield's estate was as enthusiastic as anyone could desire. Millicent was barely descended from the post chaise and was paying off her hired driver and outriders, when the duke himself, dressed in riding gear, descended the front steps just behind his butler.

"Your Grace," Millicent bowed and grinned at him. "I must thank you for ordering such fine weather."

Shoffer glanced up at the drizzling, overcast sky and laughed.

"If it were within my power, I would have requested better weather for your arrival," he said, seizing Millicent's hand and shaking it vigorously. "But with luck, it will improve tomorrow and I shall give you a long overdue riding lesson."

"I am certain, since it is the duke's command, the weather will not dare to be anything other than perfect," said Millicent. "The skies themselves are yours to command. How would it dare to cast down rain, when you say not, and put smudges on your boots?"

"You are very welcome to my home, Mr. North, fool that you are. Lest you forget, we first met because torrential rain had nerve to turn a road into a quagmire."

"Oh, but that was in Wales," cried Millicent with a dismissive wave, "heathen place that it is, and not in any civilized county."

Shoffer turned to face his butler. "See, Forsythe. I did not exaggerate. Mr. North is the most ridiculous man in Britain."

Forsythe, a rather young appearing man for such a responsible position in a duke's household, inclined his head toward Millicent.

"Indeed, sir. We were all breathless in anticipation of his visit," said Forsythe in a cool, even voice.

Millicent recoiled, her hand to her throat. "Dear God, Shoffer, what have you said of me? I shall have maidservants and footmen following on my heels in expectation of such things that even Drury Lane farces decline to perform."

"Exactly," said Shoffer.

"Good," said Millicent, relaxing from her horrified stance and bowing again. "I shall endeavor to give satisfaction."

"Do not overexert yourself, North. We did not invite you so that you might be our jester. Your company is all that is required."

"I shall be myself in good quantity, since that pleases you, Your Grace."

"Good. And put away the 'Your Graces,' I beg you, North, for I know from you that they are merely mockery. Now come inside. I have it on good authority that Beth is waiting to be gracious lady of the manor in your honor. Pray remember to be impressed. She has been fussing for the last few days that the summer drawing room decorations are too extravagant."

Shoffer led the way up a grand marble staircase and into the house. Millicent removed her hat and gloves and handed them to a waiting footman.

"Whatever made her think I was an arbiter of fashion? Did she, perhaps, contract a fever of the brain since last she saw me?"

"No, but she remembers you being humorous at the expense of another lady's drawing room in one of your letters and fears what you might say."

Millicent paused beside a grand painting, that if laid on the floor would be larger than some of the rooms she lived in, and cast a grave look toward Shoffer.

"Surely, she does not think I am so lost to good manners that I would make her unhappy."

"Of course not," said Shoffer. "Only remember, it was under your influence that she became less shy. It is to be expected that there would be the occasional backsliding to self-conscious behavior."

"I shall endeavor to reassure her."

The butler ducked ahead of them to throw wide both doors into a spacious drawing room. Millicent paused just out of sight to run her hand through her hair, brushing all the uneven locks forward to hang over her eyes. Shoffer watched her in confusion, then shrugged and entered the drawing room.

"His Grace, and Mr. North of Yorkshire, my Lady," intoned Forsythe.

Beth rose from an ornate and gilded chair to glide across the room, one hand outstretched.

"My dear Mr. North," she began, then halted as Millicent came into the room.

Millicent minced across the Aubusson carpet as if wearing high polished heels. Stopping three feet from Lady Beth, she sank into a low bow, one hand waving through the air as if clutching a large, befeathered hat. That bow would have looked bad enough were Mr. North attired in courtly garb, but as Millicent was wearing a cut away coat three years out of fashion and two sizes too big, and loosely fitting trousers over well-worn boots, the sight was hysterical.

Before anyone could speak, Millicent fell to her knees and clutched Beth's proffered hand in both of hers.

"My dear Lady Elizabeth," cried Millicent, peppering the captured hand with light kisses. "Only tell me, how did I manage to lose your favor? I am desolate without it."

And pressing the hand against her cheek, Millicent burst into simulated tears.

"Mr. North, please cease. You have not lost my regard at all." Beth glanced across at her brother. "Whatever did you say to him?"

"Only that you were concerned about his reaction to the drawing room," replied Shoffer.

Beth attempted to retreat and retrieve her hand, but Millicent shuffled along on her knees beside her.

"Oh, do stop, Mr. North." Beth tapped Millicent on the head with her folded fan. "You are quite the most ridiculous man."

Grinning, Millicent climbed to her feet. "Your servant, madam."

"Well, since Timothy has embarrassed me by calling your attention to my fears, do tell me, what do you think of the chamber?"

Millicent assumed a contemplative posture and began prowling the room, rubbing at her chin. She even when so far as to lift up a vase and examine its maker's mark, much to Beth's amusement.

"It is excellent," said Millicent, in due time, "as you well know. It is cohesive, moderate in decoration, harmonious in color, and altogether lovely, just as you are."

Beth blushed and folded her hands together.

"I do thank you," she said. "It was my mother's favorite room when we lived here. I have not changed much, merely moving furniture. I am not here long enough to redecorate. Even though it is not my work, I was concerned. I know not why your good opinion means so much to me."

"Neither do I," shot back Millicent.

"She does not believe me when I tell her something is good," said Shoffer with a pitiable expression on his face.

"That is because you are my brother and you love me," said Beth. "You would never suggest that anything I did was wrong for fear of hurting my feelings."

"Yes, Shoffer. Learn your lesson," said Millicent. "You should be cruel and precise so that your sister will always know you speak the truth."

"I am instructed," said Shoffer and bestowed such a smile on Millicent that she needed to turn away to cover her blush.

It was more painful than she had imagined to stand in the same room as him and have him look upon her so warmly.

"I cannot remember why we thought it was a good idea to invite him," added Shoffer, ignoring Millicent's momentary distraction.

"Neither can I," said Beth.

"Ah, but more important, you should wonder why I accepted," said Millicent.

Beth and Shoffer exchanged a glance.

"Well, I shall admit to curiosity," said Shoffer. "Was it the chance to enjoy the splendor of the ducal manor? I admit it is nothing to your tenant's home in Wales. Indeed, I am ashamed to show it to you, so mean are the rooms and deficient the planned entertainments."

"Nothing indeed," laughed Millicent since the duke's estate was a massive building of locally quarried stone, blessed with rooms the size of other people's houses. "I hope you will forgive me, Your Grace, but I came only in the hope of meeting the inestimable Mr. Simpson."

The corners of Shoffer's lips turned down in mock sorrow.

"Now I know my true status. I take second place to my secretary, whom you have never met," said Shoffer. "He is in the study at the moment, hard at work. Why do you wish to meet him?"

"Well, on the day I received your kind invitation, I also received a note from my cousin Felicity. It seems she has been giving the matter of her daughters' futures much thought and has decided that nothing will do but I take the girls to London for the season. And may God have mercy on my soul."

Beth clapped her hands together. "Excellent. That is good news."

"My deepest sympathy, North," said Shoffer offering a hand to be shaken. "I have but one lady to be married off, but you are burdened with two. The horror!"

"Thank you for your understanding, Your Grace." Millicent inclined her head and arranged her features in an expression of beatific suffering.

"Oh, what nonsense you men talk," said Beth. "You have not spoken of your family before, Mr. North. Who will you be launching into society?"

"My widowed cousin, Mrs. Felicity Boarder and her two remaining daughters, Mildred and Maude. The other daughter, Millicent, died last year, but her mother still speaks of her as if expecting her to return from some errand at any moment."

"Oh, how sad," said Beth. "I am sorry for it. But tell me…"

"Come now, Beth, you have said hello to Mr. North. Now you must allow him a moment to refresh himself and prepare for luncheon." Shoffer came to his feet. "Simpson is the ideal person to help. If anyone can give you useful advice, it will be him. Although, it is possible his advice will be that you hie yourself to Scotland and hide for a year or two."

"A London season is not so very bad," declared Beth.

Shoffer turned and bestowed a fond smile on his sister. Millicent's breath caught in her throat at the beauty of his face at that moment. Angels from on high coming to bless mankind should look upon their suffering with such love and beneficence as Shoffer did upon his sister. It broke Millicent's heart that she would never have that face, that love, turned upon her.

"I am so glad to hear you say that, Beth," said Shoffer, and when Beth blushed he caught her hand and continued. "Between the two of us, we should be able to advance the cause of North's cousins. That will be fun, will it not?"

"It will," said Beth, holding herself confidently. "I look forward to guiding your cousins through the season, Mr. North." Then she looked concerned. "They are not so very much older than me, are they? I would not want them to laugh at my presumption."

Millicent paused before answering. "Far be it from me to estimate any lady's age, whether young or old. Let me only say *you* are taller."

Beth laughed at that.

"Very well done. I must remember that one," said Shoffer and gestured toward the door.

Millicent bowed to Beth and followed him out. In the corridor Shoffer caught her across the shoulders and pulled her sideways into a brief embrace before setting her back on her feet.

"North, you have no idea how this aids me. I was wondering how I should be able to persuade Beth to go back for a season after the horrible experience my grandmother inflicted upon her; and now she is eager to return to the fray."

"My reasons are entirely selfish," said Millicent, turning her face away to hide her blushes, "and encroaching, I do admit it. Mrs. Fleming's ill opinion of me is confirmed."

"No matter if it is," said Shoffer. "I have to go down, anyway, for Parliament. Squiring three girls about to entertainments will be no deal more difficult than one, especially if we undertake the task together."

Millicent halted and stared up at Shoffer. "You have not spent much time in the company of young women, have you, Your Grace?"

"I shall speak to Simpson on your behalf." With that Shoffer struck her across the back and strode off.

Millicent brushed her hand over her shoulder, sighed, and thought herself all sorts of fool. How pitiable was her case if she hugged to herself the knowledge that her loved one had touched her when that touch was a brotherly hug?

They were gathered together in the hall, wandering toward the informal dining room for luncheon, when Beth returned to the subject of the season.

"When shall you be arriving in London, Mr. North?"

"I hardly know. A week or so before the festivities, I imagine, to permit the womenfolk to beggar me with their purchases," said Millicent. "That is, if the talented Mr. Simpson is able to find me a suitable house to rent. He informed Shoffer that I have left it far too late, it being a mere four months before the start of the season. All the best houses have been reserved since the year before last. I fear that all that is left is London Bridge, under the last arch, on the right side."

Beth laughed, then put on a sad face. "I grieve that I will not be able to call on you if you are forced to reside under a bridge. We can only hope that a suitable house will be found; and then I promise I shall call on your cousin and her daughters."

"Excellent. That is most gracious of you, Lady Beth. Before you arrive, I shall advise them that you have brought bent brim and wilted hats into fashion so that they will be suitably equipped and not be ashamed to greet you."

"Oh, what nonsense you talk," said Beth, as her brother choked.

"It is merely the truth," cried Millicent, leaping to her feet and bowing. "If you were to wear your hat backwards, one sleeve long, the other short, and begin walking down the street sideways, why within a week, we would see a progression of ladies on Bond Street, shuffling sideways like sea crabs."

Millicent affected a feminine air, her nose tilted toward the ceiling, and began to shuffle sideways, dragging her trailing leg along the carpet. Chuckling, Shoffer made his bow to Millicent, then the two of them shuffled sideways as if in the lines of a country dance.

"The pair of you are the most ridiculous individuals in Christendom," declared Beth laughing.

"We are only trying to make you aware of your standing in society, my dearest," said Shoffer, taking her hand and drawing her along.

"Oh, posh," said Beth sadly. "I am an inconsequential thing. A barely out of the schoolroom miss."

"Not so," cried Millicent. With a dip and a twirl she took Beth's hand and paraded back in the other direction, Shoffer matching them step by step. "Why, you have no idea the joy you gave me when you said you would call upon my cousins. Have you no understanding of your power? Why, if my cousins, country misses that they are, are greeted by you on the street, even by the merest nod, then they shall receive invitations. Should you hold out your hand to them and declare yourself 'pleased,' they will have men dance with them. But should you raise your nose and glance away, well, I should immediately be seeking out convents, for the girls will never wed, no matter how sweet their dispositions."

"I shall not have that power until I am suitably wed, so Grand'Mere said."

"Your grandmother did not want you to know, but young, beautiful, *unmarried*, wealthy women have more power than any person in the kingdom, and I include the king in that," said Millicent. "Why, with one lift of your eyebrow you will have a hundred men stampeding to your side. Should you express the existence of thirst, rivers shall be drained to bring you lemonade. In your honor, trees will be destroyed and ink pots emptied to create truly *dreadful* poetry."

By this time both Beth and Shoffer were helpless with laughter. Millicent watched them both, his short dark curls bent close over her dignified up-swept coiffure, eyes so similar, dark blue crinkling at each other, and her heart warmed. She loved them both and had the comfort of knowing that each in their way was fond of Mr. North.

"There, dear one," said Shoffer, when he had recovered his breath. "I know you do not believe me, but shall you believe this polite and indifferent acquaintance? You are the bright star of the Ton."

"And any marriage I should make shall be beneath me."

Beth looked so downcast that Millicent's heart threatened to break.

"Oh, please, if that must be so," said Millicent, "have the good grace to marry for love. Then you will not be troubled by rank or its absence."

Beth fluttered her eyelashes and fan.

"Shall you marry me, dear Mr. North?"

Millicent recoiled in mock horror, her hand clutching at her clumsy cravat.

"Whatever have I done to you, Lady Beth, that you should want your brother to run me through?"

"Silly man. I can no longer deny my feelings and must give them speech. If I cannot wed with you, then I shall wed no one."

Millicent collapsed to her knees before the snickering Shoffer.

"Your Grace, I do not know of what she speaks."

Beth held out her hand in a graceful gesture a hundred actresses could only hope for.

"Oh, my love, be brave. Even if he visits a hundred tortures upon you, I know you will be true."

"Not a bit of it," cried Millicent, seizing hold of Shoffer's coat tails. "I repudiate you this instant."

"Abandoned." Beth pressed the back of her hand against her forehead. "There is nothing for it than I must hie me to a river and throw myself in."

Still kneeling, Millicent rested her head on her fist, then glanced up at Shoffer.

"You would ask me to teach her conversation, would not you? Why did you not warn me that she came over all Shakespearian when crossed?"

"With my last breath I forgive you, Mr. North," declared Beth in a die away voice.

"And so do I," said Shoffer, tapping Millicent on the head with his knuckles. "Do get up; there's a good fellow."

Millicent climbed to her feet and tried to shake the creases out of her trousers.

"One good thing about going to London," observed Beth. "You may take Mr. North to your tailor."

"Oh, dear God, protect me," groaned Millicent.

"What is going on here?" demanded a voice.

An elderly lady, no taller than Millicent's shoulder, descended the main staircase from the upper floor, then swept down the hall. Such a lady as this would never do anything as plebeian as to stand or walk; she *progressed!* She wore garb of dark blue silk in the current high-waisted fashion which flattered her slight figure, and a frown, which did not. The lady raised her lorgnette to her eyes and regarded Millicent with distaste starting at her barely polished boots and ending with hair that needed another cut.

"Your Grace," said Shoffer in frosty tones, "I thought you said you would be taking a tray in your room, in protest of Mr. North's presence."

"It is clear that someone must be here to ensure the proprieties are maintained," was the reply. "Elizabeth, your color is too high. Have you been permitting your thoughts to be disordered? Calm yourself at once."

"Yes, Grand'Mere."

Beth folded her hands together, cast her gaze down, and all sign of humor vanished from her face.

"Grandmother, may I make my particular friend known to you?" Shoffer gestured towards Millicent. "Mr. Anthony North, this is my grandmother, Lady Philomena Shoffer, the Dowager Duchess of Trolenfield."

"An honor! I am very glad to see you, Your Grace," said Millicent, with a low bow.

"I cannot imagine why."

If the duchess's voice were any colder Millicent was convinced all the windows in the great house would frost over. Nevertheless, Millicent cast a smile in Beth's direction and replied.

"Why, but for no other reason than now that you are here, His Grace must escort you in to dine, as he is the highest ranking male and you, the female. Which will leave to me the honor of having Lady Beth take my arm."

From the shocked look on that lady's face it was obvious she had not thought through the consequences of her appearance.

"You shall not!" she said, at last.

"But it would be discourteous of me to permit her to walk so far without extending her the strength of my arm for the journey."

Beth hid her grin behind her fan, but Shoffer did not bother and grinned openly at his grandmother's consternation.

"Shoffer, you should…" began the Duchess.

"Oh, no," interrupted the duke. "You have lectured me at length about rank and precedence. My sister shall take Mr. North's arm and sit beside him and converse with him. To do less would be beneath the dignity of my table."

Fuming, the dowager duchess took Shoffer's arm in a strangling grip, which only made the duke's smile broader. Millicent made the same elaborate bow she had made earlier to Beth, then extended her elbow toward the girl. With a pretty curtsy, Beth took it and they paraded into the dining room.

The meal was as miserable as the dowager could make it. She placed herself and Beth as far as she could down the table and addressed her comments exclusively to Shoffer. Whenever Beth would make a comment, the dowager would scowl and grumble until Beth fell silent. By the end of the meal she was barely raising her eyes from her plate.

In such a chilly atmosphere, no one was inclined to prolong the meal and as soon as the covers were removed Shoffer, Millicent, and Beth rose to excuse themselves. The dowager seized Beth's arm before the girl could escape.

"Elizabeth and I have much to discuss this afternoon. I am yet to hear her version of the events at the Harrington's house party."

"I shall answer any questions you have," said Shoffer.

"It is Elizabeth from whom I wish to hear."

And with that she dragged Beth away. The girl cast one pitiable glance back over her shoulder to which the duke responded with a helpless shrug.

"What happened at the Harrington's?" asked Millicent.

Shoffer sighed. "Poor Beth, she was so bright and cheerful when we first arrived. I was well pleased with her. She chatted and seemed on the way to making a few friends; then I noticed that she again was becoming withdrawn. By the end of our time there, she was as silent as ever she was in London."

"Poor golden kitten," said Millicent. "She lacks confidence and practice, I suspect. Did you observe anyone snubbing her?"

"Not a bit of it." Shoffer shook his head, still gazing up the staircase. "She was quite popular at first. It did not last. The littlest thing would cast her down. The smallest look of surprise at her words, or hesitation by her dinner partner to respond to her jests, and she would fall silent for the rest of the day. Each day I saw her withdraw and there was nothing I could say in encouragement that restored her spirits. She only cheered up when she thought to invite you to visit."

"I will help all I can."

"Thank you. For now, I am worried what Lady Philomena will say. I hope she will exercise restraint."

"I had not thought to have the honor of meeting the dowager," said Millicent.

"Come along, North." Shoffer draped an arm over Millicent's shoulder and turned her so they could walk together down the hall. "You should not have, except that the dowager appeared with no notice yesterday. I suspect, although I am yet to question her on the subject, that Mrs. Fleming is responsible for her appearance. No doubt a letter was sent once we received your acceptance."

"No doubt," muttered Millicent. "I find myself wondering why you keep Mrs. Fleming."

"I would be rid of her if I could, but she is a very distant relative and has no other home."

"Ah, empathy. 'Tis a pity she has none for Lady Beth."

Shoffer led the way to a huge chamber whose function was not immediately clear to Millicent. There were books on a shelf, but not so many as to imply a library. Millicent wandered to the center of the room and turned, trying to figure the place out. It was not until Mr. Simpson appeared through a concealed side door bearing papers that she worked it out. This cavernous chamber was the study.

"Good God," murmured Millicent. "You could lose my house in Bath in this one room."

Mr. Simpson, a tall, dark-haired, skeletally thin young gentleman, whose appearance was more suited to the villain of some farce than a duke's man of business, paused at Millicent's words casting a worried glance toward the duke. Shoffer did no more than laugh at his friend's outcry.

"Indeed, Mr. North, and this is not the greatest nor the least of my estates, merely my favorite."

Shaking her head Millicent continued her exploration. "Do you not find yourself becoming exhausted trudging from one end of the room to the other? Perhaps you ride a horse from the dining room to your bedchamber."

"Ridiculous man, do sit down. I wish to hear your plan for Beth. Have you an opinion?"

"Not a one. I hope to have some time with Lady Beth to hear *her* thoughts."

"Very well, I shall leave it to your judgment. Only please, encourage Beth to take me into her confidence. It was disheartening in the extreme to see her become so withdrawn and have her refuse to discuss the matter with me."

"I am certain she already knows she can trust you," said Millicent diplomatically.

But Shoffer only shook his head.

Mr. Simpson cleared his throat and approached the duke. If he was surprised to find the duke taking such a common man as Millicent pretended to be into his confidence about his sister, Mr. Simpson was too well-trained to permit it to show. Instead, he offered a sheet of paper for the duke's examination.

"I have a list of houses that are vacant for the season, and I have included some that are already rented, that you might prefer for Mr. North. I can always contact the families and offer them a different house."

"That was quick," said Millicent. "I have but this moment told you of my need. Have you special horses that can fly between here and London in an instant?"

"Fool," said Shoffer without heat and began examining the

list. "These are but a few of my London properties. I lease them out without the renters being aware that they are mine. I would not like for strangers to lord it over their neighbors that they reside in one of the Duke of Trolenfield's properties."

"Oh, of course," said Millicent, preening. "How rude."

Shoffer sighed and continued reading. "Have you any suggestions, Simpson?"

"I hardly know."

Simpson glanced back and forth between the duke and Millicent, uncertain how to respond until Millicent took pity on the man.

"Do not judge me by my boots, Mr. Simpson, I am hardly poor. My annual income may not match that of His Grace's, but I am in no pain. However, the two cousins I have to set loose upon the Ton have minimal dowries. I may think of some way to improve their lot, but it cannot be counted on. Does this information help?"

Before the secretary could answer, Shoffer added, "I should like it if Mr. North is not too far from my own London residence. I expect his cousins and my sister to be much in each other's company."

"That narrows it down to these three, Your Grace."

Simpson began listing the various rooms and size of each house with the duke arguing against each. Millicent left it to the two of them to settle the matter only paying attention when actual rents were discussed. Her first shocked outcry was met with disdain by both men.

"These *are* London rents," said Simpson by way of explanation.

"Oh. Well." Millicent shrugged. "If it is London rent, what can I be complaining about? I shall pay it with *London* pounds!"

"This one," said Shoffer with finality. "It is walking distance from my home, and well situated with regard to entertainments that you can assume you, too, will be invited."

"As Your Grace commands," said Millicent, wincing when they showed her the price.

"If it is beyond your purse…" began Simpson.

"Do not let him fool you," said Shoffer. "His false economies in his dress will be corrected in London. Mr. North's purse can well stand it."

"As you wish, Your Grace."

Millicent was considering how she might further tease the duke when there was a deferential knock on the door and Forsythe entered.

"Your Grace? Lady Elizabeth has issued an invitation for Mr. North to join her in the music room?"

The confusion the butler experienced at delivering such an improper invitation was writ large on his face. Shoffer surprised him by not objecting.

"Excellent. Mr. North, if you would be so kind?"

"Your servant." Millicent bowed and rose.

"We shall work on the rental agreement while you are busy with Beth." Shoffer waved Mr. Simpson toward the great desk. "Forsythe? Have Beth's maid descend and keep them company. Mr. North, I expect a full report!"

Millicent nodded and followed the confused butler across the hall, down side corridors and, eventually, to a room containing a pianoforte and a large harp arranged upon a stage before several uncomfortable chairs. Lady Beth was seated on a window seat in the shadowed end of the chamber staring out into the garden.

"Lady Beth," Millicent made her leg and walked a few steps into the room. Forsythe pointedly flung the double doors open and stood in them until the maid arrived and settled herself on a chair near the door.

Lady Beth glanced over long enough for Millicent to see the tracks of recently shed tears, then away.

"Oh, dear." Instead of crossing to sit beside the girl, Millicent went to the stage and began running scales up and down the pianoforte keyboard.

Obviously, Shoffer's prayer that the dowager exercise restraint had not been granted. Poor Lady Beth looked as if she had been on the receiving end of a severe scolding. All undeserved, Millicent was certain. She blushed for her own part in angering the dowager. As Mr. North, she had offered considerable disrespect to the old woman – in front of witnesses, no less, and she had – he had – been engaged in teaching the previously obedient Lady Elizabeth to consider her own opinions and wishes. It was surprising that the dowager had not gathered up the servants to run Mr. North out of the house by now.

Instead the dowager had chosen Lady Beth as her victim.

Millicent drifted from playing scales to a sprightly country dance tune.

"Play something softer, please, Mr. North," said Lady Beth. "I am not in the mood for a jig."

"Are you not? It seems to me that is just the time to play one."

"Not today." Beth's voice was wistful and vague.

"Can you tell me what is amiss?"

"No."

"Or your brother, perhaps?"

Beth shook her head, hard. "No. Not him."

"This will not do, Lady Beth. How am I to retain your brother's friendship if you do not speak to me?"

"He likes you well enough for yourself alone," said Beth in such a die-away tone that Millicent stopped playing.

"You begin to worry me," said Millicent. "Come. I must have you smile."

Beth leaned further back into the window embrasure. "I have changed my mind about meeting with you this afternoon. I think I would prefer to be alone with my thoughts. Just for today, Mr. North, if you would be so kind."

"This is unlike you, Lady Beth. Only this morning…"

"That was this morning," said Beth with more sharpness than Millicent had ever heard in her voice. Millicent would have obeyed, except the strength leaked from Beth's voice and Millicent could hear the barely restrained tears. "I am not fit company for anyone at all."

"This will not do. Come now," said Millicent, turning around on the piano stool. "I shall not give over until I have made you laugh. I am uncertain at this time if you have not lost all your teeth since last we met in Wales. Come now, laugh and show me."

"Please, Mr. North. I am tired of company today."

Millicent's fingers flickered over the keyboard, a complicated trill of notes that ended with a deliberately discordant chord. She tossed her short hair, raising her hands dramatically and slashed and bashed a random set of notes.

"This is my own composition," she cried over the racket. "I have dedicated it to King George. Do you think he will like it?" She crashed her hands down a series of dark and minor chords. "It is meant to reflect his lightness of spirit and joyous reign."

Beth's head came up and she stared at Millicent. "You must be in jest!"

"Of course. Am I not always?" Millicent tried to raise an eyebrow as she had seen Shoffer do to good effect. Failing, Millicent wiggled her eyebrows instead, then put both hands behind them and wiggled her ears.

Beth's bosom heaved and she dropped her fan to press both hands to her mouth. Millicent leapt to her feet and spun around, her cut away coat tails flying before settling again, trilling in the upper registers.

"And this is to represent the pomp and dignity of His person." She twinkled the highest notes.

Beth's eyes shone with unshed tears of laughter, yet she made a great effort not to permit her lips to move.

Outside in the corridor a small group of maids and footmen roared in laughter at Millicent's posturing. Helpless in the face of their combined mirth, Beth collapsed against the cushions and gasped out giggles.

"What is the meaning of this uproar?" asked a hard, angry voice.

Beth stopped laughing and came upright, stiff and trembling in her seat. The servants scattered revealing the Duchess of Trolenfield, regal in her anger. Millicent rose to her feet and bowed.

"Your Grace. I was merely attempting to entertain her ladyship," said Millicent.

"You dare?" The Duchess took two steps into the room and glared at Millicent through her lorgnette. "The duke will have something to say when he finds you have been alone with his sister, you encroaching mushroom…"

"Yes," said Shoffer from the doorway with a folder in his hands. "He will say thank you, since he has brought laughter to my sister's lips."

"A lady," declared the Duchess, "shows her amusement by the merest upturning of the corner of her mouth, and then but rarely. She does not roar like a doxy in a bawdy house."

Beth stiffened further and fresh tears came to her eyes, this time of distress. Shoffer hurried across to sit beside her.

"Dear Beth. There is nothing wrong with laughter, I promise you."

Millicent came to attention beside the pianoforte and placed a puzzled expression on her face, tapping her lower lip with her finger. From the look on her face, Lady Philomena was not finished with her scold. A distraction was necessary.

"I must enquire, Your Grace," asked Millicent with careful courtesy, "how is it you know how a doxy laughs in a bawdy house?"

The lorgnette fell from the dowager's limp fingers to dangle by its brocade ribbon.

"What did you say to me?" she demanded.

"It is a perfectly reasonable question," replied Millicent innocently. "Since it is you who made the comparison. To be so precise in your description it can only be assumed that you speak from your own knowledge."

Beth dove immediately for the protection of her fan and raised it to cover her whole face while Shoffer collapsed, laughing and clutching his chest.

Lady Philomena's mouth worked and it was with great difficulty that she was able to force out words.

"Will you stand there and laugh at that insult?" she demanded of the duke.

Shoffer wiped tears from his eyes and faced his grandmother. "You are the one who created the circumstances of the question, Your Grace."

"You would stand there and permit me to be insulted by that ... that ... interloper? Did you realize he and your sister were all alone in this room? How do you know he has not been trying to engage your sister's affection?"

"I doubt that very much," said Shoffer. "And besides, Beth's maid was present the entire time. As it happens, I recruited Mr. North to the task of aiding my sister become more comfortable in company. She is out now, but does not speak in the presence of strangers. I have noticed that she holds whole conversations with him and is even charming and witty with his encouragement."

"She should never be in his company! I have taught her behavior appropriate to her station. Since she will outrank those she is in company with, she will have nothing to say to them, nor they to her."

"You have taught her to be silent," said Shoffer. "To be withdrawn and unhappy. I would prefer that she is able to speak confidently and with proper condescension to all she meets."

"She knows very well how to do that."

"By saying nothing at all? No. That is not right. The manner you have forced upon her does not help her to make friends."

"Friends!" The Duchess's mouth pinched at the thought. "Who is there who would presume to attach himself to her regard? I have introduced her to one or two ladies whose rank is not so far below hers with whom conversation would not be a disgrace."

Millicent raised her eyebrows at that and glanced toward the silent Beth. The fan descended and the unhappy girl glanced toward her brother in appeal.

"And how, pray, since she cannot speak to anyone, is she to engage the affections of a gentleman?" demanded Shoffer. "Or have you decided, since there are no ranks above her save prince and king, she will remain unmarried?"

Beth gave a soft little whimper at that which led Millicent to suspect the girl had met the mad King and the fat Prince Regent – both of whom were already married.

"She is to marry the Duc of Attelweir," declared the dowager.

Beth gasped and collapsed against Shoffer whose expression was equally horrified.

"That old roué !" cried Shoffer. "Are you mad? He is older than my father was when he died."

Millicent swallowed a giggle and forced herself to compose her face when the duchess shot her a quelling glance.

"He is the only man whose rank is equal to her own. Any other match would be a disgrace. As it happens, Duc Attelweir agrees with me and has given me to understand that he would not be adverse to the match."

"I will not permit it," cried Shoffer, to his sister's obvious relief. "I do not care what you have said to him, nor he to you, but that marriage would be a misalliance of the worse sort. One of temperament and morality. Attelweir is the sort of man I would not acknowledge should I meet him on the street."

"You best prepare to acknowledge him, for he is coming here tomorrow."

Beth gasped, and burst into tears.

Chapter Seven

"Here? I think not." Shoffer tightened his grip on his sister's hand and glared across the room at the dowager. "I am not in expectation of a visit from Attelweir."

The dowager raised her head and attempted to stare him down, but Shoffer would not be cowed.

"I issued the invitation. Since you indicated that you were settled here for the remainder of the summer, I thought it would be pleasant to host our own house party. I contacted some select personages, and of course, they all accepted." The dowager glanced briefly toward where Millicent stood. "You should know I have ordered your belongings moved. The room you were issued is far above your station. Since higher ranking personages will be arriving tomorrow, you will be placed in a guest chamber suitable to your status."

"Did you move me to the stables or the piggery, Your Grace?" inquired Millicent, which prompted a snort from Lady Beth even in her distress.

Before the dowager could answer, Shoffer moved between them.

"By what right do you invite someone I despise to my house?"

"I was not aware of your displeasure. However, it was my house before yours. Before you were even born!" The dowager flashed a look toward Millicent and the footman who waited near the door. "We should not discuss family matters before staff and other such."

"Such?" muttered Millicent. "Am I *such*? How very odd that I did not know it."

"Since you have seen fit to invite your friends here, so be it," said Shoffer. "Beth and I will leave tomorrow, early. Mr. North, I promised you two weeks, but I know you will understand. I'm certain your family will be happy to see you sooner. Do not worry about transportation. I shall be happy to take you up in our equipage and convey you to Bath."

"You cannot do that!" cried the dowager. "You cannot offend your guests by departing as they arrive."

"Your guests, Grandmother. Yours. Not mine by any measure. No doubt, in addition to Attelweir, you have included others of your generation, the ancient females who have lectured Beth on her behavior and provided her with no friendship. It is unlikely that you have invited anyone near her age," Shoffer's eyes narrowed, "unless you have included some chit you intend to throw at me."

At the dowager's guilty start, Shoffer shook his head.

"No, Grandmother, this will not do. I will not let you bind me with good manners into spending time with people I find repugnant. When they arrive they will be told that if they expected to spend time with myself or Beth, it was a misunderstanding on their part. Or you may tell them whatever you wish, but I have no intention of remaining in this house with them." Turning to Beth and Millicent he bowed. "If you will do me the honor of accompanying me, Beth, North, I believe we shall find the library a more congenial place to continue our conversation."

"Your servant," said Millicent to Shoffer and hastened to Beth's side. With Shoffer to one side and Millicent guarding the other, Beth was escorted past her grandmother and out of the room.

The library was a huge chamber filled with comfortable appearing chairs, well lit by floor to ceiling French windows in the daytime, and by two fireplaces and candelabra at night, but strangely lacking in books. Aside from one shelf of books bound in exactly the same shade of green leather and a scattering of London papers, there was nothing to read in the room. Millicent was not permitted to be distracted by this oddity for long. Beth claimed her attention immediately.

"Mr. North, I cannot marry him," she cried, seizing Millicent by her shirt front. "You must help me."

Millicent almost stumbled to the floor in shock, then took Beth's wrists in her hands and tried to pull the girl free before she discovered the bosom hidden beneath.

"Lady Beth, please, unhand me."

"Oh, Mr. North, please promise me that I shall not have to marry Attelweir."

Millicent cast a helpless look toward Shoffer who closed the doors before coming to his sister's side.

"Beth, my dear. Do not fear." Shoffer caught Beth around the waist and drew her firmly away. "I promise you shall not marry where you do not will."

"But Grand'Mere… You do not know her when she is determined. She wants this marriage and will make it happen unless we act to prevent it."

Shoffer rocked the small girl in his arms and tried to comfort her. Beth endured the embrace a few moments longer, then shook him off to return to Millicent.

"Mr. North, I entreat you. Promise me that should it come to that point, that you will speak for me. I cannot bear it that there be a chance that I should marry Attelweir."

"Beth, this will not do." Shoffer took her arm and tried to lead her to a chair. Instead Beth seized hold of Millicent's hand and would not be moved. "You do not need to fear. I will not permit him to trouble you."

"But I do," cried Beth, her knuckles white. "Would you just promise me, Mr. North, that you would marry me yourself should it ever come to a choice? I would go to Gretna with you, if necessary. Timothy would not mind."

"Yes, he would," said Millicent, meeting that man's eyes. "And so would I. Lady Beth, I shall not do this to you. Were I to make a promise to marry you, if ever it should be a choice between me and Attelweir – not a flattering choice, mind you – then it would weigh in your mind and twist and change in the passage of time until you came to believe that there was an understanding between us. Then, in your mind, it would become an engagement. Thereafter, you would cease to try and go about, meet with people, and seek to find the man you are meant to marry. I will not be the cause of your future unhappiness. You deserve a husband who will love you as he should. Let it be instead, I will promise should ever you need my assistance in reaching the safety of your brother's side, then I shall give my heart's blood to see it done."

"That is not good enough!"

Millicent shook her head and stepped away. "It is all I can offer you, dear Lady Beth. I do not love you as I should to be your husband."

"It is not enough," repeated Beth, and bursting into tears she fled the room.

Millicent and Shoffer exchanged looks of masculine confusion and despair.

"Why is she in such a taking?" demanded Shoffer. "Does she not believe me? How can it be that she does not trust me? Why does she turn to you? Does she not know I shall do anything that is required to be certain Attelweir is kept from her?"

"I begin to think that Lady Beth is a trifle young for marriage. Too young to be out."

Millicent turned away and considered, briefly, helping herself to a drink to steady her nerves. Of all things for Beth to demand, a marriage? If it were not so very sad it would be laughable.

"She is all of seventeen. That is not an unreasonable age to be out. Still, she is easily overset and shy. A delay of a year or so before marriage would not go amiss. I should not like to prevent her having a season this year; that would seem too much like punishment and she needs the practice of going about in society," Shoffer went to the door and closed it slowly. "I tell you in confidence, North, I do not believe my grandmother or Mrs. Fleming do her any good at all. But what am I to do? Beth must have some chaperone. There are some services I cannot provide her."

Millicent picked up and set down crystal decanters without turning her head. "If only in jest, I would suggest you find that woman of the Ton whom your Grandmother despises and install her at your sister's side."

Shoffer grunted and flung himself into the nearest chair.

"If it were a case for jesting, I might even act on your advice." He covered his face with his hands. "Be a friend and pour me a glass of something."

Instead of making use of the bottles before her, Millicent crossed the room and gave the bell pull a strong yank. When the downstairs maid appeared, Millicent sent her off for a tea tray. Shoffer dropped his hands to his lap and stared at her.

"Tea? Truly, you are an odd fellow."

"But still a friend." Millicent refused to blush. "There are times, I have noted, that a sad mood is not improved by drink."

"As you wish, then. North, I am at a loss. Perhaps your cousin can aid me? Could she chaperone Beth alongside your cousins? I would be willing to put them up at Trolenfield house in return for the favor."

"Felicity? No." Millicent did not even hesitate before answering. "No, I am sorry, that will not do. Although both her parents are of old and good stock, and her husband the second son of a baronet, my cousin must be considered by the Ton to be the wife of a tutor, since that is how her husband spent his life. She has no standing that the Ton would acknowledge and her chaperonage would not advance your sister's state."

"Then what am I to do?"

The tea tray was fetched in and the maid poured out for both of them before vanishing. Millicent obeyed Shoffer's gesture and sat in the great chair opposite his before the unlit fireplace. Millicent settled her feet on a footrest and was surprised when Shoffer's booted feet joined hers from the other side. She considered removing her feet. It was, after all, his house and his footstool. But when Shoffer merely sipped his tea and stared into the distance, Millicent relaxed and allowed herself to be cheered by his nearness. Even for an instant permitted her foot to rest against his. Two layers of leather and bootblack separated their skin and yet she felt warmed by the contact. Millicent smiled at her own foolishness while Shoffer scowled at the ceiling.

"She turned to you, North. You. If I were a lesser man, I would hate you for being the one she trusts. That she believes will aid her."

"I think, Your Grace, that there is more to her terror than we currently understand. Your sister is the only one who can explain her actions."

"Come, North," said Shoffer, after another ten minutes had passed. "There must be something you can suggest."

"Coming from my so very great experience with the Ton?" Millicent sighed. "From my history of many seasons spent in London? How can I help you? I do not even know where Attelweir is."

"Attelweir is some small province of France. The present duc escaped during the early days of The Troubles and has been living on the charity of social climbing nitwits since then. "

"He has no money, then?"

"No income, no estate, and no hope of any, considering that he is related, distantly, to the Bourbon Kings and Napoleon despises him. His lands have all been given away to the Tyrant's friends."

"Then why does the dowager favor him so much? It is clear that much of his interest must be in your sister's dowry. He has nothing to offer in return."

"Rank, and rank alone. He was born a duc. He is not considered good Ton, despite his rank, and many hostesses do not send him invitations. If I had but known that my grandmother was encouraging his attendance upon my sister, I would have acted to prevent it."

"From the way Lady Beth is behaving, it has not gotten to the point of proposal."

"True enough, and I am thankful for it. I shall take time this evening to speak to my grandmother. I shall make it clear that Attelweir will be given his congé. With luck he will accept it." Shoffer glanced toward the windows. "It looks as if we shall have fine weather tomorrow. I am sorry to miss your riding lessons. Perhaps Beth and I shall take rooms in Bath for a little while and you can present your family to her."

Millicent closed her eyes and tried to imagine close contact between her mother, sisters, and Lady Beth. Too much time spent in conversation could bring many opportunities for Felicity to blurt out the truth.

"I do not believe that will advance Lady Beth's cause," said Millicent, after a longish pause. "I think, perhaps, you should make a list of your female distant relatives and acquaintances. You could go on a tour for the last few weeks of summer and call upon them. If you are blessed you may find someone Beth feels comfortable with who can accompany her to London for the season."

Shoffer considered this, then nodded. "You are right. I have family enough that someone could be found and the traveling and socializing without the pressure of a house party would benefit Beth."

A yawn took Millicent by surprise. "Forgive me, but I have been traveling and if we are to leave tomorrow, I should pack and rest."

"Oh, yes, of a certainty. But before you retire, I promised myself there is something we would do on the first day of your visit and I am determined to keep to my plan."

"Oh?" Millicent tried again to raise her eyebrow. "Some entertainment in my honor?"

"Entertaining for me. Come lad, up. My valet is waiting to give you a haircut."

Millicent did not have to fake her collapse. A valet to put his hands on her? "No. I beg you. No."

Shoffer would not hear any of Millicent's stammered protests or excuses. It was not as if she could tell the truth. She was afraid that the experienced valet would be able to tell by some mysterious sense, by the shape of her head or some such, that she was not a man. Indeed, even as they tried to force her into the chair she resisted the removal of her loose fitting coat and refused to untie her cravat. Frustrated and amused, Shoffer threw a heavy sheet toward her with which to cover her clothing.

"All right, then, keep your neck cloth," cried Shoffer. "Do not complain to me if your neck itches for the next seven days."

Millicent sank down in the proffered chair, the cloth raised to her chin and tented around her body; she regarded the instruments of hair cutting fearfully. Shoffer's valet, a middle-aged, egg-shaped man called Ikelsby, dropped Millicent's secondhand coat onto a bench and regarded the hacked off, uneven ends of her hair with an expression of disgust.

"When we get to London, Ikelsby," said Shoffer from his position of comfort on a couch at the other side of the room, "you shall confer with your colleagues and see if we can find some strong soul who can undertake to make over our friend North."

"I beg you would not," said Millicent, shrinking away as the shears came closer.

"I believe," said Ikelsby, making the first cut and struggling to find a diplomatic reply, "that it will be difficult to find a gentleman's gentleman who could give satisfaction."

"Yes. Exactly." Millicent's eyes, wheeling in panic, focused on Shoffer. "Besides, who would give up London for Yorkshire?"

There was no way she could keep the secret of her gender from so intimate a servant as a valet. Impossible. That was one of the reasons she made no attempt to dress in a fashionable manner. Her loose coats and trousers were as necessary as the cravats around her chest in maintaining her secret.

"I was thinking some batman who lost his master on the battlefields might do," continued Shoffer. "A strong sergeant type with a bullhorn voice to keep Mr. North in line."

"It would have to be someone of that type." Ikelsby pulled on her hair and cut and tugged this way and that until her scalp ached and tears threatened.

The ordeal ended without anyone feeling much the winner.

Ikelsby snipped and combed and arranged locks, but never professed himself to be satisfied. In the end, he sighed and held up a mirror. Millicent regarded the result without enthusiasm.

"It seems," said Millicent, moving her head first one way, then the other, "that you have done as much as you could with such poor goods. You have at least left me my ears."

Her only emotion, in viewing herself, was relief to have survived without being revealed. Shoffer regarded the results unhappily.

"We shall never make you a Corinthian, Mr. North. Nor shall you give Brummel any point for concern."

"Neat and clean is the best we can hope for," added the valet, sadly. "With no reason for ambition it would be difficult to find a valet for Mr. North. Our role is to turn our masters out as best they can be, but Mr. North…"

His voice trailed away and all the men in the room nodded together. Mr. North would never be a fashionable man. Millicent stared at her reflection, wondering why it was that she was tall and plain as a woman and still unhandsome as a man. It hardly seemed fair.

"Your cousins," said Shoffer, with some hesitation, "do they much resemble you?"

Millicent considered the question odd and thought before answering.

"The ladies are generally considered to be pleasing in their looks and address," she ventured, and seeing Shoffer's shoulders relax, Millicent laughed. "Oh, dear. Were you fearing you must give consequence to ladies who are not worthy of your attention? Poor duke. How sad. No, do not worry. All the good looks in the family were granted to the ladies, as is to be preferred. They are both charming and pretty."

Rising from the chair before some other attack be planned, Millicent tossed the sheet onto the floor and retrieved her coat.

"With your permission, I shall retire, if I can but find out in which closet the dowager hid my bags. Or, perhaps, I should begin digging in the garden?"

Shoffer gave the bell pull a tug. "The upstairs maid will direct you. Considering the weather, if you rise early enough we shall go riding before departure. I shall send a note to Beth to ask she join us."

"Oh, will the fun and frolic never end?" drawled Millicent and bowed herself out of the room.

The upstairs maid was approaching already and Millicent begged to be guided to her bed. As they walked past the dowager's chamber, Millicent could hear that lady's voice raised in a scold. She considered returning to Shoffer to let him know someone was being harangued, but decided she did not want to overstep. Besides, if it were Mrs. Fleming on the receiving end of the sharp edge of the dowager's tongue, then it was no more than that lady deserved. Instead, she took herself off to bed to dream that it was Shoffer who combed her hair and it had miraculously grown, her shirt and trews turned to silk ball gown and her beauty was revealed to the duke. And he, seeing her, saw how little beauty there was to be, turned away.

She awoke to a tear stained pillow and bright sunlight.

Timothy Shoffer, Duke of Trolenfield and master, somewhat, of most of what he surveyed, regarded the spread on the breakfast board without enthusiasm. He had gone, late the previous night, to try again to speak to his sister, only to be told by that lady's chaperone that Beth was retired for the night. Beth's difficulty with company was a constant source of frustration and fear for the duke and he was grateful that providence had granted they meet the one person in all England who seemed able to break Beth out of her shell.

Beth had been taken from their home after the death of their parents from a purulent fever when Shoffer was in his twenties and Beth a mere child. It had been their grandmother's decision, then. Shoffer, the dowager declared, would be too busy coping with his new responsibilities to bear with the problems of a young girl. So, away went Beth leaving Shoffer to grieve alone.

Looking back Shoffer was certain that he had permitted Beth to be taken away not so much out of the conviction she would do better with a female relative, as much as Shoffer's determination to get the duchess out of the building as soon as possible after the funeral. The guilt of that selfish act ate at him now.

Poor Beth. He had not given a thought to how she would suffer. He thought the dowager and the little girl would be a comfort to each other, but it was obvious that had not occurred.

There was nothing Shoffer would not do now to make amends for that neglect. They were both lucky to have met Mr. North, someone they could both enjoy. Mr. North possessed that unique talent of being able to make himself agreeable to company, both high and low, male and female. If they had not met, Shoffer was certain he would still be living with a silent Beth, helpless to deal with her woes.

Glancing toward the windows, Shoffer took note of the brilliant sunlight. He gestured toward the waiting footman as he took his seat at the head of the table.

"James. Have a message taken to my sister; ask her if she would like to join Mr. North and myself for a riding lesson. Then take yourself down to Mr. North's room and have him chased out of bed."

"No need," said his friend, entering the room tugging at the collar of his ill-fitting riding coat. "Here I am and ready, if unwilling, to be bounced about like a sack of potatoes."

"The sooner you learn proper posture the less bouncing there shall be."

As Mr. North made his way down the sideboard selecting a little of this and a little of that, Shoffer congratulated himself for not being misled by North's appearance of shabby gentility, nor by his humorous way of talking. In these last few months, the man had proved himself capable of good sense, when required, and celebration in its proper hour. Shoffer looked forward to receiving his letters with an eagerness he felt for no other. Of all the people he had met in his years of attending Ton events, Shoffer could think of no one whose company he had enjoyed more.

The footman returned at that moment and hesitated at the door.

"What is it, man?" demanded Shoffer.

"Begging your pardon, Your Grace. Sally, Lady Elizabeth's maid, says how her bed has not been slept in."

"Excuse me?" Shoffer put down his knife and half rose from his chair.

"Lady Elizabeth, Your Grace. Sally went in to see if Lady Elizabeth was awake and she found the room empty. She says how Lady Elizabeth did not call her last night to help her get ready for bed, nor give her instructions for this morning and now Sally cannot find her."

Shoffer shot out of the room as if attached to a firework. Mr. North dithered for a moment before putting down his plate and running after him.

"Did anyone enter or leave the house last night?" demanded Shoffer as they ran past Forsythe in the main hall.

"No, Your Grace."

Shoffer hit the stairs at a run with North, uncharacteristically stern in visage, a bare step behind him. They arrived at Beth's room just as the maid Sally emerged, shaken and pale, but not yet in tears.

"When did you see her last?" roared Shoffer.

"Have pity, Shoffer," said North. "The girl will faint if you cannot be calm."

"To hell with calm!"

"What is all this noise?" demanded the dowager, emerging from her room in her dressing gown and sleeping cap, three rows of lace outlining her face. "Shoffer, remember who you are."

"I know very well who I am," cried Shoffer, lowering his voice in the face of his grandmother's frown. "What I do not know is, where is my sister?"

Some awareness fluttered across the woman's face and she stepped back, one hand on her door. "There is no need for this fuss. She spent the night with me."

North took a half step forward and rested his hand on Shoffer's sleeve.

"I cannot imagine," he said in a near whisper, "any circumstances wherein Lady Beth would choose *willingly* to spend a night with the dowager."

"No more can I," said Shoffer. "If you would be so kind, please tell Lady Beth I wish to see her."

"She has not yet arisen." The dowager tugged on the door, half closing it.

"I care not. I will see her now."

"Shoffer, this is hardly proper. I am not ready to receive visitors this early in the day."

North, always courteous, stepped a little away from the quarreling family members and directed a few of the servants away. There was no need for them to view this argument. Then Shoffer saw him stop and stare toward the dowager's chamber.

"Did you hear that? That thumping? What is that?" North demanded, just as Mrs. Fleming's head appeared behind the dowager and vanished.

"Nothing," said the dowager, flushing.

That was the last straw for Shoffer. He pushed past her and was in the bedchamber before anyone else moved. On the far side of the room was an ancient, inlaid armoire with its door locked. From within came a muffled thumping. In an instant Shoffer was on his knees before the shaking armoire, struggling with the key.

"Oh, my God," came the whisper from North.

Within seconds Shoffer was dragging open the door and lifting his sister off the floor of the wardrobe. Shoffer crossed the room and deposited his sister into North's arms. His move took the youth by surprise and it was all the smaller man could do to prevent the girl from dropping to the floor. Instead of bearing Beth away North settled her feet on the ground and held her to his side.

"Take her," ordered Shoffer. "Have care of her while I deal with this."

Shoffer pushed them both out of the room and shut the door in their faces. Then he turned to face the dowager who retreated until she was holding the posters of the bed for support.

"Now, Your Grace," he growled, clasping his hands behind his back so that he might resist the temptation to strangle the dowager. "We shall come to terms."

Outside in the corridor Millicent found herself and Beth to be the center of many curious eyes. As she was not strong enough to carry Beth, Millicent settled for putting an arm around the girl's waist and half dragging her along the corridor toward her own room. Maneuvering around a stunned footman Millicent's brain fired to life and she glared around at the gathered servants.

"Lady Elizabeth will need a hot bath. Bring water, a lot of it. And you," she nodded to Sally. "Which other maid does Beth like?"

"Ah? Lily?"

"Excellent. Have her fetched as well. The two of you will take Lady Beth in hand and put her to bed."

"No," whispered Beth, the first sound she had uttered since emerging from the armoire. She tightened her grip around Millicent's arm, cutting off the blood. "Please. No. I cannot sleep."

"Very well, they shall help you dress and keep you company until your brother arrives."

They went into Beth's well-appointed suite of rooms. When Millicent paused at the door, Beth dragged her further in.

"Do not leave me. Please. I do not feel safe without you."

Millicent cast an anxious glance over her shoulder. This was Shoffer's place. His responsibility, not Millicent's. As Mr. North, she could not stay, but as a caring human being, she could not leave.

"It is hardly proper." Millicent glanced about the room, seeking some way to maintain Beth's reputation and still give comfort. "I shall sit here, facing the wall and if you call out I shall answer."

"Promise you will not leave."

"Not until Shoffer arrives."

With many backward glances, Beth consented to be taken to the dressing room where a bath was being prepared for her. Several times during the next quarter hour Beth called out, seeking confirmation that Millicent was still waiting. Casting about for some nonsense with which to distract the girl, Millicent found for the first time in her life she had no idea what to say, so each time she settled for a brief affirmative.

"Yes, Lady Beth. I am still here."

When Shoffer finally arrived he called out a greeting to his sister, but did not dismiss Millicent from the room. Instead he took up the matching chair and they sat side by side facing the wall until Beth emerged from her dressing room. Thereupon, Beth claimed Shoffer's right arm and Millicent's left, and between them, descended to the breakfast room.

Not since that first day when the carriage had overturned had Millicent seen Beth so pinched and pale. The girl was attired neatly in a morning dress of palest rose, her hair combed and gracefully arranged, but her lips were white and clamped tight, her eyes wide and shining with unshed tears, and her hands trembling. Shoffer guided her to the table and seated her between his place and Millicent's, then left to load a plate for her. A footman appeared with a freshly brewed pot to fill the tea cups, then departed the room in response to a gesture from the duke.

"Here, my dear Beth," said Shoffer, sliding a plate in front of his sister. "Eat this; you will feel much more the thing."

"I cannot," whispered Beth.

Millicent exchanged a look with Shoffer. There was so much anger and pain in Shoffer's eyes that it amazed Millicent that he was able to sit there so quietly. Instead of storming about the room, raging to the skies, he put a spoonful of sugar into Beth's tea and stirred it for her.

Millicent sliced a sliver off her now cold beefsteak, the scrape of her knife the only sound in the room. She could not bear the suspense for long and sought about for a distraction. After the traumas of the night, Beth needed something to occupy her hands and mind. When the idea finally came, Millicent was shocked at herself, but could not resist. It was the ideal thing to restore Lady Beth's spirits and teach her grandmother a lesson.

"Lady Beth," began Millicent, ignoring Shoffer's negative shake of the head. "I was wondering if you could take the time to teach me a skill I believe I will need before the season starts."

"I cannot," whispered Beth. "I beg you would please excuse me."

"Oh, but as you are the epitome of all that is womanly and graceful, I know you would be skilled and I should not have a better teacher."

"Please, Mr. North. Not today."

"But, Lady Beth…"

"Mr. North," came Shoffer's harder voice. "Not today!"

Millicent forced the words out before Shoffer flung her from the room. "I should like to learn to shoot!"

"Shoot?" repeated Beth blinking in shock, her eyes clearing. "I do not know how to shoot."

"How can that be? Surely, Lady Beth, there is no marksman to compare with you. You have excellent timing and delicacy of feeling and all the womanly virtues. I am certain that you hit the bullseye every time with your bullet."

Color was returning to the girl's pale cheeks and a faint smile played on her lips as she tried to answer Millicent's nonsense.

"You flatter me, Mr. North, but I have never shot a gun."

"You do astonish me," said Millicent, and pushing Beth's tea cup into her hand, she had the satisfaction of seeing the girl take one sip, then another. "Here I was convinced that I could turn to you for aid. As I told you, I am taking my cousins down to London for the season and given my superior understanding and calm demeanor, I am certain that within the first week, I shall be challenged to at least a dozen duels. I must know how to shoot."

"But I do not know how!"

"Then I shall teach you both," said Shoffer.

"What did you say?" gasped Beth, turning to meet her brother's gaze for the first time that morning.

"I shall teach both of you," declared Shoffer. "Indeed, I realize I should have taught you long since, Beth, and once I have trained you, I shall see to it that you have your own gun with you at all times. One for each day of the week. All different colors to match your costumes. James!" The duke's shout brought the footman back into the room at a run. "James, inform the groundskeeper I want targets for shooting practice set up on the East Lawn immediately."

"The East Lawn, Your Grace? 'Tis morning. The sun!"

"Position the targets so we are shooting from north to south, but it must be on the East Lawn." Dismissing the man, Shoffer returned his attention to his sister. "Now Beth, you must eat a good breakfast or you will not be able to hold the gun steady. I do insist."

Baffled but willing, Beth started eating and missed the smile that Shoffer shot Millicent over her head. But Millicent did not. The warmth of that approval she felt clear through to her bones.

It was enough, she told herself, to have Shoffer as a dear friend. It was enough.

Her hands shook as she returned to her own cooling breakfast. It would never be enough.

They adjourned immediately after breakfast to the East Lawn, Shoffer pausing briefly in his study to collect two sets of dueling pistols, powder, and shot. At Shoffer's command, the servants hurried about setting up vaguely man-shaped targets made of straw instead of the usual archery bullseyes. A table was fetched so Shoffer could arrange the pistols and demonstrate loading and preparation of the weapons. It was not long before they were ready and Beth faced the targets for the first time with a gun in her hand.

It was perhaps unfortunate that it was that moment Mrs. Fleming emerged from the house.

"Lady Elizabeth," she cried. "Whatever are you doing? Out, without even a maid or a bonnet."

"I find it surprising, Mrs. Fleming," said Beth in frosty tones, "that of all the things that have happened in this house today you find my lack of a bonnet to be worthy of comment."

Then Beth closed one eye and squeezed the trigger. The

pistol leapt in her hand, startling her, but she did not drop it.

"A hit! A hit," cried Millicent, applauding. "That is one villain who will sin no longer. You have taken his arm right off!"

Shoffer seized Millicent around the shoulders and pounded his fist into her arm. "Yes. Yes! You were correct, Mr. North. My sister is a superior markswoman."

Millicent rubbed her arm, even as she leaned against his strength, just for a moment breathing in his scent. When he released her, she did not protest, but went with him to offer Beth congratulations.

Mrs. Fleming, however, went deathly white.

"Guns! Lady Elizabeth, this must never be known. Your reputation would be destroyed in an instant were anyone to know."

"Oh, bother everyone," said Beth. "I think if it were to get out that I can use a gun, then certain people would treat me with more respect."

"Your grandmother…" began Mrs. Fleming.

"My grandmother!" Beth drew a deep breath, and gun still in hand turned to face Mrs. Fleming, then glanced up at the house behind her.

Millicent and Shoffer turned as well. Silhouetted in a window was the unmistakable figure of the dowager duchess. Now Millicent realized why Shoffer had insisted on the East Lawn. He wanted the whole parade to take place under the dowager's window. For her to see that Beth would never again be her helpless victim. Millicent smiled and Shoffer's grin was feral as he stalked to the table and seized the next loaded pistol.

"Beth, dear. Come, Grand'Mere is watching. Let us show her how ladylike you are."

He guided Beth's steps back to face the target and prompted her to shoot. The second shot again struck the bullseye.

"My years of archery practice have stood me in good stead," remarked Beth calmly. Without turning her head she added, "Mrs. Fleming, you are dismissed. Do not expect to receive a character. The housekeeper will bring you the balance of your salary, although I am quite convinced you do not deserve it. Go now and deliver one last message to my grandmother. Tell her from me that if I ever lay eyes on her again, I will shoot her myself!"

"You cannot speak to me like that." Mrs. Fleming made the

mistake of turning to the duke for confirmation of her status in the household.

"Madam, you are dismissed," said the duke. "Leave. Never let me see your face nor hear your name again or I shall surely strangle you."

Mrs. Fleming gave a squeak and staggered away toward the house. Beth watched her go, her face set and calm. Then she raised her eyes to watch her grandmother's figure disappear behind the curtains. Once both women were out of sight, Beth dropped the pistol to the ground and fell sobbing into her brother's arms. Shoffer lifted her off her feet and carried her to a nearby wrought iron seat. Millicent was left with the stunned servants.

"Oh, I think you can all go spread the gossip now," murmured Millicent, picking up the pistol and restoring it to the table. "They do not need us at this moment."

The servants retreated and after rendering the remaining pistols safe, Millicent left as well. She chose the library on the west side of the house so that no one could accuse her of intruding on the privacy of brother and sister.

It was not more than an hour before Shoffer and Beth came seeking her.

"Mr. North," cried a much more cheerful Beth. "You abandoned us. We have not yet finished your lesson. I am determined to teach you to shoot as well as me."

Millicent set aside the novel she had been pretending to read and smiled at both of them. "I thought myself de trop, dear Lady Beth, as well as much intimidated by your superior skills."

"Oh, phoo. Come out now. It is a beautiful day and I have just told the servants to prepare an alfresco luncheon for us on the East Lawn for after. Shoffer has said he will fetch out his hunting guns for us to play with."

"Play?" protested Shoffer. "Hunting is a serious matter."

"Oh, come," replied his sister. "Tell me it is not play that has you getting up at dawn to shoot things."

"If you did not enjoy it, Shoffer," said Millicent, "you would not do it. Is that not the definition of play?"

"I cannot compete with the two of you when you are being silly," replied Shoffer. "Come, North. Up, you lazy creature. You started this; therefore, you must suffer with me."

"Willingly," Millicent hauled herself out of her chair and they all headed out of the house.

They paused in the main hall to watch servants running back and forth bearing boxes and trunks. Near the front steps two carriages were being loaded.

Beth ignored the activity and stalked past, head held high. Shoffer leaned close to Millicent.

"I sent a message to intercept Attelweir and the others last night. He will know he is not welcome. Mrs. Fleming and my ... the dowager leaves today. You shall have your fortnight, Mr. North, and my thanks."

Millicent inclined her head in acknowledgement. "I hope you know I will not speak of any of this."

"Of course. You are a fribble, not an idiot. I am only sorry you lack suitable title whereby I could bestow Beth upon you," the duke added lightly, as they strolled past the laboring servants. "Are you certain you are not related to any person of rank? An earl, perhaps? That is not too lowly for consideration."

"A baron would do," cried Beth, who returned to hear the last.

"The hand of the fair maiden in reward for saving the kingdom from a dowager dragon? No. Not one," said Millicent, "and a good thing, too. Were I to admit I am twenty-seventh in line to a mere baronetcy, I would fear for the lives of those twenty-six, given the skills of our Lady Beth."

"I would not shoot all of them," said Beth, seizing both Shoffer and Millicent by an arm. "It would not be wise and should cause talk. Poison, I think, would do for half."

Shoffer recoiled in mock shock. "See, see what associating with those who are beneath you has wrought?" he cried, as Millicent dissolved into laughter.

Chapter Eight

Winter season – London.

"Are you certain they come today?" asked Felicity, as she rearranged the folds of her new dress.

Millicent glanced toward her mother, then away. Since she had answered that self-same question six times that morning, she was becoming weary of it.

Felicity, Mildred, and Maude had arrived in London a few days previously and had been driving Millicent insane since. It was not that she did not love her family, but she had spent the summer mostly alone and found being welcomed back into the bosom of her family a trifle smothering.

After spending a few weeks with Shoffer and Beth, Millicent had been called away to deal with yet another tenant emergency, this time in Dorset. From there she had gone to Cambridgeshire and Exeter. By the time she had settled matters with tenants in Oxfordshire summer had faded into autumn. Millicent was too busy to accompany her family from Bath to London as planned, so it was not possible for Millicent to prevent her mother and sisters from spending every last penny Millicent had left with them on what the Bath modiste assured them were the latest London fashions.

Informed of the delay, Shoffer kindly sent one of his "lesser" coaches and sufficient staff to carry the ladies from Bath to London in comfort. Millicent did not inform her mother whose vehicle she travelled in until that lady had arrived in London. Her ears were still ringing from the peal Felicity had rung for that particular secret. Poor Felicity had not until that moment been aware Millicent had made the acquaintance of a duke and so had not been able to boast to her Bath friends. In retaliation she was pretending not to believe any such acquaintance existed.

Shoffer, arriving in London only the day before had sent a note around that morning announcing his intention to call. Felicity had been in a taking every moment since. Up one minute, cast down the next, she could barely keep her seat in the drawing room, but would flutter about rearranging the rented decorations.

"Are you certain," began Felicity, when a heavy knock came at the front door.

Their newly hired butler stalked past the parlor door as Mildred and Maude leapt to the window overlooking the street.

"Oh. Look at the carriage and the livery," cried Maude. "This carriage is so much finer than the one that brought us. But so tiny!"

Millicent pulled the curtain back to improve her view and shrugged. "That is a town carriage. Small and light for the narrow streets. It does not need to carry luggage so has no trunk. Shoffer tells me he has purchased a new high flier as well. That will be particularly fine."

"You must buy one, Mr. North," demanded Maude. "I do insist."

"So do I," said a deep voice from the doorway.

Shoffer was arrived.

Merit the temporary butler stepped forward, determined not to miss an opportunity that might never again come his way. He had been hired by Mr. Simpson who had informed him that he would be serving in a small, quiet, genteel household; and therefore, he had not expected to be opening the door to receive a duke's calling card from the hand of a liveried footman. Merit could barely wait for his next half day to lord it over his fellows at the employment agency.

Standing tall in the doorway, he intoned with what he thought was ducal dignity, "His Grace, the Duke of Trolenfield. The Lady Elizabeth Shoffer."

Shoffer paused at the doorway, waiting for the butler to clear out of the way and studied Mr. North's family. Mr. North had not materially changed since the summer. His hair was again in desperate need of a trim; his clothing, secondhand as before, hung loosely on his too thin frame. All in all, the Yorkshire gentleman did not show to good effect. But once one looked past such easily repaired defects, one found a man worthy of friendship. Shoffer blessed the day that had thrust Mr. North to his notice. Just imagine if they had crossed paths at some Ton event. He would have dismissed the man out of hand, as well as the family to whom he was about to be introduced. On any other day and by any Ton measure, they would be beneath his notice. He scanned the room as the butler took himself off. Mr. North was standing beside a small blond woman of middle years who had retained her looks and figure well. Two young women waited, one kneeling on the window seat, the other seated on a small couch.

Fortunately, North had spoken the truth. All the good looks in the family had gone to the women. They were all small, delicate, and golden with fine features that would retain beauty until great age. He could grant them his consequence with confidence and their golden beauty would not detract from Beth's darker good looks in any way.

Shoffer crossed the room to peer out of the window.

"It does look very fine from this angle," he said, smiling at the stunned girl on the window seat.

Then he crossed to where Mr. North stood beside his cousin's chair. Beth, trailing shyly in his wake, cast a smile to Mr. North.

"Your Grace, may I introduce my family to your acquaintance?" Shoffer nodded and Mr. North continued. "This is my cousin, Felicity Boarder and her daughter Miss Mildred Boarder. Miss Maude is in the window. There was another daughter named Millicent, now deceased. We must praise my cousin for her consistency, if lack of imagination, in naming her children."

"Mister North," cried Felicity. "What a thing to say."

"Oh, do not worry yourself, Mrs. Boarder." Shoffer bowed over her hand. "I have spent some time in the company of Mr. North and know what a foolish rattle he is. I am happy to make your acquaintance."

The Boarder ladies dropped him deep curtsies.

"This is my sister, Elizabeth, who has been most eager to meet you ever since Mr. North announced you would be coming for a season."

The ladies examined each other curiously and competed to see who could make the deepest and neatest curtsy.

"I am most honored to meet you," said Felicity. "You have the advantage as Mr. North has been so unkind as not to tell us that he knew you."

"Mister North," cried Lady Beth. "What is this? Are you ashamed to know us? Shall we be cut in the street next?"

All of the Boarder ladies went white at that statement, but North only laughed.

"Oh, but my dear Lady Beth, you know what a shy and self-effacing person I am. I could barely bring myself to think that I am graced by the kindness of notice by so high a person as yourself.

How could I prattle the acquaintance about without blushing for shame?"

"As if you have felt shame at any time in your life." Lady Beth slapped his arm with her fan and advanced to shake hands with Mildred and Maude.

"You have my deepest sympathy," continued Lady Beth, in solemn tones even as her eyes sparkled with humor. "It must be such a sore trial for you to be burdened with such a relative."

"We would hide him in the attic if we could," replied Mildred, recovering fastest, "with the bats and broken furniture, but he keeps escaping."

"Shall you take tea?" asked Felicity, uncertain what to do in the face of so much informality.

"Oh, please, I must ask something first," cried Mr. North, one hand over his heart. A pose that Shoffer knew well by now presaged one of his more ridiculous suggestions. "A favor, Lady Beth. A boon, if you will. The fulfillment of a desperate need. My cousins realized they had been misled before they left Bath and purchased clothing that simply will not do. As soon as they saw people walking down London streets they realized the problem and have spent the last two days buying enough fabric to upholster Ireland. Of course, as soon as they brought their purchases home they started such a wailing that you would think someone had died thinking they had bought the wrong thing. Please, of your mercy, will you approve their purchases? The fabric is laid out in the other drawing room."

"Oh, please, would you?" cried Maude who was staring with frank greed at Elizabeth's embroidered pelisse and befeathered hat. "You have been to London so many times and know what is right. We so need your guidance."

"I would be happy to; although, I am no expert," said Lady Beth, and consented to be dragged from the room by Mildred and Maude.

"That was well done of you," said Shoffer, when the younger girls left. Catching the baffled look on Felicity's face, he smiled and extended his hand to her. "Please sit and let me explain. You know from your own experience what kind of man Mr. North is. I asked him to help my sister be more comfortable in company. You see now the improved Beth. But I think there is still more to be done."

Felicity sat, stunned to find her hand held by a duke and glanced back and forth between her cousin and Shoffer.

"More?" asked North, seizing the bell pull. When the maid appeared, North requested tea be sent to the other drawing room and sent her on her way.

Shoffer glanced toward the closed door and spoke softly. "The summer did not go well even after you spent those weeks with us. Poor Beth flowers whenever she is teasing you and me, but seems incapable of speech in other company. She confessed to me she has no idea what to say in response to them. I think she needs to rehearse with you."

"You pay me too high a compliment, Shoffer…" began North.

"I am certain that it will help her to have your cousins to squire about. Even so, if you could spend some time…"

"Shoffer, you do me much honor, but I have never been to the type of Ton events you speak of. How can I prepare her for something I know nothing about?"

"I hardly know, except that you must. The damage the dowager did lingers still. When she is in company with me and you, she is charming and clever, but let another enter the room and bit by bit she retreats."

"Introducing my cousins about will improve her, surely. She will want to impress them with her consequence."

"And perhaps she will falter in the crowd, fall silent, and do them no good at all."

Felicity, who was turning from one to another following the conversation, finally found her voice.

"Now, what is this? What are you about with this girl? I do not like it when I hear gentlemen plotting and planning for a young woman."

"Elizabeth?" asked Mr. North. "We mean her no harm at all."

"It is entirely innocent, my dear Mrs. Boarder, although your concern does you much honor. Beth is my only sister. She has lived many years with my grandmother who is a very strong and controlling person. Beth, on the other hand, is shy. Now that she has made her come out, poor Beth does not know how to go on."

Felicity considered this. "Mildred and Maude are bold, but not too bold. Mildred, I think is older than your sister and a good steady girl. Maude is about the same age and sensible. They will naturally defer to Lady Elizabeth for her rank and previous experience and certainly will turn to her with their questions. If you will permit, Your Grace, letting my daughters follow in your sister's train will force Lady Elizabeth to make decisions. Perform introductions. Lead, when in the past she has followed. I will speak to the girls so they will consult with Lady Elizabeth often in such a way that will raise her confidence."

"Thank you, Mrs. Boarder, that is what I desire." Shoffer turned his most dazzling smile on her. "It would help if you would agree to attend some events with Beth. I can obtain invitations to balls and such for you."

"You do us more good than we deserve in return, Your Grace," said Felicity.

"Mama, come and see," cried Maude, bursting through the door. "Lady Beth has the latest copy of *La Belle Assemblee* with her. She knows all the best places for gloves and hats ... although, she keeps saying something odd about wilting straw bonnets with rain water."

Mr. North rolled his eyes. "I have not yet told the family that joke. Come, Shoffer, let us brave where few men dare and sit with the ladies while they prepare an assault upon the shopkeepers of Bond Street that would put Napoleon to shame."

"Is it too late to flee to Scotland?" inquired Shoffer rising and offering his arm to Felicity.

"Far, far too late," said Felicity, smiling up at him.

What with one thing and another, Shoffer and his sister overstayed their allotted quarter hour for a morning visit by several hours. Dusk was falling when they finally took their leave.

"Ton events have already begun," said Shoffer to Millicent as they dawdled on the front steps while the ladies said their goodbyes. "Although the season does not get into full flow for another few weeks, we should give the ladies a little time to improve their wardrobes – it is a task they never fully complete – and then begin to take them about. I have already begun to receive invitations."

"I have not. Not surprising, since I have no acquaintance in London besides your good self."

"Do not worry. I have decided that Lady Englethorpes' ball this Saturday shall be the first I accept. I shall see to it that your family also receives an invitation. That will give you three days to get some sort of evening dress."

Millicent paused and put her hands in her pockets to prevent herself from wringing them together. A Ton event as a man! She had never considered that she would have to take her masquerade to such a level.

"Do not worry, I have it all in train," continued Shoffer. "Lady Englethorpes senior is the dowager, the widow of Sir Edmund Englethorpes. It is their spinster daughter Edith, a rather interesting and charming woman, who is Beth's chaperone this season. They shall send you an invitation tomorrow."

"Interesting and charming?" Millicent felt a demon of jealousy rising and her hands clenched into tight fists. "Are we in exception of an announcement of some nature?"

"Do not be a fool, North. Edith Englethorpes is twice again my age. She has the virtue of having a sense of humor and Beth is not frightened of her. They do well together."

"I am pleased to hear it."

"As for you, I do not trust you to shop for yourself, so gird your loins and prepare to go about with me tomorrow. While the ladies empty Bond Street of its treasures you shall meet my tailor. Mr. Nestor will find you his greatest challenge."

Millicent went pale, which amused the duke and he and his sister took their leave well pleased with the visit. Millicent took Mildred's arm and dragged her into the house and up to the family's private drawing room on the second floor.

"Mildred. You must help me."

"Millicent, you have gone so very white. Whatever is the matter?"

"Tomorrow, I must undress for a tailor! In the presence of the duke. What am I to do?"

Mildred simply stood and stared. "I have not the faintest idea."

As the ducal carriage traveled the short distance back to his London residence, Shoffer patted his sister's hand and smiled in the dim light. Yes, that first visit went very well, as far as Shoffer was concerned. Little Maude looked well on the way to becoming Beth's confidant, cheerfully asking advice about hairstyles, and Mildred asked enough intelligent questions about navigating London streets that Beth was delighted to discover herself regarded as an authority on the subject of the capitol. The three young women were full of plans for shopping trips and on the way home Beth was beside herself with the excitement of preparing another woman's wardrobe. Shoffer could not remember seeing her so animated.

Yes, the Boarder family was just what Beth needed.

Millicent managed to avoid the trip to the tailor for one day by sending a note around the next morning before breakfast, claiming the need to deal with some problem associated with her estate. Shoffer responded with one of his own, declaring that, ill or not, busy or not, dead or not, the visit to the tailor's would take place the next day or else Mr. North would not be fit to be seen on Saturday.

Millicent smiled as she waved off her mother and sisters when Beth and her new chaperone, Lady Edith, collected them, a smile that lasted not a second longer than the women were in sight. Alone, Millicent retreated to her rooms and wore a hole in the carpet pacing.

Around midday Millicent dressed herself in the least disreputable of her secondhand coats and flung herself out of the house. The hackney that Merit fetched for her was driven by a red nosed, barely coherent drunkard, but the man recognized a gold sovereign when it was waved before his bloodshot eyes. Very willingly he took Millicent around town, taking her first to pawnshop row, and thence all the way to east London to Walthamstow Market to go over piles and piles of shoes of various vintages and secondhand clothing of recent and slightly older styles. It was in a hastily assembled tent behind a market stall that Millicent tried on a selection of clothing, stolen or sold, but of recent fashion, until she found some that fit well enough.

Shoffer, she knew, would die of shock if she suggested appearing in public in such smelly secondhand clothing, so she would not ask him to countenance it.

With luck and a little fast talking, her alternate plan would carry her through.

When Shoffer collected her the next morning, he was surprised to see her carrying several packages bound up with brown paper and string.

"It is customary to return from shopping with burdens, Mr. North," said Shoffer, poking one with a fingertip and wrinkling his nose at the odor that rose from it. "Not depart."

Millicent arranged the packages on the seat beside her and refused to respond to the hint. "Shall we go to Tattersall's after the tailor's? It is my observation that carriages move so slowly along the streets that a horse is better for getting about if the distance is too far for walking."

Still staring at the parcels, Shoffer responded. "I brought down that mare you favored from my own stables. It is in the mews behind my house. Have one of your footmen run across to fetch it whenever you need it."

"Oh, excellent. That is very kind. And speaking of kindness, my cousin is overwhelmed to receive her first Ton invitation. If it were not necessary to present it at the door, I believe she would have it framed and hung in the front hall."

Shoffer smiled.

"She may frame it with my blessing. We are all invited to dine with the Englethorpes before the ball begins. A singular honor, I hope you know. I shall come by to collect your family so she will not be required to present her invitation."

"Oh, excellent. The ladies will be pleased."

The journey to the tailor's was an unusual one in Shoffer's experience. His own first trip to London had been accomplished in the presence of his late father and uncle, both of whom discouraged youthful curiosity and bouncing about by dent of much frowning and scowling and one slap across the back of his head. Mr. North felt no compunction toward restrained behavior in Shoffer's presence. Indeed, Shoffer was convinced that even his father would have found it difficult to keep North in his seat. Disdaining even the appearance of fashionable ennui, North slid across the polished leather seat from one window to the other, dropping the glass and leaning out the better to peer at the buildings and the fashionable people strolling the sidewalks. There was nothing that did not excite his interest and Shoffer found himself cast into the role of tour guide for his country friend.

"You will save yourself much humiliation, Mr. North, if you remember not to display your ignorance in society," scolded Shoffer, when they disembarked at the tailor's shop front.

"Oh, bother that, Your Gracefulness." North stood, hands full of his damned packages and gazed openly up and down the crowded street. "I will not laugh at jokes if they are not funny nor pretend to understand gossip if I do not. And I shall not remain in ignorance if there are books that can enlighten me."

With that the annoying man detoured toward a publisher's shop just two doors away from the tailor.

"Oh, no," cried Shoffer, seizing his friend by the upper arm. "Books are for later. A reward for good behavior." He dragged North forcibly through the door of the tailor's establishment, bundles and all. "Lord above, you are worse than a litter of untrained puppies."

Mr. Nestor was a tailor so exclusive, so proud and disdainful, that he routinely effected to be offended when approached to sell his wares. More than one presumptive Ton buck crept out of his store empty-handed, ashamed for having suggested Mr. Nestor engaged in something as demeaning as "trade."

It could, therefore, be assumed that Mr. Nestor had never met anyone resembling Mr. North.

Shoffer watched in amazement as North pushed aside the fabrics delicately arranged on a table and began undoing the knots of his parcels.

"There you are," he cried, as Mr. Nestor emerged through a curtain. North opened the package revealing a neatly folded coat of uncertain provenance. "My friend the duke here informs me you are a dab hand with the needle. Excellent. As you can probably tell even across a crowded room, I am in dire need of new clothes." He paused and smiled at the shocked Mr. Nestor. "I do not expect you to make me over in the duke's image. I know I lack in many respects, the necessary … ah … style? Gravitas? Shoulders? However, I do know what I want."

North pulled out the coat and held it up for the tailor's inspection.

"This style suits me, well enough I think, or close to it. Be a good fellow and do me a couple like this, the size is close enough, in a good blue and black." He pulled trousers and satin pantaloons out of another package. "And these, they are my length. Waistcoats, I suppose I shall need. Maybe I should leave the colors to you, assured as I am of your superior judgment."

By this time the tailor was gasping for air – for many reasons, including the stale stench rising from the secondhand clothing.

Next, North reached into his coat pocket and drew out his purse, counting out, as the tailor's eyes grew round as saucers, a pile of gold sovereigns, which he tossed onto the pile of clothing.

"I expect I have to go elsewhere for silk stockings and linens," said North.

The tailor raised a trembling hand and pointed in the opposite direction of the bookstore.

"Excellent. Such a helpful fellow. Goodness, it is a relief to lessen the weight of that purse. It was beginning to make me walk lopsided. Well, now. I do not need anything immediately for day wear, but I shall need something for a ball on Saturday. Make me all that you think necessary, suitable for Ton events. Have it sent around when you are finished. My card." North dropped a card, so newly printed that the ink was still scented, onto the pile of clothing and money and granted the tailor a bow. "I know we shall get along famously. Your good health, sir." And with that Mr. North swept from the store, a gasping duke trailing in his wake.

A few steps past the tailor's, Mr. North stopped and turned to face Shoffer, such an entirely innocent expression on his face that the duke collapsed laughing.

"One thing I must say about you, Mr. North," said Shoffer, when he had regained his composure. "Life is never dull."

"Your servant," said North with a grin.

"Although, you do yourself no good at all by paying so much in advance. The shopkeepers will never accept your account when it gets out."

"I shall survive."

"But the others of the Ton. The ones who live on credit from quarter day to quarter day, they will hunt you down for paying cash!"

"Shoffer," came the cry from a nearby open carriage. "Back in town, are you?"

Shoffer recognized the voice and took his time turning. Not so quickly as to indicate an interest in the person who hailed him so familiarly, and not so slowly that offense could lead to insult.

The carriage contained three men past their prime years, but not yet in the dotage. All were dressed in the first stare of foppish fashion, which was a shame since the brilliant red, blue, and purple hues of their waistcoats only enhanced the similar colors of their noses.

"Ah," said North, in a voice so soft only Shoffer could hear. "So *that* is what dissipated looks like."

"Degenerate, also," muttered the duke and took only one step closer to the carriage. "Mickleton, Benson, and De Clerk. Yes, as you see, I am back for the opening of Parliament."

"And for the season," said the tallest, leaning across to speak in a confidential manner to his fellows, but without lowering his voice in the slightest. "He has a sister to fire off. Such a sweet little morsel. All pink and creamy softness."

"Oh? Really?" A pale, balding gentleman with watery blue eyes replied. "Perhaps we should call? When is her at-home?"

"Do not exercise yourselves," said Shoffer, allowing just enough coldness to enter his voice to make the polite words a threat. It would do Beth no good at all to have that clowder of old cats cluttering up her drawing room.

"Shall you present your new friend to us?" inquired the last, and eldest. "He has a fresh country face. I can see you have taken over the dressing of him. That can only be to his benefit."

"Tell Nestor not to waste too much fabric on his unmentionables," said the first and all three broke into giggles.

Shoffer found himself feeling almost as protective of Mr. North as he was of his sister. Despite all his clowning, North was an innocent. There was no malice in his jests. No harm at all. He would not for the world expose North to such degenerates, but there was nothing for it; the forms must be observed and introductions performed.

"Mr. North of Yorkshire, the Earls of Wallingford and Trentonlie and the Comte of Le Forhend."

The men exchanged head bobs and bows. To Shoffer's complete surprise his friend did not begin his usual clowning. In fact, beyond the neat bow, he made no move to acknowledge the existence of the other three. After a pause containing no conversation the Earl of Wallingford affected to check his fob watch.

"We must be going, Your Grace. We are expected at … well. We must not be stingy. There are any number of at-homes that we must honor with our bachelor presence."

"Do not let me delay you," said Shoffer and stepped back out of the range of the splatter from the wheels.

"Those three should be beyond the pale," continued Shoffer, when the carriage was well away. "Warn your cousins to stay clear of them."

"Do not worry for my cousins." North's eyes were uncharacteristically shadowed and grave. "They know very well how to keep their shoes clear of horse droppings. They seemed pleased to see you … in the same manner as a fox regards a chicken. Why is that?"

"I know not and care less. They are not of my set, being older and more degenerate than any in London. Avoid them, insult them as you please. I will not be offended." Shoffer paused and added. "Attelweir travels with them when he is in London."

"That is information enough," said Mr. North, folding his hands neatly. "But we should not let them put a damper on the day. Silk stockings, I believe, are next on my list. And I have a whim to put silver buckles on my garters."

"Dear God," sighed Shoffer.

"'Twas your idea to change my dress." North reminded him, maliciously, Shoffer thought.

"And here I receive my just punishment."

The formal dinner at Lady Englethorpes' residence was the first foray into London society for the ladies of the Boarder family. Beyond the immediate Englethorpes family, there would be few guests at the pre-ball dinner. Shoffer and Beth were the guests of honor and would have been placed at the head of the table except for Shoffer's particular request that the girls of the Boarder family be placed near Beth. Mildred's and Maude's manners were genteel enough to show their earlier upbringing was good, but lacking in a few finer points which Lady Beth gave softly to them between the courses. Altogether, Shoffer was confident he could present the Boarder ladies without being ashamed of their acquaintance.

It was a shame Shoffer did not feel the same enthusiasm for Mr. North's clothing. Poor Mr. Nestor had done his best considering he was unable to take measurements or have a fitting and perform adjustments. No. He was forced to take Mr. North's word for the fit of the clothing. Consequently, Mr. North was preparing to parade before the highest levels of society in unfashionably loose clothing. Worse, he had chosen the style of older, more dignified persons – pantaloons, silk stockings, silver buckled shoes, and a frock coat of deep blue velvet. He appeared more like someone's undernourished child dressed up for an adult party than the intelligent gentleman Shoffer knew him to be.

North's reaction to Shoffer's pained expression and critique was to bow and laugh. Silly man.

Dinner went well, Mr. North having been placed at the undistinguished end of the table and having been threatened by his cousins with terrible punishments if one toe was put out of place, spent the meal in near silence.

After, as they awaited the beginning of the ball, Mr. North spent a few moments with the new chaperone. Lady Edith Englethorpes's only besetting sin was a tendency to regard people as devices whose only purpose was to carry around adornments and her conversation was therefore filled with commentary about feathers and flounces, diamonds and rubies. She was good natured, kind, and uniformly cheerful, which gave Mr. North hope for the season.

The Boarder family passed early down the receiving line – for the sake of practice – and went into the ballroom. They found a good corner with several chairs and a long couch where Beth, Mildred, and Maude arranged themselves to their best advantage with Lady Edith and Felicity seated nearby, and prepared to be admired. Mr. North and Shoffer prowled the outer edges of the ballroom as it slowly filled with guests.

"When does the dancing start?" asked Mr. North, as they circled the room for the fifth time. "If it is not soon, I am convinced I shall be exhausted from the promenade and never have the strength to waltz."

"In half an hour or so. Ah," Shoffer turned and headed toward the stairs leading down from the main hall. "I know those names just announced. They are members of my club and are not complete cabbage heads. Let us take them over and introduce them to the ladies. I do not want to be in the position of leading Beth out for the first dance. It does not do for a young lady to be dancing always with her brother and last year, I suspect I was her only partner."

Shaking his head Mr. North trailed along behind the duke to collect two young aspiring Corinthians. The taller, Nigel Wentworth, second son of the Earl of Brigham, had skinny legs not shown to advantage in his tight trousers and the other, the Honorable Mr. Micheal Offen, square faced and pimply, wheezed when he made his bow to the ladies. Shoffer presented them to his sister as acquaintances of his with a smile upon his face. A smile that withered away as the minutes passed. Mildred and Maude fluttered and flattered and received invitations to dance, but Beth was struck dumb and sat unmoving on her couch. Mr. North waited for Lady Edith to move or speak on her charge's behalf, but no, that Lady's attention was caught by the complicated decorations on a nearby turban and she did not notice Beth's withdrawal.

"Do something," demanded Shoffer, digging his elbow into North's ribs.

Mr. North tried to catch the chaperone's eyes and was ignored. "I think we need to replace Lady Edith with someone interested in people more than sparkly things."

"Mr. North!" hissed Shoffer and repeated his nudge.

Millicent sympathized with Shoffer. The man had no way of understanding a shy sister and poor Beth, wanting so to please, was sitting watching the conversation going on before her and completely unable to find her part in it.

By this time there were significant clusters of women, both old and young, arranged along the walls, and gentlemen slowly promenading. The ladies nearest were casting hungry glances toward the tall figure of the Duke of Trolenfield, of which he was entirely unaware. No doubt they were hoping to catch his eye since every time he glanced around the room there was a wave of curtsies. Unfortunately for his admirers, Shoffer's attention was entirely upon his sister. Millicent's eye, however, was caught by a small group of débutantes fanning themselves idly who stood just beyond her sisters' chairs; and an idea struck her.

"Lady Beth," cried Millicent. "Have I told you my most recent observations on the subject of cats?"

"Mr. North, I do not think this is the right time for a discussion of cats," growled Shoffer. "This is a ballroom!"

"How can you say that, Your Grace? The cat is the most honest of God's creatures, and our best guide for society."

Since Beth immediately sat up and paid attention, as she did whenever Mr. North began one of his entertainments, Shoffer raised his eyes and hands to heaven and yielded.

"Oh, very well, Mr. North. Teach us about cats."

"How can cats guide us in society?" asked Beth, always willing in her role as foil for Mr. North's nonsense.

Mr. North leaned conspiratorially toward the watching débutantes and with a bow, drew a befeathered fan out of one of their hands. "My thanks, Lady. Cats, as you know, communicate with their tails, as ladies do with their fans."

The ladies tittered and a few idling gentlemen drew closer.

"Ah, come, of course you know this. When a lady wishes a gentleman to attend her she does thus with her fan." And Mr. North barely opened the feathered fan, put it on his shoulder and beckoned with it so that only the very tips of the feathers waved in the air. There were a few giggles as another man came from that corner of the room, a puzzled look on his face, to find out what was going on. "And when a cat is angry, she moves her tail thusly," and he whipped the fan rapidly from side to side, to another ripple of giggles. "Any man seeing a fan moving that way would be wise to be cautious."

Indeed, the man who had been approaching paused and walked away in another direction.

In a few moments there was a fascinated crowd listening to Mr. North demonstrate the many waves of a cat's tail. With each move, each flutter of feathers, came an increasing chorus of laughter. Shoffer was entertained by it, but could not tell if it was doing any good. Under the concealment of another move, Shoffer saw Mr. North gesturing to Beth to stand and dropped her a wink.

"And when you are to be punished, the tail strikes you thusly," said Mr. North, and Shoffer jumped when his forearm was smartly struck. "Then there are the gentle movements. Come, Lady Beth, you demonstrate. How does a little golden kitten signal that it wishes to be petted and made much of?"

Lady Beth raised her embroidered silk fan to her eyes, opened it just a little and moved it sinuously through the air; the audience laughed and a pretty blush rose in Beth's cheeks. Mr. North turned to his young cousins. "And when the cat has been offended?"

The crowd roared as two closed fans rose fast and stiff before Mildred's and Maude's faces and whipped away slicing through the air – at neck level to the watching men.

"Exactly so," declared Mr. North, clapping his hands as the first strains of the orchestra were heard. "Oh, dear. I am so very sorry. Here are these gentlemen waiting to beg for dances and I am being silly." Mr. North returned the fan to the giggling débutante, stepped back, and waved the young men in. "I do apologize."

Those who had crossed the room to find out the reason for the noise suddenly found themselves facing rows of expectant faces. Good manners could not provide an escape. Each gentleman bowed to one of the ladies and begged an introduction. The pairing off took a little time and at the end Shoffer was pleased to see his sister pausing to write one gentleman's name on her dance card before being led onto the floor by yet another for the opening set.

Shoffer turned to face the dance floor, prepared to watch his sister dance with paternal pride, but he had not counted on Mr. North.

"Here he is," he heard Mr. North say from a few feet away. "He will vouch for me. Come, Your Grace, admit that you know me." Shoffer glanced over to see Mr. North with a young lady on each arm, facing off with a determined appearing mother. "His Grace will tell you I am a fribble and a wastrel who cannot be trusted with a bent penny. However, I do enjoy dancing."

Shoffer sighed and bowed. "Madam, I am the Duke of Trolenfield. Mr. North is my particular friend. I can assure you that he is indeed a fool and a clown, but as I trust him with my own sister, I believe you may trust him with your daughters for the measure of a dance."

The lady's expression cleared when she heard the word "duke" and she gave her permission with a smile.

"Here, Your Grace. This one is Miss Mary and this one is Miss Joy. I will pass Miss Mary to you, as tonight, I wish to dance with Joy." And with the giggling girl hanging off his arm, Mr. North found a place in the lines forming for a country dance. Shaking his head, the duke followed.

Later in the evening Shoffer and North were commanded by a brilliantly smiling Lady Beth to fetch refreshments. North muttered and mumbled to himself while a footman poured lemonade into tiny cups. Shoffer, pleased to see the bright glow in Beth's eyes, the animation of her conversation, obeyed with a light heart.

"Tell me," demanded North, "How is one to carry these perishing little cups while wearing gloves?"

"It is a gift." Shoffer regarded the dance floor with satisfaction. His sister had not sat out a single dance, and while Shoffer had claimed her for the supper dance, she stood up with complete strangers for the rest of the evening and chatted with them all.

"Of your kindness, Your Grace, it is what you may give me for Christmas."

Eventually, North persuaded a footman to hook each little cup onto his fingers and then pour in a measure of lemonade. His concentration was completely on the task. Shoffer watched, amused, and wondered if he should bother to offer advice.

"Shoffer! My dear duke, it has been far too long. I am so pleased to see you again."

Shoffer turned to find himself face to feathered headdress with Lady Holudin, one of his grandmother's cronies, traveling underneath. He would not call Lady Holudin one of his grandmother's friends, being that she was merely the wife of a baron, the dowager regarded her as inferior, but they were much of an age and were presented at court at the same time, which gave them a bond of sorts. She was one of the highest sticklers of the Ton and well known for her biting comments. Shoffer was not pleased to see her.

"Lady Holudin." Shoffer bowed and extended a hand to indicate his friend. "This is Mr. Anthony North from Yorkshire."

Lady Holudin gave a very small nod in response to North's bow. Instead she tucked her hand in Shoffer's elbow and turned him about. "Come with me." And with that she led him across the floor. Shoffer cast one apologetic glance toward his friend in time to see Mr. North roll his eyes at the flounces and lace around the hem of Lady Holudin's gown.

Poor North. Shoffer had intended to relieve him of a couple of those little cups once he had suffered a few minutes longer, but now he would have to manage crossing the ballroom alone and thus burdened.

"Well, that is well done," declared Lady Holudin in a satisfied tone. "You are well free of that mess."

Shoffer glanced about. He could not see anyone doing anything in particular. "My Lady?"

Lady Holudin continued walking. "You owe me a great deal for rescuing you from that upstart. I shall hold you to that for a favor, so do not forget."

Shoffer's brows drew together as a suspicion formed.

"Madam, I have not the pleasure of understanding you."

She paid not a bit of attention to him, but halted where they could see Beth and the Boarder girls in the center of a group of flattering bucks. The heightened color in Beth's cheeks and her laughter filled Shoffer's heart with joy. This girl, this happy center of attention was his sister's true form, not the pale and unhappy wallflower of last season.

"Look at that," demanded the lady, pointing with her lorgnette. "Have you ever seen the like? I have tried twice to shake your sister free of those encroaching mushrooms, but they will not be shifted. We must move quickly before your sister's reputation is tarnished by association. They are nothing. Mere country gentry. She must not be seen to be giving consequence to such riff raff."

"May I take it, madam, that you have brought me here to object to my sister's companions?" Shoffer's voice was chill.

"Of course! I know not what your grandmother would say if she knew your sister to be associating with those ... those..."

Shoffer pulled himself up to his full height and stared at Lady Holudin until she took a step back. "I have approved Lady Elizabeth's association with this family. Consider, madam, that no favor is owed you."

And with that he turned back toward the refreshment table and almost groaned. In the few seconds his attention had been elsewhere, Mr. North had managed to get himself into more trouble.

Chapter Nine

At the refreshment table a group of young swells surrounded Mr. North. Their leader, his watch chain decorated with so many fobs that he rattled as he walked, had his nose so high in the air that he not so much looked down his nose at Mr. North, but rather looked at him through his bucked front teeth. The silly fop was settling snuff on the back of his glove in an affected manner and stared audaciously at North, scanning him from recently trimmed hair to polished dancing shoes. The sneer on his lips intensified as he took in the collar points that barely reached midway up Mr. North's neck, unlike these pinks of fashion who currently could not look from side to side lest they put out their own eyes. Likewise, he disapproved of Mr. North's loosely fitting clothing and the overly baggy pantaloons.

From the slight smile turning up the corners of Mr. North's lips, Shoffer knew that this group appealed to his sense of the absurd, but it would not do his cousins or his case good to offer offense to these overly decorated idiots. They were bachelors of good families after all and *someone* might want to marry them.

Dodging through the suddenly crowded room, Shoffer headed for the refreshment table to rescue his friend. The orchestra played the last bars of a waltz, then stopped, allowing Shoffer and most of the surrounding guests to hear the conversation.

"Good God, sir," drawled the fop. "Does your tailor hate you?"

"I should hardly think so," said Mr. North. "As he has been generously paid, I assume he holds me in some esteem."

This statement only seemed to confuse the crowd.

"Your coat is a disgrace," declared the fop. "You have no fashion at all! I am shocked, shocked that you should have the gall to appear in public before acquiring some polish."

Mr. North shrugged.

"Where are you from?"

"Do not answer. Wait," muttered Shoffer, as he dodged behind a dowager with a badly dyed wig.

With a half bow his friend replied. "I am Mr. Anthony North of Yorkshire."

"Yoooooorkshire," with a glance over his shoulder to his snickering cronies the fop scanned Mr. North's attire a second time. "I see that they have no style in Yoooooorkshire. You must be very grateful to have reached the center of civilization, London, and be eager to learn our fashions."

Shoffer ducked past a footman, almost upsetting his tray and reached the other side of the table in time to hear Mr. North's reply.

"Indeed, sir, I am. When we leave our mud and wattle huts, up in uncivilized Yorkshire, and go about barefoot in the muck, why we find it very cold and uncomfortable. Imagine my surprise to discover that Londoners have invented these things called 'shoes.'" Mr. North peered down at his footwear. "Why, as I go about the streets with my feet warm and dry I cannot but be grateful for the invention. I do commend them to you, sir."

Shoffer halted, his hands resting on the table and lowered his head. He should have had more faith in his friend. There was a round of titters from the listeners and the fop preened, not realizing that the laughter was at his expense. Shoffer glanced up again and his stomach clenched. Both he and the fop caught sight of an elegantly attired man at the same moment.

"I say, Brummel. Come tell us what you think of this man's cravat?" cried the fop.

The Beau halted, offended at being hailed in that familiar manner, but came across.

Brummel! Shoffer smothered a groan. Why did it have to be Brummel? That posturing poser could ruin a man's reputation with a careless shrug. Before Shoffer could intercede and freeze Brummel into retreat, Mr. North had turned already to face this new threat.

Lemonade cups still in hand, Mr. North first reared back in shock, then leaned forward to minutely study Brummel's elaborate neck cloth while Shoffer almost swallowed his tongue.

"Oh, I am awestruck," cried North before any other could speak. "I know what my cravat looks like. It looks like a one-armed, blind, drunken sailor was struck with a seizure while trying to fit me for a noose before he fell down dead. Which is in truth what happened. Out of sympathy for the fellow's memory, I left my cravat just as he made it. But you, sir. You… Surely a flock of angels descended from heaven, and dancing to a celestial choir, wound themselves around your person, draping the silk in folds at the direction of God Himself. And once done they fell to earth weeping, for surely in all of God's creation, nothing will ever be as perfect as your cravat."

Shoffer's fingers tightened, gripping the tablecloth as the Beau examined Mr. North through his quizzing glass. Then to everyone's surprise, he laughed.

"Why, yes, that is in truth exactly what happened. I commend your perception." The Beau made a graceful leg. "And who might you be?"

"This," declared the fop, "is Mister North from Yoooooorkshire."

He grinned, fully expecting to witness one of the Beau's famous set downs, but instead North and Beau exchanged nods and smiles.

"My honor, sir," said North.

"I am pleased to meet you, Mr. North," said the Beau, then he wandered away.

After a moment the fop wandered off as well to try, vainly, to report the exchange for in truth he had not understood it. But the Beau had laughed. Surely, if he repeated the tale he would gain laughs as well. He did, but not for the reason he supposed.

"Dear God, I thought my heart would stop," declared Shoffer coming around the table.

"I as well," said North. "One of the cups started to tip and I feared I would be wearing lemonade for the rest of the evening. Be a good fellow, Shoffer, and take a couple of these. I cannot manage."

"North?" Shoffer worked two cups free of the gloves. "You do realize what just happened? Do you know to whom you were speaking?"

North raised his eyes to the duke's and for a moment there was an expression of genuine puzzlement, but it did not last long. A broad grin overspread North's face and lit his brown eyes with mischief.

"Oh, yes. Of course, I know. That nit does not have enough wit to realize he's been insulted."

"No. The other one. Beau? Beau Brummel. He was not expected or else I should have warned you. He can be quite withering."

Mr. North shrugged. "He seemed perfectly pleasant to me."

"Do you have any idea how close you came to social disaster?"

"No." After another moment of blank staring, he flashed Shoffer a dazzling grin. Turning, North started off across the ballroom, Shoffer trailing in his wake. "Yes, of course I did. I am not so much a fool as I pretend. Fortunately, the Beau has a sense of humor."

Shoffer grinned at his sister as he handed over a small cup of lemonade. The ladies accepted the refreshments politely, though they had no need of it. The Boarder ladies and Lady Elizabeth were surrounded by young men competing to hold their fans, fetch drinks, and otherwise entertain them.

After examining his sister's dance card and approving it, Shoffer retreated. Lady Edith and Mrs. Boarder had the situation well in hand. After checking that his cousins were happy, Mr. North rejoined him.

"Well, Shoffer, it appears we are not needed. Come, it is time we did our duty by the wallflowers."

"Again?" Shoffer paused, then stared at his friend. "I was about to suggest we retreat to the smoking room."

"Never. Do you tell me you do not like to dance, Shoffer?"

"I like it well enough."

"Excellent." North took him by the sleeve and drew him through the crowd. It was turning into a veritable crush, which would please their hostess, but made navigation difficult.

"North, what are you about?" demanded Shoffer.

North cast a grin over his shoulder.

"The truth of the matter is I love to dance. One of the many advantages of being male, Your Grace, is that when I wish to dance I need only ask. But a lady? She must wait to be asked. And wait and wait and wait. Do not imagine that if you grant a wallflower one dance, she will expect to receive an offer. We can dance quite safely."

With that Mr. North came to a halt before a cluster of stunned wallflowers. There was not a one in the group that Shoffer recognized; although, by their ages it was possible that it was a third or fourth season for some of them.

"Ladies." Mr. North made a graceful bow. "I come seeking a dance partner. I promise to step on your toes not more than twice. Would anyone care to do me the honor?"

"This is hardly proper, my friend," said Shoffer. "You have not been introduced."

"Oh, we know who he is," said a rather spindly, red-haired girl with a regrettable number of freckles over her face and décolletage, and she waved her fan in a gentle curve like a cat's tail. "He is Mr. North of the cats."

The other young ladies giggled and imitated the move.

"My reputation precedes me. And do you know this tall fellow with me?"

There was a chorus of "Your Grace" and another wave of curtsies.

"Well, then, who shall volunteer to be steered about the room?"

Despite the haphazard manner of the invitation, it was accepted with enthusiasm. Shoffer bowed and accepted his fate. It was not until three dances later, as he stood side by side with Mr. North awaiting the beginning of a quadrille that he realized he was enjoying himself.

The wallflowers, one and all, were so grateful to be granted some small portion of his time and consequence that he was almost embarrassed by the thanks he received. Indeed, if not for Mr. North he would have quit the ballroom, but there he remained as one after another young lady promenaded down the dance on his gloved hand.

They were standing side by side waiting for a jig to begin when Shoffer gasped and seized North's arm in a grip so tight the man cried out.

"Shoffer? What?"

"Do you see?" demanded Shoffer. "Look, that is Brummel heading toward Beth. Damn it, North, what if again she is struck dumb?"

Shoffer was about to commit the extreme social faux pas of leaving a dance in progress and charging across the room to his sister's side when North gripped his arm and held him back.

"Stop, Shoffer. Think and wait. It will do your sister's confidence no good to have you embarrass her this way."

"But…"

"She will think you do not trust her to be able to deal with one overdressed poseur."

North's grip was as strong as wilted celery, but the glare he directed toward Shoffer held him pinned in place. Helpless, he watched as the Beau was presented to his sister and her friends by their hostess. There was an exchange of words that they were too far away to hear; then the Beau bowed, and said something to Beth which set her laughing and waving her fan sinuously through the air. The conversation continued for a few moments; the Beau laughed at some comment of Beth's and all conversation died across the room.

The Boarder sisters made a few observations which were well received by Brummel; then it was over. The Beau, still smiling, bowed over Beth's hand, nodded to the Boarder family, and took himself away. A corridor opened before him permitting him to leave the room unmolested and then the noise level of the room rose as the gossip resumed. As soon as the Beau had vanished, the crowd of men about Beth doubled in size.

North nudged Shoffer's arm, directing his attention to his partner and the ongoing dance. Shoffer granted the débutante a dazzling smile and took her arm even as joy bubbled in his heart.

Her rank gave Beth a place in society. Mr. North's nonsense gave her confidence and conversation, but the Beau's bow had brought her into fashion.

Beth's success this season was achieved.

Never in his life had he felt more like dancing. As they passed each other in the dance, Shoffer and Mr. North exchanged matching proud smiles.

It was midday before Millicent made her way downstairs the next day. Mildred and Maude were before her, for a miracle. Waves of feminine laughter drew Millicent to the formal parlor. Pausing at the door Millicent peered in. Beth was there, which raised her eyebrows, and was helping Mildred and Maude read the notes that accompanied the masses of flowers filling the room.

"Great God," said Millicent, "What is a forest doing in here? Shall I summon the gardeners to beat back these overgrown shrubs? Do we need a gang of servants to slice a way through the jungle?"

She wandered into the room, picked up a nosegay, and inhaled the fragrance.

"Is not this wonderful?" cried Maude, waving toward the banks of flowers. "All these on this side of the room are mine."

Mildred paused and selected a few blossoms from one arrangement and placed them into a vase. "These are mine, but they could have been better presented."

"And to what do we owe the honor of your appearance here this morning, Lady Beth?" asked Millicent.

Beth laughed, her eyes brilliant and dancing. "Oh, I could not sleep and I was awake when my own flowers were delivered. If you can believe it, I have just as many at home as your cousins…"

"And you came over here to crow about your achievement?" Millicent mock scowled at her. "Proud infant. How unkind."

"No. No. I finished my thank you letters and wanted to come over and advise Mildred and Maude on the phrasing of theirs. That was one thing that Grand'Mere taught me well. How to write exact letters."

Millicent tried vainly to raise one eyebrow, an exercise that never failed to send her sisters into giggles. "Exact letters?"

"Oh, you know, how to use the exact phrase to suppress pretensions and what to write when you want to encourage someone."

"Well, be careful in your writing, ladies, for if we have as many dandies as you have flower arrangements come into our parlor, our floor will surely crack under the weight."

"Do not fuss," said Mildred calmly. "We shan't have that many callers. It is not as if anyone knows where we live. We are not exactly well known about town."

"Mildred, dear," said Millicent patiently. "They must know in order to send the flowers. Do not worry, your admirers shall find you. As for you, Lady Beth, should you not be on your way home? You do not want your own tribe of poetry writers to be disappointed when they come to worship at your feet and find you gone."

"Oh, phoo. There was no one last night I wanted to encourage."

Again, it occurred to Millicent that Beth was a trifle young for the marriage mart. Then she noticed the intent and adoring look on Beth's face directed toward herself; her heart chilled and she backed out of the room.

"Well, enjoy yourselves, ladies, I shall be out and about doing … things and will not be home until late."

"Oh, no," cried Beth, reaching out to Millicent. "You must be here. I shan't know what to say if you are not."

Millicent dodged, seizing her hat and gloves from a waiting footman, and backed toward the door.

"Mildred and Maude will be here to aid you. Besides, the gentlemen will be doing much of the talking. I would not be surprised if there were a sonnet or two already composed to your eyes."

"What shall I say if I do not like it?" Beth reached for Millicent's sleeve requiring her to dodge again. "I cannot offend a gentleman by saying his work is bad."

"Say that you find you prefer Shakespeare."

And with that Millicent fled the house without the benefit of breakfast.

Uncertain what to do with herself since her plans for the day had been to take a leisurely breakfast followed by reading letters from her tenants, Millicent paused at the side of the road and scowled at the footpath.

"What did the sidewalk do to offend you, Mr. North?"

Millicent glanced up, warmth replacing the chill in her chest at the sight of Shoffer astride his favorite grey horse. Following him on a leading rein was the small mare on which Shoffer had taught Mr. North to ride properly.

"My God, I must be in a bad way if I am glad to see you here ready to go riding," said Millicent.

Shoffer laughed.

"Poor Mr. North. Have the ladies driven you from your own house? Come on up, fellow. A ride will clear your head." When Millicent hesitated, Shoffer continued. "In your case, it will not matter that you are not in riding clothes."

"I am more interested in finding something to eat since I was driven out before breakfast."

"Well, if that is the case we shall ride to White's. I intended to introduce you there once your wardrobe was improved, but since you have proven that is a futile hope, I may as well take you now."

"I do not mind where we go as long as they serve coffee."

Millicent hauled herself into the saddle and found that she could not return Shoffer's cheerful grin. After riding for a few minutes, Shoffer turned in his saddle to regard her thoughtfully.

"You are not yourself this morning, North. Is something troubling you?"

Millicent concentrated on persuading her horse to follow its stable mate. She had no idea what to do. Shoffer had asked her to aid

Beth in gaining confidence with her conversation all the time believing that Beth was safe from forming an attachment to Mr. North. But from the girl's behavior this morning, an unrequited attachment was becoming a distinct possibility. Millicent was reluctant to risk her own friendship with Shoffer by revealing her concerns. The only reason Shoffer continued the acquaintance was the belief that conversation with Mr. North was good for Beth. After only one Ton party, Mildred's and Maude's entrée into good society was still dependent on the duke's good opinion. Were he to withdraw his support, no invitations would arrive.

Some part of Beth's enthusiasm for Mr. North might come from the fact that he was not the Duc of Attelweir. Once her brother was able to convince her that there was no risk of a marriage Beth might pay attention to other gentlemen.

"North?"

"Forgive me, I am a little fatigued. I had no idea Ton parties exited so late."

"Generally, gentlemen do not aspire to dance every dance," said Shoffer. "Although, I do not say that to criticize. I am certain the young ladies appreciated your labor."

"My feet may never forgive me," said Millicent with a tired grin. Indeed, her feet were very sore and she would have to get a new pair of evening shoes, or two or three, if she intended to repeat last night's performance.

"It was your own doing," said the duke with complete lack of sympathy. "But I shall not be distracted. You are quiet and solemn. An uncommon enough circumstance that one familiar with your moods would be wise to take note. Come, I have sufficient respect for your intelligence to listen when you speak your mind. Is it about Beth?"

Millicent almost fell off her horse. Did the duke know about Beth's childish partiality? If the child had repeated that declaration that she would wed only Mr. North, the duke would be well within his rights to run her through and chase Felicity and the girls all the way back to Yorkshire.

However, Millicent realized as she brought her horse back under her control, he would not be so calm if that were the case.

"Mr. North, you begin to worry me."

"Please, Your Grace, am I not permitted a quiet moment like any other mortal?"

"Now you have gone and fully aroused my curiosity. What troubles you?"

Millicent sighed. She had no one to blame but her own transparent nature.

"I would call it nothing serious; except, well, I think Lady Beth is still entertaining an attachment to me that I swear to you I have done nothing to encourage."

"Good God, does she still have the idea that she needs to be saved from Attelweir? I thought I had dealt with that entirely."

Millicent shrugged. "Perhaps to your satisfaction, Shoffer, but not to hers. Forgive me for being intrusive, but have you and Lady Beth ever talked about her being put into the armoire by her grandmother?"

"I have assured her that it will never happen again."

"But perhaps," said Millicent softly, "you should find out how many times it has happened *before*."

Shoffer turned in his saddle to stare. "You cannot be serious."

"I wish I were not. It occurred to me at the time that Mrs. Fleming was entirely too calm about the matter. If it was just the one occurrence at your home, one would hope that Mrs. Fleming would have become disturbed and raised an outcry. But the fact that she seemed to accept the … event … indicates to me that it probably was not uncommon in the duchess's household."

Shoffer closed his eyes, bending forward for a moment over his saddle.

"Dear God, forgive me," he moaned. "I left my poor sister in her hands."

Millicent risked her balance to reach across and briefly squeeze Shoffer's wrist.

"I may be wrong. Indeed, I hope I am. Let us not judge the duchess so harshly without full knowledge."

Shoffer drew a deep breath and sat straight, his face calm even while his eyes burned with suppressed rage.

"You are right, my friend. I should speak to Beth, no matter how hard it may be for both of us. I must find out all the threats and punishments that were levied on my poor sister as I cannot promise to protect her unless I am fully informed." He pulled his horse to halt outside a rather plain building. "This is White's. There is nowhere else in London with better coffee and chocolate."

"I would beg you, Your Grace, not to have any expectations of my application to this august body. I am not interested in politics, or cards and gossip, so would have nothing in common with the gentlemen here."

Shoffer grinned as he dismounted and passed his reins and a few pennies to one of the urchins who hung about outside the club.

"You were driven from your house this morning by the women of your family. You have more in common with the gentlemen here than you imagine."

The proffered breakfast was substantial, but essentially tasteless with the exception of coffee, which was well deserving of White's reputation.

Millicent was contemplating the last dry scone when three gentlemen crossed to stand beside their table and await the duke's notice.

"Mr. Wentworth. Mr. Offen," said Shoffer. "How do you, sirs?"

"Well enough, thank you, Your Grace," said Wentworth. "I wonder if I might make my friend known to you? The Honorable Mr. Joseph Martindale was with us at Cambridge."

Shoffer gave a slow nod in acknowledgment of Martindale's bow. Millicent swallowed a smile and the last of her coffee when the gentlemen turned to her.

"And this is Mr. Anthony North," said Shoffer. "I believe you spent some time in company with his cousins yesterday evening."

"Indeed," said Wentworth, looking Millicent up and down as if he could not believe such well turned out young ladies could possibly be related to the shabby man before him. "Charming gels."

"I will be sure to tell them you said so," said Millicent. "Although, such extravagant compliments to their beauty are likely to turn their heads."

Shoffer grinned and settled back in his chair to watch. His friend had shaken off his odd mood and was back to his humorous self. For the next ten minutes North chatted, joked, and expounded on the most illogical thoughts until the three interlopers were quite confused.

"You look to be of an age with us," said Wentworth. "I do not believe I saw you at Cambridge. Did you perhaps attend

Oxford?"

He said the word as if Oxford were the same as the trash that was never completely cleared from London's streets. Considering the legendary enmity between the two schools, Shoffer considered the fribble was trying to gain the upper hand over North.

"Hardly, sir, I was educated at home by my ... m ... other."

The other gentlemen did not know how to respond to that answer and stood speechless.

"Poor witty mother, witless is her son," came a stentorian voice behind them.

Shoffer gritted his teeth and turned. The Duc of Attelweir, tall, white-haired, and as dignified in his bearing as he was degenerate in his morals, posed in the center of the dining room, his coterie of cats, the Earls of Wallingford and Trentonlie and the Comte of Le Forhend, arranged around him.

"Shakespeare, *Taming of the Shrew*, Act Two, Scene One," cried North, clapping his hands. "Who shall offer a quotation next? Although, I do not believe you quoted it properly, so I suspect it does not count."

Shoffer, accustomed to North's lightning changes of subject, merely smiled. The others stared.

"Such a charming collection of young men you have gathered around you, Your Grace," said De Clerk, the Comte Le Forhend, with a smirk as he stroked his hand down Wentworth's sleeve, then fell silent when Attelweir waved his lorgnette.

"I am so pleased to have found you, Shoffer. When I called at your house this morning I was told that both you and your sister were from home. I was most distressed not to be able to pay my respects."

Shoffer said nothing, merely nodding in reply.

"Perhaps I shall call this evening..."

"Do not bother, Attelweir. I have instructed my butler not to admit you." When their listeners gasped, Shoffer continued. "It is a pity that you did not take me at my word; it would have spared you this embarrassment. I was quite clear in the letter I sent you. I will not permit you near my sister. If you approach her at any time, at any social event, I shall have you dragged from the room."

Attelweir paled, but a faint smile curved his lips. "You should be more careful how you phrase yourself, Shoffer. One might think that Lady Elizabeth has not behaved in a manner suitably virtuous for your fine English sensibilities."

Shoffer paled at the insult and would have risen, except North joined the conversation.

"Oh, do not worry about Lady Beth," said North grinning. "She is well able to protect her own reputation. Anyone foolish enough to offer her impertinence in either word or deed best know a good sawbones for she is a prodigious good shot."

"Shot," gasped several voices.

"Yes, shot." Shoffer sent a grateful glance toward North. Thank goodness North had remembered Beth's unusual talent. "Lady Beth has a pistol for every day of the week. If a gentleman she despised were to approach her, or to spread rumors about her, why he might find himself standing on some misty meadow at dawn facing her pistol and I would give not a tinker's damn for his chances."

Shoffer stared into Attelweir's eyes, hoping the man would make a move that would justify Shoffer driving his fists into his face until that perfectly benign countenance was a broken mess, to match the degenerate soul within. Unfortunately, Attelweir was wise enough to do nothing. With a bow he turned and with his friends arranged about him, stalked away.

The young bucks remained until North made shooing motions with his hands.

"Away you go. Have you not gossip to spread?"

Wentworth, Offen, and Martindale glanced toward Shoffer who raised an eyebrow in return.

"Oh, no. We would not dream of saying a word," cried Wentworth, proving himself the brightest of the lot, and gathering his friends, they escaped.

"Well, that was fun," said North, returning to his seat and investigating the contents of the cold coffee pot.

"Was it?" Shoffer's voice was cold.

"Of course not. It was perfectly dreadful. Being the center of such a scene turns my stomach." North leaned back in his chair. "What are we going to do about that leech? Will the gossip that you have cut him be enough to keep him from Lady Beth?"

Shoffer folded his arms across his chest. Attelweir's pockets were notoriously to let. The man supported himself with gambling, but luck was inconsistent and dowries the size of Beth's more certain. As long as Beth was unmarried, there was a risk Attelweir might do something, possibly conspire to compromise the poor girl and force her into marriage. He was not to be trusted, the snake. Despite his own best intentions, Shoffer could not stand guard over Beth every moment. A balance must be struck between safety and captivity.

Shoffer pushed the back of North's chair, almost toppling him to the ground.

"Come on, man, up," cried Shoffer. "The day is wasting."

"What? Are we late for an appointment?"

"You have reminded me; I have not bought the guns I promised Beth."

North threw a few coins onto the table and scrambled after him. "I hesitate to remind Your Great Graciousness, but 'tis Sunday. The stores are closed."

Shoffer halted and turned to face him. North grinned and recoiled, one hand coming up to shield his eyes.

"Oh, oh, the ducal stare. Spare me! How could I forget? Mere law and day of rest cannot stand against it."

"Try not to be more of a fool than is needful," said Shoffer and led the way from White's.

"That is a hard path to walk," muttered North and hurried along behind.

Chapter Ten

Trolenfield House was in a state of carefully managed and genteel uproar when they returned later that afternoon. Despite the heavy parcel that filled his arms, Shoffer managed to enter the main hall and pass halfway up the stairs toward the private chambers before his butler appeared. Shoffer's first impression was that the man, wide-eyed with his remaining hair standing on end, was fleeing some threat.

"Whatever is wrong? Is the house afire?"

The butler halted and settled his coat. "Not that I am aware of, Your Grace."

"Then why are you running?"

"I do apologize, Your Grace. The household is somewhat disturbed by the unexpected arrival of the dowager duchess."

"Traveling on a Sunday?" observed North. "Most unexpected."

Shoffer could feel the air seize in his lungs.

"Where is my sister?" he gasped.

"Her Grace and Lady Elizabeth are taking tea in the wi…"

Shoffer charged up the stairs and ran down the corridor to the upstairs parlor. He burst through the door, not waiting for a footman to open the door, and came to a sudden halt facing his grandmother. His sister was seated on the same chaise lounge as his grandmother, her eyes downcast and hands folded on her lap. Despite his labors she was back to being the little mouse she had been under their grandmother's tyranny.

"What are you doing in my house?" demanded Shoffer, then caught Beth's warning glance toward the window. He turned to find himself facing Lady Sally Jersey.

Of all the people to be there to witness this scene, this was the worst! The patroness of Almack's held a tea cup in one hand, a marzipan in the other, and stared at Shoffer open-mouthed. Of those persons frozen in the room, Lady Sally recovered first.

"Good heavens, Your Grace, are you unwell?"

There was a glitter of malicious curiosity in the gossip's eye. Shoffer swallowed a groan, but gave the old woman a respectful bow.

"You understand my concern, dear Sally," murmured the dowager with unruffled calm. "Shoffer is a man with a great number of responsibilities. It is just as well that I recovered enough to come for the season to relieve him of the burden of taking his sister about. He is so fatigued that he has quite forgotten his manners."

Shoffer straightened out of his bow and glared at his grandmother. He did not doubt that this scene had been arranged, although he was at a loss as to how she had managed it. To have arrived, settled in, and summoned Lady Jersey in the short period of time he had been out of the house was impressive.

Annoying, but impressive.

His grandmother was not a fool. She would want the perfect witness to inhibit Shoffer's protests. Given the importance of Almack's to any young woman's social standing, the dowager probably thought having Lady Sally Jersey in the room would stop his mouth.

She was about to learn how ill-advised this move had been.

Shoffer pulled himself up and stalked across the room to yank the bell pull. While he waited for a response only a few seconds in coming, he crossed to take his sister's hand and help her to her feet, then held her close against his side.

When the butler arrived Shoffer spoke with as much calmness as he could manage.

"Apologize for me to the staff for adding this burden to their Sunday, but my grandmother's house in King's Square is to be readied for her occupation before nightfall."

The butler paled, but instead of protesting the impossibility of accomplishing such a task, he thinned his lips and nodded.

"Make certain that all of the dowager's baggage and servants are taken there at once." Turning to the stunned old woman he continued. "Enjoy your tea, Your Grace; I am certain everything will be ready for you, alone, by nightfall."

"Your Grace?" Lady Jersey regarded the dowager with surprise. "I was under the impression you were residing in Trolenfield House for the season?"

"Oh, do not mind him, my dear," said the dowager, once she had recovered her voice. "My grandson has come under the influence of a most disreputable personage of very low estate and you can see what damage it has caused."

"That would be me," came a voice from the doorway and Mr. North bowed his way in.

Shoffer tightened his grip on his sister's hand, hoping to convey reassurance, but until Mr. North entered the room Beth had remained downcast and trembling. Shoffer gritted his teeth, angry for two reasons. One, that his sister was reassured by North's presence, but not his own. The other was to have all his good work undone so quickly was beyond tolerance. No matter that there were witnesses; the dowager must leave. Mr. North, a paper-wrapped parcel tucked under his arm, advanced into the room until he stood between Beth and the dowager. He made a creditable leg toward that fuming woman before turning smartly to face the infamous Lady Sally Villers, Countess of Jersey.

"This reprehensible creature is the one of whom I spoke," said the dowager before North could speak. "I have no understanding of how someone with no rank and such a weak chin could gain influence over my grandson, but there he is. A more degenerate, repulsive, reprobate individual you could hope never to meet. No doubt he will end his days dangling from a rope."

Shoffer sighed and added. "Lady Jersey, my friend, Mr. Anthony North."

North paused, rubbing his chin with his free hand. "Jersey? Jersey? Surely, I know that name. Ah, yes, one of the patronesses of that assembly place ... what is its name? Oh, dear. It has quite escaped me." He focused on the frowning woman. "But surely that cannot be you. I heard that was a woman of a certain age. You are far too young for such responsibility."

Before Lady Jersey could reply the dowager snorted. "Do not think to ingratiate yourself with Lady Sally. Almack's is one portal through which you shall not pass."

North turned his head just enough to regard the dowager. "Surely, madam, I may have some aspiration to invitations. I may be not of noble blood, but I am of an old and respectable lineage. Added to that I may claim an annual income of twenty thousand pounds. Someone must marry those girls presented on the marriage mart. I dare to think that should I present myself, appropriately clad, at Almack's door that the patronesses will pause a moment to consider my application before I am thrown to the curb."

"Possibly," said Lady Sally, causing the dowager to gasp and stare.

"You cannot be serious," cried Lady Philomena. "This fellow is beyond the pale."

But the words "twenty thousand pounds" had their own power. Lady Sally flicked a glance up and down North's form, no doubt imagining him appropriately attired. Then she examined Shoffer's face. Since the duke did not immediately declare North was exaggerating his fortune, Lady Sally's eyes narrowed and she nodded to herself.

"What do you have to accuse him of?" asked the countess.

"Nothing at all," replied Shoffer. "My grandmother is a snob and sees no virtue in friendship outside of the rarefied heights of our class. As I wish to have conversations with more than eight persons in the realm, I will consort with intelligent, educated persons even if they have no rank to dignify them."

Shoffer could almost see the thoughts passing through Lady Jersey's mind.

"In comparison to our own rank, yours is a recent creation," Shoffer smiled. "I should not, in my grandmother's opinion, be speaking to you. Nor should my sister attend Almack's being that those gathered within those portals are so far beneath her that to speak to them would be a disgrace. A degradation. I am certain you have heard my grandmother say so."

Shock and offense passed across Lady Sally's face as she rose to her feet. "I am not..." she began.

"Of sufficiently ancient rank," Shoffer nodded sympathetically. "Sadly, no. But all of London, except those few who share my grandmother's preoccupation with rank, do not think less of you for your family history, Lady Jersey, despite your scandalous relatives. I shall continue to urge my sister to take advantage of your entertainments during the season. I cannot make the same promise for my grandmother."

"Do not put words in my mouth," protested the dowager, coming to her feet. "Your manners have degraded far further than I had feared. It is painfully clear you are not the appropriate person to promote Lady Elizabeth. I am certain Lady Sally would agree."

"W..." began Lady Sally, but Mr. North stepped forward.

"Now, what is all this? Surely we have interrupted the ladies at tea, my dear duke. And here we are with birthday gifts for Lady Beth that are already late."

"Of a certainty," agreed Shoffer and pushed a brown paper and string wrapped parcel into Beth's hands. "Here you are, my dearest sister. The first installment of the gift I promised you. Open it now, so we may admire the fit."

Beth cast a baffled look in his direction, then crossed to place the heavy parcel on a nearby table. It was the work of a few minutes for her to unwrap and open the box within.

With a gasp Beth flung her arms about Shoffer's neck and kissed his cheek.

"You remembered. You remembered. I feared you would not."

"Of course, my dear Beth. I knew how important it was to you."

"What do you have there, Shoffer?" demanded the dowager, attempting to peer around North's obstructing body.

Beth reached into the satin lined box and pulled out a dueling pistol, turning it over and over in her small hands.

"Oh, Timothy, they are wonderful. Look at the chasing, so delicate!"

"Pistols!" shrieked the dowager. "Shoffer, do you intend to fully destroy Elizabeth's reputation?"

Shoffer cast a narrow-eyed stare in her direction. "If Elizabeth chooses to take up shooting I have no doubt she shall bring it into fashion. But that is irrelevant. I have promised that she shall have a pistol for every day of the week, one to match each of her costumes and so she shall."

Under the weight of his stare the dowager sank back. Beth clutched her new pistol in both hands and spine straight and chin up, faced her grandmother.

"I am sorry your visit will be of such short duration, Grand'Mere. Please have your secretary keep us apprised of which entertainments you choose to attend so that I may go elsewhere. There are so many hostesses and so few of ducal rank that we must distribute ourselves to the greatest effect. For now, I pray you will excuse me," she smiled at Shoffer and North. "Come with me to my private sitting room, Timothy. I want you to help me display my new pistols to their best advantage."

With that she proceeded from the room, Shoffer and North on her heels.

"I hope you will like the pistols I have chosen," said North. "His Grace chose one of English manufacture, but mine are all the way from the Americas."

"We were at war with the colonies," said Shoffer.

"I am well aware of the uprising against the lawful overlordship of King George by those ungrateful colonists, but that does not mean that their guns are of poor workmanship!"

Beth led the way along the corridor and around a corner. A footman appeared to open a door for her. Before they could enter Beth's sanctum rapid footsteps sounded behind them. They turned in time to see Lady Sally hurrying down the grand staircase and away.

"The gossip that we are estranged from the dowager will be all over London before the end of the day," said Shoffer with some satisfaction.

"All the hostesses will know that if they want you to attend, dear brother, they may not invite Grand'Mere. Since you are unmarried and she is a harridan, I know who the hostesses will prefer." Beth grinned broadly and waved her pistol toward the blue parlor. "She was so shocked when you gave me this weapon I thought her eyes would fall out of her face."

North placed his parcel on a side table and crossed to stare out of a window.

"I hope this will not ruin your cousins' chances of vouchers for Almack's," said Shoffer to North.

"Oh, fear not, we were not in expectation of such a thing or I would not have been so bold with her." North smiled over his shoulder at them. "Wednesday will be, for my family, a day of rest while you suffer in overheated rooms, drink weak lemonade, and dance with giggling vir ... young women."

"Oh, but you must come with us," cried Beth. "If you appear at the door in our train you will not be denied."

North gave her a lopsided smile. "I have no wish to appear encroaching. Or more encroaching than we already appear. To do so would validate Her Grace's opinion of me. No, do not worry about us, dear Lady Beth; we do not repine. Invitations to other entertainments are already arriving."

"But..."

"There are other matters to discuss." North gave Shoffer a speaking look.

Shoffer frowned. If there was something he had agreed on with North, then the events of the afternoon had quite driven it from his mind.

"I do not know if this is the best time." North tried and failed to raise his pale eyebrows. "The armoire?"

Beth paled at the word and sank onto a tapestry chair, pistol clenched until her knuckles were white. Shoffer considered, briefly, dismissing his friend's advice. Beth was too affected and should be permitted to keep her own counsel. Time would make that horrible episode fade in her memory. Reminding her of it would do no good, of that he was certain.

"My dear," Shoffer covered her hand with his own. "Do not think on it. I urge you; put it out from your mind. It will never happen again. I am certain once she gave the matter some thought, Grand'Mere regretted doing that to you."

Beth burst into tears. Shoffer cast an angry glance toward his friend. They should have left the matter alone since reminding her only distressed Beth. North's face was set and stern even in the face of the tears.

"Dear Lady Beth," said North. "How many times did…"

"I lost count!" cried Beth.

"Oh, God!" Shoffer wrapped his arms around his sister and held her close. "Dear girl, I am so sorry."

"I never knew what would cause it. A word, a look and I would be locked in."

"Where?" asked North calmly.

"Always in Grand'Mere's armoire. When she put me in I must be quiet as a mouse. If she heard me moving about, waking her in the night, she would hit the armoire with her father's cane. If I ruined her clothes she would shout and shout."

"You will never live with her again." Shoffer tightened his grip on Beth's shoulders, marveling at how tiny she was. He had left this fragile person in the claws of her grandmother and never thought to check whether she was happy. He might never forgive himself. "Do not think on it. You are safe now."

"I was worried that you would be ashamed of me. Angry at me."

"You were wronged, my love. I should never be angry with you for this."

"I need you to teach me to shoot really well. If she comes near me again, I shall … shoot the feather out of her hat!"

Mr. North laughed. "She has grown her claws, our little golden kitten. We should take care not to offend her."

"Oh, you do not need to be afraid," said Beth, her eyes glittering with unshed tears. "I would never shoot you."

"I appreciate the sentiment, Lady Beth and thank you. I shall leave my gift for you to examine later." So saying, North rose to his feet.

"No, you cannot leave yet. Stay a while. Until my grandmother leaves, at least."

"So kind an invitation, but I cannot."

"But…" Beth reached a hand to the departing North.

Shoffer caught it and drew Beth's attention to himself.

"My dear sister, Mr. North must go. We have much to discuss, you and me. Alone and private. I wish to know all that the dowager did to you. I must know the whole no matter how painful it may be for you to remember and for me to hear it. In future when I promise to protect you, to see to it you do not suffer at the dowager's hand, I want you to know that I understand the extent and shape of what I am promising."

So saying, Shoffer handed over a larger handkerchief to replace the scrap of lace Beth was pressing to her face. North, wise fool that he was, slipped from the room and faded away.

Aside from deciding he should thank the man in the morning, Shoffer put him from his mind and concentrated on his sister. By the time Beth had finished explaining all that had happened to her, he was ready to have the magistrate arrest the dowager and throw her into Newgate prison. Since that particular satisfaction was denied him, Shoffer growled and grumbled and let the matter settle into the back of his mind.

This, all this, was the reason his sister did not trust him. Damn that woman. Lady Philomena was never again to be alone with his sister.

The next night Shoffer took up the Boarder family and extended his invitation to a soirée to include them. Mr. North spent part of the evening deconstructing the subject of feathers. Feathered hats, feathered fans, feathered fashions, all were subjected to his wit.

The following evening they all attended a musicale where during the intermission Mr. North expounded on his theory that it was a deaf, bald gentleman who liked to comb his one remaining long hair with a narrow comb who accidentally invented the violin.

The next night they attended a ball where Mr. North tried to teach how to judge if someone were an Englishman, a Scots, or a Welshman by the way they dismounted a horse. Each night more people sought him out and hung on his every word.

On the fourth day when the Boarder family gathered for luncheon, Millicent stared in astonishment at the huge pile of gilt edged pasteboards Merit carried in on a silver salver.

"Good Lord." Millicent lifted one, then another invitation. "Who would have thought there to be this many parties being held in London?"

"The season is begun, Mr. North," said Felicity, rising to run her hands through the pile. "This is all due to the duke. I hope you will thank him for us."

"And the Beau," said Maude. "Mr. Wentworth informed me that the Beau referred to us as 'charming.'"

"He said the same of Lady Beth," said Mildred. "We shall have to coordinate with her. We should make a list of the invitations we have received and see which ones we have that match."

Felicity resumed her place and, ignoring her food, started shifting through the pile.

"We should not assume that His Grace will take us in his carriage. Indeed, I would prefer he did not. We do not wish to appear country cousins to him and the other evening when I was ready to go home His Grace and Lady Beth were about to go on to another party." Felicity fixed Millicent with a piercing stare. "We should have our own carriage."

Millicent sighed and concentrated on her meal. Another expense. Still, she could not bring herself to deny her mother and sisters anything they required for the London season. Guilt made her generous. Guilt from knowing she still had not told them about the late Christopher North's will and their lack of dowries.

As yet no gentlemen approached her asking about settlements and expectations and as long as no one did, she would avoid discussing the matter with her family. At least until she had thought of a solution.

"This is odd," said Felicity, holding out a strip of paper to Millicent. "The hostess has added the strangest postscript."

Millicent accepted it and read: "The Countess Fenton is eager to receive Mr. North as her guest."

"Odd indeed," agreed Millicent.

"Look at this one," said Maude.

Millicent glanced toward her sister. While she was distracted by her thoughts, Felicity shared the pile of invitations with the sisters.

Maude held up a scented cardboard.

"Lady Johnson-Fife is enthusiastic about the prospect of seeing Mr. North at her gathering."

"Is she now?" said Millicent.

"Please assure Mr. North that the Honorable Mrs. Edward Pike is eager to have Mr. North attend!" added Mildred.

"This is very strange," said Millicent. "I doubt this is how ladies approach gentlemen for an affaire."

"Do not be silly, North," said Mildred. "It is all very simple. You have become fashionable!"

"What?" cried her family.

"Only think," continued Mildred. "Last night there were near fifty people listening and laughing while Mr. North was telling his stories. At one point there were more people listening than there were on the dance floor. Tonnish hostesses are quick to pick up on fads and fashions. If you continue to be humorous, Lady this and that will say to their friends, 'Oh, you must come to my party. Mr. North will be there!'"

"Dear God," sighed Millicent, sinking back in her chair. "I have become the court jester to the Ton."

"And you must continue to be silly, without being dull or repetitive, or else we shall not receive invitations."

Millicent covered her face and groaned.

The next morning found Millicent presenting herself at the door of the duke's London residence.

The duke's London butler was exactly the archetype of the species. Tall, proud, skeletal with a hooked nose proudly raised and clothing of immaculate fit. Millicent paused on the doorstep staring at the man for a full minute before removing her gloves one finger at a time.

"No. Not the father. No. Are you, perhaps, the uncle of the Somerset estate Forsythe?"

The butler did not even blink. "Sir is entirely correct. I congratulate sir on his perspicacity. Within the family I am referred to as Forsythe senior."

"If you permit, I shall as well. I am Mr. North. I expect His Grace has warned you about me and you have, therefore, declared your intention of manning the battlements, taking up the draw-bridge, and barring my entrance."

"Indeed not, Mr. North. By His Grace's command, I am to render you every courtesy.

"How very kind of him. Dare I hope to be so fortunate as to find him home?"

"If you would wait, I shall inquire."

The butler directed Millicent into a gilt edged, formal receiving room more suited to the dowager than the current duke. Millicent occupied herself examining paintings until Shoffer arrived, out of breath and smiling. He held out both hands and shook Millicent's in a firm, enthusiastic grip.

"North. Excellent. Dare I hope you are here to request my aid in improving your wardrobe? If necessary I shall accompany you to Nestor's and add my voice to yours in the hope he will accept your apology."

Millicent waved her hand, dismissing the offer. "I called upon Nestor two days ago. If you ask him I think you will find he likes me well enough."

"Indeed?" Shoffer stepped back and examined the lines of Millicent's baggy clothing with an air of disbelief. "Why ever for?"

"I paid off one of Beau Brummel's debts."

That set the duke back on his heels.

"Good God, why? I hope you do not expect him to thank you."

"I have no intention of informing him of the action at all." Millicent began prowling the room. "It is enough for me to know that I have done so. When he took notice of my cousins he raised them from simple country *gels* to London sophisticates and I am grateful. And, before you ask, I did speak to Nestor about my clothing. He had heard enough rumors about my appearance to be – let us not say eager – but resigned to accept another commission from me. And since I promised to enter and leave through the back door until he is satisfied with me, we are in good humor with each other."

"Well, then, I see that I am not needed in the matter of your wardrobe."

Millicent smiled while behind her teeth the words, "I shall always need you" begged to be spoken. He was particularly handsome this morning in a dark green cut away coat and fawn buckskins hugging his muscular thighs. Even at rest in his home Shoffer radiated strength and authority.

"I should thank you, Your Grace," she said instead. "The invitations that you promised even now rain down upon my household. When I left the ladies were creating a calendar for the rest of the season and arguing over which entertainments to attend."

"I am pleased to hear the Ton has taken you to its bosom; although, I will take little credit beyond the first. Your cousins acquitted themselves well and you have been well received, despite your unfortunate clothing."

Shoffer grinned at his own joke and relaxed in his chair.

"All good things come with a price," sighed Millicent. "If possible, I must apply again to Mr. Simpson for aid."

Shoffer sent a loitering footman off with the message and directed Millicent to a chair. Mr. Simpson appeared almost immediately.

"There is the fellow, the miracle worker," cried Millicent. "Again I throw myself at your mercy, Mr. Simpson."

"How may I be of service?" inquired Mr. Simpson.

"Oh, it seems I must have a town carriage. The ladies of my household have been cheerfully going hither and yon in hackneys these past few days, but, woe is me, once they had been taken up in His Grace's equipage nothing would do but they have their own carriage."

"I have seen the floor of a hired hackney," said the duke. "They are disgusting; therefore, I find I am in sympathy with the ladies. You will find, my dear Mr. North, that carriages take some time to build. You ought to have commissioned one the same time you looked for a rental house."

"Commissioned? You mean *new*?" Millicent allowed both eyebrows to rise. "My dear duke, I thought you knew me. Certainly not *new*. I was going to ask Mr. Simpson, who knows everything about everybody, if he knew of anyone who was planning on selling an old carriage. Surely, there is someone who has gambled what he should not, or another who has a new carriage and who now has a used carriage I might purchase."

There was a moment's silence, then the duke raised his hand to heaven and began to laugh. "Why am I surprised? Why?"

"Certainly, I wonder that myself," said Millicent. "After all, I do have two young ladies to fire off. I must make economies where I can."

Simpson by this time was shaking his head as he made a notation on a scrap of parchment. "When I have the names for you, shall I make an appointment for you to view the equipages?"

"Certainly not. Take them around to my house and ask the ladies to choose. They are the ones who shall be using it, after all. I find I prefer to walk."

If he was surprised Mr. Simpson declined to show it.

"I shall begin inquiries immediately." Simpson nodded to Shoffer and disappeared into the depths of the house.

"And you, Mr. North," said Shoffer, "now that you have discharged your errand, how are you planning to occupy yourself today?"

"This is my first visit to London. I thought to see the House of Lords and the Palace. I cannot go back to wild and untamed Yoooooorrrrkshire and say that I never visited the King!"

Shoffer laughed.

"Oh, very well, we shall embarrass ourselves by appearing the awed and impressed country bumpkins and gawk at the fine houses."

"It is not necessary for you to accompany me. I do not mean to impose."

"Bother that, North, it is no imposition. I have just left my sister who needs me not at all. She informed me that she intends to call upon your family and take them to see those sights that young ladies so admire."

"Bond Street," sighed Millicent.

"Indeed. So you best prepare for another round of invoices."

Millicent groaned.

"Go home," commanded Shoffer. "Put on your riding gear. I shall come fetch you in a quarter hour. You do not know the capitol well enough to be allowed out alone. Perhaps by visiting some of the stately buildings and historical monuments you might begin to acquire some much needed town bronze."

Millicent rose to leave. "Bronze? My dear sir, the most you can hope for in my case is tin."

True to his word the duke followed her home, then accompanied Millicent on an extended tour of the city. They rode for a time, sampled ices at Gunter's – Shoffer extracted a promise from Millicent that Beth would not be told of this indulgence since the promised visit had not yet taken place – and generally wandered.

Millicent could not remember a day she had enjoyed more. Shoffer was a charming and well-informed guide. Patient with her questions. Indulgent with her jokes. When they paused at a coffee shop to rest, and Millicent found herself listening to his description of the doings of Parliament, she hugged the moment to her heart and enshrined it in her memory.

He would never have relaxed so in the presence of one of the many débutantes who cluttered up the capitol. His own wife would not share a public meal with him like this. There were many advantages to being Shoffer's friend. She could bask daily in the sunshine of his smile.

Today was the most perfect day of her life.

Chapter Eleven

Her good mood lasted only until she reached the rental house. Merit opened the door and almost dragged her in by the collar.

"Oh, sir, thank God you are home. The ladies are in such a taking I do not know which way to look."

"Which one of the ladies?" began Millicent, then heard her mother's shriek. "Ah, I see." Millicent handed her hat to the butler and began removing her gloves. "How long has this been going on?"

"Near to an hour, sir."

"Then tea will not do." Millicent shook her head. "Have brandy sent up ... and have a glass yourself."

"Thank you, sir."

Shrieks and sobs, interspersed by Mildred's tired voice drew Millicent to the family bedrooms. The noise, she discovered, was coming from Maude's room. Standing in the corridor Millicent wondered if her father had ever hesitated in this manner. Given that he was married to Felicity for two decades it was more than likely.

Drawing a deep breath she knocked on the door frame.

Inside the room her mother was kneeling on the floor, her hands covering her face while Mildred and three maids hovered about trying to calm her.

"Oh, Mr. North," cried Mildred, looking up. "I am so glad to see you."

"I imagine so," sighed Millicent. "What has set her off this time?"

"Can you not see?" sobbed Felicity. "Oh, my poor daughter. Ruined. Ruined."

"We have only been in town a few days," protested Millicent. "How could she be ruined in that time?"

"Look at her hair!"

Millicent climbed over her mother's recumbent form and walked to the bed where Maude lay burrowed under the quilts. Whether to hide from her mother's wrath or the noise, Millicent had no idea. With Mildred's assistance she pulled down the blankets. Maude was curled up in the middle of the bed, her hands over her recently shorn head. Instead of the long gold hair that Millicent had envied, Maude's hair was now a short cap of gold curls.

"Good Lord, Maude," said Millicent. "What has happened to you?"

"You do not like it," wept Maude, reaching for the coverlet.

"I did not say that," Millicent exchanged a frustrated glance with Mildred. "I only asked where and who trimmed your hair."

"Trimmed? They shaved her bald!" cried Felicity.

"Felicity, please, you are not helping." Millicent spotted Merit and Felicity's maid waiting outside and beckoned them in. "Come, cousin, sit up and take a sip of brandy. It will calm you."

While Felicity was being helped into a chair, Millicent drew Mildred to one side.

"Tell me, quickly, what happened?"

"Lady Beth invited Maude over for tea after we spent the morning shopping. I came home, for I was tired. While Maude was there, Lady Beth's maid cut Maude's hair. From what I can tell, as soon as it was done they both regretted it. Maude came home with a blanket over her head and Mother has been crying ever since."

"They will think she is fast," cried Felicity. "Her reputation will be ruined. No good man will marry a girl with such wanton hair."

Maude shrieked and dived back under the covers.

"Oh, dear God," sighed Millicent.

"Perhaps Maude could wear a wig," suggested Mildred.

"A wig? Why, for heaven's sake?" Millicent lifted up a corner of the covers. "I think she looks very well, what I can see of her."

"Yes, a wig." Felicity bounced to her feet and started pacing, jabbing her finger at Millicent. "You must go at once. Get a wig. In the Grecian style. Yes, that will look very well. We never could get Maude's hair to cooperate for that style."

"Cousin Felicity, there is nothing wrong with curls. It is all the rage. We have seen women with just that style at every party we have attended. Personally, I am jealous. My hair is straight as can be and nothing can make it look the latest style. You should be pleased she looks so fashionable."

"A wig, Mr. North." Felicity pulled herself up to her full height. "We shall none of us attend any events until Maude's head is decently covered."

"Do not be unreasonable…" began Millicent, then noticed the close attention the servants were paying to them. Good gossip was currency to servants. Their own status in the world depended upon who they worked for and what the latest on-dits were.

Glancing around Millicent realized she was standing in the middle of her sister's bedroom, a place no unmarried gentleman should find himself. Bowing to her mother she drew herself up and retreated. At the doorway she paused.

"I believe, once you have calmed, you will realize that Maude's hair is not the disaster you imagine. Her new maid is quite skilled in the latest London styles. Have her put a few ribbons through Maude's hair and put on her best dress. You will see how well she looks."

"A wig," shouted Felicity. "We shall not leave this house until one is found."

The door slammed in her face.

Millicent turned and wandered through the house not realizing that Merit was following her until the butler cleared his throat.

"Yes, Merit?"

"I believe I can aid you with your task. I can recommend a talented barber, sir," said the butler. "My last employer was a gentleman with an unfortunate bald pate. Every week, it seemed, I was sent to obtain a new wig or to have his current one restyled."

"Does he provide for ladies as well?"

"Oh, of a certainty."

"Then, if you would be so kind, go and see this barber and bring back a selection of blond women's wigs." Millicent reached for her purse. "How much will you need?"

"Oh, he knows me, sir, so he will let me have a few on account and I will take back the ones that do not suit."

"Thank you, Merit."

Once the butler was gone Millicent checked the time by the grandfather clock in the hall. Ton events kept Ton hours. Although it was past seven in the evening, it was still too soon to leave for dances that did not start until nine or ten, or later.

If they were leaving at all.

It was unlikely that even Merit would be able to obtain a wig tonight and even if he did Felicity was in such a state that she would not enjoy the tension and crowds of a successful Tonnish event.

The rattle of plates and shuffle of feet in the dining room told her that the family planned to dine before embarking on this evening's entertainment and the servants were busy preparing the table. Millicent stood in the hall and wondered what to do. Should she dress for the evening or not? Did Felicity's prohibition on leaving the house apply to her, Mr. North?

Since the last thing Shoffer had said to her was that he looked forward to that evening's entertainment and the plan was that he would send around his second coach for the Boarder family, Millicent went to the study to draft a note. It was possible Shoffer already knew about the disastrous hairstyle from Beth. Still he should be advised that he need not have his horses put to or have his grooms labor unnecessarily with the carriage.

The note sent, Millicent peered into the dining room. The table was set, food prepared, and servants waiting to serve. Even though she was not dressed properly, Millicent went into the room, sat alone, and dined. If the ladies of the house wanted food they would have to come down and get it, since Millicent also directed that no trays be taken to rooms that evening.

There were, Millicent decided, as her orders were obeyed without protest, some advantages to being male.

Mildred arrived before the covers were taken away.

"Are you going out tonight?" she demanded without preamble.

Millicent shrugged. "I have no idea. I assumed not so sent a message to Shoffer saying we would be spending the evening at home."

"Oh, bother." Mildred sat and stared at the empty plate before her.

"Do you want something to eat?"

"Oh, the dessert will do," Mildred smiled at her sister. "I commend you for the cook you hired. He has a way with sponge cake that I admire."

"Thank Mr. Simpson. He took care of all that. And you, was there a particular reason that you wanted to go out tonight? A beau, perhaps?"

An attentive servant placed a dish of poached pears with clotted cream before Mildred.

"Beau? Me? Good heavens, no, North. It is my concern for your current status that prompts me to suggest you should not miss an event where you are expected. You are fashionable at the moment. It would not do for the hostesses to discover you could not be relied upon."

"You have a point, and Lady Fenton did approach me personally last night to confirm my attendance." Millicent leaned back in her chair, eyes closed. "What should I do?"

"While a lady cannot attend a party alone without causing comment, a gentleman may do so at will."

"I do know that, Mildred, but the entire point of us coming to London is for you and Maude to parade along the marriage mart."

"I could come with you. A male cousin is an unremarkable escort. We sent in our acceptance. Someone should go." Mildred grinned. "I only say that since it would be impolite not to."

"Yes, I see you are motivated by sincere disinterest." Millicent nodded, even as she shared a smile with her sister. "I suppose we could walk over. Shoffer was right. This house is close enough to walk to most of the best parties."

"Walk? Walk to an evening engagement? Never! Mr. North, have you forgotten, we have our own equipage!"

"Really? Since when?"

"Since the very efficient Mr. Simpson brought it around."

"I did not know that. No one discussed the pricing with me. What size is it? Where do I go to hire a driver or reserve a place in the Mews?"

"Oh, Mr. Simpson took care of all that." Mildred waved her hand airily toward the rear of the house. "All we need do when we want to go out is to ask Merit to send for it. Shall we do it now? I should like to make my first foray into society in my own carriage."

"Your carriage? Oh, well. But, I should like to know, how much is all this costing?"

"Does it matter?" asked Mildred.

"Well, yes, a little," cried Millicent. "We are not all that wealthy and this year has more expenses than Mr. North's estate usually carries. Added to that, I was required to grant more than a few of our tenants extensions on their rents or reductions due to it being a poor season."

"How am I supposed to know?" Mildred's raised voice gathered more than a little attention from the watching footmen. "You say nothing to us about money. You say nothing at all that cannot be taken as a joke."

Millicent flushed as she realized the truth of that accusation. Like many men of the Ton she had considered the women of her family unable to comprehend the complexities of finances. And she was a woman!

"Please, Mildred…" Millicent stammered. "I am so sorry. I should have done better."

"You certainly should have, Mr. North. You used to talk to me about everything and this last year we barely saw you, heard from you. If you do not share your troubles and concerns with me, you cannot expect me to be able to help!"

"Dear God," moaned Millicent, hanging her head and pressing her fingers to her temples where a headache threatened.

"And moderate your language in the presence of ladies. I have noticed a regrettable tendency toward swearing of late. Most ungentlemanly."

That at least brought a smile to Millicent's face.

"More and more I begin to understand Shoffer's point about club membership." Millicent laughed, as she leaned back in her chair. "I am sorry to distress you, Mildred, dear. Things are not so bad as you suspect. I can afford to keep a carriage, and a few more servants will not be the difference between comfort and the poor house."

"Are you certain? I can speak to Mother and Maude. We need not go about with Lady Beth shopping as much now that we have our wardrobe for the season. Although, I do need a larger reticule suitable for evening engagements. Lady Beth has brought them into fashion."

"Dear Mildred, do not worry. Go ahead and enjoy your shopping trips. I would appreciate it if you kept to your budget, though, if it is not too much trouble."

"I do not understand. I know there is something that is troubling you. There has been for a while."

Millicent nodded. Turning to the nearest footman she said, "We shall take tea in the front parlor."

Offering her arm to Mildred they traveled silently through to the parlor. After settling her sister in the most comfortable chair, Millicent paced the room for a while before standing with her back to the fireplace, her hands clasped behind her back.

"You know," said Mildred thoughtfully, "there are times when you remind me much of our father."

Millicent smiled at that. "Who do you think I took as my model?"

"Father never joked about as much as you do."

"Granted, but he worried about money more and now that I have the role of man of the house I find that worry is no longer the appropriate word. There is no word to describe the vacillations between security, confidence, and uncertainty."

Mildred went pale. "Please, Millicent, tell me. You begin to frighten me. What is the matter?"

Millicent crossed the room to the chair nearest her sister and leaned close. Even then she kept her eye on the door and her voice low.

"The late Mr. North was not a miserly misery for no reason. He inherited the tendency. I have seen a copy of *his* father's will. In it the late Mr. Christopher North insulted our Mr. Anthony North by declaring him to be a degenerate wastrel. Christopher put strict limits on what Anthony could spend and forbade him from selling any part of his inheritance. Our Mr. North was only regarded as a place holder until he died, then the rightful heir, Perceval, was supposed to inherit everything." Millicent sighed and ran her hands over her face. "It is a constant worry to me, the fear that I shall not have the correct amounts in the bank if I should die. The late Mr. North described to a penny what should be in the accounts. Should I permit you and mother and Maude to buy all you wish I might overspend and…"

"And what?" cried Mildred. "Shall Perceval North drag you out of your grave to hold you to account? What a ridiculous thing to worry about! When you are dead what more can be done to you? Surely you do not think that the North family has influence over God or the devil so that they might petition that you make good on the missing funds from beyond!"

Millicent gaped at her sister for a moment before laughing.

"Oh, Mildred, I should have told you ages ago. I should have known that you would put it all in proportion! But, dearest, do you not see? By the terms of this dreadful will I cannot make over a dowry to you or Maude!"

"Can you not? I cannot see that being much of a problem; after all, when we are wed the money goes into the keeping of our husbands. Mr. Perceval would find it difficult to get it back once it has passed out of your hands. It is not as if he is able to go to every tailor you bought clothes from or every butcher who supplied your meat and demand the money back. Once you have spent it, it is done!"

"The tailors and butcher, I grant you, are beyond his power, but if he were to sue for the return of any money I gave you as a dowry, it would be quickly gone. Solicitor's fees do rack up at an alarming rate."

"Hmmm. You do have a point. Perhaps Maude or I will marry a lawyer. It is not as if we have caught much attention amongst the Ton."

"Marry into trade," cried Millicent, in mock horror, one hand pressed to her cravat. "Mother will expire from the shame."

They both giggled, unable to stop even when a knock at the door heralded the arrival of the tea tray.

Millicent rose as the door opened and resumed pacing. A maid carried the tray across to set it beside Mildred's chair. Millicent waited until the girl was gone again before continuing.

"I worry from time to time what shall happen to you all if I am found out," she said. "They will hang me and all the money will go to Perceval."

"They will not hang a woman," declared Mildred.

"Why not?" asked Millicent. "They beheaded a queen or two in the past, did they not? I do not fear for myself so much as I worry about the three of you. I must find some way to provide for you all."

"That is what marriage is for," said Mildred.

"Which brings us back to tonight's gathering," said Millicent. "Shall we go out? All joking aside, we are unlikely to find your husband lurking in our parlor."

"I should like to. It will not take me long to prepare."

"Cousin Felicity will not approve. She did declare no one was to go out until Maude has her wig."

"Oh, bother Mother. She has taken to bed with a sick headache brought on by her snit. It is likely she will never know."

"As you wish." Summoning the maid Millicent said, "Inform Merit we need the horses put to and the carriage prepared. We shall go out in an hour."

Millicent approved the carriage Mildred selected as she settled back against the gently broken in leather squabs. The brilliantly polished lanterns' glass inserts were intact and the floor clean – a great improvement over a hackney. They arrived at the ball just before the receiving line ended and were met with such enthusiasm by the hostess as to be very gratified.

"Mr. North. You are here!" was the cry when the hostess spotted them climbing the stairs toward the ballroom. "I was beginning to despair of you."

"I do apologize, Lady Fenton," said Millicent, bowing over her hand. "My new coachman could not believe that such a rattle as I would be invited to your sophisticated revels. Convincing him I was worthy took a few moments."

Lady Fenton tittered politely as she led them down into the ballroom, ignoring all the other late arrivals waiting to greet her, Mildred following on Lord Fenton's arm. The hostess undertook to introduce "Mr. North" to all those of importance in the room, thus guaranteeing that Mr. North's presence at her gathering should be gossiped all over town.

Millicent did her best to satisfy the reason for her invitation. She joked with a parliamentarian about the subtle insults with which the Tories and the Whigs described each other. (The Right Honorable Bastard from West Cumbria is no Gentleman!) When faced with a gathering of dowagers and match-making mamas, she teased that the number, color, and positioning of the feathers in their hair was a coded signal, sending messages to their spouses and children. Released into a crowd of wallflowers Millicent continued her "cult of the cat tail" jest and signed as many dance cards as she could.

Mildred, to her own satisfaction, danced with a number of young bucks eager to claim they had spent a few minutes in conversation with the famous Mr. North, or failing that, his cousin.

Millicent was quite satisfied with the evening right up until her descent to take breakfast the next day, when she was greeted by Felicity waving a copy of a London gossip sheet.

"What, may I ask, were you thinking?" she demanded. "How could you do this to me?"

Millicent flushed to the roots of her hair.

"Cousin? I have not the pleasure of understanding you."

"Look. Look. That is your name plastered all over the gossip page. Mr. North said this, Mr. North graced that party. Mr. North. Mr. North. Mr. North. The pages are full of you. Have you lost your senses?"

As the page passed under her nose for the third time Millicent managed to take hold of it and, reading as she went, entered the breakfast room.

It was as Felicity described. The attendees at last night's party competed with each other to describe the "irresistible humor" of Mr. North, some quoting at length the text of her jokes. Millicent set the sheet aside and nodded to the hovering footman who poured coffee before retreating.

"Well?" demanded Felicity, "what do you have to say for yourself?"

"That I am happy my name is a simple one to spell correctly." Millicent sat and took a sip of coffee before glancing up at her mother. "What would you have me say, Cousin Felicity? That I am ashamed of myself? Of all the things I could be ashamed of, I have to say that being counted as popular cannot be one. Only yesterday you were pleased that my humorous nature caused you to receive a number of invitations. Now you are offended? I do not understand you."

"That is beyond the point. You have made yourself a public mockery. A fool."

"Cousin Felicity, I have always been a fool. That was the plan. Have you just this moment realized?"

"But your name is in the paper! People will read it."

"Yes, I do realize that, though I admit I had no plans to have my name in print. I see no reason to be so excited about it." Millicent waved her cousin to a chair, only that moment realizing that she had seated herself while a lady was still standing. Immediately she rose to her feet. "My dear cousin, consider, I shall never have my name in the paper as a participant of a duel, nor shall I be the cause of a marital fracas, nor be involved in an infidelity. Compared to those greater sins being a humorous guest at a Ton gathering is hardly a crime."

"But ... but," Felicity sank into the proffered chair, "but you should not make yourself such a public figure."

"I am fashionable and the Ton is fickle. Wait but a moment, my dear cousin, I shall fall out of favor soon enough and no one will utter my name again."

"The duke does not object," Mildred pointed out. "Surely he is a better judge of what is acceptable than we."

"I suppose," Felicity stared mournfully at the paper at Millicent's elbow. "It hardly seems proper for a young person to draw so much attention to h..."

A cough from the doorway interrupted the discussion. Merit the butler stood there with two footmen burdened with several hat boxes.

"Sir, as you requested, I have some ... items for your review."

Millicent stared at him blankly for a moment. Merit wiggled his eyebrows, twitched his shoulders and gave meaningful looks toward Maude who was wearing a turban on her head, until Millicent finally realized what the man was trying to subtly convey.

"Oh, yes, items! Please have them taken up to Mrs. Boarder's sitting room."

"Mine?" Felicity shook her head. "I have not purchased so many hats."

"It is the head wear you requested for Maude," said Millicent. "A selection for you to choose from. Those you do not like will be sent back."

"Oh, yes." Felicity leapt to her feet and hurried from the room. Her voice could be heard echoing back down the hall, demanding Maude attend her.

Maude sighed and obediently left her breakfast to follow her mother.

"No thanks given to you for the speed of delivery," observed Mildred. "Mother is impolite from time to time."

"Oh, it is no matter. Merit is the hero of this hour. He has distracted Felicity's attention from me. I shall thank him later."

Millicent spent the day peacefully dealing with her correspondence. A note came down from the upper floors informing her that the ladies would be taking their luncheon on trays, but they fully expected to attend the scheduled musicale that evening.

Millicent passed that piece of information on to Merit with a request for the carriage to be readied and promptly forgot it.

It was not until she was dressed in the "best" of her formal attire and waiting in the front hall that she saw what had been occupying the ladies all day.

Felicity was first to descend, a self-satisfied smile on her face. Millicent could only gape. Instead of the faded blond tresses liberally graced with grey arranged in a dignified chignon which was her mother's usual hairstyle, Felicity Boarder wore a brilliant blond tower of curls, with three ringlets dangling before each ear. Mildred followed beneath a wig styled with masses of ringlets at the back and six kiss-curls across her forehead.

Maude's was the worst. The hair was styled in a manner more suited to the previous century with three formal white feathers rising over her tower of hair to dangle before her eyes. A string of pearls and three silver ribbons were twisted through the mass.

The weight of the thing was such that Maude was frowning in her efforts to keep her balance. Despite her work she stumbled on the last step. Immediately her hand flew to her head, to no avail. The hair slipped forward and sideways.

"Oh, Maude, be careful," cried her mother. "You will ruin it."

"It is impossible to anchor properly." Maude used both hands to force the wig straight. "My hair is too short."

"This is beyond enough," shouted Millicent, surprising even herself by the volume. "I shall not appear in public with any of you if you insist upon wearing those monstrosities."

"Mr. North," began Felicity.

"No. In this I am deadly serious. I am a fool for the entertainment of the Ton, but this is beyond anything I should undertake. Maude, your own hair could not be more ridiculous than that wig. Take it off; I insist. Go upstairs at once, have your maid comb out your natural hair, and be done with it. Mildred, you as well."

"I shall keep mine," declared Felicity, holding her head high.

"That is your privilege, Mrs. Boarder," shot back Millicent, "but think on this. You wear that in public and I shall spend the entirety of the evening making jokes about people who go about wearing cats instead of turbans on their heads. Do not think that I will not."

Felicity went pale, then red. "You would not dare."

"I promise you," growled Millicent. "I am content to be a figure of fun, but these ... I declare to be too much."

Felicity sulked and argued until she realized that both of her daughters were already disappearing upstairs in obedience to Millicent's commands. Maude, when she returned was smiling, her bright gold curls fluffed about her head like a halo and threaded through with narrow green ribbons that matched the trim on the bodice and sleeves of her virginal white gown.

Felicity turned with a huff and went upstairs to redo her toilette.

"You look better," said Millicent to her sisters.

"Oh, much," said Maude. "It was somewhere between the third and fourth wig that I realized that there were worse things than my haircut. I now think I look very well with short hair, compared to the alternatives."

The final touch to her confidence came when Shoffer, upon seeing Maude reared back in surprise, smiled, and kissed the back of her hand and declared that none in the room could compare with her beauty.

Millicent was strolling about the outer edges of the ballroom and trying to decide which group of wallflowers to honor with a dance when Shoffer stiffened and tried to disappear behind Millicent's back. His expression was one of such horror that Millicent first checked to see that her sisters and Lady Beth were well before looking about for the danger. A London ballroom was not the place to fear brigands or cut purses, but the cause of Shoffer's distress was soon apparent. A glowing débutante – all white silk and pink flowers – appeared at his side.

"Your Grace," she said, "I fear you have forgotten our waltz. You did promise to dance with me at the Longstride soirée last year before you were called away to attend your sister. You did promise and I will hold you to it!" She tittered and simpered in what she imagined was a fetching manner.

Shoffer glanced desperately toward Millicent who was tempted to leave Shoffer to deal with the matter himself. That whim lasted just a moment. Listening to the girl's high pitched titter, Millicent winced and moved between them.

"Oh, no, Your Grace, you cannot," Millicent laid a restraining hand on his sleeve – though Shoffer made no move toward the débutante. "Remember what your physician said this afternoon."

The hopeful virgin's eyes opened wide. "Physician?"

"Oh, yes," said Millicent. "His Grace had a dreadful accident today. He was dismounting from his horse and his foot landed in a pile of, well, I cannot go into details which are not fit for a lady's ears. Let it be said only that slipping while half on and half off a giant stallion such as His Grace rides, well … we can only hope that he recovers." Millicent glowered at Shoffer and shook her finger under his nose. "I believe you were warned that the injury would be permanent if you exercised yourself. You should be at home in bed!"

"Well…" stuttered Shoffer. "My sister… The hostess … I could not disappoint."

Millicent seized Shoffer by the elbow and began directing him toward the nearest door. "I act your physician's part in this. If you do not rest, you will be a disappointment to your future wife. Now, come along." And with that she hustled Shoffer from the ballroom.

"My thanks," said Shoffer, as they made their way down the less crowded corridor past a gathering of gentlemen hiding from the dancing. "What injury am I supposed to have suffered? In case I should have want of the excuse again?"

"You have herniated yourself."

"What?" Shoffer began laughing. "What made you think of it?"

"Oh, the local blacksmith was dismounting once and fell. He hurt himself in the … the." Millicent could not prevent the blush that rose to flood her face, even while she grinned broadly. "The poor man fell, clutching himself in an area gentlemen do not usually admit to the existence of in the presence of ladies, and screamed for such a long time. It was pitiable. Later his wife said he was not much good for anything at all. It was odd. The blacksmith's wife popped out a child a year for the first five years of their marriage, but since then, not a one."

Several men who were nearby all winced and groaned at that information. Shoffer pushed Millicent along before him.

"Thank you very much for starting that rumor about my vigor and future fertility," he hissed. "Come, North, let us find the billiard room and rest my supposedly wounded pride."

Their host, a man who understood that sometimes it was necessary to hide from the female of the species, had set up a comfortable seating area in the billiard room complete with a set of footmen standing ready to fetch drink or anything else that might be required. Shoffer led the way toward a grouping of leather armchairs near the window, far from the occupied ones near the fireplace and nodded acceptance of the whiskey offered by the attentive staff. Millicent waved it away.

"You know, North," said Shoffer after he had taken a fortifying sip. "I do not believe I have ever seen you drink."

"I take wine with dinner," replied Millicent.

"Yes, I know, but never at any other time."

"What, Your Grace, would you have me turn drunkard?" Millicent laughed. "'Tis no very great deal. I do not drink because when I am drunk I am far sillier than you could imagine."

Shoffer put a horrified expression on his face and flinched away. "No. Say not so. You? Silly? I will not credit it."

Millicent took a cigar out of the humidor on the nearest table and threw it at Shoffer. Another footman appeared instantly with a taper to apply light to the tobacco.

"The truth?" continued Millicent, with reluctant honesty since Shoffer appeared to be waiting for an answer. "I do not like to risk what I might say, what I might do when I am disgusted. I am fool enough sober, I find I do not like myself drunk."

Shoffer puffed on the cigar and released a long stream of smoke. "You are your own best judge, North."

Millicent felt the tension unclench in her stomach. That was the complete truth. She knew herself to be chatty, but the one and only time she had taken too much wine she had talked endlessly, telling secrets of much less consequence than the ones she currently held.

Several moments passed while Shoffer smoked and sipped. He studied the end of his cigar with interest far beyond that piece of burning leaves deserved while Millicent shifted in her chair uncomfortable with the silence. During the last few days there were more and more occasions when the duke was silent. Pensive. His preoccupation worried her, though she had no idea why or what she could do to ease him. In so many tales, the legends of the gods and demi gods of ancient times, the hero ventured off in company with a loyal companion to see what could be discovered. Once or twice while reading Millicent wondered why those companions had not gone and had adventures of their own. Now she knew. They could not bring themselves to be parted from their beloved heroes. Sitting so close to him and yet not able to touch was agony, but not one she was willing to surrender. Even as a young woman, or miracles, a wife, she would not have the same access to his time. He would be off with his friends, seeing to his business, and she would have a few minutes over meals before he escaped to his club. But as North she could travel in his shadow by day and by night, listening to his confidences and sharing his life the way no woman could.

And if he never knew of her love, no matter, she would have the daily blessing of seeing his face. Hearing his voice. She closed her eyes and commanded her tears not to fall. When she composed herself she leaned forward, catching his gaze.

"May I inquire, Shoffer? How long shall we hide here?"

"Are you impatient to return to the ballroom and your devoted audience, Mr. North?"

"Hardly. Even I must rest. But, remember, there is dancing tonight."

Shoffer gave an indulgent laugh.

"Just a little longer, then. Just long enough to be certain that Miss Morris finds another poor soul to take her in to supper."

"We should check on my cousins, your sister…"

"Do not worry, North. I examined their dance cards earlier. A quite unexceptional Major of the Guards is taking Beth in to supper. Your cousins both have respectable gentlemen to attend them and with Lady Edith watching over them, they should do very well."

"Ah, well then…"

"Your Grace! Mr. North. How do you, sirs?"

A tall gentleman whose appearance niggled at Millicent's memory approached them and bowed first to the duke, then to Millicent. She frowned for a moment. Surely she had seen him before. Yet another of those dancing attendance upon her cousins or was he one of Beth's followers?

"Mr. Wentworth," said the duke. "We are well enough. And yourself?"

Millicent rose to shake the youth's hand. This one, if she remembered correctly, was the Honorable Mr. Wentworth, second son of an earl , and the youth had danced with Maude once or twice. Added to that he had been there in the club when Shoffer gave Attelweir his conge.

"I am well enough," said Wentworth, obeying the duke's gesture and settling into another heavy leather chair. "I went to a lecture recently by an explorer returned from the wilds of South America. He said there were rivers filled with fish that could strip the flesh off a cow, down to the bones, in seconds. Damn, if I do not think of those fish every time I cross a ballroom."

Shoffer and Wentworth laughed, but Millicent, more in sympathy with the young ladies desperately seeking their own security by attaching themselves to a man of fortune, only shook her head.

"Please do not be offended, Mr. North," continued Wentworth, seeing her disapproval of the joke. "I do not include your cousins in that. They are modest and unassuming girls."

"Yes, they are," said Millicent dryly, thinking of how loud Mildred could be when she was in a snit. "One can hardly credit we are from the same stock."

"No doubt," said Wentworth, accepting an offered drink from a footman, "when you seek a wife you shall take one as jolly and chatty as yourself."

"Oh, no," said Millicent making herself comfortable, leaning back in the chair, and putting her feet up on a short table. If there were any advantage she enjoyed as a man it was not having to sit as upright as a stick. She ran a finger under her collar and loosened her cravat just a touch. "My wife would have to be the listening sort, or the two of us would forever be chattering and there would be no one to hear a word."

"She will have to be tolerant of your nonsense, North," murmured Shoffer. "Else she would kill you before the year is out."

"True. True." Millicent fiddled with a cigar. She detested smoke, but found no one objected or offered her anything else if she just held one. "Should you happen to see a jolly sort, who is also quiet and has no objection to sharing her living quarters with a chatty, unfashionable fribble, please do bring her to my attention."

"Immediately," said Wentworth. "And you, Your Grace? What do you seek?"

"Oh, him. He dare not express an opinion," said Millicent. "If he states his favorite color is polka dot and his favorite music is bagpipes played by a drunk, then we should have a whole tribe of inebriated, polka dotted, bagpipe-playing débutantes staggering down Bond Street the next day."

Shoffer's lips quirked and he sank deeper into his chair. "It would almost be worth it to see such a sight."

"For myself, my tastes are simple," said Wentworth, glancing toward Millicent. "I am seeking a fair maiden, of grace and good sense … and curls. I have a preference for gold curls."

"It would be better if you preferred silver curls," said Millicent, after a moment's thought. "The gold fades soon enough."

"Gold coins do not," observed Shoffer.

"That is true," said Wentworth who shot another glance at Millicent and waited.

Not knowing what he was about, Millicent ignored him. After a few idle comments, Mr. Wentworth sighed and excused himself to return to the ballroom. Millicent watched him retreat in some confusion.

"What was that man about?"

"He was fishing for information," said Shoffer.

"Information?"

"Your cousin, the little one who cut her hair, quite fashionably I note, and now has gold curls; he was trying to find out if she is well dowered."

"Oh? Oh, really?" Millicent sat up in her chair to take another look at her sister's presumptive suitor, but the youth was gone. "Little Maude has an admirer? I must remember to tease her."

"Have pity on the poor lass."

Millicent shrugged and subsided. Shoffer tilted his glass this way and that watching the liquid slosh gently.

"I have often wondered what type of woman would please me," he said softly. "I cannot bring her to mind. It is such a nebulous thing for me I cannot even state a preference for height or feature or form. Blond, red head, brown, I cannot say if there is an advantage to any."

The words caused an acute pain in her breast. Shoffer, married. A woman with a claim on his time, his company. His body! She closed her eyes and swore she would say nothing. If she were blessed, then her silence would turn him from the subject.

And yet, as one does when a tooth hurts if pressed by the tongue just so, and it is irresistible to press it again to measure the depth, the intensity of the pain, she raised the subject herself. She tightened her grip until her prop cigar was crushed and the scent of tobacco filled her nostrils.

"Perhaps her nature?" said Millicent. "Do you prefer a certain sort of girl? Studious? Vivacious? Dazzling? A diamond? A blue-stocking?"

"How can I tell? And would I know it if I saw her?" Shoffer emptied his glass with one swallow and set it down on a table with a thud. "I swear to you, North, I wish to God that there were some sign, some flash of light, a heavenly choir so that one would know. Would that be too much to ask? I look about and see some marry for money, others for need, but I do not need to do that. I am wealthy and free to please myself. Free to be happy. And yet the woman who would make me happy stubbornly refuses to appear."

Millicent could not speak through the tears that filled her throat and tangled her breath. It seemed that Shoffer was not through torturing her.

"I love women, in general. The softness. The heat. The joining, when done well, is an exquisite agony. My wife could be tall or short. Dark or fair. I even enjoy those with nice cushiony curves, all the better to hold in the dark, but I cannot find her. The special one. How would I even know her if I saw her?"

Millicent turned away and so did not see the tight expression that passed across Shoffer's face. Shoffer slammed his glass on the table and tossed the stub end of his cigar into the fireplace.

"Come, North. The ladies will be looking for us. We have neglected them too long. Even if we cannot dance you might entertain them with your chatter."

The abruptness of the command took Millicent by surprise, but she rose and followed on his heels.

Chapter Twelve

Shoffer first became aware something was wrong when he stopped into one of his clubs a few days later to check the betting book. Given the propensity for gambling about every subject under the sun he knew from experience that if a young buck had ambitions to marry his sister Beth, that information would be recorded in the betting book long before any other sign could be detected.

Beth's name did not appear, although his own was linked to a number of ladies – both reputable and of the demimonde. To his complete shock he found Mr. Anthony North's name. Smiling slightly, and wondering which young woman allegedly had caught his friend's eye, Shoffer read on. The smile vanished when he saw that the bet was that Mr. North would be arrested before the end of the season for "gross indecency."

The criminal euphemism almost took the breath from his body.

North? A bugger? No, never! Shoffer had spent days, weeks in the man's company and could attest without reservation that he was an honorable gentleman.

Determined to call the person perpetrating this slander to account, Shoffer glanced down at the names of the gentlemen placing that bet and saw the Earl of Wallingford's signature.

Swearing softly, he settled back on his heels.

Damn the man. Of all the people to be creating this gossip the earl, well known to be "light in his slippers," was one who would be believed at every turn on this subject alone.

Like would well recognize like, people would whisper.

Slamming the book closed he turned on his heel and stormed out of the club, noticing as he passed that a couple of young bucks glanced at him before whispering together. Shoffer granted them the "ducal stare" as North called it before sweeping out of the building.

He was on his horse and halfway down the street before he realized what the whispers meant.

He, Shoffer, was constantly in North's company. It was not beyond possibility that those who believed such a reprehensible thing about North might think *him* guilty of the same propensities.

Shoffer tightened his grip on his reins, causing his temperamental mount to bridle and shift sideways, before taking control of his temper.

He continued his self-appointed rounds, visiting every club to which he was a member now looking for two pieces of gossip. In every book he found the same damned lie, written by one of three hands. The Earl of Wallingford, the Earl of Trentonlie, or the Comte of Le Forhend had made the bets; to Shoffer's mind there was one man behind the creation of this rumor. This lie.

Attelweir.

It had to be his revenge for the cut Shoffer had dealt him.

Poor North, with no good and noble name behind him, with few friends and his cousins to fire off, was vulnerable where Shoffer was safe.

No matron of the Ton would dare cut the Duke of Trolenfield from her guest list, nor would she offer any impertinence to his sister. But North? He would find his new acquaintances avoiding him, his cousins' matrimonial options limited or nil, and not have any way to defend himself against the purulent gossip.

Damn Attelweir.

By the time Shoffer exited the last of his clubs, it was evening and the day was turned cold, wet, and miserable. He could, if he wished, go back into the club, wait in comfort and warmth while he sent for his carriage. Except that when he glanced back toward the door two gentlemen of mature years were entering and they smirked at him as they passed.

Damn. Damn. Damn.

Shoffer set his heels into his horse's flanks and directed the startled beast along the slick street.

Damn.

Of all the accusations to have made against a man, this was the worst, since it was so difficult to disprove.

One could say North was a lecher and a rake and the Ton would shrug. Call him a despoiler of young maidens and they would keep their young charges closer, but not cut him. After all, the man had money. One could accuse him of being up the River Tick and he need only open his purse to prove them wrong, but buggery? It was an accusation against which even marriage was no defense.

Shoffer scowled as he rode. He was now in the unenviable position of having to explain to his young friend that his time in London was about to come to a sad end. He could advise North to retreat and let his cousin, Mrs. Boarder, take her girls about. That separation might preserve the girls' chances of a good match. That and a good dowry might save the Boarder girls' hopes.

Possibly.

More likely if North retreated it would be considered confirmation of the rumors and his reputation and that of his family would be permanently tainted.

Shoffer's primary responsibility was Beth. Beth who had flowered under North's gentle teasing. Beth who would tear London down with her own fingers if she knew her dear Mr. North was under suspicion of a crime that would, if ever proven, get him hung by the neck until dead.

Perhaps he should let it happen.

A cold and remarkably uncomfortable chill passed down his spine at the thought and he suppressed it immediately. It was entirely due to jealousy. Even after all his efforts to gain her trust, little Beth seemed to prefer the silly fellow to her own brother.

For a moment Shoffer faced his own demon. Yes, he could permit the Ton to unjustly reject the little man and when he was gone Beth would have no friend or confidant beyond her brother ... and he would hate himself.

He could not let her know the trouble Mr. North faced. Beth gave her friendship with her whole heart and would not pull back. She would risk her own reputation to defend his. Shoffer frowned as he examined the depths of Beth's affection for the man. No, North made no attempt to engage Beth's affection. He never went beyond the realms of proper behavior. Beth's affection was based on Mr. North being the first person to tease her out of her shyness. Shoffer could clearly remember North declaring that he would never marry her.

His scowl deepened. He believed it. At no time did he ever consider Beth in danger from Mr. North. Could it be that he had always known, that he had realized without examining his belief that North would not compromise his sister? That North truly was ... guilty?

Damn. Damn. Damn.

No. He could not doubt his friend. Not until he had proof of his own certain knowledge.

But proof one way or another changed nothing. Accusation was enough to ruin Mr. North's reputation.

Damn.

Shoffer's bad mood communicated itself immediately to his household staff. Forsythe senior took one look at his thunderous brow and brought the brandy decanter. Shoffer accepted the glass and stared at it a long time before taking a drink. But once he had begun continuing was easier. The bottle was half empty and the evening well advanced by the time a familiar irregular knock came at the door.

Groaning, Shoffer sank back in his chair even as he listened to his butler's soft footsteps as he went to answer the door. Shoffer prepared himself to utter the refusal only to hear Forsythe welcome North in without first confirming if His Grace was home to visitors.

"His Grace is in the Chinese drawing room," intoned the butler.

"Thank you, Forsythe senior. Is Mr. Simpson with him?"

"No, but I shall relay the message that you are seeking him," said Forsythe.

Shoffer stared blankly at the doorway where Forsythe appeared in short order to announce "Mr. North," before departing to fetch the duke's secretary all without asking permission or consent.

A clear indication, thought Shoffer, of the degree to which Mr. North had ingratiated himself into his life.

North paused just inside the doorway, gazing about in the vague, awed way he had when he was pretending to be a country innocent for someone's amusement. Once he had finished his examination, North stared at the polished floor and began to walk, heel toe, the length of the chamber, counting out the paces. Instead of stopping to greet the duke he continued to the far wall before turning.

"This room is seventy-five feet long!" he cried and was about to measure the width, when Shoffer rose to seize him by the arm and gave him an ungentle shove toward a fireside chair.

"If you have an absolute need to know the dimensions of my home, I shall have them measured by the servants and sent to you."

The words uttered so coldly had Mr. North's head coming up and the smile fading from his face even as he sank into the chair.

"I have no wish to cause anyone extra work," murmured Mr. North and Shoffer waved his comment away.

A footman entered a few steps ahead of Mr. Simpson and gathering the brandy decanter and humidor offered both to the duke's guest and secretary.

"Most kind." North waved away both brandy and cigar and grinned up at Mr. Simpson. "Here is the fellow. Good evening to you, Mr. Simpson. My cousin, Felicity, wishes me to thank you for the house. It is, she tells me, everything that is gracious and fashionable. I expect, before the season is over, she will declare it dreadful, dark, and demeaning, so I will give you the compliment now and leave it to her to deliver the insults later."

"I am pleased to be of service." Mr. Simpson sank down on a straight backed chair and regarded North solemnly.

"And Miss Mildred is dazzled by the carriage you found. Again, my thanks."

Mr. Simpson colored a little, then nodded. "I am informed you inquired after me."

"Yes."

North smiled across at Shoffer with his expression open and friendly as a puppy. Shoffer's stomach churned with the knowledge that he would have to cut this friendship if he wanted to continue in the Ton's good graces. North might be a fool, but he had feelings and sensibility and would be hurt by the cut. There might be no member of the Ton whose friendship he valued more than North's, but he had to consider shy Beth first and foremost. She could never endure being gossiped about. The sideways glances. The sneers and whispers would cut Beth's fragile confidence to the bone.

"I hope, Your Grace," North continued, "that I might impose on you by again borrowing your secretary."

"I would be pleased to be of service," said Mr. Simpson, reminding Shoffer he had already ordered his secretary to do everything to make the Boarder family's stay in London comfortable.

"Actually, I need you to listen to me and tell me if, in your judgment, I have a good understanding of the late Mr. North's will." Mr. North reached into his coat and pulled out a much folded bundle of papers.

"You would be best served seeking the advice of a lawyer."
Despite that comment Mr. Simpson reached eagerly for the papers.

"Eventually I may, but for now I seek the advice of intelligent men of goodwill instead. His Grace is already aware that my father's will is an odd object. He was with me when I learned the full extent of my father's opinion of my character and abilities. The late Christopher North was compelled by *his* father to grant me half of the estate and he did so, but reluctantly and with a proviso. As I read the will, it is expected that I shall die before my brother. The late Mr. North, may he burn in hell for a few years – I am not cruel – was specific in his instructions as to how I should maintain and hold all that I received from his will so that it might be given to Perceval upon my death. The list is complete in every detail. Every groat and penny itemized. Although Christopher North does not say what punishment he arranged should I fail in this, I suppose he had some expectation of petitioning God that I should be flogged in the afterlife."

"I do see that list." said Mr. Simpson after a pause, his eyebrows rising as he examined the length and extent of Mr. North's holdings.

"It is my belief," said North slowly, "that I am not required to surrender anything *more* than that list. That the profits of my labor, the excess of my rents earned after inheriting, revenue from my investments, which are not included in this list, are mine to do with as I will."

Mr. Simpson and Shoffer exchanged a glance and Shoffer, his interest engaged, crossed to sit beside his secretary, accepting each page as Simpson completed it and reading carefully.

"Your father even listed the amount in his Mercantile account," said Mr. Simpson. "Do you have more than this now?"

"Oh, of a certainty I have more, much more," declared North, with a laugh, "Although, my cousins are industriously trying to correct that situation this season. I am a dreadful skinflint, do not you know." At Mr. Simpson's shocked look, North continued. "What, do you think I have done nothing but gamble and whore since coming into my inheritance? I hate to disappoint you, but that is the exact opposite of what I have done. Remember, it was to be considered a contest between myself and Perceval to see who best managed his inheritance. It was all very biblical."

"From my reading of the will," said Mr. Simpson "your understanding is correct. Because your father and his solicitor were so precise in what you must hold available to be rendered to Perceval, anything in excess should be considered yours."

"Excellent," cried North, leaping up and pacing before the fireplace. "This is wonderful news."

"I should take advice from a lawyer to be certain," added Mr. Simpson.

"Oh, I shall do better than that. I plan..."

"I hesitate to ask," said Shoffer coldly, covering his eyes with his hands. "Heaven protect us from Mr. North with a plan."

Millicent paused and glanced back at the duke, puzzled by the tone of his voice. His voice, his entire manner since she had arrived had been withdrawn and antagonistic. He had never spoken so slightingly of her before. She could not think of anything in their current discussion which would offend him so much. Indeed, in the past when she had raised this subject he had been supportive of her intention to dower Mildred and Maude. His manner today was entirely unexpected.

Mr. Simpson glanced back and forth between them, as if equally surprised. "If I might know it, I might offer an opinion."

"It will not go forward without His Gracefulness's cooperation."

"What do you intend?" demanded Shoffer, his voice hard.

Millicent hesitated and spoke only when Shoffer made an impatient gesture in her direction.

"Come on, out with it."

"Very well. I thought that I should take some monies, above what is described in the will, and put it in the Exchange for my cousins. If I frame the matter properly, then they shall have an income even if they never marry."

"The Exchange?" Shoffer nodded. "That is simple enough. I can introduce you to someone who can make the investments on your behalf."

"It is not the investments which concern me," said Millicent. "I can ask the manager at the Mercantile to make them and to see to it that the ladies receive their quarterly dividends. No, my concern is the possibility that once I die, Perceval should come and protest the use of the money."

"You could indicate in your will ... oh," Mr. Simpson glanced down at the papers in his hands. "I see your difficulty. Perceval North can argue that the money belongs to him, claiming the will of Christopher North supersedes your own, and demand the money be returned. If he is a man with no sensibility, that is. But what man would take the only income of a family of ladies?"

"Oh, come now, how can you doubt it? Many men do so every day and think nothing of it. I think you can safely assume that Perceval has no qualms," said Millicent. "Certainly, I expect Perceval to demand every penny. If I could create a will, I would give the girls a decent inheritance, but I cannot."

"But you have a plan," said Shoffer.

Millicent paused and stood facing the fireplace. "If I have lost your good opinion, Your Grace, then I have no plan at all."

"Good God, man, out with it!" When Millicent hesitated, Shoffer rose, seized her shoulders, and shook her, then released her so abruptly that she staggered. "No one knows from one moment to the next what you shall say or do, Mr. North. For heaven's sake, what do you want of me?"

Pale and confused Millicent stepped back and slowly corrected the lay of her clothing and kept her gaze directed toward the lush colored carpet.

"Only that when Perceval discovers what I have done, I hope you will hold my cousins' concerns in your heart. Should I appoint you executor of my estate, then Perceval will have to deal with you. Should you regard him through a lorgnette as if he is some strange form of toad, then he will retreat and leave the girls in peace. That is, if you are willing."

"Is that all?" abruptly Shoffer stalked back to his chair. "Really, Mr. North, you make such a production of every little thing! I would have thought you were going to ask for my life's blood!"

Confused, Millicent watched Shoffer pour brandy into his still half full glass. Usually Shoffer was in the best of moods when they were together. In fact, unless someone was insulting his sister, Shoffer was the most even tempered of men. Millicent reviewed the conversation and the previous few days trying to think of something she might have done or said that carried now to the duke's ears that would set the man against her. Him. Mr. North. There were so many things she had done and said, but at the time Shoffer merely had laughed. What had happened?

Shoffer slouched back to his chair and cast an unreadable look toward Millicent.

"Is this all? It seems you need very little from me, which is a surprise given the production you made of it."

"I do apologize for wasting Your Grace's time."

"Good God, North, how you do carry on."

"I think," said Simpson, still appearing confused about the tension between the two friends, "that since Mr. North cannot create an ordinary will that His Grace should have some letter of intent. A request he have guardianship of the ladies' finances until they marry."

"Yes. That is a good idea." Millicent glanced toward the duke and away. "I am in no haste to write my will, expecting that neither God nor the devil is in any hurry to see me. Nevertheless, I shall write a letter tonight and send it across."

"Oh, write it now and be done with it." Shoffer waved a careless hand. "There is paper enough over there. Use paper with my crest on it. Simpson shall sign as witness. I shall sign acknowledging this was done with my consent. Let us see if your brother can argue with that."

Millicent crossed to the writing desk where perfectly trimmed pen, strong ink, and soft paper awaited her. An imp of mischief decided her on what to write. Instead of a formal letter, in the style of a will, she wrote out her plan ending with, "Trusting to the good will and temperate nature of the Duke of Trolenfield, I do beseech him to supervise the distribution of my estate after death. If I could but divide the estate I hold equally between my cousins, I would, but the malicious actions of the late Mr. Christopher North prevent me. Therefore, I ask His Grace to extend his benevolence to my cousins and protect their interests as he would his own. I extend to them a sum of money as if they were a charity – being both widow and orphans – and bestow the sum of five thousand pounds upon each of my cousins to be held for them in the Exchange so as to serve as their income for life and dowry. As a charity cannot be compelled to return a donation, equally, my cousins, widows and orphans as they are, should not be robbed after my death by Perceval North."

And she signed it Anthony North in such an illegible hand that Mr. Simpson frowned at her, but Millicent could not explain the true Mr. Anthony North, being almost blind, could barely write.

"Is there any other way we can aid you, Mr. North, since you have your own bank selected to act as investors?" Shoffer barely glanced at the page Mr. Simpson held to him before affixing his signature and seal. "Put that somewhere safe, Mr. Simpson. I do not expect to need it any time soon."

"Yes, Your Grace."

"Actually, there is something Mr. Simpson can do for me..."

"I wonder that I bother entering the room," snapped Shoffer, scowling into his cup.

Millicent colored despite her desperate wish to avoid blushing. "I do apologize, Your Grace. I should not trouble your man of business."

"Be damned to the Graces, North!"

Millicent and Simpson carefully avoided meeting each other's eyes and remained silent awaiting the duke's next action. Millicent was breathless with fear that the next words she would hear would be Shoffer banishing her from the house. She knew not how she would bear not seeing him, not spending time in his company. But, perhaps, it was for the best. She should not be torturing herself with the unattainable forever. It hurt too much to be so close and never to touch. Sighing, she straightened and prepared to take her leave of Shoffer.

"Oh, forgive me, both of you," said Shoffer rising and briefly resting his hand on Simpson's shoulder. "I have been a bear with a sore head all day and it is neither of your faults. North, I am pleased that you have managed to figure out a solution to the problem of your cousins' dowries. Truly, you are the most confusing man – a generous skinflint." He gestured toward Millicent's secondhand finery. "You neglect your own appearance, but place no limits upon your care of your family. And you, Simpson, as far as it does not interfere with your other duties, I would appreciate it if you would render what assistance Mr. North requires. I know he will compensate you for your time. He has the money to spare since he spends near to nothing on his clothing."

And just that quickly the tension in the room vanished. Millicent exchanged a confused look with Simpson, but both were too grateful to have the calm and cheerful duke back to risk comment.

"For what else do you require him?" asked Shoffer.

"I only wished to know to whom and for how much I

should make out a note of hand for the carriage and its upkeep. Mildred settled the matter with Mr. Simpson without my being aware of the details."

"I shall write it out for you immediately, Mr. North."

"I should pay for the carriage as soon as possible, I think," said Millicent. "I expect the person who sold it is in need of the funds."

"Oh, yes, indeed," murmured Simpson.

"Very well. Will tomorrow suit you, Mr. North?" asked Shoffer. "For visiting lawyers and setting up a trusteeship for the Boarder family? There should be something formal in place to defeat your brother."

"Certainly, Your Grace."

"Very well. I shall … I shall collect you about ten and after we have dealt with your issues at the bank, I am taking you to meet with my tailor. Again. This time I will not permit you to delope."

"You are most kind, Shoffer."

She waited for a moment, certain that she had been dismissed, but uncertain as to why Shoffer was suddenly cheerful once more. Shoffer did not explain and she could not work it out. Confused, Millicent bowed and departed. Today was a most unusual day. She could think of no reason for Shoffer to behave as he had. It was more likely that it was nothing to do with her at all. After all, he attended the House of Lords which meant other, greater responsibilities than the petty concerns of a country gentleman. She should limit the demands she and her family put upon his time. It was only right.

Quelling the hurt in her heart, she walked home, not noticing that some of the Quality who saw her crossed the street or stared at the sky instead of running the risk of meeting her eye and creating the need for an exchange of greetings.

The season rolled on its merry way. Millicent attended events at Felicity's direction trusting that her mother had sense enough to choose events which were most appropriate for the ambitions of Mildred and Maude. Lady Beth and her chaperone attended most with them, although Millicent noticed that the little girl was coming out of her shell more and needed familiar faces less and less.

But most of all, Millicent noticed that Shoffer was not there. Beth explained that while Parliament was in session her brother was busy during the day and could not give up all the hours of the night to entertainments. Millicent accepted that reason with a smile even though she missed him like a lost limb. The pain of his absence weighed on her so much that one hostess was moved to comment – with a frown – about Mr. North's morose expression, reminding Millicent that her family's acceptance by the Ton depended a great deal on her foolery.

Millicent shook herself out of her pensive mood. Worrying about her friendship with the duke gained nothing. Since that one strange night, Shoffer was polite enough on those rare occasions she saw him.

She was standing on the sidelines for a change, watching the dance, when the Earl of Trentonlie and the Comte of Le Forhend approached her. Millicent frowned as the two men circled her like hawks hovering over a freshly harvested field. For a few circuits the men did nothing more than circle until they gathered the undivided, if surreptitious, attention of the guests nearby. Their intention, Millicent did not doubt, although she had no idea why they were making such a show of themselves. Millicent watched their progress with a blank expression on her face.

Benson, Earl of Trentonlie, tilted his head as he passed behind Millicent and examined her pantaloons.

"My dear Mr. North, did not His Grace advise you on the fit of your trousers? You should enhance what nature has given you."

"I prefer comfort to fashion," replied Millicent coolly, "and make my own decisions regarding my clothing. In consultation with my tailor."

"It is clear you do not take your tailor's advice." Standing before her the comte raised his lorgnette to his eyes as he scanned Millicent from head to toe.

The urge to raise her arms across her breasts had her hands trembling. Millicent flushed and kept her hands at her sides through will alone. Her disguise had survived for months, but she had never been subjected to such intense scrutiny. The comte glanced down at her hands and smirked at this proof of her nervousness. Turning away from his examination Millicent smiled at one of the nearby ladies and with a bow appropriated her fan. By now no lady would consider refusing Mr. North's request for a fan. This lady would boast to her friends for weeks and probably save the fan as a memento, such was Mr. North's current reputation. For now waving it gave Millicent a little confidence and helped calm down the flush that threatened to become a wholesale burning blush.

"My tailor requires that I enter from the alley and not reveal his name," said Millicent, smiling at a nearby wallflower. "I do not blame the fellow as I do not display his works of art to their best effect."

"Oh, I think with a little effort you could be improved," purred the comte. He pointed at Millicent's thighs and crotch with his lorgnette. "A little padding here and there and you would receive the acclaim of the crowd."

There were a few snickers from those listening.

"I believe I am receiving as much acclaim as I can accommodate," said Millicent, "there being only so many hours in the day and so many days in the season. Poor mortal that I am, I can attend only so many functions."

"You have a high opinion of yourself for one of such low estate," murmured the comte.

"Oh, sir, you are mistaken. At least two of my estates are at the top of hills and my hunting box is on one of the higher mountains of the Pennine Chain! They are not low at all."

The listeners laughed louder at that.

The comte flushed at that since every member of the Ton knew that he was title proud and penny poor since the Grande Revolution had robbed him of all material goods.

"I suppose," continued Millicent, as she waved the fan under her chin, "when considering padding one's clothes, I prefer honesty, since at some point in one's life one is required to provide proof and one does not wish to disappoint under those circumstances…" She allowed her voice to trail off, then continued, "as you well know, my Lord Comte."

His flush deepened as those mature ladies within earshot either giggled or nodded. The débutantes pretended they did not understand the jest.

"I would be willing to testify as to your honesty, Mr. North, after a suitable period of examination," said the earl.

Millicent permitted the fan to still and she regarded the earl through narrowed eyes.

"I have no need of *your* testimony on any subject, nor at any time," she said in the most chilling tones she could summon.

Before the earl could manifest his offense at her reply Millicent noticed one of Lady Beth's young admirers hurrying through the crowd toward her.

"Mr. North! Mr. North, you must come at once!" He clutched Millicent's arm and turned her about. "She has gone quite pale and he will not listen to any of us. This is to be my dance and he dismissed me. Me!"

By this time Millicent recognized the lad as being the heir to a respectable baronetcy. As far as she could tell from the lad's babble there was some quarrel about precedent within Beth's circle. Since Shoffer had given Lady Englethorpes a list of those who were approved to dance with Beth, Millicent was tempted to refer the lad back to the chaperone, but at that moment the crowd parted and she could see Attelweir looming far too close to a cringing Beth. Her approved suitors were hovering a few feet away watching with expressions of distress, but making no move to rescue her.

Lady Englethorpes was wringing her lace handkerchief, frowning. Obviously, she lacked the spine to dismiss a duc on the hunt.

Millicent took one step forward, then halted as her arm was caught in a surprisingly sharp grip. She glanced down first at the beringed hand that held her, then up to meet the comte's glittering gaze.

"Uh, uh, ah," said the comte, waving a finger under her nose. "No, you will not. It is not for you to interfere in the concerns of your betters."

Millicent seized the littlest of the comte's fingers and yanked it back, hard. The man screamed shrilly and released her.

"There are pigs in their wallows who are better than Attelweir," Millicent hissed, then crossed the room at as close to a run as she could manage, given the crowding.

Millicent did not bother with subtlety or jests. She pushed through the watching crowd and placed herself firmly between Attelweir and Lady Beth. As soon as she was in place, Lady Engelthorpes moved in, hartshorn in hand, to support the girl who was, from what Millicent could assess, actually near fainting.

Millicent turned her back on Attelweir, a move sure to set him to fuming and leaned close to Beth.

"My dear girl, whatever is the matter?"

Beth's only reply was to close her eyes. Her lips were pale and tightly clenched and she shivered in the embrace of her chaperone.

"His Grace has been speaking to Lady Elizabeth of matters unsuitable for a girl of her age," Lady Englethorpes glanced toward Attelweir and away, "When His Grace's conversation grew too warm, I chastised him and reminded him of Lady Elizabeth's youth and innocence and his response was quite crude."

Millicent stared over her shoulder at the duc. "Sir, you should be more careful in your speech."

"As should you be," shot back Attelweir, "or do you presume to correct your betters?"

Millicent straightened. "Before God, I swear I do not regard you as the 'better' of those gathered here. But our opinions of each other does not matter. Lady Beth does not wish for your company. You should honor the young lady's wishes and depart."

"I shall not since a courtship requires a maiden to be persuaded of where her best interest lies, even if at first she does not realize it." Attelweir smirked and attempted to push past Millicent, but she stepped sideways and blocked him. "Now, get out of my way, you mushroom. You..."

Before he could gain traction for a rousing tirade, Millicent leaned forward and hissed in his ear for a few moments, then leaned back and laughed, full-throated and loud. Attelweir gazed at her in shock.

"What? What did you say?"

Millicent leaned in again and whispered. "You may outrank me, Your Utterly Gracelessness, but you cannot defeat me. I am the joker, the royal fool. I may with impunity mock the pompous, heckle those of High Estate and make light of their pretensions."

She stepped back and laughed again. All around her the matrons, the débutantes, the young bucks, and older gentlemen laughed with her. Attelweir glared around, confused by their imitation.

Mr. North had not made a joke and they could not possibly have heard what he had said. Why were they laughing?

"What you do not understand," continued Millicent with a smile, whispering again in his ear, as she stalked around his taller form, "is that I have a reputation for outlandish jokes and subtle insults. No one here wishes to admit they cannot hear my joke or that they misunderstood it." She broke off to laugh again, echoed by the crowd – louder and longer. "Tomorrow it will be all about the Ton that I mocked and ridiculed you and you were disgusted at yourself for being destroyed by it."

"I am not disgusted!" cried Attelweir and colored when all near him burst into gales.

From one side of the hall to the other all the guests were looking at them, all laughing and pointing, some near to tears with hilarity. Attelweir turned burning eyes on Millicent who smiled and bowed.

"Your servant, Your Grace." Then Millicent took Beth by the hand. "Let me take you in to the supper room, my dear Lady Beth. I think you need a little sustenance to restore you."

Millicent did not glance behind. She could judge by the stares of those she passed that the other guests continued to watch Attelweir. Lorgnettes turned to follow him as he stalked through the room and away. Out of the corner of her eye she saw the comte and earl hurry after him.

More fool them. In Attelweir's current state, they were likely to receive the toasting that Attelweir was thwarted from raining down on Mr. North.

"He will have his revenge on you," said Beth, leaning heavily on his arm. "Oh, Mr. North, I am so sorry for being so weak. If only I had a stare like Timothy's, I would have sent him away, but I am too young."

"Oh, please Lady Beth, do not worry so. The ducal stare is granted only to the duke. With it he can ignite the coal in the grate when the mood is upon him. If age would grant such a thing, I would have it myself, but, poor, pathetic creature that I am, I cannot even cause a dry leaf to wither."

It was a feeble joke, but Beth chuckled anyway, and straighted her spine. Millicent glanced about and caught the eye of the youth who had alerted her to the problem. A nod of the head was enough to bring – what was his name? – running to draw out a chair for Beth. Millicent studied the room and caught the eye of a few others of Beth's approved court. Within a few minutes the chosen table was filled with chattering young men, flattering and gently teasing Beth into a better frame of mind. Millicent did not think for a moment that Attelweir was permanently routed. She would have to consult with Shoffer and determine the best way to go on.

Chapter Thirteen

Millicent reported the exchange in full to Shoffer that night, waiting in the ducal study until near dawn when Shoffer returned from a night's dissipation. She tried not to feel hurt that Shoffer chose to spend time with other companions when he was supposed to be sleeping off Parliament. While it was a compliment of sorts that he had trusted her with his sister, it hurt to think Shoffer spent time with ladies of a "certain reputation" rather than with Millicent and Beth.

Consequently, Millicent gave a brief report of Attelweir's actions, and stated that Mr. North was available to offer whatever aid was required and departed.

At home she lay sleepless in her bed for hours.

The season was half done and the family sitting at the luncheon table, silent and preoccupied, when Felicity recalled Millicent to her primary responsibility.

"I do not understand it," she said. "We have gentlemen visitors every day, flowers in every room, and still the girls have received no proposals. There is nothing for it, Mr. North, you must increase their dowries and make certain all the gentlemen know about it."

Felicity had not been informed about Millicent's concerns regarding dowries, merely the result, and she had to be prevented from literally putting an announcement in the papers once she had heard about Millicent's solution.

Two girls, pretty and talented with Five Thousand Pounds in the Exchange, to be wed. Apply at Maricourt Place ...

Millicent shuddered to think of it.

"I hardly think that is the way to go on," Millicent glanced down at the plate before her and was surprised to see she was eating fish. Generally, she despised fish. When neither of her sisters spoke she looked around the table. "You are all quiet today."

"Silence is not a crime," said Mildred.

"Oh, I do grant you that, it is just unusual in this house. Perhaps you are all tired. We need not go out every night. It might be as well that we stay at home tonight and be comfortable beside the fire."

"Oh, no," cried Felicity. "Tonight is the Earl of Decrent's ball. We must go for Maude's sake."

Millicent blinked at that information and sat up to regard her youngest sister with interest. "Oh? Am I to expect a visit from a gentleman of that family?"

"I doubt it very much," said Maude stiffly. "You need not put yourself out for me; we can stay home tonight with my blessing. I have no expectations."

"Maude, what are you saying?" said Felicity. "You know very well that the earl's second son has been paying you the most pointed attention." She turned to Millicent. "He danced twice with her at the Henderson's ball and took her in to supper there and last night at the musicale he was most attentive. When we go walking in the park he appears most days to keep us company."

Millicent glanced toward her youngest sister who was studying the contents of her wine glass with particular attention. "I think if we were to ask Maude we would find that the earl's son has been dancing at her heels for longer than a few days. Did you not meet him at your very first ball?"

It took only one glance at Maude's reddened cheeks for Felicity to judge the truth of Millicent's words.

"I wonder why has he not called on you here?" asked Felicity. "He has had enough time, it seems, to be certain of his affections."

Maude declined to answer. To stave off an inquisition from Felicity, Millicent rose from her place at the head of the table and went to sit between her sister and mother and instead asked the necessary questions gently.

"Are you being courted? Are his eyes framed with dark lashes?" teased Millicent. "Do his legs show to good advantage in stockings?"

A dimple appeared in one of Maude's cheeks and she shot a sidelong look toward Millicent. "He looks very fine and is very graceful in the dance."

Millicent leaned a little closer and whispered in Maude's ear. "And how does he kiss? I admit, I am a little jealous that you are the first of us to find out about kissing."

Maude blushed again as Felicity began to cry and fuss. "Kisses? Oh. Oh. The scandal."

"Oh, be still, please," said Mildred, from her place on the other side of the table. "Kisses behind curtains in ballrooms do not a scandal make. It would be more of a scandal, or at least a cause for shame, if we managed to get from one end of the season to the other with neither of us kissed at least once."

"Mildred, how can you be so casual?" demanded Felicity.

"Because I have been at Maude's side at every event, just as you have. I know very well Maude has had no opportunity for truly wicked behavior. And I have been in her confidence. While the earl's son is handsome and an excellent dancer, he is also impoverished. He has come to the conclusion that Maude's dower is far from sufficient for his needs and he has so informed her."

"Oh," cried Millicent, drawing back. "The scoundrel. I shall seek him out and teach him better manners. To say something so unkind to a young lady is unforgivable."

"Oh, no. It was not like that," Maude clutched at Millicent's sleeve. "Please do nothing to him. I know you and the duke could discredit him up and down the whole of town, if you wished. No. I told Mildred that he said how very sad he was he could not pursue a courtship with me however much he might be tempted to. He does not have an independence and cannot keep me as well as I deserve."

"Was this before or after a kiss?" demanded Millicent. When Maude lowered her gaze to the table, Millicent rose and began to pace the room, swearing under her breath.

"Please, Mr. North, do not be cross with him. I am not." Maude pulled a kerchief from her long sleeve and sniffed into it. "I forgive him. He is not responsible for his secondary status or his family's lack of estate. But I would prefer not to discuss the matter and I would rather go to a different entertainment tonight."

"You are too disinterested." Millicent paused in her pacing and turned to face her other sister. "And you, Mildred. Am I to expect a caller on your behalf?"

"No."

Felicity and Millicent exchanged a glance.

"No? Just no," said Millicent. "I am certain that is not so. Surely, I have seen you with a half dozen bucks dancing attendance upon you each evening."

Mildred shook her head. "They are no one of consequence."

"Now I am confused. I would have thought from your manner that you found them pleasing. Has no one engaged your affection?"

This time Mildred did not answer. Maude, happy to have the family's attention on someone else, leapt into the fray.

"Oh, ho. Silence speaks loudest. Mildred has a beau!"

"She has not," declared Mildred, with some heat. "She has no such thing and is in expectation of remaining … alone."

"Come, Mildred," demanded Millicent. "I must know. Have you met someone?"

"I have met several people."

Millicent waited for more and when there were no words forthcoming, again began pacing. "This is impossible. Have you forgotten you can confide in me? Mildred? Am I so changed that I am unworthy of whispered secrets?"

There was stunned silence from the three women, then Felicity, for a change, shook herself as if coming out of a trance and laughed. "You cannot be cross that your disguise has worked so well. Are you truly shocked that we keep feminine secrets from you, the man of the house? I thought that was the objective!"

Mildred and Maude began to giggle. Millicent stopped and crossed her hands over her chest.

"And now you do look as stern and cross as Papa used to," observed Maude.

"I now understand his reasons," muttered Millicent.

"Sit down and eat, Mr. North," commanded Felicity, amused at Millicent's frustration.

Millicent stood for a moment completely stunned, then burst out laughing. When she regained her composure, Mildred smiled upon her sister.

"I am sorry, dear. You have been out and about dealing with the tenants, making money, and other such masculine things and I have not had a chance for a long coze with you for months. I have come to rely more on Maude in your absence."

"I suppose I have only myself to blame. Please forgive me, I have been neglecting you." Millicent sighed. "I have been busy, but that does not mean I do not want to know if some young buck has caught your eye. For both masculine and feminine reasons."

"Not a young buck," said Mildred softly. "A gentleman."

"Oh?" Felicity, Maude, and Millicent all leaned forward eagerly.

"Do tell," commanded Millicent.

"If you must know…"

"Yes," came the chorus.

"Mr. Simpson," whispered Mildred, then she blushed.

"Who?" cried Felicity and Maude.

"Mr. Simpson," cried Millicent. "The duke's private secretary and creator of miracles, that Mr. Simpson? When did you meet him?"

Mildred gave her sister a look of mixed amusement and disdain. "Mr. North, you sent him to me yourself."

Millicent stared at her in confusion. "When?"

"The coaches, Mr. North. The coaches. Mr. Simpson appeared one morning with four coaches, complete with drivers and outriders and demanded someone must make a decision. Since Mr. North declared that the ladies of the house were going to use them, the ladies must decide. Four secondhand coaches cluttering up Maricourt Place, with all the staff of our neighborhood sitting on the steps and staring, while Mr. Simpson and I climbed in and out of the wretched things examining the fixtures and commenting on the squabs."

"Oh, dear God," Millicent covered her face. She could well imagine the disruption four complete coaches could create in their small and fashionable square. Poor Mildred, the subject of those stares. "You did not say anything at the time. Just that we had a coach."

"It was nothing." Mildred shrugged and tried to return her attention to her food.

"Obviously, it was something."

Mildred threw down her napkin in disgust. "Very well, it was. It was the merest hint of interest. It was noticing that the gentleman has nice eyes, that he spoke to the servants kindly no matter how impatient they were. It was the slightest thought crossing my mind that I would like to speak to him again and judge if it were possible, if the acquaintance persisted, that I might conceivably enjoy his company."

Maude choked on her wine while Millicent and Felicity frankly stared.

"That is a good deal of words to describe a bare interest," said Millicent.

"Well, it was not as if I was in his company for more than a quarter hour."

"You were out for over two hours," declared Maude. "And when you came in you were blushing to your toes."

"The wind was chill. I had been exercised climbing in and out of coaches."

"Now, girls!" Felicity raised one hand and both sisters subsided back into their chairs.

"Well," said Millicent. "I may not be about to do anything about the penurious son of an earl, but I can do something about Mr. Simpson. Cousin Felicity, dear, please ring the bell."

"What? What will you do?" cried Mildred, rising as Felicity rang the little silver bell at her elbow.

"Why, I can arrange for you to spend a few minutes furthering your acquaintance with Mr. Simpson." When Merit appeared Millicent beckoned the butler nearer. "Be so kind as to send a footman over to the Duke of Trolenfield's residence. Present my compliments to Mr. Simpson, his secretary, and ask him if he will do me the honor of taking a cup of coffee with me this evening."

Merit bowed himself out. Millicent observed that the butler glowed as he left the room. Any opportunity to communicate with the household of the duke fairly made his day.

"So glad I can make someone happy," she muttered.

"Milli ... Mr. North, you cannot send for him. I will not allow it."

"How can you stop me? The message is already sent."

"I will not see him. It would be too humiliating. I will stay upstairs."

Millicent again regarded her fish, sniffed it suspiciously, and set the plate aside. "It is not humiliating. It is merely coffee. The Duke of Trolenfield has asked his secretary to hold himself available should I happen to need something, and tonight I have decided to need his company."

"Well, you cannot tell him you need a husband for me!" Mildred came to her feet.

"How ignorant do you think I am?" Millicent laughed. "Dear Mildred, I am only providing you the opportunity to decide if further acquaintance ... I do not remember what you said exactly, but you wanted another opportunity to examine him. Therefore, I provide it. It is my duty to provide what you need."

"But what will you say when he comes?"

"I will think of something."

Mr. Simpson arrived promptly at six. He first made his bow to Mildred, seated beside the coffee service.

"Ah, Miss. Boarder. I do hope the coach you selected is giving satisfaction."

"It has four wheels and does not turn over," said Millicent before her sister could reply. "What else do we need?"

Mildred granted Millicent a frosty stare that would have done credit to the highest stickler of the Ton.

"Mr. North has no understanding, and since he would walk from engagement to engagement if we were to permit it, he sees no need for the carriage." Mildred offered Mr. Simpson a plate of cakes and a smile. "The ladies of the house, on the other hand, are very grateful for your assistance."

"My pleasure."

Millicent found herself staring at the familiar face of Shoffer's trusted secretary. The man was hardly handsome by conventional measures and she could not tell by examination of his features if he were worthy of being trusted with her sister's future. Would he turn into a drunkard as years passed? Would he be short-tempered and intolerant of the noise children made? As if suddenly aware of her thoughts, Mr. Simpson turned and gave Millicent a weak smile.

"His Grace asked me to apologize for his neglect the last few days. He has been busy with parliamentary business."

That startled Millicent who missed him dreadfully, but had not thought gentlemen offered each other apologies.

"Oh, has he neglected us? I hardly noticed. But then, we can hardly expect such a high ranked gentleman to be always dancing attendance upon us." Millicent shrugged as if she were not painfully aware of each of the hours and minutes since last she had seen him. Of the hours spent speculating on with whom he had spent those hours and minutes. On the possibility that he had set up a mistress or was seriously courting some young woman out of Millicent's sight. "Please tell His Grace that we continue to go on as planned. Lady Beth is happily escorting my cousins about town and they have come over quite popular, if the number of invitations on my desk is any indication."

"His Grace will be gratified. Now, what service may I provide you?"

Mildred winced and almost spilt scalding coffee over her guest's hand. Her agitation was understandable since Millicent had teased her all afternoon, claiming that she was going to announce that she needed someone to take Mildred off her hands, would Mr. Simpson have any opinions to offer? After all, he was so efficient in finding a house and carriage, would husbands be that much more difficult?

Given that Millicent's humor was unpredictable, Mildred was still not certain what she would say.

Neither was Millicent.

She had been so busy that afternoon that she had put aside any thought of the excuse she would use hoping to be struck by inspiration.

Fortunately, Mildred had her own plans.

"Mr. North, nipfarthing though he is, has granted us permission to host some form of entertainment, provided we do not beggar him in the process," she said.

Mr. Simpson raised both eyebrows. "I hardly think I am the best person to ask for advice in such matters."

"You are the only person we know, Mr. Simpson, that we can ask," continued Mildred. "After all, you selected this house, which is far too small and lacking a ballroom for traditional Tonnish entertainment. We were hoping you would be able to suggest an assembly hall or some such we could hire."

Millicent groaned, all in the interest of staying in character, she told herself. To her surprise Mr. Simpson did not turn to her in male sympathy, but continued to concentrate on Mildred. Millicent found her own eyebrows rising. Could it be that Mr. Simpson returned her sister's interest?

"We have been offered such kindness by the hostesses of the Ton and it would be impolite to consume without offering reciprocation," continued Mildred.

"Impolite, but inexpensive," muttered Millicent and was ignored.

"A rental hall is not that unprecedented," said Mr. Simpson, "since not all houses have the necessary facilities. Some hostesses take over the pleasure gardens for the evening, but I would not recommend that since it is generally regarded as a low class sort of entertainment with many opportunities for scandalous behavior."

"Oh, no, of course not." Mildred's gasp was suitably shocked.

"Might I suggest an afternoon tea party? A picnic at one of the public gardens. An area can be reserved..." Mr. Simpson glanced toward Millicent. "At a reasonable rent."

"And extra servants and food and tea," muttered Millicent. "And new dresses and hats."

"And an open carriage in which to arrive," added Mildred.

"And parasols for when it rains," shot back Millicent.

"I would recommend pavilions for the tea area itself, with both inside and outdoor seating, should the weather be unfavorable." Mr. Simpson directed a smile to Mildred. "I would be honored to assist you with arranging the rentals."

"Thank you, Mr. Simpson, but I simply could not take up so much of your time," Mildred blushed and lowered her eyes. "If you would just direct me to the most reliable providers."

"Oh, no. No trouble at all. It would be my pleasure."

Millicent threw up her hands at that point. Mr. Simpson, it appeared, was as taken with her sister as her sister was with him. And the upshot was Millicent was going to have to pay for a party, and eventually, a wedding.

Fortunately, Mr. Simpson already knew how small a portion Mildred would have for a dowry. Since he was employed by the duke it was likely that for a wedding gift, Shoffer would grant him a small house for Mildred to occupy to begin her wedded life. Millicent could count on Simpson having well paid employment lifelong and a reasonable exposure to country society for Mildred to enjoy.

While Mr. Simpson and Mildred moved across the room to the escritoire to begin making lists for the party, Millicent began totting up in her mind the expenses of Mildred's future life. Perhaps the amount in the Exchange could be added to annually? A gift for each child?

Mr. Simpson did not leave until quite late. Millicent escorted him to the door.

"I understand from His Grace, he intends to go to White's after escorting Lady Beth to Almack's tonight." Mr. Simpson paused in the process of pulling on his gloves. "He did say something about applying to the patronesses for vouchers for your sisters."

"I wish I had known," said Millicent, "I would have begged he would not. An evening at home is not to be sneezed at. I find myself looking forward to Wednesdays."

"Well, if you wish to find him, that is where he shall be. You are well enough known now, Mr. North, that if you were to go to White's some other fellow might escort you in."

"I have no intention of hanging about outside White's like some ill-mannered dog banned from the house for chewing rugs with my nose pressed to the window waiting to be let back in. Tomorrow is soon enough to talk with Shoffer."

Mr. Simpson gave her an odd look, but shook her hand without comment and departed. Millicent watched Mildred float up the stairs, her eyes glowing with the twin joys of becoming a society hostess and the promise of future meetings with Mr. Simpson to plan the details of her party. Sighing, Millicent retreated to her study.

She had no idea how other land owners managed during the season. Despite her efforts during the summer months to see to the properties and the conviction that once the harvest was in she could rest until next year, letters continued to arrive from her various tenants. Roofs, it seemed, waited until winter to leak, stock chose the worst weather to become ill, mines to flood. With her night hours caught up with taking her sisters about to Tonnish events, the days spent visiting shops, Millicent found she had little time to manage those things that made the others possible. And, all the time in the back of her mind was the worry that one day her stewardship would be judged insufficient, the money would run out, and her deception would all be for naught.

After all, she was a young lady under this masculine clothing. With every letter that brought another potential farming disaster to her attention came the fear that she was missing something important. Something Mr. North, as the true heir to all this knew and she, as his mere secretary, had never learned.

Millicent settled at her desk reading and rereading her correspondence. She did not hear the clock ticking and chiming the hours of the night, nor the knock at the door that had one of her footmen shuffling to answer.

Shoffer's voice, however, was enough to penetrate her concentration.

"I saw the lights still on downstairs. Are the family still awake?"

"Mr. North is in his study," came the sleepy reply. "The ladies are abed."

"If you would inquire…"

By that point Millicent was out of her chair, through the door, and facing Shoffer.

"Your Gracefulness, I did not think to see you tonight. Did Almack's close its doors forever? Is White's out of brandy? Come in. Come in and be comfortable. Is there anything you need?"

She could not wait to welcome him into her study. These were the times she enjoyed the most. Not those times when they walked and talked at balls, or explored London, but the quiet times seated near a fireplace. Shoffer's face and body at rest, slumped in one chair while Millicent watched and admired and lusted from the other. These times when she alone held his attention. She did not need to be silly or strive to entertain him. Despite her disguise, these were the times when she was most herself and he was most desirable. Sometimes he would discard coat and cravat and she would be blessed with a rare opportunity to admire his form. She would watch his well-shaped lips form words and bathe her soul in the warmth of his voice and no one was the wiser.

Never for any money would she permit him to know her thoughts on such occasions. The heat filling her nether regions, melting her in that mysterious way, making her feel empty and hungry, was her own private pleasure and agony.

"We could not be so lucky," said Shoffer wearily. "Almack's survives still. No, I provided Beth with escort there and took her home and now I was thinking to spend the evening at one of my clubs. I thought you might wish to come along. It is past time you gave up your solitary ways and joined one or two. Boodle's, perhaps. I am certain the gentlemen there would enjoy your conversation and company. I would be pleased to put your name forward. You need to make more friends than just myself, North."

"Hardly that," Millicent looked closely into his dear face. It hardly seemed possible that she could love him more when she saw him less, but that was the truth. He did look tired, even sad. "You do not look your usual self, Shoffer. Was Almack's legendary lemonade worse than usual? Did you dance with every young lady and wear out your shoes?"

Shoffer sighed and glanced toward the footman currently leaning against the wall outside with eyes half closed.

"No, this cannot be avoided. I wish a private word with you, North."

Millicent could feel the blood draining from her face. Whatever had happened to make Shoffer stern?

"Go to bed, James," she said to the footman. "I shall find the brandy for His Grace."

"I do not need brandy, thank you."

The footman shambled off, too tired to remember to bow. Once the study door was shut Shoffer refused a chair and every other courtesy Millicent offered, choosing instead to stand, hands clasped behind his back, staring into the fireplace. Millicent hovered behind him.

Shoffer struggled to unclench his jaw. The words he needed to say sealed his mouth. Gossip at the clubs had intensified over the last few days. The betting books contained all manner of subtly phrased bets. Now it was not only that North would be revealed as a person of degenerate morals, but the location and who else would be caught as his partner in crime was being discussed. No one dared to name Shoffer as yet, although the look in some of the Ton elders' eyes hinted that speculation was rife.

Shoffer was forced to bite his tongue and ignore the looks, the snickers, and an unsubtle hint from one old roué that he would be happy to join him in his frolics.

He did not, could not, *would* not believe it true. He knew the rumors were not true of himself and North was an innocent, ignorant of the worse debaucheries of the world and Shoffer had no wish to be the person who ruined the virginity of his mind.

And yet he could not permit North to go wandering about in society unaware of the rumors that chased him. It occurred to him that if North was better known by his fellow gentlemen then the rumors would die. Who meeting North would think him capable of such a thing? Yes, he was a silly rattle. Yes, he found more opportunities to jest than seemed reasonable, but no, he was not degenerate in his person, opinions, or actions. A truly honorable, gentle, man.

Shoffer himself with rank to support and protect him was safe, but North was a mere country gentlemen and his cousins, ordinary misses, were particularly vulnerable to the worst damage gossip could cause.

Something had to be done, and soon, else the family would be cut from all good society.

"Shoffer? Your Grace?" There was a note in North's voice that tore Shoffer's conscience. "If I have offended…"

"No. No, North, you have not offended." Shoffer turned to face his friend. "It is not you. It is the gossips of the Ton. Purulent minds who see in innocent friendship degenerate intentions."

Those words set North back on his heels. "I have no understanding of what you are saying."

"I am certain that you do not and I wish I were not the one tasked with delivering this information, yet I cannot permit you to go on as you, as we, are!"

To Shoffer's shock he saw a hint of tears forming in North's eyes that were rapidly blinked away.

"We? What have *we* done? Has some father objected to our dancing with his precious daughter? Have my cousins done anything they ought not?"

"It is not their daughters they fear for, North, but their sons."

"My cousins have not attempted to trap any gentleman into an unwelcome alliance."

Shoffer grimaced and shook his head.

"Not your cousins. You."

"What?" North shook his head. "I have not challenged any young man to a duel or tried to separate one from his sweetheart. What harm could I have done?"

His astonishment, his confusion were so sincere that Shoffer felt his heart lifting. From the first moment he heard the rumors he feared that someone saw something that Shoffer did not. North's manners were so odd that it was possible … but, no! There were foppish dandies aplenty who wandered about the Ton without scandal with odder mannerisms than North's. It was not possible it was true.

And now, North's protests were so innocent, it could only be that he was, in fact, innocent!

Shoffer let out a weak chuckle and pointed to the chair on the other side of the fireplace and waited until North was seated before he sank into its twin.

"My de … Mr. North, I am sorry to be the one to advise you on a subject that should not have to be raised, but there is a rumor going about that you and I … that we spend so much time together … that we are closer friends than we should be."

"But why? I may not have rank, but I am a gentleman. The North family tree can be traced back to Henry's time. And I am not so far beneath you in income, either."

"None of that matters, North. It has been suggested that our friendship is…" Shoffer sought about for a polite way to phrase it, "of an *illegal* nature."

"Oh?" said North. "Illegal? How can friendship be … oh. Oh!" His eyes widened and a deep blush overspread his cheeks. "Oh!"

"Yes, indeed. Oh."

The high color fled North's face as fast as it filled it leaving him white with shock. North went to clutch Shoffer's hand but halted, then backed away. Shoffer grieved for the gesture that spoke volumes more for the injury he had inflicted than any amount of blood shed.

"Your Grace," cried North when he had recovered his voice, "you know this is not true!"

"Of course, North. But that is beyond the point. The accusation has more weight than truth." The worst of the news out and now his own soul satisfied that it was not true, Shoffer relaxed. "I suspect the story is being put about by Attelweir as revenge for my separating him from any hope of gaining Beth's dowry. It is just the sort of foul thing that he would do."

North did not comment, but stared blank faced into the fire.

"I heard the story a few days ago," continued Shoffer, "which is why I have absented myself from your company, but I did not think I could continue to stay away without giving you some sort of warning. A few foolish souls of the Ton might begin to cut you and your cousins, and you cannot defend yourself unless you know what sort of gossip is going around."

That was enough to bring up North's head.

"I have noticed no one cutting me. Mildred and Maude have not reported anything and I have seen no drop off in invitations. Do you think we shall have some invitations withdrawn?"

"Perhaps. I hope not."

"I see. Thank you, Shoffer, but if there is any risk of harm to Beth … may the girls still call upon her? I should not go with them. Or perhaps we should leave London."

"No. No, that you cannot do. To disappear from society would give the impression that you are guilty. That would do more harm than you could imagine. It is only necessary that you and I be less in each other's pockets."

North attempted to raise his eyebrow, an attempt which drew a reluctant laugh from Shoffer.

"Gentlemen travel about with each other all the time," protested North. "Is it because I cannot claim that I went to Eton with you or to Cambridge that I am unworthy of your company?"

"No! It is more that gentlemen tend to travel in larger groups, or with more variety of companions. These last few weeks, it is said, that one cannot see one of us without the other. That is the only fuel this fire has. Do not take this to heart, North. It is a comment on my actions as well as yours. Usually when I come down for Parliament, I make choosing and setting up a mistress one of my earliest actions. This year I have been so caught up with advancing Beth's cause that I have neglected that task."

"My cousins and I have taken up much of your time as well."

"And I regret none of it, North. Believe that. If it were not for Attelweir, then this rumor would not have started. However, now that it has it is necessary for us to adjust our arrangements. In addition to seeing less of each other I think it important that we both choose and set up a mistress. If you require any assistance…"

North blushed. "Enough! Good God, please, I beg you stop! Your Grace, say nothing more! This is one subject on which I will not accept your advice."

Shoffer laughed and raised his hands. "I do apologize."

North's expression was particularly pained and embarrassed and for a moment Shoffer speculated about North's experience with women. Surely, a gentleman so popular with the ladies would have been intimate by now … surely. Then again, maybe not. North was too kind a man, too honorable to debauch a virgin and too respectful of others' feelings to chase after another man's wife. Whatever North's arrangements were it would not do to embarrass the poor man to suggest he was unable to establish a relationship. That he was still a virgin at his advanced age of four and twenty.

"Very well, I shall leave you to it, North. As for me, I shall find an occupant for my house in Wesley Square."

"Wesley Square?"

"I maintain a house there for my mistress, whoever she is. It is being wasted this year with no occupant."

"You will find an occupant so easily?"

"I am a duke." There was no modesty in the statement, but no arrogance, either. It was merely truth.

"And Ton gatherings? Shall we divide up the duties of attending your sister and my cousins? Shall you send me a note telling me which events you will be attending so that I may know not to go? Or should I stay at home until the gossip dies away?"

"Heavens, no! You are popular yet with the hostesses with your nonsense. It is just we should behave toward each other with less ... less..."

"Less," repeated North, downcast. "Yes, I see."

"And during the day you should try to develop more friendships. Gather some fellows about you. Let there be more than just myself who benefits from your company. I keep urging you to join a club or two and go about gambling and such as is appropriate for a man of your station."

"I understand," said North in as solemn and soft a voice as Shoffer had ever heard the man use.

"We shall continue to be friends."

North rose to his feet, his hands behind his back and chin high. "I appreciate all you have done to make my entry into good society as easy as it has been and I shall do all in my power to quell these rumors that snap at the heels of your good name. With that in mind, I think you should go and be seen yourself about town tonight. Go to a brothel, find yourself a woman, find ten and prove your vigor!"

The last was said with some heat.

"North!"

"I apologize," said Millicent, after a moment, and forced her hands to unclench. "You have been everything that is noble and kind and I am ashamed for my part in this embarrassment."

"It is not your fault, my friend."

Millicent closed her eyes and tried to calm her ragged breathing. "What is to be done?" she cried, ashamed to hear her voice travel up into her feminine register. Coughing she covered her face, half of her hoping Shoffer did not notice her slip and the other desperately hoping he had.

"For myself," said Shoffer, "I shall be attending Lady Algrieve's Venetian Masque tomorrow. It is the ideal place to find a lady with whom to behave badly."

Millicent winced at the thought of Shoffer with another woman, but her responsibilities held her in a prison of her own making. Her honor might be battered. Society in general might despise her as a degenerate, but she would continue on as Mr. North. Gathering her courage she turned to face the man who held her heart and said the most painful words she had ever thought to utter.

"You should not be here at this hour of the night, Your Grace. Stay away from me. Your welfare, and that of dear Lady Beth, are more important to me than you can know, so I beg you, stay away!"

Shoffer gathered himself stiffly and bowed.

"Call upon me if you have any great need."

"I suspect I shall be busy elsewhere for some time," said Millicent, "and have no expectation of needing any aid."

"As you wish."

Millicent rang the bell summoning the footman from his rest.

"I think a witness to your departure is required," she murmured.

"As you wish. Good night, North."

"Go away, Duke of Trolenfield!" whispered Millicent, but only once the door closed behind him. "Go away and never come back."

Chapter Fourteen

There was no justice in the universe, decided Millicent, as she watched the minutes of the night drag past. If she had not been so miserable, she might have found the situation funny.

Tears had been shed in good measure and now she was in a dreadful state of exhaustion and self-pity. She wished, begged for, sleep to swamp her and allow her an escape from the pain in her heart

It was unjust.

She, Millicent Boarder, loved the Duke of Trolenfield, but could not have him. Never touch or dance with him. Never flirt with, or heaven help her, kiss him. Never taste him. Painful though it was to be near him, she bore that burden; she accepted it as the price she paid to be Mr. Anthony North and provide for her mother and sisters.

Now to be accused of a criminal love for him and to be banished from his presence was beyond cosmic irony. In truth, she had committed a crime that would justify hanging if she were found out, but not the crime of which the Ton suspected her. That society gossiped about.

She lay buried under layers of pillows and duvets as the dawn light crept into the room. The breakfast bell rang elsewhere in the building and was ignored. Indeed, she did not move until late morning when Mildred barreled into the chamber and pulled the blankets down off the bed and onto the floor.

"Mildred, that is hardly proper. This is a gentleman's bedchamber, after all." Millicent seized her blankets and hauled them back over her head.

"A gentleman who has kept the women of his household waiting a full hour past when he promised to take them to Bond Street."

"You have clothing already," mumbled Millicent.

"I told you, I need a few new walking dresses and a pelisse. If I am going to be walking out in the park with Mr. Simpson, I wish to impress him. I cannot be wearing the same costume always."

"You cannot be buying different outfits always. He may flee you judging you to be too expensive for his pocket."

Mildred again pulled the blankets off.

"You promised to take us shopping, Mr. North. Come, it is not as if you are keeping the money to spend on yourself!"

Groaning, Millicent sat upright and ran one hand over her swollen eyes. "I will have you know it takes a great deal of effort to appear this shabby."

"Effort? Yes. Money? No. Come along. The late Mr. North proved you cannot take it with you when you die so we may as well spend it now." Mildred opened the curtains and turned to face her sister. "Good heavens, you look dreadful."

"Thank you so very much." Millicent swung her legs out of bed and staggered over to the wash basin to splash water on her aching eyes.

"What have you been doing? Have you taken to drink?"

Reluctant to discuss Shoffer's revelations of the previous night Mildred settled for a different truth. "Reading letters from my tenants. Roofs that leak, ill stock. All manner of bad luck that must be put before the landlord. It seems not one day goes by that I do not receive a letter complaining of unexpected expense that I must take a share in."

"You know," said Mildred, tugging at her lip, "it could be they lie to reduce their rents unfairly thinking you young and inexperienced."

"Of course, I am aware of that," snapped Millicent. "But as the only way I can be certain is to visit and see for myself..."

She paused and considered. That might be a solution. Some time away would give the gossips time to find another scandal to latch onto. Time for Shoffer to find a mistress. She closed her eyes and pressed her hand against her chest. The thought of Shoffer loving another woman was agony. Mildred caught the look of pain that crossed Millicent's face and took her by the arm.

"Millicent, are you unwell? Truly, you do not look yourself."

"That is because I am Mr. North and you should not be in my room."

Mildred was not to be put off. "How may I help?"

Smiling slightly Millicent shook her head. "No, dear. If you would but go downstairs to wait, I shall be with you shortly. I beg you; have coffee sent up while I dress."

"If you truly are unwell, you need not accompany us..."

"Only I should send my pocket with you?" Millicent turned and headed into her dressing room. "Fear not, fair cousin. I shall be dressed and downstairs in but a moment."

Millicent spent the day trailing her female relatives from shop to shop in a perfect imitation of a much put upon, bored male, if she but knew it. It was not until they were in the fourth modiste's shop that she revived a little. An evening gown of honey brown colored silk with ivory lace upon the bodice and trailing down from the high waist in a demi train adorned a dressmaker's form in the center of the waiting room. Her interest caught, Millicent wandered across to stroke the cap sleeve between her fingers.

"I like this one," she murmured, then raised her voice. "Do you not agree, cousin? This is beautiful."

"Do not be silly, Mr. North," said Felicity, glancing across. "That will never do for the girls. This season they may only wear white and I do not wear brown."

Millicent shook herself out of her preoccupation. Of course it would not do for her sisters. They were honey blonds themselves and this color of silk would make their hair appear washed out. In truth the colors suited the late Millicent's darker hair and stronger features. Noting the modiste's attention Millicent stepped back and regarded the dress from the side.

"They will not always be in débutante white."

"Really, Mr. North," said Felicity, "allow me to know what will and will not suit my daughters."

"I know someone it would suit," murmured Millicent, but Felicity was no longer listening.

Once Felicity and the girls were tucked away in dressing rooms the modiste appeared at Millicent's side.

"If you wish, sir," she said in a low voice, "you might send your lady friend around. This dress was commissioned by another, but not completely paid. If you pay the balance you may have it at a discount. I would be discreet and not tell your lady friend the price. She will regard you as generous once she sees the quality of the lace."

Millicent stammered and blushed even as her mind raced. The modiste thought she was shopping for a mistress!

Shoffer had suggested she set up a mistress. She could not! There were undeniable physical reasons why she could not. After a pause, Millicent smiled at the modiste. She could create the illusion of one. A few purchases here and there might do the trick. After all, what was one more lie?

Reaching into her pocket, Millicent drew out a handful of coins. "If you would package it up, I shall take it with me. The … uh … her lady's maid can make what adjustments are necessary."

With a reluctant nod, the modiste whisked the dress form away and returned shortly thereafter with an innocent appearing bundle. She gave Millicent a knowing look which again set her to blushing. No doubt she looked a fool, but if she were lucky, the modiste would gossip up and down Bond Street that the famous Mr. North was seen buying clothing for a lady who was not his cousin.

On their return home Millicent was pleased to see that, as yet, there was no fall off of invitations. A respectable pile adorned Merit's silver salver. They adjourned to the family parlor for tea and reviewed the latest.

"Lady Peling requests the honor of our company for an evening of cards," read Maude. "She especially desires the presence of Mr. North."

"For cards?" asked Millicent. "Hardly. I enjoy the company of my money too much."

"An evening of music with the Forthingtons on Friday next," read Mildred. "The daughters of the family will be performing on harp and pianoforte. Mr. North is expected."

"Never," said Felicity. "The Forthington girls will expect to have the attention of any males there as reward for their labors. Attending would be a waste of time."

"I do not know," said Millicent. "Can they play their instruments with skill?"

"That hardly matters," replied Felicity.

"Oh, look at this. The Countess Greylin is having a small gathering of friends this evening," Maude clapped her hands. "We must go."

"Rather late to be sending an invitation," remarked Mildred. "Why did she wait?"

Millicent glanced up from a puzzling calling card Merit had handed to her separate from the invitations. A lawyer, Mr. Johansen, had called that afternoon while she was out and left it. On the back was a request for an appointment at Mr. North's convenience, but no reason was given. Millicent tossed it onto the side table when Maude called for her attention.

"What is it, dear Maude?"

"Countess Greylin's gathering, Mr. North. We must go."

"I thought we were going to the Hendrickson's ball." Millicent paused. Actually, there was good reason not to go. How had Shoffer phrased it? They should not be in each other's pockets.

"We can go later," cried Maude, "but we must go to Countess Greylin's."

"Why ever for?"

"Because she is dear friends with two of Almack's patronesses and they are sure to be there."

"Almack's." Millicent groaned, rolling her eyes. "My dear, you cannot be serious."

"Why ever not? Do you not think we are worthy of Almack's?"

"You are too good for that place. I am too good for that place. There are mudlarks along the banks of the Thames too…"

"We shall go to Greylin's," declared Felicity, "but, Mr. North, it would be better that you did not. If the girls are to have a chance to impress the patronesses with their style and sophistication they cannot do so when you are wittering on and joking about."

"I cannot think why you should want to go to that place. Do you not receive sufficient invitations? Are you not welcomed by the Duke of Trolenfield and his sister?"

"You are right, Mr. North; we have nothing to complain of," said Mildred, "but it would be nice, when we are old and grey, to be able to bore our grandchildren with tales of our come out, and if we can include Almack's in the list of our adventures, we shall be happy."

Millicent groaned and covered her face. "Do what you will. I have work to do."

"Mr. North, I do wish you would not refer to work," said Felicity, rising. "It whiffs too much of trade. Say rather that you are consulting with your man of business."

Millicent thought for a moment of the laundry and floors they had scrubbed, the food they had prepared, but refrained from reminding her mother of their time as servants.

"I do not have a man of business."

"Then you should get one. Consult with that nice Mr. Simpson when next he comes to call about how to get one. Come girls, we should choose your gowns for tonight, then rest."

The ladies of the house withdrew leaving Millicent scowling at an empty room. It was, perhaps, a good idea for the girls to come out from under Lady Beth's social wing and establish their own circle. It might be a ring or two down from such rarefied heights, but more suited to Millicent's pocket and their mother's connections.

It also would probably be good for Millicent to put the story about that she must go and see to some of her properties. While Felicity might fuss about *work,* any sensible male of the Ton would know that tenants must be supervised or the rental incomes would decrease.

She could put it about that she was leaving town for a few days only, then decide if it were worth her while to return. The season had but a few weeks left to run. Felicity, or Mildred, rather, could manage the house quite well in Mr. North's absence.

Rising, she retreated to her study to create a list of problems. For the better part they were niggly things that could be dealt with by letter. None of them justified leaving in the middle of the season. Well, that was neither here nor there. She needed an excuse; this would do. She did not need to state what the "great emergency" was that drew her away from the season's entertainments.

A knock at her door shattered her concentration. Merit paused at the door, a half-opened paper wrapped bundle in hand.

"Ah, sir. The ladies inform me that this dress was added to their purchases in error."

"Really?" Millicent accepted the bundle, turned down a corner, then blushed. It was the gold-brown gown she had bought to create the illusion of a mistress.

Merit, seeing the blush, nodded and dropped his voice to a confiding murmur.

"In future, sir, it would be best to have the modiste deliver items for *other* ladies directly to them. It does not do to let your lady relatives find you are purchasing clothing for … ahem … from the same modiste they themselves patronize. They tend to be put out."

"Oh. Thank you."

"And the lawyer, Mr. Johansen, has called again. Are you in?" Merit offered the card on his salver.

"No. Why is he calling?" Millicent accepted the card and was scowling at it when Merit continued.

"Will you be going out this evening, sir?"

"Oh." Millicent tightened her grip on her bundle. "Well, the ladies are … that is, they will need the carriage. I … have not decided. I may."

The look Merit bestowed upon her could only be described as sympathetic.

"So Mrs. Boarder informed me. However, a gentleman cannot always be in the company of his family. If you wish a note taken around, with the parcel, I can send one of the footmen. Though you may not be aware of the way things are managed here in London, generally it is wise to take one's butler into one's confidence. I shall need to know your lady friend's name and address to better serve you."

Millicent tightened her grip on the bundle.

"No, thank you, Merit. I shall deliver it myself and take care of any necessary communications. After the ladies have departed."

"Yes, sir."

Merit vanished and Millicent sank back, eyes closed.

Her butler thought her a scattered and inexperienced virgin. Male virgin. Gossip was that she was a shameless, what, catamite? Her best friend was afraid to appear in public with her unless she possessed a mistress that everyone knew about.

If her life became any more complicated, she was going to go screaming mad and retire to either a nunnery or a monastery, she could not decide which.

Maybe she should have accepted the advice Shoffer offered on how to choose a mistress. Except then he might continue to ask her about her success in that field. Would know if she had created an agreement with the woman he had suggested. A heated blush filled her face. It did not bear thinking on. Even a false mistress was too much of a complication.

Package in hand Millicent retreated to her room and prepared to toss the damned thing into the back of her armoire; but, then she halted. The dress was particularly fine and did not deserve to be treated so shabbily.

Alone in her room Millicent unwrapped the parcel, held it up, and admired the image of herself draped in soft, glowing silk in the pier glass.

Felicity was right. It was not a color that would do for her sisters, but for the late Millicent, it would have been perfect. Millicent, dead as far as the world was concerned for the last ten months, had not attended a ball, nor worn a dress this fine, nor danced with a duke. And that would never happen.

Millicent cast the dress onto her bed. She was no fool and had no wish to hang for the crime of stealing her late cousin's name, fortune, and life.

It was time to leave London, but she was going to entertain herself on her last evening here on her own terms. She could go and make one last splash as Mr. North. Be as entertaining as some hostesses required. Be seen publically without the duke. Be remembered as the Ton's favorite fool.

But she would not.

Be damned all of them. The rumor going around suggested not only that Mr. North was attracted to the Duke of Trolenfield, but had acted on that attraction. Her stomach burned as she paced in her study. The hell with them. How could they taint the love that she held for Shoffer in that way? She blinked rapidly to clear her eyes of tears of rage and loss.

Shoffer would never, ever think of his friend Mr. North in that fashion but … she paused and pressed a fist against her chest … but under these ill-fitting clothes was one deeply unhappy woman who hungered for an opportunity to experience that love. If she left now, like as not, she would carry a torch lifelong for the duke. He had never seen her as a woman and had not had the opportunity to snub her, as she deserved. If he had, maybe in the fullness of time her heart would heal. Her chin firmed and tilted up. But, perhaps, he would not. In that beautiful gown upstairs Millicent Boarder would be the equal of any lady of the Ton – if she could remember a lady's graces. Her lip twisted. Well, probably not, but like Cinderella's ugly stepsisters, she would like to hazard her chance at winning the heart of the prince.

The duke had stated his intention of honoring Lady Algrieve's Venetian masque with his presence. And hence, would go Millicent.

She smiled at her folly even as she charged up the stairs. Like as not she would be a wallflower at this event since there would be no one to provide an introduction. Even so, to wear a soft gown and gloves again was beyond temptation. This was her chance, possibly her last chance, to be a woman. To dance and to flirt. Possibly to be admired.

Possibly with Shoffer.

Oh, God, please let it be Shoffer who danced with her!

She pressed the heels of her hands against her eyes even as she acknowledged that impossible hope.

There was no way of knowing if she would catch his eye for even an instant. More likely, she would huddle behind a potted plant with the other wallflowers and watch him dance and flirt with shameless widows and other accommodating women.

Perhaps she should not go.

Clenching her hands into fists so tight her nails dug into her palms, she stood and scolded herself. She was no coward. At no time this year had she drawn back from any action in the defense and support of her family.

This she would do for herself!

In future, during the season, Mr. North would stay at one of his country properties. Felicity and the girls, now established with friends amongst the hostesses of the Ton, would be able to go about without his governance.

Mr. North and family had been invited to Lady Algrieve's Venetian Masque, but Felicity had ruled it inappropriate for her daughters, as such events had bad reputations, but for Millicent, tonight it was ideal.

It took all of her self-control to be calm during an early supper with her family and it was with relief that she waved them off in the carriage with a vague promise to join them later. No sooner had the door shut behind them then Millicent was off, pounding up the steps to her bedchamber.

Trying to get into the dress without assistance was difficult, but soon enough she was gowned and facing herself in her mirror as a young woman for the first time in a year.

The modern fashions for high waists suited her much more than her smaller sisters. The glowing silk brushed over her hips enhancing their curves and outlined the length of her legs, a smooth waterfall of shimmering gold.

The only problem was the bodice. There was very little fabric and it was cut oddly so that her breasts were not concealed in the slightest. What fabric was there existed to embrace each breast, highlighting them, enfolding them as gently as gloved hands. In fact, the cut of the tiny bodice lifted them up as if on a platform and put them on display for the admiration of the crowd as if they were buns in a bakery window. Millicent stared at her silhouette turning this way and that in front of the mirror. The bodice was so tight she could not even wear a chemise under it. Compared to her masculine clothing, she was very nearly naked!

But in no other costume had she ever appeared voluptuous.Was that not just wonderful? She clenched her fists and rested them on her hips. A fashion that flattered her had waited until she was no longer a woman to appear.

Damn it.

Maude might have gotten away with the current fashion for short hair, since once properly cut her gold hair curled naturally, but Millicent's hair was straight as a bone, brown and dull and with no time to play with curling papers. Her shoulders sagged. That was it; she could not appear in public dressed like this. Then she froze, remembering Maude's panic when she had cut her hair. The wigs Felicity had demanded were still boxed up in her room waiting to be returned to the barber.

Millicent hurried down the corridor to her mother's room, cursing the unfamiliar restrictions of a skirt. The wigs took a while to find since Felicity had buried them in the back of her traveling chest. Of the Grecian-styled blond wigs, one was more natural appearing in color, style, and configuration. It took a few minutes to work out the arrangement of hooks, tapes, and strings that combined to hold a wig in place, but finally Millicent lowered it onto her head and stared at herself in the pier glass.

Astonishing. She actually looked fetching. The pile of hair, curled, beribboned, and dignified that had been too much when worn on Maude's smaller, rounder frame looked very well when worn by the taller Millicent. She ran smoothing fingers over the wig, settling it straight, looked herself in the eye and smiled – a slow feminine upturning of the lips that the dowager duchess would have approved.

In all honesty, she did not just look feminine, she looked wicked! Taking advantage of her mother's cosmetics she layered a little color on her cheeks and lips and was ready to go.

Millicent caught up her sister's spare evening cloak and reticule, collected a little money and her key from her room, pulled the hood up over her head and started downstairs, pausing from time to time to see if any servants were about.

She waited, crouched at the turning of the main stair until the footman was summoned below for supper before scuttling out her own front door.

Out on the street, she discovered that her fashionable neighborhood was a different world for an unaccompanied lady at this hour of the night. A female servant hurrying on some private errand glared at her before putting her nose in the air and stalking past. The hackney driver who stopped in response to her hail sneered at her and demanded payment in advance, adding – "You do business in me cab and I wants me cut!"

Millicent ignored the assumption she was a hackney whore (five shillin' round trip, g'vner – sightsee, screw, and shilling tip for driver), tossed him a coin, and requested to be let out a short distance from her destination. She had chosen to arrive after the receiving line was finished and so needed only present her invitation to a bored under butler. At this time of the evening, and at this type of an entertainment, there was less supervision of the proprieties. A woman arriving unattended did not so much as raise an eyebrow. The assumption was she was a married woman escaping a more conventional party to indulge in a little naughtiness.

Her evening gown attracted no comment. Not all who were there chose to wear costumes. Instead she was directed toward a table bearing a selection of masks. With what she hoped was a feminine giggle – she was out of practice after all – she selected a gold embossed papier-mâché mask that went well with the color of her dress and breezed into the party.

Drink was flowing freely and more than one guest had over-imbibed. Voices were shriller, laughter louder, and no one was obeying the rule regarding the amount of distance between bodies during the waltz. Some had taken license to appear in public in costumes hardly decent. A portly man dressed only in thin bedsheets with a bunch of grapes hanging from a belt about his waist, had his arms about two ladies whose skirts did not reach the floor, nor even their ankles.

She stood for a moment at the top of the staircase leading down into the ballroom. Of Shoffer there was no sign. Damn the man. He had probably changed his mind and gone to some event with Lady Beth and after she had gone to such trouble with her toilette.

Then again, she could hope that he had not yet arrived. She closed her eyes for a moment and dismissed her dismay at his absence before gazing out across the ballroom. She was here to dance; that was the important thing. She was here to celebrate her womanhood once before the Ton. The Duke of Trolenfield be damned, she was going to have fun.

Millicent barely made it down the steps onto the dance floor before she was approached by a cavalier, who bowed and requested the honor of a dance.

Millicent did not hesitate. Her hand was on his shoulder and his arms about her waist and they were inscribing sweeping curves across the dance floor in an instant.

Whereas more respectable parties permitted only three waltzes, it seemed this orchestra knew no other music. After the cavalier, Millicent waltzed with a pirate, a gentleman in a domino, two Roman soldiers – one after another – and a person in the smelly remains of inherited, unwashable Tudor garb.

Sending her last partner off in search of refreshments, Millicent escaped through French windows onto a broad, but barely lit patio. Steps down into the gardens were lit by paper lanterns, but the expanse of the gardens had only scattered illumination. Millicent ran her fingers under the uncomfortable weight of her wig and closed her eyes as the cool air flowed onto her overheated scalp.

"It appears your cicisbeo has lost you," observed a voice in the darkness as her last partner wandered past inside the ballroom, a cup of something in each hand.

A familiar voice. A voice she heard nightly in her dreams.

Shoffer.

Millicent snatched her fingers out of her hair and turned, searching the patio, heart pounding in her throat.

Draped in a domino cape, Shoffer was almost invisible in the darkness. Seeing her panicked gaze he stepped forward to bow. He wore a plain black mask, with an air of reluctance, Millicent thought, and conventional dark evening clothes instead of a costume.

Millicent dropped a hasty curtsy, thankful for the mask that concealed her own features. Now she had just to attract him. Convince him she was experienced and willing.

Millicent cast another glance at him. He did not recognize her. In fact, if she were not mistaken – the dim light and mask made it difficult to be certain – he was not looking at her face, but at her bosoms neatly displayed on their shelf of golden brown silk.

The thought set her to the blush and had her drawing a deep breath. Shoffer's matching inhalation confirmed it. She could feel her loins heat and nipples tighten, and her lips curved.

Shoffer, beloved Shoffer, was admiring her breasts.

Timothy Shoffer, by the Grace of God and King, Duke of Trolenfield was not in a good mood.

Yesterday, Beth was less than pleased to be dragged off to Almack's, particularly once she was told that her friends, the Boarder girls, and their charming and silly cousin still would not be there. Shoffer did not expect his sister's intransigence. He insisted they attend Almack's, as a demonstration of Beth's superior, improved social skills, but they were there a bare hour before Beth demanded to leave. She wanted to go to whatever social event North and the Boarders were gracing. Told that the family was staying at home that night she near demanded to go there instead. It was necessary for Shoffer to sit with his furious sister in the ducal carriage for another hour and explain the necessity of weaning themselves from that family – a frustrating endeavor since he could not explain the reason. Hinting at rumors of unspecified crimes only aroused her ire.

"I do not care what rumors are going about," declared Beth. "You and I both know that North could not have committed any crime. He is the star of the season! If Brummel can overcome his rumored penury and other behavior and still be acceptable, then North can as well. Besides," she marshaled her best argument, "if we cut him the rumors will be judged as truth. We must continue to see them to protect them!"

"Beth, dear," began Shoffer. "Your own reputation is my greatest concern."

"Are the rumors true?" the girl demanded.

"By no means."

"Then I shall continue to count them all as my friends." She folded her arms, raised her chin, and glared at him.

Shoffer sighed, closing his eyes against the sight of his beautiful, caring sister with the stubborn jaw. Truth was he missed them as well. Little Maude with her curls, Mildred with her soft voice and gentle good humor, and North with his good sense hidden behind silly jokes.

"I am not saying we see them not at all, simply less. And you should take up with other young ladies as well."

Beth put her lower lip out mulishly.

"I shall choose my own friends. In fact, they should not be banned from Almack's. I shall go to Greylin's party tomorrow and I shall tell Lady Jersey they should be issued vouchers."

"I beg you would not."

"I shall. You cannot prevent me. I am a person of some influence amongst the Ton; you have taught me that yourself; and I choose to extend myself in the interests of my friends."

Eventually, the only way Shoffer was able to prevent Beth attending the Greylin party was to claim a previous engagement and refuse to give Beth his escort.

It was the first serious fight between brother and sister and several times during the day Shoffer had wished for North's presence, if only to tease them both out of their sulks. It was all very well for society to demand Shoffer socialize broadly, to maintain friendships from Eton through Cambridge and all the way to the grave, but North was his best friend, despite inferior birth and indifferent education. With North about, he did not need those other chatterers. He did not need to drink to all hours, to play deep at cards in order to be entertained. He could sit quietly and read, or gossip endlessly about nothing; with North on the other side of the fireplace, he was content.

Shoffer intended to spend the evening at one or another of his clubs, but he put that thought aside. He was too preoccupied with North, that much was true and while he did not entertain any licentious thoughts toward the man, it was necessary for him to find a woman tonight. Set up a mistress. Be seen behaving inappropriately with a lady. If he set those rumors aside, then he could try and find a balance, ration the time spent with North and his family, and Beth would be happy again.

Fortunately, there was a party tonight that was just the place to be seen, to be a suitably vigorous male of his rank.

While normally he spurned masquerades as beneath his dignity, it was well known to be an ideal place to find a woman with whom to behave inappropriately. On arriving at the Masque, he was grievously disappointed to discover that none of the women present pleased or attracted him. They were uniformly over perfumed, over familiar, and unappealing. The gathering was boring, the available women lacking in sensibility, and the orchestra discordant.

He tried to retreat to the smoking room only to back out rapidly. Two couples had chosen that room to … well … couple! He went out onto the patio and was considering going home when a slender woman, escaping an overly familiar dance partner, emerged in the doorway and ducked out for a breath of air.

A golden statue come to life was his first impression. The lady's form was encased in shimmering gold silk, her breasts smoothly molded by the fabric. Her bright eyes behind the mask told him she was well aware of her charms. He smiled slightly at her to reward her with the appreciation that her bosom deserved. He shifted position so that he was no longer blocking the light behind him, permitting it to highlight the lady. She made no attempt to avoid his gaze, but continued to regard him calmly even as his eyes explored her body.

She moistened her lips, bringing his attention to their fullness, and spoke in a soft, warm contralto.

"I wonder," she said, "have you ever wished that a celestial light would shine down when one meets the person who is one's fate? That a chorus of angels would cry out, 'Here! Look! This is he!'" She sighed. "It would make life so much simpler."

Surprised to hear his own words, his own thoughts repeated to him, Shoffer stepped forward, his eyes on her mouth.

"Have I? Yes, I have. Have you ever desired from the first whisper of silk, the first touch of the hand to hold, to taste, to possess? To drown?"

Her eyes drifted closed, then opened again to regard him with a heated gaze. Her answer was a mere breath of sound and she crossed the intervening space to stand close enough that her breasts brushed his vest.

"Yes. Yes, I have."

He put one hand on her waist and took hers in the other and began to guide her in a small circle. Instead of the grand sweeping curves of the ballroom waltz, he danced her around that small section of the balcony, drawing her closer into his arms with each circuit. Finally, they were breast to chest, hip to hip, as they moved back and forth, her hand on his chest and her cheek nestled against his neck.

The hand that had been resting on her waist for the movements of the waltz slid up to the underside of her breast and his thumb brushed over the peak of her nipple. She gasped, but made no move to escape. Emboldened, he curved his other arm about her back supporting the length of her body against his. Tilting his head, he brushed his lips along and down the line of her neck. She shuddered and sighed at the feather light touch and pressed closer. He could feel her lips move first to kiss his jaw, then the corner of his mouth. That was all the encouragement he needed to take matters further.

His arms tightened around her, pulling her up to him. His mouth descended to claim, to consume. Surprised, her lips parted and he took advantage, his tongue delving in, again and again, to explore and drown in her sweetness. She was untutored in the matter of kissing, he realized, when she recoiled from the invasion of his tongue, but once instructed she opened her lips beneath his and met his sweeping touch with her own, moaning, trembling in his arms, and returned his kisses eagerly.

This was no experienced, shallow, unfaithful wife. No. Her perfume was subtle, light. The sort of fragrance preferred by the débutante crowd. Sweet, fresh, and unassuming.

He drew back to gaze down at her flushed face, her swollen lips, and half lidded eyes. She rested against him, using his solid strength to hold herself upright.

This was no idle, no wanton, bored woman seeking illicit thrills; he would stake his fortune on that. For all her enthusiasm for his caresses, his kisses, he knew from her brief hesitations that she was inexperienced in dalliance.

As an honorable man he knew he should shelter her from her own folly. Take her home, back to the protection of her family.

Even as he prepared to release her, make the speech that would put her to the blush, she rose on her toes to press another kiss to his lips and looked him directly in the eye.

"I wish to love…"

Her voice died away and she stiffened; whatever she saw in his eyes made her draw away. He tightened his grip to prevent her escape.

"Truly? Love?"

His hands firm on her buttocks, he pressed her against his growing erection. Her body tensed away for a moment, then she wrapped her own arms around his waist and held him tight. He groaned and covered her face with kisses. She tilted her face up to meet his heated gaze. His eyes were dark with passion as his hands roved freely over her curves.

"Well, no. I have no right to such expectation." Her voice was stronger now. "However, I would wish to experience *lovemaking* at the hands of a skilled man."

"I have standards, you know. If there is a husband at home, a father who will protest..."

"My use of *my* body? No," she whispered, "there is no one. No husband. No father. None with the right to nay say me."

"Do you swear it?" he pressed his lips to her forehead, even as she swore that she was alone. "If so, tomorrow, I will meet you..."

"Now!" He could feel rather than see the heat of her blush. "I am sorry to be so forward. If not tonight, then it may well never be. I leave the city in a few days..."

"Then we should not waste time," he drew back to stare into her masked eyes. "Swear to me; I have no wish to cuckold; swear you belong to no one else."

"Only to myself."

Shoffer swung her in a circle, his face resting against her smooth hair. He closed his eyes and swayed with her, enjoying the soft pressure of her breasts against his chest. She would do as well as any other lady. Already, he could feel his body heating, growing heavy with need and lust.

"Come then."

He seized her by the wrist and drew her back into the ballroom and through the dancing throng, making no attempt to conceal his departure. Indeed, given the rumors going around about him the more public a departure with a woman on his arm, the better. Halfway across the dance floor, he realized how futile that plan was while wearing a mask. As he reached the footman guarding the steps to the ballroom, he drew off his mask and handed it to the man, then turned to face the ballroom. A slight widening of eyes and indrawn breath and a rapid increase in the chatter told him he had been recognized. The host of this gathering likely would hear very soon that the Duke of Trolenfield left the party with a woman and the gossip would spread throughout the Ton before dawn.

The lady herself kept the company of her mask. He released her only long enough for her to retrieve her cloak from the cloakroom. By the time she had returned, his carriage was waiting. He handed her in himself, not wishing to give up even that small touch to his footmen.

Once inside he reached past her to lower the light from the brass lanterns. His golden lady glanced toward him, then away to her hands folded in her lap. Shoffer watched a blush steal up her silken cheeks to vanish behind the mask.

"If you wish," he said softly, "I could escort you home…"

"No," her voice was nothing more than a breath. "I wish to be with you."

He waited, for the first time uncertain how to begin a seduction. The lady took matters into her own hands. She slid across the seat to his side, raised his arm and pausing just long enough to gain his nod of consent, placed it about her shoulders before nestling her face into his neck. He was not certain, but it seemed that she breathed in his scent, eyes closed, before wrapping her arms about his chest. He smiled, content that she had made the first move and enjoyed her gentle embrace until the carriage lurched into motion; then he shifted her back against the squabs to kiss her.

Given the degree to which she had aroused him, initially, there was no urgency to possess. His hands did not wander, but merely pressed silk against skin, supporting her. His mouth explored hers, with slow kisses and gentle pressure. He had never consummated the sexual act in his carriage and it seemed inappropriate now. It had been so long since he had been with a woman that he was not going to be uncomfortable. A bed and soft sheets were necessary. Instead, he was content tasting the sweetness of her mouth, pressing his lips to the curve of her chin and neck, enjoying the softness. The scent.

For a moment he considered ending the interlude. Untutored kisses hinted that she had lied, that she was the wrong person for a seduction, but the scent of her warming body filled his mind and she fitted his arms so well, that the thought of setting her free melted under the pressure of rising passion.

Chapter Fifteen

Despite the lassitude that had filled her in the aftermath of their interlude on the balcony Millicent's primary sensation was one of safety. Even as his mouth left hers to a leisurely exploration of her cheek, her throat, the upper curves of her breasts, she rested in his arms, certain of her security. This was Shoffer, honorable, wonderful Shoffer. He would care for her, even not knowing her identity. He would see to her passion, the satisfaction of her body, the realization of her secret dreams.

In the morning she would be gone, back beneath the mask of Mr. North, but tonight she was woman. Shoffer's woman.

The jerk of the carriage halting penetrated the fog of passion. Her eyes were glazed, but she did not hesitate when he assisted her down to the footpath. Shoffer paused only long enough to dismiss the carriage.

"I shall make my own way home, John," he said, waving away his servants before leading the way down the short path to the cottage where he usually lodged his mistresses.

He let them into the house with his own key. The housekeeper appeared just as he was guiding the woman to the staircase, but only put her head around the servant's door long enough to confirm it was the duke and not a robber. With a deferential nod she disappeared. His lady's quick intake of breath told him she had seen the servant and he glanced back in time to see another blush fade. Shoffer stopped and leaned down to her.

"My dear, if you but say, I shall take you home."

Her reply was immediate. "No. I will stay."

"This is your first time?" He did not define it further. He did not want to know if she were a virgin. Honor would require he stop at once. "No. Do not answer, I beg you."

"Children would be a bad idea," was her only reply.

"Trust me; I have what is needed."

His body was one hungry ache. It was far too long since he had last enjoyed a woman and he was not going to deny himself. The woman gave him a hesitant smile and squeezed his hand. When he reached for her mask, she moved her head just out of his reach. Nodding his acceptance of her wish to remain unknown, he led her up the remaining steps and down the corridor to the bedroom.

His servants did not disappoint. The room was warm and well aired. The sheets fresh and sweet smelling. He pulled the blankets down with one rough motion and turned, expecting the woman to be cowering in the far corner. Instead he was seized about the chest as she crushed her lips to his. It took him a moment only to take control of the kiss, sinking into it, claiming her mouth with his tongue. She moaned and pressed closer and he could feel the bite of her fingers through his clothing.

Her enthusiasm was gratifying and certainly arousing. Shoffer tightened his grip on her, in case she recovered her mind and drew away. There were only a half dozen little buttons holding her bodice in place. Before she realized his intent, the buttons were slipped free of their moorings and the gold silk drawn open, exposing the breasts that had captured his attention less than an hour before.

"Oh, my dear, you are beautiful."

He swung her up into his arms and laid her gently on the bed. His lips were like warmed velvet, brushing over the sensitized skin of her breasts. His fingers smoothed over her shoulders, her upper arms, and eased down the little cap sleeves. While she was distracted by the gentle suckling of his mouth at her breasts, he drew her dress down to her waist.

Her arms freed, Shoffer captured both hands with one of his and raised her arms over her head; with the other hand he laid siege to her body. Warm and strong his hand captured, cupped her breast, with gentle pressure he raised the nipple to near painful arousal. The touch of his tongue did not ease the ache, but sent arrows of passion to her center which flowered with moist heat and need.

A groan escaped Millicent's lips even as her head fell back against the pillows. Shoffer accepted the invitation and moved above her, onto her, pressing her further down into the feather bed.

The pressure of the pillows on her hair pushed it forward down over her nose and the mask down over her mouth, near blinding and suffocating her. Shoffer's hand hesitated above her head as if reluctant to remove it, fearing what he would find. Millicent grabbed for the misbehaving hair, the smothering mask to push them back into place, but her movement was too rough, too fast, and the wig tumbled back off her head.

Shoffer was on his feet in an instant. The short, poorly cut hair, the square, open face thus revealed must be as familiar to him as his own!

"North!" he cried, "What are you doing here?"

Millicent pulled the sheet up over her body and dug in her heels until she was seated upright with her back against the headboard. Shoffer stood there, the damned wig clutched in his hand, staring at her as if she were some strange beast never before seen in England. Even as she labored to use the bedding to conceal her chest he, pulled it down to stare at her breasts, then up again at her shorn head and familiar face. Millicent pulled the sheet up, Shoffer down. Again and again he uncovered her breasts to stare at them, open-mouthed.

"Oh, stop that," cried Millicent. "Anyone would think you had not seen breasts before."

When Shoffer tugged on the bedsheets again, Millicent lost her temper. Boxing his ear firmly she pulled the sheets up to her chin, folded her arms across her breasts and glared at him.

"Stop that," she commanded. "By now you should be confident that they exist. You were content with them just a moment ago when you were…" a fierce blush flooded her face, "entertaining yourself with them."

Shoffer smiled at that and raised his eyes to meet hers.

"Oh, yes. Very entertained. And I believe you were not adverse to the activity either. But, how can this be? Who are you?"

Millicent sighed. "You mean, who am I or how can I be Mr. North or who is the woman with Mr. North's face?"

"Either. All. Both." Shoffer shook his head. "I understand this not at all."

"Very well, I am Millicent Boarder," she held out one narrow-fingered hand, "how do you do?"

Shoffer took it and held it rather than kissing or shaking it. "Millicent *Boarder*? Why does that sound familiar?"

"How soon I am forgotten," sighed Millicent, gazing up at the ceiling. "I am the eldest Boarder daughter. You remember, I, that is, Mr. North, told you about the sister who died of a fever last winter?"

"And yet, here you are before me," Shoffer glanced down at her barely covered breasts again, "in the all too living flesh."

"You were not complaining earlier," shot back Millicent.

"Granted, but earlier I thought I was embracing a woman."

"You were," said Millicent, "you are, or do you doubt the evidence of your own eyes … and lips?"

The corner of Shoffer's lip curled up. "Perhaps I should taste again, to be certain."

Millicent raised her hand and Shoffer leaned back out of range, laughing.

"Oh, very well, but you must understand my confusion. Only a moment since I was engaged in…" He smirked at the blush rising again in Millicent's face, "you always did blush easily, Mr. North. As I was saying, I was pleasuring a young woman, but now I find my arms about a woman with the face of my old friend *Mister* North. How does this come about?"

Millicent started to answer, then paused. "I hope you understand that I put more than my own self in your hands by telling you."

"You know you can tell me anything. Well, apparently not, but tell me now. How comes this about?"

"I suppose, under the circumstances, you are entitled." Millicent sighed and her expression became far-away. "Four years ago my father died, leaving me, my mother, and my two sisters alone in the world. What little income we lived on died with him, an annuity from his grandfather and what money he earned as a tutor. Felicity appealed to all of whom she could think, relatives, friends, and the only person who offered us shelter was Mr. Anthony North, our distant cousin. We considered ourselves fortunate right up until the moment we entered his house and discovered he intended that we should become his servants, unpaid, since it was not necessary to pay relatives, only offer them food and shelter. Having spent our last penny to get to his house, we were rather at a loss for options, so we stayed."

"So there was an Anthony North!"

"Oh, of a certainty – a truly horrible person. Everything I purport him to be, he was, quite sincerely. The most discontented, greedy, pinchpenny, misogynistic miser one would hope to avoid. Last winter, when a purulent fever swept through the village, he died. Instead of telling the truth and making ourselves helpless and homeless, again, we put about the story that I … that Millicent Boarder had died. He was buried under my name and I assumed his. We spent a few months in the workhouse once, dreadful place, and I would do anything to protect my mother and sisters from going back. What were we to do? Anthony's only living relative was Perceval, and from what Anthony told me, Perceval was more of a miser than he was himself. When we had first appealed for aid, Perceval had not even franked the reply he sent refusing us! It cost us sixpence to be rejected and insulted. You can understand, I hope, why we felt there was no other choice than for me to assume Anthony's identity. It was not as if Perceval did not already have enough money himself."

Shoffer gave a half nod, too caught up in the tale at first to react to her words, but when the import of them sank in, he shook himself and stared at her.

"North, sorry, Millicent, you do realize what you have done is a crime?"

"Of course, I do, what sort of fool do you think I am? I could hang for this. And when you came and told me I was accused of … of … well, what a horrible condition to be in. You come and tell me I am accused of a crime where the only way I can prove myself innocent of it is to reveal that I am guilty of another capital crime." Millicent dragged both hands through her hair and groaned. "You are lucky I was too surprised that night to act; otherwise, I would have strangled you."

"Another capital crime," murmured Shoffer with a grin.

"This is not funny," cried Millicent.

"No, I grant you it is not and you have put me in the most untenable position. When the truth comes out no one will believe me to have been in such close quarters with you and unaware of your deceit. I shall, both Beth and I, be ostracized."

Millicent sniffed and stiffened her spine. "Oh, I do apologize. Forgive me, do, I beg you. While I am hung by the neck until dead and my mother and sisters deported to Botany Bay, I shall most certainly grieve for the six parties and two soirées a season for which high sticklers will not send you invitations."

It was Shoffer's turn to groan and clutch at his hair. "I do not mean to deny the danger you are in, but you should have considered the whole before…"

"The whole? My dear duke, do not be more of a fool than me! On one hand, I ran the risk of death from starvation, abuse, and degradation. On the other hand, I could protect and provide for my family. Can you swear to me, sir, that if our positions were reversed, you would not have done the same? But wait, you have no knowledge of deprivation. In your whole life you have never missed a meal, except by your own choice, or gone cold and hungry to a flea ridden bed you must share with half a dozen unwashed strangers."

"Enough, I beg you. I am not completely unfeeling, but it would be best for all concerned that the deception end!"

"Oh, do not worry. My excursion tonight was my last appearance in London society. Mr. North leaves soon on a protracted tour of his estates. My sisters will put about the story of some 'disaster' I must attend to, and I shall not return."

"You misunderstand me. You must give up this deception entirely. Mr. North must be permitted to die in truth."

Millicent gasped and stared at him open-mouthed. "You cannot be serious. What shall we do? When Mr. North is declared dead, all shall go to Perceval. We will be destitute, again!"

"As it should have been last year. Oh, do not look so distressed. You have had your year and granted Maude and Mildred a coming out and their dowries. Be content."

"Content? You arrogant ass. What would you do if anyone were to suggest you give up even a small part of your property? Is it because I am a woman that you dare suggest such a thing? I should call you out, except that Lady Beth is a better shot than me. Perhaps I should ask her to act in my stead."

"She is angry enough at this moment to do it," Shoffer stared at the woman in his bed. Why was it he was so calm? Surely, there should be some other emotion he should be experiencing. He should be shocked. Horrified. Offended. A woman in men's clothing? Disgusting. A woman presuming to present herself to the Ton as a man of property? Never! He should be angry, except, he was not. Instead his lips curved until he found himself grinning broadly. "Oh, my dear Mr. North, of all your jests, I find this one quite takes my breath away."

Millicent glared at him for a moment before snorting out a laugh. "My dear duke, I should be enraged at your presumption, but I find I cannot stay angry with you." She watched him thoughtfully, then continued in a softer tone. "I suppose I have been in love with you too long to wish to spoil this moment."

"You love me?" Shoffer was off the bed in an instant, his expression so horrified that Millicent could only laugh.

"Oh, my dear duke, do not fear. It is not Mr. North, a man who says this, but Millicent, a woman."

Shoffer's gaze drifted down to her bosom. This time Millicent did not move to cover them. Instead she watched and waited until he returned to sit on the edge of the bed.

"You love me?" Shoffer was genuinely astonished by the news. "For how long?"

"I think since the first moment I saw you." A corner of her mouth curved up. "You did appear to good effect with your buckskins molded to your thighs by the rain. No detail was concealed."

"Oh?" A faint blush stained his face.

"I thought you were a statue come to life," Millicent continued. "A Greek athlete or Roman god. Beautiful beyond my understanding."

"You do not want to know what I thought of you."

"You called me a fool for the first time." Millicent shrugged. "It has occurred to me that I owe you an apology. It could be that something I have done, or some look I have given you contributed to the beginning of these dreadful rumors. I thought I controlled my features, but I admit there have been times when I have been thinking 'I love you,' and looking in your direction while witnesses were about."

"No, Nor ... Millicent, I am certain that is not the cause. Attelweir and his clowder could have chosen any number of rumors to put about, but the most damaging rumor is the one they chose. The one that cannot be disproved by any means."

"Certainly I cannot challenge it without risking the gallows."

Shoffer leaned forward close enough to inhale the subtle scent she chose, resting the palm of his hand on the headrest above her.

"You say you love me."

"Yes, for months now."

"What an odd thought. I have been fond of you as Mr. North, but I hope you understand I cannot be expected to transfer that affection to Millicent."

"Indeed, I do not expect it. Nor do I think you should get into the habit of referring to me as Millicent. Millicent is dead."

"We shall have to consider what name to refer to you by, once Mr. North is dead," said Shoffer, ignoring Millicent's frown.

"You presume a great deal."

"Milli … my dear, you do not have to fear a penniless life without the deception of Mr. North. I will take care of you."

Millicent stiffened. "Will you now?"

Shoffer tried for a reassuring smile and took her hand in his, pressing a kiss to the palm. "I came out tonight with the intention of setting up a mistress. Your beauty caught my eye and you cannot say that the idea of making love with me displeased you. Up until the moment the wig betrayed you, you were … enthusiastic. I find I like the idea of a liaison with someone I like, and who loves me."

"Well, how very nice for you." There was a warning note in Millicent's voice that set Shoffer laughing.

"Be reasonable. You cannot continue this deception indefinitely. Let Anthony North die. You have made arrangements for the settlement of Mildred and Maude. I shall deal with Perceval as you have requested, and it will be no inconvenience for me to find some place on my estates for Felicity to settle. Please, permit me to provide for you. I think we shall do well together."

"As mistress and protector?" Millicent's voice was now cold as ice. She reclined against the headboard permitting the bedsheets to drift down fully exposing her breasts. "By your reasoning there is nothing left but to set my price. I warn you it will be high as I have a good opinion of myself."

The mercenary words chilled Shoffer more than the tone.

"I believe I can meet your price."

"Can you? I want twenty thousand pounds a year."

"North!"

"No, do not nay say me. You want to remove my income, very well, you must replace it, or else tell me, by what right do you declare that I am unworthy of these funds? Christopher North divided his property in half between his two sons. By that measure Perceval has no complaint, having twenty thousand per annum of his own. If anyone was to attempt to deprive you of what you hold, you would run him through. Why should I be more complacent?"

"It is not yours by right! You stole it from a dead man! Besides, how can you continue going on as you have? Someone is sure to discover your secret."

"Really? Did you? Has anyone? The rumor going about is not that Mr. North is a Miss, but that he is a bugger. An exclusively masculine crime, if I remember correctly. I had everyone, including you, completely fooled."

"But it cannot go on! Sooner or later some event or other will result in your being revealed. Retreat now before you end up facing the scaffold."

"Bah! I do not believe you are motivated entirely out of fear for my life."

"I admit, I should like to make love to you. That is the reason we are here."

Millicent pulled up the sheet, unable to meet his eye. There was a gleam to them, and a seductive curve to his mouth, which sent a blush climbing her cheeks.

Shoffer laughed to see it.

"How could I not suspect? You blushed so easily."

"I have seen men blush."

"But not as prettily as you."

Millicent grunted and tried to turn her back on him. Shoffer climbed further onto the bed and pulled her into his arms.

"Oh, come, let us not quarrel. We did not come here tonight to fight, but to make love."

"We need not," muttered Millicent, her lips so close to his chest he could feel the warmth of her words. "I might disappoint you, masculine person that I am."

"Never."

"I do not understand your confidence."

Shoffer permitted her to push away far enough that he might see her face. "Dear Millicent, I am certain we shall do very well together. I do not doubt that you will approach the act of love with the same enthusiasm with which you approach all aspects of life. Do you not dance with joy? This is another form of dance." He smiled at her. "And, you love me."

Chapter Sixteen

Millicent did not comment, but she did not miss that, yet again, Shoffer had said that *she* loved him, but did not state his love for her. It was only to be expected. Why should he? Millicent Boarder was a stranger to him. Anthony North was a mere friend. Brotherly affection was not kindred to passionate love. She should not and did not expect that he would love her simply because she loved him.

However, at this moment, his body was warm and hard under her fingers. She rested her forehead on his shoulder relishing the firm support. Those few moments she had spent under his fingers burned in her mind. Honesty being the best policy, she admitted to herself that she ached to resume the interrupted act.

Enthusiastic was a good description of her attitude.

"Just for this one night only, Shoffer. Tomorrow, I return to being Mr. North, and if you cut me from your acquaintance, I shall endure it. But I shall not give up being my family's only source of income. I will not!"

"Tomorrow," murmured Shoffer against her cheek. "Tonight you are a woman and you are mine!"

He drew a long tin out of the table drawer and opened it to reveal several tan tubes decorated at one end with a ring of ribbon. Millicent rose up on one elbow to watch him.

"Whatever are they?" she demanded.

For the first time in their acquaintance, Shoffer blushed deeply.

"Avoiding pregnancy is your only concern, my dear. These will take care of that matter."

"How?"

Shoffer could not meet her eyes.

"Really, if you wish to continue here you should not question me about this."

"How else am I to learn?"

"Oh, for pity's sake. They are from France. Do not ask what they are made of, for I do not know. They enclose me and prevent pregnancy. There, are you content?"

"Excellent," she lay back. "You shall tell me where they are purchased and I shall tell my family."

"You cannot discuss this with the women of your household! North, you cannot be so lost to sensibility."

"I am a lady and may speak to the ladies of my household as I choose!" She smiled. "Or have you forgotten already?"

Shoffer only shook his head.

"I am confused."

"Well, if I am too confusing," said Millicent, levering herself up as if to get out of the bed, "perhaps I should leave."

Shoffer's arm, iron hard and as immovable, pushed her back down. He huffed a breath into the tube then stripped off his clothing. His member sprang free of his trousers eager, and was soon enclosed by the strange tube. Shoffer fastened the ribbons in a neat bow and stood naked and proud before her.

"Blue, to match your eyes," observed Millicent.

"Next time," said Shoffer, climbing onto the bed and bracing himself upon his forearms above her, "gold to match *your* eyes." He kissed her, lowering himself to press her into the mattress. "Then pink for your blushes. White for your skin. Red for my passion."

Shoffer ran his hands over the curve of her shoulders, outlining the smooth line of her breasts and down to the swell of her hips. It was, he knew, a woman's body under his – soft, warm, welcoming.

He knew it and yet it was necessary for him to continue examining that body with his lips, his hands, his tongue to confirm it. He closed his eyes the better to concentrate on the scent of her, the brush of fingertips over her swelling breasts and, heaven be praised, the sensation of her hands traveling over his shoulders. Her lips pressed to his skin. Her touch at first was tentative, but grew bolder with his murmured encouragements. She passed her hands down his spine, seizing and squeezing his buttocks at his command. His erection, already painfully hard, swelled and rose only to become captive of her hand and increase further.

"God, woman, what you do to me," he gasped and she laughed.

"What is this?" her eyes were dancing. "What shall I do with it?"

"Receive it," he rose over her, parting her thighs and settling himself between them.

Now he could meet her eyes without doubting this was indeed a woman, soft and willing, her heat open to him. He hesitated at the entrance, unwilling to cause pain, but she rose to meet his thrust unafraid. He tensed as he entered her velvet heat, pleasure so close to pain. She froze beneath him, but did not resist his withdrawal or his return. The muscles of his back and shoulders corded under the strain of control. He would not ravage, pillage. Her ease, her pleasure were his obligation and joy. He sank slowly into her, giving her time to stretch and receive him. Once he was in to the hilt, he waited until her tight clenched eyes opened again and she smiled her welcome of his possession. Now she was ready for him, slick and hot, he withdrew until a bare inch was still within. He settled into the ancient rhythm, welcoming her sighs and whimpers as his reward. Need claimed them both, drawing them onward. Her movements beneath him became demanding as her body sought, then claimed, the pleasure that was love's reward. As her body clenched around him, he followed her into joy.

He pulled her close against his chest, even as his breath heaved and body shuddered in the aftermath of pleasure. He thought at first the vibration rising from her chest was laughter, then choked on his own amusement when he realized she was purring.

"Again cats, Mr. North?"

Now she laughed.

"What better guide, have we? Cats, when well petted, purr."

Early the next morning, dressed only in a borrowed powdering gown, Millicent picked up her silk dress, then dropped it in disgust.

"Whatever is the problem?" asked Shoffer from the other side of the room where he was wrestling with his cravat.

"I cannot go home dressed like this," cried Millicent. "It is morning already. My staff will be up and about and, even with my own key to the door, I am sure to be spotted. Can you imagine the fuss?"

"Yet another reason why Mr. North must die," muttered Shoffer, running his hand over his stubbly chin.

"Leave off that nonsense, Shoffer; it will not happen." Millicent again lifted her dress, still staring at Shoffer. "That is not the same shirt you wore last night."

"Of course not. I am in the habit of leaving a change of clothing…" he stopped and raised both hands. "No. No, Millicent. I will not give you my clothing."

"Why ever not? They will be of finer make than my usual clothing and it will not matter that they do not fit. Mr. North never appears in tailored clothing, anyway."

While Shoffer stuttered protests Millicent walked past him into the dressing room. The main armoire was occupied by half a dozen women's dresses of different styles and colors – the sizes were much the same, which told Millicent that Shoffer usually chose women of smaller stature than herself, but better endowed about the bosom. In the corner were a chest and a trunk containing Shoffer's clothing. It was the work of a moment for her to locate small clothes, linens, and a suitable set of evening clothes. The only problem she was left with was shoes. Somehow it had never been necessary for Shoffer to leave shoes behind. She dithered for a moment about wearing her evening slippers, then decided not. Going about in her socks was unusual, but she could explain that she had ruined the shoes somehow. No one would care about that. But appearing in women's shoes? No, that would start rumors she sincerely feared.

Shoffer was standing in the middle of the room scowling at the floor when she emerged from the dressing room attired in his clothing.

"I want you to know I disapprove of this," he said.

"Of my borrowing your clothes or the masquerade?"

"Both!"

Millicent laughed. "And yesterday, when I was Mr. North, you trusted me to stand guard over your sister, your most precious treasure. You are a hypocrite, Your Grace. My deception may be an inconvenience to you, but as it is life and liberty to me, I suggest that if it offends you so much, you just do not look!"

Shoffer gave her his back, his face thunderous. A rattle on the cobbles outside had them both turning to the window.

"My carriage is here. Come along, I will drop you off at your home."

"I think not, Your Grace. 'Twould attract comment from your staff here if you arrive in the night with a woman and depart in the morning with a man, and from my staff if we arrive together after a night of dissipation. No. I will find my own way home. But, if I might request it, please make a fuss as you depart and attract the attention of all of your staff. Have them join you in the front hall so I may slip out the back."

"You cannot travel through London unattended!"

Millicent sighed. "Shoffer, you turned not a hair when I traveled the length and breadth of England alone this summer. Kindly, do not be more of a fool than me."

Shoffer snarled, then left the room without another word. Millicent folded her mother's wig into the evening dress and searched the room for something in which to carry the bundle. She found a pile of brown paper sheets and string in the bottom drawer of a chest. Her head came up as she heard Shoffer's roar from the front of the house. Snatching up the paper she hurried from the room and down the servant's stair. She stopped and clung to the shadows while the maid-of-all-work hurried past, obviously confused at being summoned to the front of the house. Once that lady was gone Millicent dashed through the servant's area out into the tiny back yard. It was a well maintained garden, as she expected for one of the duke's properties and the hinges on the gate that lead to the mews were well oiled. Cursing the cold ground and the dew that rapidly soaked through her socks, Millicent hopped from foot to foot as she roughly wrapped up her precious dress and wig; then she crept away down the mews. She emerged in time to see the rear of Shoffer's carriage as it rattled away.

Clutching her package as if it contained nothing important and trying to walk as if she were indeed well shod Millicent started off in search of a hackney.

She was cursing her pride by the time she reached home two hours later, soaked to the skin by a sudden rain shower, footsore, tired, and wounded in her heart.

When she was safely behind her bedchamber door, she stripped to the skin and stood naked before her mirror. Strange that her body should be so unfamiliar to her this morning, as if the act of loving had transformed her. She studied her face and eyes intently seeking some sign – a knowing look or wanton gleam – to mark her as a fallen woman. There was none. Indeed, once she was bathed and dressed in Mr. North's attire, no one could see the little bruises on her neck, the glowing red abrasion across her breasts. But she knew.

She knew she was changed. These last few months, she had entertained herself with imagining receiving affection, acknowledgement of her femininity from Shoffer, usually in the form of a kiss. Since she possessed little knowledge of kisses until last night, her imaginings were rather unsatisfying. Not so the actual act. Even now, remembering was enough to melt her hidden core and set it to painful longings. She wrapped her arms about her chest and squeezed, remembering the strength of his embrace, the hunger aroused by the weight of his body on hers. Her breath hitched and quickened and her body warmed. There was no denying she wanted again to experience last night's passion, but it was dangerous beyond all consideration.

The risk was not worth the price.

She would have to be strong and deny herself and him repeated pleasure.

Oh, but it hurt. It hurt. She sank to the floor, hugging herself, refusing to give in to the tears that burned her eyes and throat.

She had hungered for so long to know the ecstasy of Shoffer's touch and now that she had experienced it, the memory was intolerable.

She had loved him before as a virgin, now she loved him as a woman, with a woman's full knowledge of all that was possible.

In the eyes of the world she was a man, and necessity demanded she remain a man.

She would. There was no other choice. She would care for her family. At the price of her own happiness, she would ensure theirs.

It seemed to Shoffer that he had spent the whole year in a dream. Nothing he had considered real or true was so. That he had been deceived to such a degree when he was accustomed to considering himself clear-eyed and perceptive stunned him, and now, to discover how completely he had been deceived? Intolerable.

He had gone to bed as soon as he had returned home, expecting to lie wakeful and in turmoil, but instead had fallen into a dreamless sleep that had lasted until evening.

After he had bathed and eaten in a leisurely fashion he had sent a message to Maricourt Place requesting Mr. North attend him. His intention was to lecture the stubborn Millicent Boarder until she finally saw sense, but to his consternation his messenger had returned with the news that the Boarder family and Mr. North were attending the Jensen-Smythe ball and had already departed.

He was out of the house, dressed for the evening, within a quarter hour – leaving his stunned valet in his wake. On arrival at the ball, where he had not been expected, he had been little better than rude to his hostess in his impatience to locate Millicent.

Shoffer charged from one overcrowded room to another, ignoring everyone who tried to catch his attention.

He found the object of his search, again attired as Mr. North, holding forth to a group of wallflowers and a few gentlemen who were attracted by the laughter. Shoffer halted and stood to watch Millicent cast her spell.

It was amazing, now he was in on the secret, how clear it was that Millicent was no ordinary man. The movement of her hands was too graceful, her manner cheerful and all encompassing. She made no attempt to cut out other gentlemen to increase her own status, but included them in her humor. Her attention to the needs of wallflowers should shout for all to hear that this was a gentle lady trying to advance the cause of less bold and less favored ladies, and yet, no one could see.

He shook his head. Blind. They were all blind. It was incomprehensible. It astonished him and, then again, it did not. The masquerade was masterful. The costume, all things considered, perfect. No one looking at Mr. North would ever think that "he" was anything other than a unique individual, but still a man.

Her audience was captivated. Shoffer stepped closer to stand behind her just as she wound her way to the end of a joke.

"... his wallpaper was Chinese silk and there was an Egyptian sarcophagus in the corner. Statues of Greek and Roman gods stood on pedestals all about the room and he was wearing French fashions and drinking scotch whiskey. He pounded himself on the chest and declared to me, "I am proud to be an Englishman," and I thought, 'Pray, sir, how am I to tell?'"

The wallflowers tittered behind their fans and the gentlemen laughed whether they understood the joke or not, such was the power of Mr. North's reputation. Millicent turned her head, catching the opening bars of the next set.

"Ah, I distract you. Surely, these gentlemen have come to claim their dances. I apologize for monopolizing the ladies."

She bowed and stepped back leaving the gentlemen face to face with hopeful wallflowers. The ploy had worked yet again. Shoffer watched a smug smile cross Millicent's lips as she watched the pairings.

The stunned gentlemen dithered and muttered, but could not escape. No. They were surrounded by steely eyed mothers and soft, willing virgins before they could gather their wits. Introductions were provided. Offers were made and accepted and the wallflowers were led onto the dance floor. Millicent glanced back over her shoulder and smiled at the duke.

"I knew you were there," she said. "I could sense your presence. Why did you not join us?"

Shoffer shook his head at her. "I came to rescue you."

Her eyes opened in surprise.

"From what? The Ton? I thought you had realized by now I have them all well in hand."

"From ... from exposure."

Millicent laughed, a deep husky laugh that to Shoffer was seductive and reminiscent of the bedroom, but apparently to all others little more than a gentleman's ordinary laugh.

"Ah," still smiling Millicent lowered her voice. "Poor Shoffer, now that your eyes are opened, you think I am exposed to the general throng? No, my dear sir, as you see the mask is still in place."

"I cannot decide if that pleases me or not." His voice sounded petulant even to himself.

"It pleases me." Hands clasped behind her back Millicent took her place at Shoffer's side and they began to stride about the room as they had so many times before, watching the ranks of dancers prance and dip their way across the floor. "I will not give it up, Shoffer. I gave the matter serious thought today. Believe it or not, I enjoy it. There is a freedom in being a man that is addictive. Once I tasted the privilege of being able to walk down a street alone, go across country unattended, and of being treated with respect rather than condescension at inns and shops, I determined that I had no wish to give it up."

"And what of us?" Shoffer said softly, nodding distantly to an acquaintance.

A pained shadow crossed Millicent's face and she struggled not to turn and throw herself into his arms. Instead, she smiled at yet another matron who simpered and curtsied in response, then fluttered and gossiped with her friends, pleased to have received Mr. North's notice.

"We remain friends, I hope."

"We cannot," whispered Shoffer. "You know there is foul gossip circulating about us and while people fear to cut me, your cousins' status will suffer."

"There will be less gossip when I depart London. Attelweir and his friends will consider they have won. You will continue to protect your sister, so my aid is not required. I grieve to yield the ground to them, but I must. Felicity and the girls are not important enough to cut so their consequence will not suffer."

Shoffer pulled her into an alcove. The ducal stare was enough to keep all others at a suitable distance. Millicent attempted to leave his side, but was pulled back.

"You do nothing to reduce the gossip by acting this way, Shoffer," she said shaking his hand off her arm and glaring at him.

"Be damned to them all," Shoffer hissed. "What of us? I want to be again with Millicent."

"Do not say that name," hissed Millicent. "She is dead."

"Then how shall I name her ... you?"

"Oh, for God's sake. Call me ... call her Helene Winthrop, if you must."

"Will this Helene protest your assumption of her name?"

"I think not. Helene was one of my mother's cousins from Cornwall. She died about the same time as my father."

"Another lie. Lie upon lie," Shoffer swore and clenched his fists at his sides. "Each one necessary to conceal the greatest lie. I wonder why I ever considered you an honest man."

"Well, therein is your essential problem," said Millicent calmly. "I am neither."

Against his will and despite his anger, Shoffer laughed.

"Oh, very well. When shall I see Helene?"

"Never." Millicent stared up at him, her eyes clear of tears by willpower alone. "I thought I was clear. We would be together one night only. I shall be leaving London in a few days. My ... Felicity does not know why and she is less than pleased, but they have enough invitations to keep them busy for the rest of the season. I have left them money enough to enjoy themselves, so she has no good reason to complain."

"Be damned to your cousins, North. What of … Helene and me? I have no wish to end the liaison after only one night."

"You will have to learn to live with the pain," Millicent's eyes grew sad, "as shall she."

"That is not satisfactory, at all." Shoffer turned his back to those curious persons in the ballroom. "I wish to continue a relationship with … Helene. Surely, one night was not enough for her. Especially after she has declared her love for me."

"You are the oddest person, Your Grace," said Millicent, smiling despite the stab of pain to her heart. "Surely a man in your position would run a hundred miles rather than continue to spend time with a mistress who has professed her love?"

"Love? Good heavens, Your Grace," came a voice from the other side of the concealing house plant. "I had not thought any lady had caught your eye this season!"

Millicent's heart stuttered as panic caught her breath in her throat. How much had the listener heard? Who was it?

Shoffer spun to face the intruder, effectively blocking Millicent's view of the ballroom. She slapped at his shoulder to no effect. Silence stretched, which made her suspect Shoffer was subjecting the interloper to the ducal stare. Her suspicion was confirmed when she heard stammering and stuttering.

"Do you have something to say that I wish to hear, Wentworth?" asked Shoffer.

Maude's suitor. Millicent's stomach unclenched. That little weasel was so self-concerned that he would pay little mind to other people's troubles.

Still, Wentworth's presence was annoying. Shoffer was as aware as Millicent of the youth's pathetic courtship of Maude and was just as offended. The boy had to have some spine to still be standing there having endured the ducal stare.

"I was hoping to have private speech with Mr. North, regarding his cousin," stammered Wentworth.

"Oh? Well, here he is." Shoffer stepped to one side permitting Millicent to see Wentworth for the first time. "Are not such private conversations traditionally conducted in a gentleman's study during the daylight hours? I was not aware that they were conducted in public venues."

Wentworth had the grace to blush. "Please do not misunderstand. It is not *that* conversation, exactly." He met Millicent's eye. "If I might have a moment of your time?"

Millicent folded her arms across her chest. "I do not know that I wish to speak to you, Wentworth, on any subject. I do know that my cousin is saddened by the mere mention of your name. Why should I subject myself to your company?"

"Please? Sir, it may not be important to you, but it is life's breath to me."

The youth went paler and looked, to Millicent's older and wiser eye, near to tears with some soul deep distress. Very poetic, to be sure, but not much use.

Millicent groaned and glanced toward the ceiling. "Dear God, spare me from… Oh, very well. Come along. Shoffer, do you have any suggestions where this gentleman might have private speech with me?"

Shoffer considered the request. The card room would be crowded and any stray corner at this hour of the night was likely to be occupied by those determined to engage in a little scandalous activity.

"The garden it will have to be," Shoffer declared. "Thank God it is not raining."

Shoffer gestured toward the nearest French window leading out onto the terrace. Millicent led off, followed by Wentworth. To that young man's increasing distress, Shoffer trailed along behind. Millicent permitted herself a small smile. There was no way Wentworth would be able to summon the spine to dismiss a duke should he choose to join the conversation.

From the terrace, they descended into the garden, choosing a path that was better lit than the others. The deeper dark of the garden was reserved for lovers. Eventually, Millicent stopped where a set of stone chairs were arranged about a fountain and chose the one that looked like a throne for herself, permitting the other two men to arrange themselves as they saw fit. Wentworth remained seated for a heartbeat only. He leapt back to his feet and began pacing. Shoffer and Millicent watched him without sympathy.

Eventually, Wentworth could endure the silence no longer.

"Has Maude any other relatives?" he demanded.

"Besides me? Beside her mother and sisters?" Millicent leaned back in her chair and steepled her fingers. "Interesting. Why would you concern yourself with Miss Maude Boarder's family?"

Wentworth closed his eyes for a moment before continuing. "Indulge me, please. Has she any elderly aunts or such that would be willing to state they have included her in their wills? Some grandparent or uncle of good estate near to death?"

Millicent and Shoffer exchanged appalled glances.

"No. Not a single solitary soul," said Millicent.

"Are you certain? Think again!"

Millicent regarded him solemnly. "I should be expected to know my family tree. Frankly, in this generation it is more like a twig, a walking stick than a tree. Think of something with very, very few branches and even fewer of them with funds."

With an agonized cry, Wentworth sank onto a bench, his head in his hands. Shoffer and Millicent exchanged a long, steady glance.

"Is he ill, do you think?" asked Millicent.

"We can only hope."

Wentworth shook himself and sat up. "Please understand my distress. I have only one hope, that Maude did not know the extent of her finances. But it seems what she told me was the complete truth." Wentworth turned eyes as wet and watery as uncooked egg on Millicent. "A mere five thousand in the Exchange? Perhaps she misunderstood and it is five thousand per annum?"

"You impudent pup," cried Shoffer coming to his feet. "Is this how you approach a gentleman about his cousin's *dowry*? About settlements? How dare you…"

"Peace, Shoffer," Millicent rose and stopped Shoffer in his tracks by placing one hand on his solid chest. Her fingers tingled with the remembered pleasure of the previous night. For a moment she could not remember where she was or what she had been about to say, but could only stare at her lover. Shoffer caught her distraction and grinned at her. Then they both shook themselves and turned to face a pale Wentworth, who fortunately noticed nothing amiss.

"I am so very sorry, Mr. North," said Wentworth. "Not for anything would I lose your good opinion. I spoke to my father about Maude and he demanded that I get reliable information about the extent of your estate and responsibilities. I tried to assure him that you held your cousins in high esteem and would provide for them when they married, but he said you were still young and could marry yourself and would, of necessity, keep all your wealth to impress your wife's family. My only hope was there was another relative who could write a letter to my father and assure him that Maude was an heiress."

"And I thought I was the oddest fellow in London," said Millicent. "Here is a man who seems to be well ahead of himself. He is imagining that he will receive money from me and my hypothetical family. I am at a loss to think as to why I should do this."

"Oh. I thought you understood. It is only because of her paltry dowry that I have not yet offered for Maude."

"Miss Boarder to you!" Millicent shot a burning look at Shoffer. "You are closer; you hit him!"

Shoffer reached out and slapped a hand over the back of Wentworth's skull. The youth paled at the insult implied by the location of the blow. Obviously, Shoffer considered him unworthy of a blow to the face.

"You insolent little pup," said Millicent mildly, while Wentworth clutched at his head. "You have never entered my home to chat with the ladies when they are at-home. You have never called to take Maude riding in the park, nor appeared at her side at any public venue except for the duration of a dance. In short, you have never performed any of the usual courtship courtesies. And now you are here whimpering that the girl is too poor for your consideration! Am I supposed to cry 'Oh, I must increase her portion so that this idiot, this beggar, this weak and pitiable example of a wastrel will find her worthy of receiving his hand?' Do you know, I do not believe that will happen."

"It is my father that insists that the girl I marry have a certain amount of the ready," cried Wentworth.

This time Shoffer did not wait for Millicent's command and again slapped the youth, this time over the ears. The contempt in that gesture as well as the stinging pain brought tears to the boy's eyes.

"I say, Shoffer. That is uncalled for," said Wentworth.

"What? Are you going to take offense? Are you going to call me out?" Shoffer stepped closer and glared down at the younger man, who cringed away. "I thought not. Go away you pitiful excuse of a gentleman."

"And stay away from Miss Boarder!" added Millicent, as Wentworth scuttled away.

Millicent waited until the boy was out of sight before giggling.

"Silly fool."

"You best be careful," warned Shoffer. "If he approaches Maude as a wounded and rejected suitor, he may persuade her to improper behavior in the hope that after marriage he might be able to compel more funds from you. Or compromise her and threaten not to do the right thing in order to blackmail you."

"Maude is no fool."

"My dear North, London is filled with families who believed that their daughters had more sense than to be taken in, and found to their regret that young girls quickly forget their lessons when faced with poetic eyes and soulful glances."

"Really?" said Millicent, looking at him over her shoulder. "Then I should warn *all* the women of my family to beware any man who seeks to persuade them to do something their good sense advises they should not."

Shoffer snorted. "I do not mean you and me."

"I suppose not," said Millicent with a laugh, then she sighed and stared up along the garden path. "Poor Maude, she liked him, even when she did not want to."

"She shall do better. They both will. A gentleman will come who will value them for their many talents and good sense."

"Ah. Perhaps I should warn you. A certain gentleman has taken an interest in Mildred."

Shoffer's eyebrows winged up. "Oh? Why do I need to be warned?"

"Mr. Simpson has been visiting my house quite often since Mildred has asked his aid in arranging her first Ton event."

"So? That means nothing. I asked him to keep himself available should your family have need of him."

"He is spending his free hours in my front parlor choosing table linens and discussing flower arrangements for a tea party," said Millicent with a smirk.

"Oh, by God," cried Shoffer, clutching at his heart. "The man is sunk."

"Exactly my thought."

They stood staring at each other, then both burst into shared laughter at the fall of another bachelor. The laughter faded, but their gazes held.

"Millicent," whispered Shoffer and took a step toward her.

"Ah. Ha ha!" Millicent retreated, waving a finger at him. "No. No. No. Do not use that name!"

Shoffer's eyes darkened and his gaze settled first on her lips, then traveled down her form. There were no curves to admire, but his memory of what was hidden under the layers of cloth was excellent and warmed his blood.

"I beg you; come, spend the night with me."

"We cannot," cried Millicent.

"Please. Do you not desire me? Last night did we not all the passions prove?"

"Do all your family come over Shakespearian when crossed?"

"Please, the quote is Mallory, not Shakespeare," said Shoffer and he smiled, a slow curving of the lip revealing a hint of perfect teeth. A predator's confident smile.

Millicent could feel her legs weakening and heat pooling in her loins; she could barely force herself to continue backing away. She desired him too much. One taste of the forbidden fruit only had increased her hunger.

"How? And where?" she cried. "We cannot go to your mistresses' place. Two men arriving late at night? The story would be around London before dawn. There is no place for us to go to be together. How could we do it? I cannot change clothing in your carriage, your footmen would notice. I cannot bring you to my home, my family would know. Stop that. You are not listening to me."

Shoffer smiled, ignored her words and continued walking and Millicent continued to back away, not noticing that the section of the garden they were in grew darker and was enclosed by high hedges. Shoffer moved closer, his arms outstretched. Millicent shook her head and tried to dodge only to find herself blocked on every side.

"We cannot," she protested even as Shoffer laid siege upon her lips, dragging his hands over her body.

Masculine clothing was no barrier to his exploration. Her shirt was unbuttoned in a trice and his teeth seized and tormented her nipples until she writhed and bit her own lip to keep in her cries. His hand caught and cupped her buttocks, kneading and squeezing even as he lifted her up onto the base of a statue. The falls of her trousers were undone to permit the invasion of his fingers. Even as she melted under his assault, he drew down her trews to her ankles, parted her thighs and plunged.

"You cannot. You cannot," she gasped, even as her hot, velvet canal clenched about his shaft.

"I beg you," Shoffer slowed his movements with a groan, and pressed his face against her neck. "I need you."

"No children."

The relief that swept through him almost brought him to pleasure at that moment.

"Trust me," he gasped and thrust anew.

Millicent clung to him, arms, legs holding him tight in her embrace as her head fell back. She could not move with him, trapped as she was between statue and solid man. She could only endure the rising heat, the burning pressure as he filled and retreated. She could not escape the pleasure when it came, but trembled helplessly as it tore through her body. She barely noticed that Shoffer withdrew from her with a curse to spend himself upon the ground.

They stayed together as their breathing slowed. Millicent was the first to move, pushing Shoffer's face away from his resting place on her neck.

"You have quite destroyed my cravat," she complained.

Shoffer laughed and kissed her. "Who would be able to tell?"

"Brummel," was the reply and he laughed.

They separated and made use of a small fountain nearby to cleanse themselves.

"We cannot do this again," declared Millicent as she straightened her clothing. Shoffer merely nodded. "I am serious. We have been gone from the party too long and suspicions will be aroused. Whatever happened to not living in each other's pockets?"

"We shall return to the party separately the better to preserve your reputation." Shoffer saw Millicent's hand go up and dodged back out of range. "You should be more careful, my dear North. Slap anyone other than me and it might be misunderstood as a challenge."

"Oh." She thought for a moment, not lowering her hand. "Shall we have trouble with Wentworth?"

"That pup? Challenging either of us? No, that will not happen. He has not the courage!"

"I shall watch for him in any event." Millicent finished buttoning up the falls of her trousers. "You should go in first."

"Oh, no. I shall not leave you alone in this darkness. Who knows what might befall you. You go in. I shall watch to see that you are safe."

"What? Some lecher will fall on me from the shadows and have his way with me? That terrible event has already befallen." Millicent shook her head. "You will have to stop being so protective, Shoffer; someone will notice. In any event, you will not be able to watch over me after next week. I shall be gone."

Shoffer pressed her up against the tree in an instant, trapped between the implacable strength of his body and the rough bark.

"No, you will not." He rested his forehead against hers. "Stay. Stay with me."

"I cannot. You know I cannot." But she clung to him, relishing the heat of his body.

"We could spend the summer together," continued Shoffer. "I have properties that could benefit from a visit. I should not trust my secretary and business manager with everything. We could travel together. Alternate one of your properties with one of mine. Spend every day and night together until we have burned out this need."

"Simpson might be busy with other matters next year and appreciate the respite," Millicent murmured into his neck cloth. "But we cannot any more than we could be together here. Do you think staff in country inns gossip less than London servants?"

"There must be a way."

Millicent only shook her head.

"You could visit my house," suggested Shoffer. "We have spent hours together in the library without comment."

"With your sister in the house? Visitors and servants in and out at all hours? No. It will not do."

"Damn it, North, the season has only a few more weeks to run. There must be a way."

"We could visit your mistresses' house…"

"Two men going to a house of assignation where no woman resides? You are correct. I do not pay the staff there enough to keep that secret."

"Then we are back to my first assertion. It is not possible."

"And, yet, I am unwilling to end this liaison before I am sated."

Millicent drew back and regarded him calmly. "How romantic."

She could almost hear his teeth grinding.

"Damn it, North, you know what I mean. We have been together one night only. This does not count! You cannot say that I have exhausted your desire for me any more than I have tired of you. If we could but find time this season, we might wear out this need and return to being friends."

Millicent swallowed her shock and found herself speechless. Lack of romance was one thing she must accept. After all, she could not expect flowers and poetry when attired as a gentleman, but to baldly state his expectation that passion would fade quickly took her breath away.

"I suppose," she said when she could form words, "I should be grateful that you envision us remaining friends. You will have considerable power over me once this affaire is over."

"Oh, North, give over. We were friends long before we were lovers. If we are careful and do not quarrel too much, I do not see us enduring some terrible rupture. Besides, Beth would not permit me to cut you when the rumors of your perversion went about; she is unlikely to give up your friendship for any lesser reason."

"Perversion," repeated Millicent and dropped her hand down to seize and squeeze his buttocks. "The perversion was not mine alone."

He laughed, released her, and stepped back.

"We should return to the party. For now, North, we should give serious thought to solving the problem rather than protesting impossibilities. You have more experience in deception than me; therefore, I have great faith in your inventiveness."

"As Your Grace commands."

Chapter Seventeen

"What are your plans for the day, Beth?"

The breakfast room at Trolenfield house was grey and dreary, despite the bright colored wallpaper. A dismal driving spring rain rattled the tall windows, necessitating the lighting of lamps despite the early hour. Beth was not usually up before noon, but today she was neatly attired in a warm walking dress and tucking into her food with determination.

"I am assisting Mildred's cause," said Beth. "Today, I shall go to as many at-homes as I can and tell everyone that we both shall be attending her afternoon tea. Whether it rains or not!"

By the end of the sentence Shoffer was paying attention to his sister's every word. Anything to do with the Boarder family had the power to claim his complete attention.

"My apologies. Why must you do this?"

"Mildred's invitations have been out for two weeks and she has yet to receive a single acceptance, beyond ours that is. I suppose she is not considered high enough ranked for her invitations to be coveted."

Two weeks. Shoffer suppressed a groan. Two weeks of the season fled and Millicent was still avoiding him. Whichever event Shoffer chose to attend, he would find Mr. North had just left or was expected later. If he remained, North would not appear and if he left, he would find himself trailing from party to party in North's wake.

Pitiable, poor, pathetic moon-calf.

Not, he knew, the best way to suppress rumors.

Shaking his head he forced himself to pay attention to Beth.

"That surprises me, considering how popular Mr. North is," continued Beth.

Shoffer did not comment. The rumors about Mr. North must be well distributed by now. His star could well be fading and the Boarders' place in society with it.

"Well, certainly we shall attend Mildred's party," said Shoffer. "I was not aware that there were any difficulties. As Mr. Simpson took a hand in the arrangements, it should be a success."

"It shall be, if only we can persuade the Ton to attend. Poor Mildred is beside herself and threatening to cancel. I keep telling her not to. If she retreats now, she will never risk trying again."

Shoffer smiled at Beth. The girl had matured this season. No longer the fragile little shadow she had been after last season, she stepped up and became a dignified lady aware of her own power. A woman of character and strength.

However, her brother still regarded himself as her protector. If an action of his could further a cause of hers, then he would act. Besides, even though he had warned Millicent that there was a risk of invitations falling off, he had no wish for the end of the Boarder ladies first season to fizzle after such a dazzling beginning. He was fond of Mildred and little Maude and wanted them to be happy.

"What entertainment is planned?"

"I told you, there will be music. Mildred has hired a well-regarded small orchestra to play while people converse, but there is no expectation that people will dance. Mostly, they are expected to stand about, eat, and talk."

Shoffer considered for a moment.

"Might I suggest the soprano Mademoiselle Therese be invited to sing?"

Beth's eyebrows rose. "Does she not have a ... reputation?"

"Indeed, but it is an afternoon event and she will be gone long before dark so husbands will be safe from her. I only suggest it as then I can speak of the gathering in my clubs. The presence of the beautiful Therese will cause a few of the eligible gentlemen to attend. We can pass *that* gossip along to the marriage minded mothers who might then consider bringing their daughters."

Beth considered that. "I do not know that Mildred can afford to hire M. Therese."

"I could visit her and suggest she accept an invitation, instead. I know the lady desires some illusion of acceptance by the Ton. She might forgo her salary in exchange for a proper invitation."

"Oh? Would she do that for you? I had no idea she was your mistress."

"Beth!" cried Shoffer. "What a thing to say!"

"Bother that. I am old enough to know about such things as mistresses."

"You are not even old enough, in my opinion, to put up your hair and dance. Have pity for my grey hair." Shoffer patted his hand on his chest. "You will stop my heart entirely saying such shocking things."

"Oh, phoo."

"Besides, she is not under my protection. I only suggest it as a way of creating interest in Mildred's gathering."

"I shall consider it." Beth fiddled with the eggs on her plate for a moment, then continued. "I know. You will invite that handsome tenor so that the ladies will have someone to swoon over and some other stars of the stage, as well. We shall create a sort of afternoon salon. A socially acceptable way for the ladies of the Ton to meet actors. Usually we cannot call on them or visit them after performances, as that would be scandalous, but to see them in the afternoon, to praise their acting, that would be entirely proper."

"I suppose," said Shoffer, not entirely convinced he wanted his sister in the presence of actors.

"Surely, you and North together could persuade them to come."

Shoffer cut his beefsteak. Considering the changes in her personality, he could not take the risk Beth might not take it into her mind to go visiting the theaters should he refuse. "Very well."

"Excellent." Beth rose to her feet. "Up brother, and away. You have much to accomplish."

Shoffer grinned back at her, then turned to the nearest footman. "Please send a message for Maricourt Place. Inform Mr. North he must attend me while we go about guaranteeing his cousin's party's success!"

By not writing a note, he forced the footman to announce the command. North, he knew, would be forced by his own family to go out with him. There had to be a way for him, in between their errands, to find time alone with Millicent in the same room as a bed.

Shoffer was arguing with his valet about the complexity of his cravat – wanting something simple he could recreate without assistance if he was lucky enough to disrobe that afternoon – when the message arrived.

An unscented, folded, and sealed corner of parchment with his name scrawled across the front lay on the footman's salver. Suspecting it was some excuse from North he flipped it open and read the signature. Immediately his body tightened and came to full arousal.

She had signed it "Helene." Her female name. The female he had enjoyed for one night and who had tormented him and left him sleepless every night since.

Helene.

And if she had signed her name Helene, it was obviously a signal that she wanted him to enjoy that female body, again. Shoffer was entirely in favor of that idea.

Fortunately for his blushes, his valet was distracted and the footman had already turned away. Shoffer pulled free of his valet's hands and stalked across the room to stand staring out of the window until his body had calmed.

"Your Grace? Is something the matter?"

Shoffer did not turn. "No, Ikelsby. You may go, I shall finish here myself."

There was a moment's silence, then the door closed, marking Ikelsby's departure. Shoffer again opened the note and smiled as he read.

"Your Grace, please meet me at your *other* house at two. Helene."

Helene!

Millicent.

Tucking in the ends of his cravat as he ran down the stairs, he called for his horse rather than the carriage. He wanted to be there when she arrived to answer the door himself, just in case she arrived in her disguise as Mr. North. He did not want her loitering on the doorstep an instant longer than necessary. Never before had he ridden at such speed through London's crowded streets. He was directing his horse around the last corner when he spotted a lady strolling along the pavement. Tall and dignified, her pacing firm and her parasol raised proudly over the feathers in her bonnet, her hips swayed in a manner that caused more than one man to turn his head to watch her walk away. She was attired in a costume that suited her very well, while still being somewhat out of fashion. He recognized that step, that form, that economy instantly and his lips curved as he came alongside, swung down to the ground and faced her.

Ringlets framing her face beneath her bonnet, Millicent smiled up at him as she offered her gloved hand in greeting.

"Your Grace," she murmured, bobbing a small curtsy.

He bowed over the hand, then turned it over to kiss the inside of her wrist.

"My dear M…"

"Ah, ha?" She waggled a finger at him.

"My dear *Helene*. I have missed you beyond words."

"Have you? But I have hardly noticed your absence."

"Oh, cruel. When you are the sunlight of my day," he waved at the overcast sky, "it is dismal and grey without you."

She inclined her head toward him. "How flattering."

"Minx."

"Lecher."

He tucked her hand into the crook of his elbow and they strolled along the last few yards, Shoffer leading his horse. At the house, Shoffer knocked rather than let them in with his own key. The housekeeper's husband appeared immediately, peering around the door, then squeezed past them to deal with the horse. When the housekeeper arrived, Shoffer reached into his vest pocket and handed Millicent his key.

"Mrs. Fosters, this is Helene Winthrop. She will be visiting me here from time to time."

Mrs. Fosters was polite, but her eyes remained unimpressed as she bobbed a curtsy. Millicent was not surprised. No doubt Mrs. Fosters saw an ever changing parade of ladies through these doors, and was confident in her employment. She was here before the ladies and would be there long after.

"Do you require anything?" asked Mrs. Fosters. "Tea? Sherry?"

"No, thank you," said Millicent.

"And your luggage?"

"Thank you, but I shall not be living here. His Grace and I will visit only."

With the introductions over, Shoffer took her arm and guided her up the stair.

"I was very pleased to receive your note, my dear," he said. "How did you manage to ... escape?"

Millicent laughed as he escorted her to the upstairs bedroom. "Ah, well, for a while I considered changing in a hackney, but you are correct, the floors are filthy and the drivers are not drunk enough to ignore a male passenger entering and a female alighting. Then I considered leaving my home before the servants were up and about, but that would not do. Do you have any idea the hour they get up? Then," she drew off her bonnet and her curls and tossed the wig and hat onto a nearby table, "I found a house for rent that backs onto the same mews that runs behind this house."

"So close?" Shoffer seized his cravat and dragged it free, throwing it across the room. "Excellent. But will *your* servants not comment?"

"I have not hired any staff. I cleaned one of the rooms myself and set it up as a dressing room." She loosened the bodice of her pelisse and shrugged out of it. "If I am careful no one shall take note of my comings and goings. I shall enter through the mews as a man and exit the front door a lady."

She turned to face him and found his arms open wide. Two steps brought her into his arms to receive his kiss. They clung together, swaying and moaning as the kiss deepened and swept them away from such mundane matters as the journey. The only thing that mattered was the destination – each other's arms.

As the sweat dried on their bodies, Shoffer pulled Millicent close and ran a soothing hand down her spine. So soft and feminine a body to hide beneath all those layers of masculine attire, he smiled as he repeated the gesture possessively. He was the only man who would know her like this. The only one to have joy of her. To see her soft and replete in the aftermath of pleasure.

"If you stop doing that, I shall hurt you," said Millicent, her eyes still closed and a gentle smile curving her mouth.

"I shall never stop."

"Silly man, it would look very odd when we are strolling along Bond Street."

Shoffer laughed. "Speaking of Bond Street. We should find time to go there, with you dressed as a woman. There is no need for my mistress to go about attired in last year's fashions. I shall buy you whatever you need."

Now her eyes snapped open. "What is it about me that compels you to change my dress? First, Mr. North, now Helene? Have you no other occupations?"

"Undressing you has its pleasures, as well." They both laughed at that. "But it occurs to me that we should be seen about town together. Helene and Timothy taking the air in the park and visiting shops and the theater will help with putting down the rumors and I should enjoy your company."

"The rumors about you, which are not very strong to begin with, but me," her gaze traveled down his long, strong legs. "You would not look as well in women's clothing as I do in men's, and we would have difficulty explaining the pelt on your décolletage. I cannot see taking the air with Timothea on my arm."

She tugged at the curls on his chest even as he rolled her onto her back.

"That will never happen," he growled.

"Not even for me?" she fluttered her eyelashes.

Shoffer laughed and pressed his face to her neck. When he recovered and pulled back, he watched her with a thoughtful gaze. "I have never laughed while making love before."

"Why are you surprised given present company? Do you like it?"

"I find that I do." He took hold of her breast and feasted for a while upon her nipples. When he raised his head again his eyes were dark and his expression feral. "Yes, and I believe you do as well."

It took two attempts to get them out of the house that afternoon as they both were easily distracted and seduced by the other. By the time they succeeded in getting fully dressed the Bond Street stores were closed and most of the Ton were retired to their homes to rest and prepare for the evening's entertainment. Shoffer rode a few streets away and loitered about waiting for Millicent. She arrived soon enough, mounted on a horse from Shoffer's own stable, attired in Mr. North's loose clothing. Shoffer smiled to see her. Millicent regarded his satisfied expression as she approached and replied with a frown.

"You cannot look at me as if I am a sweet cake when I am North. No wonder people talk!"

"You are entirely correct." Shoffer's smile vanished in an instant. "That will not do. Of your kindness, remind me if I should do that again."

"Certainly, and you must stop insisting on accompanying me home. I can find my own way."

"We are not going directly home. We have errands to run for your cousin, Mildred."

Millicent tried to raise her eyebrows. "Why would Mildred appeal to you?"

"Actually, Beth told me. She wants us to persuade a few of the more interesting actors and actresses currently fashionable to attend your Mildred's afternoon tea in the hope that it will encourage the Ton to attend."

"Is that wise?" asked Millicent, after some thought. "Will that not lower the tone of the event?"

"It has become necessary."

"Oh?"

"Or else we two will have to eat a tea for two hundred without assistance. Did they not tell you, no one has responded to the invitations?"

Millicent's hands tightened on her reins and the horse protested and bridled.

"They had not told me."

"Do not be offended. It is possible they hoped that the situation would change before you heard of it and they may have feared you would command them to cancel the arrangements."

Millicent closed her eyes and groaned. "I am not really a pinch-penny. Why can they not tell me these things?"

"The cry of all males when considering the motivations of their females," replied Shoffer. "But we can aid them. Before we return home, we shall visit Covent Garden and The Strand theaters, speak to a few of the better-mannered thespians, and see what bribes are necessary to guarantee their sober attendance."

Appearing at the stage door with a duke at her side was an educational experience for Millicent. Lacking any interest in setting up a mistress, she had no reason to pursue an acquaintance with the ladies of the theaters. She was, therefore, astonished to see the degree of undress that those ladies considered appropriate for receiving visitors. Once she and Shoffer were ushered through the dim and dusty backstage corridors to a shabby sitting room, voluptuous women dressed in little more than chemises and perfume emerged from the depths of backstage – driven by the mere hint of a rumor that a duke had entered the theater. Millicent was astonished to discover that Mr. North was known here by reputation. A plump, pink lady whose turn included singing "naughty" songs forced her way through the crowd to lay claim to Millicent's lap and nothing could turn her away. Millicent considered appealing to Shoffer for aid, but after one look at his grinning face, she changed her mind and resigned herself to having her knees crushed and all four of her cheeks pinched.

The singer flung one arm about Millicent's neck and pressed her face into a pillowy bosom. It would have been tolerable, even amusing, if the lady was in the habit of bathing regularly. As it was, the scent of fermenting flesh, rancid perfume, and greasy makeup turned Millicent's stomach.

Fortunately, the singer was not on Shoffer's list of prospective invitees.

Mademoiselle Therese, seated at Shoffer's right hand, draped in a peignoir of lace and satin, was flattered and teased into consenting to grace the tea with her presence. If she was under the impression that the duke himself was hosting the party, that was her misunderstanding and not his fault. As the duke had hoped, the poor Mademoiselle wanted desperately to receive social acceptance and was willing to forgo performance payment for such a prestigious invitation.

It was obvious she also expected to receive an offer of protection from Shoffer. Millicent closed her eyes rather than watch the two flirt. Jealousy was an unpleasant emotion that she was determined not to indulge. Besides, if a wife could not expect to spend as much time in her husband's company as his friends, then a mistress could expect much, much less. Millicent knew she would not exchange her place in Shoffer's life for anything.

The male actors took less time to persuade than the ladies. Millicent and the duke visited Shoffer's selections in their dressing rooms, stated the date and time, and received immediate acceptances.

They were ambushed by ambitious actresses as they attempted to leave. Millicent was struggling to free herself from her plump admirer when a group of gentlemen were escorted in. Millicent recognized two of them; Shoffer, it appeared, knew them all. The eldest recoiled in shock to see Millicent and Shoffer well occupied by the opera dancers.

"Setting up a mistress, Shoffer?" cried the youngest, seeing Shoffer with one on each arm and another pressing her assets against his chest. "I say, play fair. Leave one or two for the rest of us."

"The race goes to the swiftest … and wealthiest," replied Shoffer blandly.

"And Mr. North," said another, affecting to be greatly shocked. "I had not thought to see *you* here."

"How can I resist the manifold charms of a well-acted play?" asked Millicent, ignoring the unspoken message. "The powerful words. The high emotions. The histrionics... the cleavages."

The plump singer giggled and tightened her grip on Millicent's arm.

"But we are late," said Shoffer. "The ladies of our households will not be pleased if we delay their departures for this evening's entertainment."

He worked his way free of the actresses, kissed the fingers of one, then nodded his farewell to the gentlemen. Millicent found it more difficult to free herself, but eventually she was standing in the fetid back alley. The singer followed her to the door, and waved a handkerchief. Millicent managed to send her a smile, despite a tightly clenched jaw. Her mood was not improved by Shoffer's broad grin.

When Millicent raised a threatening fist in his direction, Shoffer dodged out of range.

"Come, now, North, it is all to the good. Just give it a few hours and it will be all over London that you are setting up a mistress."

"Oh, yes, that *is* good news." Millicent stalked past him toward where an urchin waited, holding their horses. "And the story will go that I require you to hold my hand and guide me in the selection of a courtesan. That will certainly enhance my reputation as a gentleman."

Shoffer grinned. "You cannot tell me that it is not better than the current story."

"I do not know," snarled Millicent, turning to face him and raising her voice. "Shall we start the same about you? That you are such an innocent, helpless virgin that..."

"Lower your voice!"

Millicent smiled and passed a coin to the waiting boys.

"Do not worry, Your Grace, I shall keep your secret. No one will suspect that you have reached such a great age without *knowing* a woman."

"Insults and abuse?" Shoffer threw himself into the saddle. "This is my reward for aiding your sister?"

"Perhaps you should appeal to her in person if you wish kind words and flattery."

Mildred's reaction to Millicent's and Shoffer's labors was not exactly what they had expected. Millicent greeted her sister with a report of their afternoon's activities upon spying that worthy as she descended the main staircase. Mildred first went pale, then red; then the shouting began.

"How dare you?" shrieked Mildred. "What were you thinking? No. You could not have been thinking and done such a thing. Mr. North, you, I believe, are capable of any foolishness, but you, Your Grace, I thought you possessed better sense, better understanding of the Ton!"

With that she burst into tears and ran back up the stairs, leaving Millicent and Shoffer open-mouthed and gasping in her wake. Millicent recovered first.

"You told me this was a plan! I assumed that you had received instructions!"

"I...I..." Shoffer stuttered into silence. Now that he came to think of it, he was uncertain how it had come about. "We were talking, Beth and me, about how your sister's party was looking to be a disaster and..."

"And you, in your magnanimity, decided to interfere in an event that my sister has been planning for weeks. Her debut as a hostess to the Ton?" Millicent drew herself up to her full height and glared, hot and fierce, at the duke. "You arrogant son of a bitch. How dare you? Do you not understand that there are some matters where one would rather fail by one's own efforts than be rescued by a superior, smug, know-it-all!"

Merit, who had emerged to take personal charge of the duke's hat and gloves, turned ice pale and his knees gave way. The nearest footman dropped Millicent's hat to seize Merit by the arm. The two staggered and fell, knocking the hall table with its burden of bric-a-brac to the floor. Even as the echoes faded, Millicent turned and followed her sister up the staircase. Shoffer stood abandoned for a few moments before shaking himself, collected his own gloves from the floor and departed. He was so disturbed that he forgot the horse waiting for him and walked the darkening streets to his home.

Ignoring his own butler and footman, Shoffer kept the company of his hat and gloves, strode through to his study, and poured out a generous amount of brandy. It was not until he had drained half the glass that he noticed that he still wore his gloves.

Cursing women in general, and all the women of the Boarder household in particular, he tore off his gloves and threw them on the nearest flat surface with enough force that they bounced and landed on the floor.

"Your Grace?" ventured his butler.

"Where is my sister, Forsythe?"

"Upstairs, resting in preparation for this evening, Your Grace."

"Well, wake her and inform her there is no need. I have decided we shall not be going out tonight."

To do him credit, Forsythe hesitated before speaking. "Not going out?"

Shoffer did not reply. Forsythe hurried from the room to carry the message himself, instead of delegating it to younger legs.

Beth appeared within five minutes having run through the house in her dressing gown and slippers rather than take the time to dress for the interview.

"Timothy? Whatever is the matter?" she demanded.

"Lady Elizabeth," replied Shoffer in the coldest tones he had ever used with his sister. "Pray tell me, when did you discuss the need for changes to be made to Mildred Boarder's tea party with Miss Mildred herself? When did she approve your intervention?"

Beth stared at him open-mouthed. "I … that is, I saw that Mildred was upset and I wanted to help…"

"Did she ask? Did she specify that she desired you to act?"

"Well, no, but I had to. I could not bear it if she was humiliated by the Ton."

"So you decided to humiliate her yourself?"

"No. No." Beth went pale and pressed her fingers to her lips. "I did not mean to."

"This was poorly done by us, sister. I include myself in this, as I did not verify that my interference was requested. I undertook to carry out our plan, involving Mr. North in its completion, without considering the opinion of Mildred Boarder, the hostess. Were we to do thus for any other lady of the Ton we would be justly shunned."

"Oh, no!" cried Beth.

"She is justly displeased with us, and has included her cousin in her ire, who is innocent in this."

"Oh. Oh, I am so sorry. I shall speak to Mildred tonight at the ball and apologize. She will understand."

Shoffer shook his head. "Not tonight. You go nowhere tonight."

"But we are expected."

"Consider it a justly deserved punishment, Beth. We shall take no entertainments tonight. Tomorrow, we shall present ourselves as penitents to the family Boarder and make a formal apology. I suggest you spend this evening drafting a letter since I judge that a verbal apology is insufficient."

Beth opened her mouth to protest, then colored and nodded. "Of course, Timothy, you are correct. Must I stay in my room?"

"Is that where your writing desk is located?"

"No. The upper drawing room. I can have it moved."

The question puzzled Timothy for a moment, then he saw how pale Beth had gone, how thin her lips, and he remembered when he had seen her thus before. He smiled and crossed the chamber to give her a hug.

"Dear Beth, do not be afraid. I am not going to lock you in a closet. I am cross with both of us and do not think there is an armoire in the house large enough to hold us both."

Beth giggled at the image and relaxed.

"I shall be ready whenever you decree tomorrow, Timothy. Thank you."

Shoffer gave her another squeeze, then let her go. As he watched her, he could feel his anger fade, to be replaced by the glow of pride. It was not until he was alone, again, that he remembered Millicent's fury and sighed. How complicated his life had become, but all things considered, he would not give up any part of it. He settled in the large wing-backed chair beside the fireplace and stared at its empty twin, imagining Mr. North grinning at him and expounding on some piece of nonsense.

He missed him. Missed her.

He growled and sank further into the chair's embrace. Mr. North, Millicent, Helene – the woman possessed more faces, more lives, more lies than any other person of his acquaintance. Knowing what he did about her facility for falsehoods, he should spurn her, cut the acquaintance. Certainly he should not permit his sister to continue associating with the man – who was a woman – about whom everything he knew was a lie.

He covered his face with both hands and tried to rub some sense into his tired brain. The truth was he liked and trusted Millicent … North … Helene.

Whoever she was.

Despite the lies, the absolute disgraceful impropriety of her deception, she was the most honorable person of his acquaintance. When she was near, he depended upon her good sense, her insights into human nature, her refusal to kowtow to the pretenses of the Ton. For the first time, he was enjoying the season, seeing the posturing and pretensions through her eyes. He missed her conversation, her good humor.

His body heated and his groin grew heavy. Truth to tell, he missed her smooth curves and willing body.

Male friend and feminine lover, she was everything he needed.

If only he could find a way to have both of her identities in his life, he would be a very happy man.

Chapter Eighteen

Shoffer and Beth presented themselves at Maricourt Place at the earliest hour for a morning call. Merit opened the door to them and actually kept them waiting in the hall while he verified that Mildred and Mr. North were at home. Shoffer nodded his acceptance of this unspoken rebuke, to Merit's relief.

A few minutes later Merit descended the steps to inform the duke and his sister that the family was indeed at home and would be down in a few minutes. They were guided to the formal drawing room. North and Mildred arrived together, Mildred's hand resting lightly on Mr. North's sleeve. Beth came her brother's side to echo the posture. Both men bowed and ladies curtsied and they stood facing each other.

Millicent's lips twitched. Shoffer raised an eyebrow, then the tension broke and all four started laughing.

"What a load of bu…" began Millicent.

"Mr. North, there are ladies present," interrupted Shoffer.

"I was going to say Ton. Yesterday, was a lot of Bad Ton."

"Really?" inquired Mildred. "That is not what you called it last night."

"It is not what *you* called it, either," shot back Millicent. "I was quite impressed by your vocabulary. So were three sailors who happened to be passing."

"I admit I am surprised to see you so well disposed toward each other," said Shoffer. "I thought there might have been bloodshed."

"And you came so quickly to my aid," said Millicent dryly, drawing her pocket watch out and examining it. "It only took you ten hours to find your way back here."

"Oh, Mr. North apologized and explained last night," said Mildred. "In fact, there was such beating of the breast, moaning, weeping, and wailing that I was required to accept his apology much earlier than I would have, as I was afraid the neighbors would complain and the servants give notice if I did not."

Beth giggled, then held out a neatly sealed letter. "I should like to apologize for my presumption. It was very wrong of me to interfere in your preparations. In case I became nervous and forgot what I wished to say, I have put it all in this letter."

"I shall be certain to read it and admire your phrasing, in case I am ever in the same position," said Mildred, accepting the note and tucking it away in a pocket, unread.

Before she could continue Merit appeared at the door.

"Mr. Simpson," he announced and withdrew reluctantly.

Poor Simpson hesitated at the door staring at the assembly.

"I apologize for the disturbance." He wrung his hands, his eyes flickering from North to Mildred to Shoffer and back to Mildred. "I have come in hope of a private word with Mr. North."

Mildred's indrawn breath was the only hint she knew what the private word was about. Millicent affected unconcern and regarded the duke's secretary calmly.

"Why, Mr. Simpson, how are you today? Have you found something else for me to buy or rent? Dear heaven, I hope I have enough blunt at hand. Is it tea or cake that you come to discuss?" She took Simpson by the elbow and turned him about. "Do come along and tell me all about it."

Just outside the room she paused and glanced back at Shoffer.

"Oh, no," laughed Shoffer. "I am not so much an arrogant, smug know-it-all as to intrude on *private* conversations."

Millicent wrinkled her nose at him and gave him her back, leading Simpson down the corridor to her study.

Since that room was her "masculine" preserve, it was not much tidier than old Mr. Prichart's, the Welsh farmer. Papers and broken pens covered all flat surfaces. Filos and boxes of documents were stacked beside her chair.

Simpson sank into the offered chair and folded and unfolded his hands.

"Oh, do stop fussing, Mr. Simpson. I am not an ogre." Millicent glanced about, seeking some masculine device with which to comfort her visitor, but as she did not smoke or drink, she kept neither in her retreat. "Shall I send for tea?"

"No. No. That is not necessary."

When Simpson started to climb to his feet to pace, Millicent put a firm hand on his shoulder and pushed him back.

"The only thing I can think of to put you into such a state, would be if you were seeking my cousin's hand in marriage," began Millicent.

There was such an expression of relief in Simpson's eyes that Millicent began laughing.

"What, you think to surprise me? I have been discussing your dowry with His Grace this last week or more."

"*My* dowry?" gasped Simpson.

"Why, yes. You thought I would not inquire? I sought out His Grace for confirmation that you will not come empty handed to this marriage."

Simpson shook his head, confused, then caught the glint of humor in Millicent's eyes.

"Oh, Mr. North, you quite took me in. You were joking."

"Exactly so," said Millicent, with a smile. "I am acquainted with the high regard in which His Grace holds you and assume that you will continue in his employ for some time. My concern for your ability to care for and support my cousin is therefore dispelled. As to the matter of rank and connections, you and my cousin are equals as both of you are distantly related to an earl. Not the same earl, fortunately."

"Yes. Yes."

"And I assume that you offer from affection."

Simpson continued to nod, smiling broadly.

"Excellent. Then the only matter still to be discussed is which one of my cousins did you prefer?"

Simpson stared at her blankly for a few moments, then began to laugh. "And to think I feared to approach you. I should have known better."

"Oh, do not think me so eager to get my cousins off my hands that I would accept any offer for them. I know Mildred has the greatest respect and affection for you; and, therefore, I bow to her judgment in the matter. I must trust that you promise to care for and look after her?"

"Yes, Mr. North."

Mildred nodded. "And you know how small her portion is, since you have been present at all my discussions with His Grace on the matter."

"Yes."

"Then you have my blessings. Shall I send her to you so you may make her cry?"

"Please."

Simpson rose and began pacing before the fireplace while Millicent left the room. Tea had been served in the formal parlor and Shoffer, Beth, Maude, and Mildred all looked up, falling silent when Millicent returned. Millicent met all their expectant gazes with a calm one of her own before turning to Maude.

"Maude, dear, may I speak with you privately please?"

"Maude? *Maude?*" cried Mildred, coming to her feet, her eyes blazing.

"Well, yes," said Millicent, her expression blank. "Mr. Simpson just asked for the honor of marriage with my prettiest, most serene, beatific, talented cousin. Of course, I knew he meant Maude."

Mildred snarled at Millicent and pushed her against the wall as she charged past on her way into the hall. Those remaining in the room laughed.

"Actually, Your Grace, Lady Elizabeth, I do need to speak briefly with Maude. If you will excuse us a moment?"

Shoffer and Beth exchanged a puzzled glance. Shoffer nodded and Maude followed Millicent to the second, less formal front parlor.

Millicent waved Maude to the couch and came to sit beside her, taking Maude's hand in hers.

"You frighten me, Mr. North," said Maude, paling. "Has Mr. Simpson asked to wed us both? How very Moorish."

"No, dear girl. Although, I am pleased to see your sense of the absurd is intact. No, I have meant to speak to you for some time, about Mr. Wentworth."

"Him?" Maude waved a hand dismissively. "He is nothing."

Millicent's shoulders sagged. "Dear girl, I am pleased to hear you say so, but why? How has he lost your regard? I admit I have my own reasons for sending him on his way. I wanted you to know that I would not be accepting his pursuit of you."

"Oh, I am glad to hear you say that. I cannot stand the man. He had the nerve to suggest to me that I ask you to give Mildred's dowry to me because, he said, Mildred was so old and dull featured that she should never marry, and therefore, might live with you and look after your household and not need the money."

Millicent reared back and gaped at her. "He wanted Mildred's dowry in addition to yours?"

"Horrible man. As if I would steal my sister's money. He is not worthy of my regard and I told him so."

"I am very glad to hear it. Shoffer suggested he might come to you as a poetical rejected suitor and persuade you to do something silly. I was afraid to raise the matter with you for fear of making him more attractive by being forbidden. Nor do I want you to be motivated by jealousy of your sister's happiness with Mr. Simpson to make a foolish decision."

Maude sneered and sniffed at that suggestion, reassuring Millicent of her sister's good sense.

"Well, I am glad that is settled." Millicent rose, extending a hand to her sister. "Let us go back to the others and see if we might cancel this dreadful afternoon tea that has been the cause of so much trouble."

Alas for Millicent's hopes, Mildred was still determined to have her party.

"I see no reason to cancel," declared a glowing Mildred when she and Mr. Simpson returned to the formal parlor. "I am quite looking forward to it."

"But the only reason we beg…"

Mildred pinched Millicent's arm, hard. Millicent fell silent and let the remainder of the discussion wash over her. It was not until tasks were assigned that she again paid attention. Shoffer and Millicent were given a list of "interesting people" to whom personal invitations were to be issued. The actors and singers already invited were still to attend, but Mildred decided to expand her afternoon tea into a full blown *event*. If the presence of persons of interest would bring the rest of the Ton, then Mildred wanted everyone. Shoffer was even commanded to see what could be done to ensure the presence of the Prince Regent – to his complete horror – and Millicent was ordered to fetch Brummell. Shoffer and Millicent exchanged long suffering glances, made their bows and left, leaving Mr. Simpson to bask in the admiration of his fiancée.

It was not until Shoffer and Millicent were standing on the footpath that Shoffer became aware of some lack in the morning's events.

"Where is your cousin Felicity? I have not seen her this morning at all."

"Oh, last night's shouting and apologies gave her a headache. She gave us strict instructions not to wake her this morning unless the house were burning down."

They both turned to stare at a house that was entirely unaffected by heat, smoke, or flame. Millicent cast a wicked grin in Shoffer's direction as his footman let down the carriage steps.

"Cruel, Mr. North. You are cruel. I am filled with admiration."

"Thank you."

Arriving back at Maricourt Place that afternoon, they found it in a state of polite uproar.

Beth, pleased that her dear friend and her brother's useful secretary were making a match, announced her intention to host a ball to celebrate the engagement. Felicity, made aware of the engagement, immediately protested. As mother of the bride, it was her responsibility to host any such party – but her house contained no ballroom. The argument bounced back and forth – the comments prefaced with such terms as "my dear Mrs. Boarder" and "with all due respect, Lady Elizabeth" – as the two women debated precedence and rank.

It was into this debate that Millicent and Shoffer walked, all unaware.

"Timothy. Timothy," cried Beth, leaping to her feet. "Please, my dear, support me. We have a ballroom and I have a larger guest list to use. We must host the ball."

"Which ball?" inquired Shoffer.

"It is hardly proper," cried Felicity. "Mr. North, I insist we must do it."

Millicent glanced back and forth between the two women, even as Beth seized both Shoffer's and Millicent's arms to draw them further into the room.

"You are a person of sense," said Beth to Millicent. "Inform your cousin that her suggestion simply will not do."

"I beg you, leave me out of this," said Millicent. "My duty, as far as my cousins are concerned, is to pay for their entertainments. I have no other role."

"This is far more important. As the head of our household, your voice is final." There was a note in Felicity's eye and a hardness to her voice that promised all manner of punishments if Millicent spoke against her mother's plan, head of the household or no. "You agree with me that we will host Mildred's engagement ball."

"Oh, but I thought we were having a garden party," said Millicent weakly. "An afternoon tea. It is all arranged and paid for."

"That," declared Felicity, "was arranged for an entirely different reason. The engagement requires a separate celebration."

"Oh, heaven," sighed Millicent sinking into a chair. "Another expense."

"Do not be a skinflint. This is your dearest cousin. You cannot be so miserly as to deny her an engagement ball."

"Actually, I rather prefer Maude…" began Millicent, grinning.

"No," cried Felicity, echoed by Beth.

"Enough," cried Mr. Simpson, overriding all voices and stunning his future mother-in-law into silence. "Ladies, as much as I appreciate your efforts on my behalf and the enthusiasm with which you wish to welcome me into your family, I must insist any engagement party be in proportion to my rank. While I am a member of the cadet branch of a good family and my dear Mildred is distantly related to an earl, a grand Ton ball is not the appropriate manner for announcing our engagement. A simple dinner party with friends is all that is required."

He beamed at them all. Millicent glanced toward her sister in time to see her nod her head in support of her future husband. Astonishing! Beth and Felicity growled and grumbled at having their plans dismissed, but soon turned to quarreling about which household would host the dinner. Shoffer caught Millicent's eye, then Simpson's and summoned them both with a jerk of his head. Without offering apologies to any of the ladies, the gentlemen retreated.

"Could I possibly impose upon you," said Millicent to Simpson, "to provide a home for your mother-in-law after your marriage?"

"Mr. North, how can you say that?" asked Simpson, with a grin. "I thought you liked me."

Millicent looked back at Lady Beth, her chin firm and lower lip pouted, her sisters glowing with shared happiness, Felicity, happy to have one daughter well settled, confident enough in her position to quarrel with the sister of a duke, and started to laugh. It took a moment for Shoffer to work out the reason, then he joined in. Simpson waited until after the ladies of the two households began to giggle before he surrendered to the general merriment.

Eventually Millicent regained control of herself. Looking Shoffer directly in the eye, she whispered, "I have never been so happy in my life."

"Nor have I," replied the duke.

After giving the matter serious thought, Beth announced over breakfast the next morning that she had resolved the matter of the engagement celebration.

"Did you not learn your lesson?" interrupted Shoffer, regarding his sister over the coffee pot. "The Boarders will not thank you for your presumption. It is their place to celebrate the engagement!"

"Oh, phoo, Timothy. I am not so much a fool as that. I intend to present it to Felicity in such a way that she will think it her idea. And when Mr. North protests the cost, then I shall step in and offer to share it."

Shoffer winced at the enthusiasm in her voice. He was learning to mistrust that tone. It seemed to presage all manner of difficulties for him. Although he could not bring himself to regret Beth's emergence from her shell, it was occasionally inconvenient.

"That is not proper at all, poppet. You cannot be giving money to Mr. North."

"Oh, do not frown so, Timothy, it is not so bad. I thought only to suggest that we go to Vauxhall for the evening. A small party. Just Mr. North and his family, Mr. Simpson, and ourselves. If there is any member of the senior branch of Mr. Simpson's family in town, we may invite them, as well." When Shoffer did not comment, she continued. "Only think, Timothy. What other entertainment in London is so egalitarian?"

"Egalitarian? What have you been reading?"

"Nothing you would not approve. Well? Shall you come with me to see the Boarders?"

Shoffer made a show of rolling his eyes and groaning. Before he could open his eyes warm arms were wrapped about his neck.

"Please. Please, Timothy. Say we can go. It will be so much fun."

"Dear sister, how can I refuse you when you are choking me to death?"

Beth loosened her grip, laughing.

"Little hoyden. What a bad example we have set you. Strangling people to get your way. Shocking little minx."

"'Twas meant to be a hug," pouted Beth.

"Very well. Present the suggestion to the Boarders, but be prepared to accept their refusal." When Beth gave a shout of joy, Shoffer continued. "Only because you are determined to visit Vauxhall and I will only permit you to attend in my company."

Beth bent to hug him again, and kiss his cheek before hurrying from the room.

"Thank you, best of all brothers," she shouted back over her shoulder. "Ask Forsythe to send round the carriage; I am going at once."

"Take a message for me," shouted Shoffer after her. "Tell North I shall see him later today. One o'clock. He knows where and why."

Beth waved and disappeared. A nod from Shoffer sent a footman to arrange for the carriage for Beth. After finishing his breakfast, Shoffer spent a few hours working with Simpson before departing for his appointment. It did not occur to him that Millicent would not be waiting for him. She would. She wanted him as much as he desired her.

Simpson found he was unable to hold the duke's attention to any of the matters raised. Not farm, nor mine, nor investments on the Exchange could batter through Shoffer's distraction.

"I think, Your Grace, that we are gaining nothing today."

"Are you dismissing me from my studies, Simpson?" Shoffer grinned. "Or are you seeking extra time to spend with your beloved?"

Simpson reddened slightly. "Miss Mildred is busy with her mother this morning. I was thinking more that your mind is elsewhere."

"I admit that is true. Perhaps I have spring fever. The weather is so much improved I would much rather be out and about."

Simpson's gaze flickered toward the window and back without changing expression. While it was not actively raining, the sky was overcast and dismal. It was an improvement over outright snow, sleet, or fog, but only a man blind or in love could imagine it a fine day.

"I have correspondence to attend to, Your Grace, if you wish to finish for the day."

"Bother the correspondence, Simpson. Go visit your fiancée. Steal her away from her family for a walk or some such. Life is too short to spend writing letters for me."

"As you wish, Your Grace."

"And tell Forsythe to have my greys set to my phaeton."

"Yes, Your Grace."

Simpson gathered his papers and left, still frowning. Not half an hour later, Shoffer was seated in his high flier, smiling, gloved hands gently gripping the reins.

It was a beautiful day, bright with a soft breeze. He hoped North was in a good mood for he fully intended that they not waste such a day indoors. He wanted to carry out his threat to take North shopping for clothes. A man bore the responsibility and the pleasure of dressing his mistress. North, skinflint that she was, spent too much time in secondhand clothes. This season's colors for married and experienced women were bright golds and blues which would suit her coloring brilliantly. He had seen some brocaded silks from China and India that would look very well on North. Lacking a lady's maid, North eschewed stays which made seduction easier for Shoffer, but that meant that soft, sheer chemises were more important and he knew exactly which store provided the best. And he wanted to purchase a few light, lacy night rails for her, as well. Stripping her out of her day dresses was all very well, but there was something about feminine curves, encased in glowing silk, moving towards a man through candle lit gloom that enhanced arousal.

He wanted to take her shopping. To have her hand resting on his arm as they paraded down Bond Street. Then, when she was suitably attired, they would take the air during the Grand Parade and he would show her off to the Ton gathered at the park. His smile broadened. He would be the focus of the greedy eyes of envious men when they saw him side by side with the most beautiful woman of the Ton.

He blinked and shook himself, almost colliding with another carriage.

By the Gods, he was in love. He was in love with North! There was no other explanation for the odd path of his thoughts.

When had he become so besotted? When?

Love could be the only name for the warmth that resided in his chest. The lightness of his step during the day. The heat that arose in him whenever he considered her name.

He was in love with his best friend, his dearest companion: North.

North was his friend, his lover; she was the one person he could trust with his treasured sister, with his mind and his confidences.

He considered the matter for a moment. Being in love with North was not a problem. Indeed, he approved it. He had been worried that he was incapable of that emotion and it was reassuring to finally achieve it. There was only the problem on continuing in this happy state considering that *she* insisted upon remaining a *he*.

This engagement of Simpson's would work well for the ongoing affaire with North. It was only to be expected that a devoted cousin such as North would want to visit the newlyweds. Shoffer, being a considerate employer and friend to both sides of the union would offer Mr. North accommodations in his own home whenever North came to visit the family.

It was even possible that cousin Felicity and little Maude would want to live close by to Mildred. Shoffer could find a house to rent to them and the sisters and mother could keep each other company. Not too big a house. He wanted no spare bedroom kept ready for North when she visited. And in the summer Shoffer and North could travel the countryside together visiting their properties. He would give the matter some thought. He was certain there was a way for that to be possible. Did not other gentlemen travel from house party to house party in each other's company?

Since the families were bonded by matrimony and common country society who could protest the constant companionship?

Hours spent riding together. Nights spent in each other's arms. The very thought was delightful. Since they both possessed female relatives no one would raise an eyebrow should female clothes be found in North's luggage. Then, whenever they were so inspired, "Helene" could appear in public with Shoffer and keep the gossips at bay.

And, if he gave the matter some thought, he might find some small cottage in an out of the way village they might use as a house of assignation. Somewhere North could wear women's clothing. Where they could walk together down country lanes as a man and woman.

He thought, when North revealed her true feminine nature, that it would be difficult to transfer his affection for his masculine friend to the female who lurked beneath the disguise, but that had not been the case. North's feminine nature was so engaging that Shoffer had fallen into desire and lust, and now love, without seeing the hole beneath his feet.

How odd, and yet, how not, that love had grown between them.

He considered the matter as he navigated the crowded streets. All things considered together, he did not mind being in love with North. She was a handsome, even-tempered woman whose jokes never failed to make him laugh and whose smile filled his heart with joy. He enjoyed her company above all others.

Loving one's mistress was not so much a sin as loving one's wife, in the eyes of the Ton – not that their opinions mattered.

His current relationship was complicated, but he saw less reason now to end it. North already had admitted she loved him. Now he knew he loved her.

Altogether, a very happy relationship.

His plans to take the air of Bond Street went out the window as soon as he arrived. The housekeeper met him at the door with the information that "Mrs. Winthrop" was already upstairs. Shoffer nodded, then jogged up the stairs two at a time. When he threw open the bedroom door, he found Millicent already situated under the blankets. Not, however, with the flow of her hair arranged over the pillows, her hair was too short for that. Nor was she smiling seductively and raising her naked arms toward him, drawing him across the room and into her embrace.

No.

Attired only in a thin cotton chemise, she was leaning against the headboard, legs crossed, with a filo open on her knees and she was reading correspondence while chewing on a pencil. Shoffer thought he had never seen so alluring a woman.

Millicent glanced up and smiled as she watched Shoffer draw off his cravat and begin unbuttoning his shirt.

"Good afternoon to you, Your Gracefulness."

"Good afternoon, my love."

He waited a beat to see if she would react to the word, but she did not. Instead she watched avidly as each layer of clothing was removed.

"I heard your sister's suggestion for the engagement party," said Millicent, conversationally as the duke's shirt followed his jacket to the floor. "I take it you have approved the outing? I find I do not trust the girl where her own amusements are concerned."

"Vauxhall? Yes. Although, I warned her Felicity might not." The bed creaked as he climbed in beside her.

"I would take it as a favor if you would advise her I only pretend to be a miser. It is not necessary for her to offer to pay her share out of her pocket money."

"North," Shoffer caught her chin in his hand, pushed her papers off the bed. "Shut up."

The kiss burned all the way through to his soul. His fingers tunneled into her hair as he sank into her mouth. His freshly discovered love enhanced the moment. He was not engaged in coupling, he was making love to the beautiful woman who held his heart. For the first time in his life each touch was worship. Each kiss a benediction.

He trailed his fingertips down her curves, following that path with his lips. Her skin trembled beneath his exploration, warm and soft. She held nothing back from him, concealed nothing. She was his to taste, his to enjoy, his to love. No other man would know her sweetness, her passion, he was determined in that. He moved further down her body and delved into her secret spaces, felt her body struggle and writhe beneath his invasion. No one would touch her, know her like this and hear her cries as pleasure tore through her body. Her hands would cling to his hair only, to his shoulders in extremis, and the weight of his body only would press her to the mattress as they joined. Grateful that she was too distracted to comment on the colored ribbons of his condom, he thrust into her, his grip on her buttocks bruising, the pistoning of his hips fevered.

As he found his release, he wrapped himself about her body, gasping, "Mine, mine, mine."

Chapter Nineteen

Millicent gazed vacantly out of the parlor window, smiling to herself. Yesterday, she had lain in Shoffer's arms naked and helpless while he had done such things to her that she could never have imagined. Even now the memory had the power to send heat to her loins.

"Mr. North. Are you attending?"

Millicent came upright in her chair, blushing and staring about, stunned to find herself in company. Mildred and Mr. Simpson sat side by side on a small love seat directly across from her. Maude sat, spine straight and hands occupied helping Felicity sort out her silks. It was Felicity who was scowling at Millicent.

"I do apologize, Cousin Felicity, I was ... distracted."

"Well, do pay attention. We were speaking of our outing to Vauxhall."

Millicent sighed and slumped back in the chair.

"Mr. North, this is an important event in our Mildred's life."

"I am aware of that, dear cousin, but I thought the arrangements were finalized."

"That was before." Felicity folded and tucked away another length of thread with considerable satisfaction. "Mr. Simpson has just learned that his second cousin, the Earl of Edgeware, is in town. He is planning on visiting the earl and requested he attend our little party."

Millicent's gaze met Mr. Simpson and saw only resignation there.

"It is a shame *our* relatives are not in town," continued Felicity. "It would make quite the event!"

"Yes. Shame," muttered Millicent.

"You should accompany him."

"Pardon?" Millicent was about to descend back into her daydream, but Felicity's voice brought her to attention. "Me? Why me?"

"I am certain the earl will have questions about Mildred that only you could answer."

Millicent groaned.

"Felicity, can you not be content with being an acquaintance of a duke? We have no need to pay calls upon Mr. Simpson's distant relatives. Beyond an invitation to the wedding, I am certain Lord Edgeware requires no further notice."

Felicity scowled. "You will call upon him. I insist. The acquaintance should not be permitted to lapse."

Millicent opened her mouth to protest further, but was forestalled by Simpson rising to his feet.

"I have His Grace's carriage with me since the ladies will be certain to need yours."

Millicent allowed herself to be ushered from the room, given her overcoat, and near pushed out of the house. Once she stood upon the footpath, she settled her coat and stared at her cousin-in-law to be.

"Why do you want to do this? I thought you a man of sense."

"I am. Mrs. Boarder is the one who ferreted out the earl's presence in London and she who insisted we should pay a call."

"That does not surprise me." Millicent followed Simpson into the waiting carriage noting as she did so that Simpson had brought the one with the heraldic device on the side. She cast Simpson a worried glance. Simpson gave her a reassuring smile and turned to wave at his mother-in-law to be who watched from the drawing room window. The carriage lurched into motion. Once they had turned the corner and were out of sight, Simpson flipped a length of heavy wool over the heraldic device on the door.

"Thank goodness for that," said Millicent, letting out a breath. "I thought you had lost your mind."

"Let me set your mind further to rest and tell you that His Grace is aware of Mrs. Boarder's request and has granted permission for us to use the carriage this morning. Further, he suggests that you make use of it should you have any further errands this afternoon."

Millicent grinned broadly. It was almost worth the embarrassment of paying an uninvited call on a high-ranked stranger when she would have the reward of time with Shoffer.

"Mr. North…" Simpson flushed and turned away.

"Simpson? Is there … have you found something else for me to buy?"

Simpson's smile faded quickly.

"My dear Simpson, you appear troubled. Have you changed your mind about Mildred?"

"No. No! Mildred is everything that is a delight. I cannot imagine my life without her."

"I am happy for you." Millicent peered closer at Simpson. "You do not appear to be happy."

Simpson stared down at his hands. "Mr. North, I regret having to raise this subject with you, but it has been brought to my attention that…"

He stopped speaking and stared out of the window, a dark flush staining his face.

"Ah." Millicent sighed. "You have heard those dreadful rumors, I suppose."

Simpson nodded.

"Do not worry. Shoffer brought that to my attention some time ago."

"Of course, His Grace is an honorable man and the fact he continues to associate with you is taken by many as proof that the accusations have no weight."

Millicent's eyes narrowed. There was a note in Simpson's voice, a hesitation. Perhaps he thought, as others did, the opposite was true. That the continued association was proof.

"And you, what do you believe?" inquired Millicent.

"Forgive me, Mr. North…"

"Oh, no. Let us not speak of forgiveness. Speak out if you must. Have some courage!"

"Very well. I am troubled by the effect your reputation will have on my family."

"This peer upon whom we are forced to call?"

"Exactly. He is a man known for high moral principles and fierce adherence to biblical precepts."

"Spare me the details. What do you require? That I tell my cousin I suddenly remembered an important meeting and left you to face your uncle alone?"

"That would do … as a beginning."

This time Millicent turned fully on her seat to face Simpson. Her voice dropped to its deepest register and she scowled at him.

"The only reason I do not call you out is that Mildred would strangle me and Felicity would crush my bones to powder should this wedding not take place. I offered to retreat from London when the rumors started, but His Grace directed otherwise. You should keep in mind, Mr. Simpson, that His Grace has already begun planning for the summer. We shall be doing a tour of our estates, together. Accustom yourself, sir, to facing down whispers and hints and stares for they shall continue to be a part of your life if you remain in His Grace's employ, married to my cousin!" She gave a hard rap on the roof and the carriage slowed. "But for now, out of sympathy for your uncle's delicate sensibilities and the very distant possibility that he might include you in his will, I shall leave you to be Daniel to his lion."

With that she swung herself down to the street, turned her back on the carriage, and strode away. She did not pay attention to where she was and the quality – or lack of it – of the persons sharing the street for a quarter hour. It was not until she dodged a particularly foul smell emanating from an alley that she shook herself into awareness and took note of her environs. She was, she realized, in one of the worst of London's stews. The lane was narrow, the ground beneath her feet covered in filth, and the people on the street either ignored her or stared in a threatening manner. She resumed walking at her previous rapid pace, aware that several watchers fell in behind her. Millicent's throat tightened and her mouth dried. Bad enough to be outed as female by the Ton, but she would not speculate what could happen if these men discovered her secret. She tried to keep her face impassive as she sought up and down the road for some sign, some path of escape.

Outside one rickety house stood a cluster of slovenly women with dresses that the seamstress seemed to have forgotten to put bodices on. Grinning, Millicent hurried to that house. The ladies welcomed the fresh faced lad she appeared to be and ushered her into the house. The parlor was as filthy and smelly as the street and Millicent did not want to think how long it had been, if ever, since the ladies pressing against her had bathed. Smiling as gallantly as she could, Millicent bowed to the rotund prioress of the bawdy house in which she had taken shelter.

"My dear lady. I do apologize for my sudden entrance. I began to suspect the gentlemen on the street outside would deprive you of the opportunity of robbing me."

The madam smiled in return displaying a mouth in which teeth were honored more in memory than in presence. "Always ho'ored to have the fancy visit," she said, extending her hand toward the whores. "What is it yo're wanting this fine day?"

"I want to get home alive." At the madam's rude chuckle, Millicent continued. "Forgive me, dear lady. My name is Mr. Anthony North, and while I am certain that…"

She got no further.

"Mr. North," cried one of the ladies. "We was reading about you just last night."

"Really?" Millicent could not work out what made her more astonished. That the dirty woman facing her could read or that reading gossip sheets was the entertainment of bored whores?

One of the older, tinier ladies simpered. "I'd some lessons when I was younger," she admitted somewhat sadly, her accent hinting at some gentility in her history. "And the gents leave their papers behind sometimes, so I read the society gossip."

Millicent was astonished. Mr. North's reputation had reached all the way down here? What would Shoffer say?

"Dead useful for lining me shoes, papers," said a woman with unbelievably red hair.

"That use I will acknowledge," said Millicent. "I realize there is a fee to be paid for your aid, but I have wandered far from home and need assistance to return to more familiar streets."

Negotiations with the madam took some time. A messenger, the madam's grandson, was fetched and sent out to find a cabbie brave or stupid enough to come this deep into the stews. Then Mr. North paid a fee for a few of the ladies to go out and distract the men watching the house. While Millicent waited for the messenger and hackney to arrive, she entertained the madam and her senior employees with tales of the entertainments and excesses of the Haute Ton. To her complete astonishment the women demanded to be taught the "fan language of cats just like proper ladies." That occupied Millicent for over an hour. The ladies were as eager for entertainment and distraction as the most jaded matrons of the Ton.

"Do you not want to go upstairs a while with one of my lasses?" inquired Mrs. Harvey, the prioress.

Millicent shook her head and launched into another funny story. She was searching her memory for another anecdote when the brothel door crashed open and three men charged in. Millicent tried to leap up, but she was sharing a couch with four ladies and could not move. The leader of the men, an unwashed thug with a vicious slashing scar across his face, dove at Millicent with his knife only to be knocked to one side by the madam – using a chair. The second man was hailed by one of the whores who recognized him as her long absent husband and chased him from the room. The last tripped and fell upon the first man's knife.

Millicent was the only one in the room to jump back in horror. The only one to gasp and tremble. The ladies were more concerned with the damage done to the carpet.

"I am dreadfully sorry to leave you with such a mess," said Millicent when her voice returned.

Mrs. Harvey was more sanguine.

"'Tis no more than I have dealt with on other nights," she assured him. "He will find his way down to the Thames tonight. Like as not, no one will care enough to look for him."

"Well, that is ah … it is comforting to be in the presence of an efficient housekeeper."

Mrs. Harvey laughed. Not long after her grandson returned and escorted Millicent to a filthy hackney. It did not escape Millicent's attention that the boy climbed on the back of the hackney and hung on all the way across London. When Millicent finally reached Maricourt Square, she staggered up the front steps and almost threw herself into Merit's arms, so great was her relief. Shortly thereafter, she was resting in her office with a cup of tea, her feet up on the couch and issuing orders to a gathering of her male employees.

"I want hourly tours of the lower floors, in pairs," said Millicent. "One footman with a pistol in the front hall, all the hours of the night. None of the ladies are to walk to or from the carriage without escort of at least two footmen."

"How long must we keep up these precautions?" asked a pale Merit.

"Until the end of the season," said Millicent. "Mrs. Harvey is a charming individual, but I am not happy that she knows my address."

"You should have paid her off."

"I gave her quite enough. Consider that this is my paranoid nature speaking."

Merit sighed and nodded. "I must say, Mr. North, life in your household is never dull."

The butler went to the door and paused, one hand on the doorknob before returning to stand before Millicent's chair.

"Yes, Merit?"

"I must say, sir, that I have enjoyed serving your household this season."

"Thank you, Merit."

"And, if you would keep me in mind when you return next year, I would appreciate the opportunity to serve again."

Millicent regarded him with a smile. "Let me see. You have survived the worst of Felicity's outbursts and tolerated our country manners and demands with skill and calm. The only problem I see, Merit, preventing your continuous employment with my family, is that I have no plans to keep a London house, and our residences in Bath and elsewhere require a housekeeper rather than a butler."

"In what way is not a butler superior to a housekeeper? I can manage both roles."

"We do not entertain much."

"Is that your will, or the lady's?"

Millicent closed her eyes. Today's frights and starts left her exhausted to her bones, but that did not mean that she would not be rising soon to dress and prepare to take her family out to yet another night of entertainments. Last winter in Bath, Felicity had taken her daughters to every event for which she could wrangle an invitation. This year Mildred was marrying into the household of a duke. Like as not, Felicity would take advantage of that connection, and Mr. North's money, to make her mark in country society.

"I will speak to Felicity, Merit. Would you be willing to travel? Supervise a household in Bath for the winter, summer rentals at Bristol? Wherever she should be?"

"I would be honored," said Merit with a bow and departed to supervise the defense of Maricourt Square.

That, it appeared, settled that. Having Merit to bully around would keep Felicity entertained when Millicent was away.

Life was settling into patterns that would continue into the foreseeable future. Millicent would travel with Shoffer, endless summer weeks. The Boarder women were safe, their dowries and annuities arranged.

Millicent smiled into the fireplace. The only shadow on her life was that dreadful rumor. With luck and a little time, the Ton would find another distraction.

Her smile faded. As long as Attelweir continued to pursue little Beth the rumor would continue. Attelweir would see to that.

Setting her tea cup aside, she rose and began pacing the room. There must be a way to discourage that lecher. She would have to discuss the matter with Shoffer.

The bridal plans of the family of Mr. North were much discussed by their temporary staff and, in the manner of all things gossiped, the story traveled outside the walls of Number Six Maricourt Place, across garden fences, down the street, across town, and into the eager ears of the Ton matrons. And, in the manner of gossip, the story twisted and evolved until they no longer spoke of the marriage of Mildred Boarder and Edgar Simpson, secretary to the Duke of Trolenfield, but of the Duke of Trolenfield and his soon to be closer bond with the family of Mr. North.

The betrothal party of Boarder and Simpson began well. As a kindness to his long-time secretary, Shoffer collected Lord Edgeware in his own carriage to transport him to Vauxhall. Simpson and Mildred accompanied them so as to have the opportunity to converse with Simpson's great uncle; by the time they had reached Vauxhall, Mildred had dazzled the Lord with her willingness to sit silently and listen to the older man talk.

Lord Edgeware was quite convinced he had never met such an intelligent woman. Once the whole party reached the rented dining box, Felicity and Beth wrestled for control of the gathering. Beth tried to seat the guests by friendship instead of rank while Felicity wanted to place herself between Shoffer and Lord Edgeware and have all the others, in descending order of rank, radiate down from her position. Millicent retreated to the unpopular corner which placed her back to the dance floor, but gave her the freedom to stare up the length of the table to Shoffer, a view she much preferred. The party was congenial; the conversation was not brilliant, but flowed smoothly. Millicent, under orders not to offend their guest, spoke only when directly addressed and made no jokes. She did not realize there was a problem until she saw an expression of total shock cross Shoffer's face; he came to his feet, staring at the door of their dining box.

"Grandmother," he gasped. "Could that be you?"

Millicent swung around in her chair, nearly tipping it over in her haste.

There, her face and body almost concealed by a dark domino, was the Dowager Duchess of Trolenfield. At her shoulder, stood Attelweir, leering at the gathering.

"The most dreadful news came to me only an hour since," said Lady Philomena, pushing the door open and climbing into the box. "You are here for an engagement party?"

"Certainly," said Shoffer, "although, I cannot think of a reason for you to concern yourself."

"It is true, then," gasped Lady Philomena. "You are so lost to decency, to honor and rank, as to bind yourself to this … rabble."

Millicent glanced back toward Shoffer, realizing only then that Mildred was seated at his right hand.

"I did not believe the gossip when I heard it," continued Lady Philomena "I never thought you would choose someone with no lineage to recommend her. Come away at once. Repudiate this unworthy alliance."

"Ma'am, I have no objections to my secretary marrying a young woman of good family."

The dowager paused, confused.

"Your Grace," continued Shoffer, "we are gathered today to celebrate the betrothal of Mr. Simpson to Miss Mildred Boarder."

The dowager deflated, pressing a hand to her throat.

"Oh, thank the Lord. Attelweir came to me with the tale that was spreading about London that you were about to marry much below your rank." The dowager squeezed her way past the diners and seized her grandson's arm. "I feared you lost to all reason. Come away now before you are seen and this family attempts to take advantage of the rumors to force your hand."

Shoffer scowled at Attelweir and shook himself free of his grandmother's hand.

"Your opinion would have no weight, even if it were true. Since you are not here to celebrate with us, please feel free to depart."

"I must insist you accompany me, and, Elizabeth, come away at once."

"I am staying here with my friends."

Millicent was pleased to note that Beth's voice did not shake.

"We are comfortably settled here," continued Beth, "and have no plans to depart until our entertainment is done."

Lady Philomena clenched her hand, coming up as if to slap, but Shoffer stepped between the dowager and Beth and the moment passed.

"I can see North's influence over you has grown," moaned Lady Philomena. "I have heard what is said of him. How can it be that you continue to receive him? Do you not know how you are regarded? The effect upon Elizabeth's standing? How can it be that a man of wit and rank can be so taken in? If you continue this association, I can foresee that no family of sensibility will have either of you."

"Good," was Beth's only reply.

"You have no voice in whom and when I wed, Your Grace," said Shoffer.

"It is your responsibility to marry. I have told you over and over. If I have told you once, I have told you a hundred times, you must marry. And you should marry soon to bury these dreadful rumors."

"Well, there is your problem," said Millicent from her place at the poorly lit end of the table. "You have not said it enough. One hundred times! Surely you are aware that you must repeat that particular command exactly one thousand times, and when you have done so, our friend Shoffer will leap up and cry 'of course, I must wed,' and marry the first woman he sees thereafter."

The guests laughed.

The dowager glared down the table. "Your mockery is not appreciated. It is required that Shoffer should make an advantageous, appropriate match that supports the dignity of his station and remove from our family name the stain you have brought upon it."

"How very dull you make it sound." Millicent lifted her still full wine glass and studied its depths.

"Dull or lively makes no difference. I was speaking of marriage, not a Cheltenham farce. Shoffer has delayed taking up this responsibility for spite. If he bore any respect for his rank, he would have wed at my direction years ago."

"And yet, I did not." Shoffer rose and stared the elderly woman down. "But to comfort you, dear grandmother, I shall tell you. I have met the woman I would marry given the chance. But, let me be clear, if I cannot marry her, I shall not marry at all."

The dowager went pale as ash at his look and tone. Shoffer moved closer to tower over the tiny woman.

"I love – a word with which you are not familiar, dear grandmother – nevertheless, it is true. I love Helene Winthrop and if she would consent to be my wife, I would be the happiest of men."

Millicent dropped her glass, which shattered on her plate, and all heads turned toward her.

"Who, pray," shrieked the dowager, bringing all faces back to her end of the table, "is Helene Winthrop?"

Millicent's mouth worked, but she could not think of a single word to say.

Into this silence Shoffer said with deadly calm. "Helene Winthrop currently does me the honor of being my mistress. Should circumstances ever change, I hope to have the greater honor of having her as my wife."

Up and down the table came cries of shock and disbelief.

Millicent's heart turned over in her breast and she pressed her hand against that ache. He loved her. Loved her. He wanted to marry her. Despite everything, he loved her. She could not believe it. Still, no matter what he wished or said, marriage was not possible between them. Her thoughts held her paralyzed as the rest of the table roared like a swarm of angry bees.

"I say, Shoffer," Lord Edgeware chided him. "It is not done to name your bit of fluff like that, especially in mixed company."

"I am not ashamed of her and neither is she of me."

"Who is this woman?" demanded the dowager. "Mr. North, I am certain this is yet another disaster that you have visited upon my family. It is bad enough that you encroach upon us and bring dishonor upon our name for the first time in its history…"

"Spare us," cried Shoffer. "What of the third duke who slaughtered all his captives on the way home from the battlefield rather than be bothered to feed them long enough to ransom them? Or the one who tried to drink the whole family into penury? Or the one who assisted in the dissolution of the Catholic Church by raping as many nuns as could be found? My association with Mr. North – entirely innocent as it is – is barely a smudge in the deep pile of filth that so many of our allegedly noble families have as their heritage."

The dowager ignored him and went so far as to seize Millicent by her arm. "Who is this Helene Winthrop to you?"

"I…" Millicent stammered for a moment, then spoke weakly, "I am surprised that Shoffer would say her name before this company."

"I will apologize to the lady later," murmured Shoffer. "For your information, Lady Philomena, Helene is the widowed cousin of Mr. North."

"I thought as much," cried the duchess. "Another of your foul family. You encroach too far. Leave immediately, Mr. North, and take your disgusting family with you. Elizabeth, you are coming with me. I am taking you to my house and you will spend the next week in your room praying that no scandal attaches to you from your association with this degenerate."

"Your Grace," interrupted Shoffer, glaring at the dowager. "You are becoming quite overset. I must insist you leave at once."

Silence reigned as Shoffer took his grandmother by the arm and half dragged her down the few steps and onto the path beside the dining boxes. The cluster of revelers who were loitering there, hanging on every scandalous word parted like the Red Sea as Shoffer half carried his grandmother away.

"Well," said Attelweir. "That was entertaining."

"No, it was not," said Lady Beth. "Mr. North, I am sorry you were spoken to in that manner. Sometime soon, I should like to be introduced to your other cousin."

"That is unlikely," said Millicent, so desperate for an excuse she settled for the absolute truth. "In the current circumstances, she is not considered fit company for you."

"I do not care. I would dearly love to meet the woman who has captured Timothy's heart."

"Grant the poor girl's wish, North," said Attelweir with a lecherous grin. "Given the other sins, going about meeting with a mistress is such a small scandal for Lady Elizabeth to indulge in. I would not mind meeting the fair Helene myself."

"Attelweir, your opinion has not been sought! You were not invited to this gathering and should depart." Beth drew herself to her feet. "Since you arrived in Grandmother's carriage you should hurry, else you will have to find other transport home, and, if your pockets are as much to let as usual, lacking a shilling for a hackney, you will have to walk."

Attelweir paled at this frank reference, before witnesses, to his lack of blunt. He did not bother to bow to any of the watchers, but turned on his heel and vanished into the crowd.

Beth drew a deep breath, arranged her features into a pleasant smile, and beamed around the table.

"My dear friends, I hope you will not permit that … display on the part of my relatives to ruin your appetites or spoil your enjoyment of the evening. Please, do continue to eat. I am confident the fireworks will begin soon."

Millicent obediently picked up her knife and fork, but could not eat since her plate was covered in broken glass and spilled wine. Around the table conversation resumed. Everyone was avoiding, at least in audible tones, discussing the very interesting announcement the duke had made. Millicent rarely heard the weather discussed with so much dedication.

Her own thoughts kept returning to Shoffer's statement.

He loved his mistress.

Loved Helene.

Loved her.

She closed her eyes.

Shoffer loved her possibly as much as she loved him.

She could die in this moment and be content.

Shoffer returned from seeing his grandmother off in her carriage, scowling with such ferocity that people leapt out of his path. He climbed back into the dining box without acknowledging anyone present. Beth smiled at him when he resumed his place at the other end of the table and he managed a weak turning of his lips in return.

"Did you see both of them off?" inquired North.

"Both of them," repeated Shoffer. "What do you mean?"

"Attelweir. He arrived with Her Grace, remember? Did he catch up with you in time to be taken up in her carriage?"

Shoffer stared at his plate as if it contained the answer to all life's questions. "No. I did not see him."

North glanced about at the milling crowd, but could not spot the duc. "I hope the ladies will forgive me, but I think we should not stay for the dancing and fireworks."

Shoffer nodded.

"I agree with North. I apologize to you all for the disruption, but it is better so. We should escort the ladies home."

"Surely, you are being over cautious, Timothy," said Beth. "We can safely stay until the fireworks are over. Please."

"Forgive me, dear Beth. I shall arrange for you to come another night to view the fireworks, but tonight, I think it would be best to leave before the crowd. Once the fireworks are over, the pathways hereabouts will be over-full with people and it will be near impossible to locate our carriages."

It looked for a moment that Beth would continue to protest, but Felicity rose, and recruiting Lady Edith with a glance, took the girl in hand.

"I agree with His Grace. The crowd hereabouts has a rough and disgusted look about it. We best leave."

Without discussing the matter, Shoffer and North took the lead with the ladies trailing behind them. Simpson and his uncle undertook to follow behind to make sure no one was separated by the crowd. By the time they had battled their way through the massed revelers, even Beth was willing to admit fatigue and agree to go home, instead of to some other entertainment.

As the ladies were aided into the carriages by the footmen, Shoffer, Millicent, and Simpson took leave of Lord Edgeware, who was planning to take a hackney home.

"Uncle," said Simpson, "I wish to thank you for coming. I am only sorry that the evening was cut short."

"Not at all. It was unexpectedly entertaining."

Millicent scowled at the older man, which intimidated him not at all.

"The girl you are marrying seems a sensible lass," continued the Earl. "Once the settlements are arranged come and see me and I will give you advice on investing her dowry."

Millicent bit her tongue to stop herself from protesting that action and resolved to ensure the lawyers protected Mildred's interests. Simpson gave a neutral grunt, shook his uncle's hand, and aided him into the hackney. Millicent took leave of Simpson and Shoffer with a nod and climbed up to join the women of her own household. Millicent and Maude had their heads together discussing something or other and Felicity was resting her head on the squabs, her eyes closed. Millicent copied her, unwilling to engage in conversation.

All she wanted to do was pull out the memory of Shoffer declaring his love and relive it over and over.

Shoffer loved her. Want to marry her. Joy fought with pain. It was not possible, would never happen, but, oh, the knowledge he loved her that much, would marry her despite the differences in their ranks, their positions in society, she hugged to herself in the dark. Even her fictitious widowhood and position as mistress had not stopped him from declaring his intent before witnesses.

So deep was her preoccupation that she noticed no passage of time until they drew up outside Maricourt Place. Millicent descended first and turned to offer her hand to Felicity.

"Your pardon, sir," came a voice from the shadows.

Millicent turned even as her footman leapt down from the rear of the carriage and seized the speaker by the collar.

"Stop," cried the newcomer. "I am no robber. I only wish to speak to Mr. North."

"Which one?" asked Millicent, even as her heart leapt into her throat. This was it, the moment when she was revealed as a liar, a fraud. With hope, she would have a few moments to warn her sisters and mother, perhaps send them on to Shoffer's house. He would protect them.

"I am seeking Mr. Anthony North. I am Mr. Johanson, Mr. Perceval North's lawyer. I have left my card many times to no effect."

"Oh, dear God preserve us," cried Felicity and fell into a faint.

Millicent leapt to stop Felicity's insensible body from falling to the pavement. Mildred seized Felicity by the arm and the footman released his captive to take hold of Felicity's torso. Merit, summoned by Maude's cries, bounded down the stairs followed by half the staff. Millicent blessed the confusion that gave her another few moments to think.

How had Perceval discovered her ... his ... Anthony North's presence in London? Perhaps he had read the gossip pages of the London papers? How much did he know? Had she broken some unknown rule of the inheritance? What if Perceval wanted to meet with Anthony? Why was the lawyer looking for her and how could she get him to go away without revealing the deception?

Maude and Mildred near fell out of the carriage in their eagerness to be of aid to their mother. Millicent tried, but was unable to get Mildred's ear to advise her of their late night visitor's identity. In all the confusion, Mr. Johanson followed them into the house. Millicent was trying to regain command over her household when a familiar voice came from the door.

"North! North! Is Beth here with you?"

All in the hall fell silent and Millicent spun to face Shoffer and Simpson.

"Heavens, no, why would you think so?"

"My carriage left without us," said Shoffer, his face ashen pale. "I thought perhaps Lady Edith and Beth thought we would travel with you and went on ahead home, but when I got there I found that they had not arrived."

"Oh, dear God," cried Felicity, and fainted anew.

"Attelweir," said Maude, charging across the hall to seize Shoffer's arm. "But where would he take her? Surely, he does not imagine he could take her to Gretna, not with her chaperone along!"

"I can only pray that Lady Edith stays with her," said Shoffer. "But we cannot be certain he has headed north. He might hold her somewhere in London. But where?"

"Oh, poor Beth, in the hands of that scoundrel," cried Maude and burst into tears.

Mildred was nearest and quickest.

"Have some sense," she said, shaking Maude by the shoulder. "It's more likely she's stopped in traffic or she might have directed the coachman to take Lady Edith home first. Do not leap to the worst construction before anything is known for certain."

Maude sniffled and retreated.

"We should check both possibilities," said Millicent.

Shoffer nodded. "Simpson, go home and wait. If Beth arrives send a messenger to find me. North, you go to Lady Edith's home and I shall go to Attelweir's rooms. If he is planning on leaving the city, it is likely he will stop there first for his belongings."

He had taken two steps toward the door before Millicent halted him.

"Shoffer, I cannot imagine Attelweir persuading *your* servants to drive him out of the city, particularly if Lady Beth was kicking up a fuss."

"You are right. Unless, of course, he overpowered them and was driving the carriage himself."

"The coachman and four footmen, plus the tiger, all overwhelmed by Attelweir?" Millicent shook her head. "If he can do all that, I must begin to treat him with respect."

"We must be mistaken," said Simpson. "It would not do to overreact and start a panic. Beth is likely delayed. Or home again. We are all over excited by this evening's quarrels."

"I will come home with you to be certain," said Millicent. "I would not be able to rest not knowing if Lady Beth is safe."

They hurried from the house. Fortunately, her carriage had not yet been taken back to the mews. It was not until Shoffer swung himself into the waiting carriage that Millicent remembered the lawyer. Perceval's lawyer. What if the man spoke to her sisters while she was away? She paused on the step, considering whether she should go back, dismiss the man, before leaving.

No, there was no reason to fear. Good manners would have the man leaving the house quite soon after her departure. It was late and the man of the house was gone. Merit would see to it. Felicity was being taken to her room and Mildred was sensible. Even if the man cornered her, she would refuse to speak.

Millicent leapt into the carriage and sat beside Shoffer, shoulder to shoulder, hip to hip.

The carriage lurched into motion throwing Millicent against Shoffer. Simpson, on the facing seat, clung to the wall for balance.

"She is likely home by now," repeated Simpson.

"Do we even know where Attelweir resides?" asked Millicent. "He is not on my sister's guest list."

"Nor mine, though I am certain my grandmother knows," replied Shoffer.

It was not necessary to dismount from the carriage at Trolenfield House. Forsythe, oil lantern in hand, stood at the top of the steps before an open door. He descended, hope shining on his features, when the carriage pulled up, but when he saw Beth was not with them his face fell.

"Still not here," whispered Shoffer. "Am I being over concerned?"

"Where your unmarried, beautiful, and wealthy sister is concerned, I think not," said Millicent, laying her hand lightly on his arm. "I do not wish to encourage you in fearful thoughts yet I cannot help being worried myself. Attelweir is scum. I would not put any crime past him."

"And he has your grandmother's approval, publicly stated," continued Simpson.

Shoffer and Millicent exchanged a glance.

"The dowager…" Shoffer paused. "You are correct, North. Beth would cause Attelweir endless trouble were he to try and take her out of London, but if he were to redirect my carriage to the dowager's residence, she might go. My servants would not protest the command."

"Would the dowager protect Beth from Attelweir or would she conspire with him against Beth's wishes?" Millicent shuddered as the thought chilled her.

"Simpson. Go to Lady Edith's residence. Find out if Beth is there. Whatever the news, send a message to me. I am going to call on my grandmother." Shoffer turned and charged down the stairs again. "North, with me!"

Chapter Twenty

The carriage ride to the dowager's residence was spent in complete silence. Since Simpson was no longer with them, Millicent risked reaching across the wide seat to grasp Shoffer's hand. He returned the grip with such ferociousness that she knew he was in the clutch of, if not terror, then at least strong fear for his sister's safety.

When they arrived, Shoffer did not wait for the footmen to open the door and lower the steps, but leapt from the carriage to the ground and raced up the staircase. Millicent, descending slowly, took a moment to glance about.

"Shoffer, your carriage," cried Millicent, pointing. "It is heading down the street!"

Shoffer glanced toward her and away. He did not knock on the door so much as pound it open.

"Thomas, with me," cried Millicent and ran down the road after the ducal carriage. Fortunately, since the North family and the Shoffers kept their equipages in the same mews, the coachman recognized Millicent's footman and obeyed her shouts to stop.

"Come about, my good man," gasped Millicent. "Go back to the dowager's residence and wait. We may have need of you soon."

The coachman sighed and muttered something about horses and the whimsies of the *fancy*, but nodded his understanding.

"Thomas," said Millicent, grasping her footman's arm. "You and the others stand ready. We may be leaving at speed."

"Yes, sir."

With that Millicent turned and ran back toward the house.

Inside Shoffer ran down the main hall, up the staircase, and down a corridor toward his grandmother's favorite sitting room. Winter, summer, made no difference, the dowager received visitors in a room she had decorated in the image of the Queen's drawing room. He was halfway down the corridor when he heard Beth's voice raised in anger.

"You may say what you will, Attelweir, I shall not consent!"

"Fetch a special license, Attelweir," came Lady Philomena's voice. "We shall have her safely wed before morning."

Shoffer hit the door like a cannon ball and was in the midst of them. In an instant, he assessed how things stood. Lady Philomena was seated, regal and judgmental, in her throne-like chair. Attelweir was near the door holding his nose, which had been struck when Shoffer burst in, and Beth, brave and darling Beth, with Lady Edith at her side held the center of the room, holding Attelweir at bay with her pistol. She took one look at Shoffer and started to cry.

"Oh, Timothy, I am so glad you are here. I have only one bullet."

"My dear, in the right circumstances, one is just enough." To the dowager, Shoffer showed his teeth. "I shall be taking my sister home, now, Your Gracelessness, and if I ever see you again, ever, in any circumstances, I shall shoot you myself."

"I am leaving now," said Beth, relaxing from her shooter's stance and rushing toward her brother.

As she passed Attelweir, he leapt, seizing first the gun, then the girl.

"I think not," said Attelweir, pulling Beth tight against his side. "Carrying a gun? Pointing a gun at me? I shall teach you better manners once we are wed."

"I shall never marry you," cried Beth, struggling within his grip, "and you should pray I do not, since if you do force me to marry, one dark night when you least expect it, I shall cut your throat."

"Well done," cried Shoffer, as Attelweir paled and looked suitably horrified at the threat.

At that moment, North rocketed into the room, hitting Attelweir at waist height and sending him bouncing off the wall. Beth fell out of his grip and sprawled across the floor. Attelweir's hand spasmed and the pistol spoke, shockingly loud in the chamber. North and Beth cried out together as North collapsed to the ground, clutching his stomach. Dark red blood leaked between his fingers, staining his shirt.

Beth crawled on her knees to his side as Shoffer leapt over them and smashed his fist into Attelweir's face.

"Stop, stop," shouted the dowager and was ignored.

All of Shoffer's attention was on the hated person of Attelweir. The aging roué could not match him in strength or passion. Again and again Shoffer's fist drove into Attelweir, breaking his nose, blacking his eye. A rib broke beneath Shoffer's fist and even that was not enough to satisfy his rage.

"Murderer," came Beth's voice. "You have killed Mr. North!"

Shoffer froze, then turned to stare at his sister kneeling beside North's silent, bleeding form.

"No," he whispered as his hands sagged toward the floor. No. It could not be so. North could not be dead.

"I shall see you hang," continued Beth in a quivering voice. "I shall pay for all the hunters of Bow Street to track you down, no matter where you flee, you bastard. You murderer. I will see you dead for this."

Attelweir rose up, desperation fueling him, and sent Shoffer sprawling. Then he ran past Beth and North, charging out into the night.

Silence reigned after his departure only to be broken by the dowager's voice.

"Pray remove the body," she said. "That rug he is bleeding on is quite valuable."

Given who Mr. North was and his general reputation within the Ton, it should not have been so much of a surprise that his funeral became the *place* to go and the *event* to see and be seen – the most glamorous and significant gathering of the season. On the morning of the funeral, old St. George's Church was full to overflowing with people and flowers. Common people, distracted and attracted by the procession of the Ton dressed in deepest mourning, lined the street two deep in some places trying to find out who was being buried. Considering the fuss, they whispered to each other, it must be a royal cousin at the very least! Faded bunting, left over from the last royal wedding was fetched out of attics and hung hastily along the streets.

The London modistes had good reason to bless Mr. North's memory. So late in the season, demand for new clothing tended to die down as budgets were stressed and parties decreased, but most of the women of the Ton were determined to appear in some degree of mourning clothes for Mr. North's funeral, and therefore, kept dressmakers and seamstresses busy to all hours in the days preceding the funeral. Even the brightest tulips of the Ton disdained their colors that day and went about in Brummellian black. Members of the military put on their least faded formal parade uniforms and strutted about for the entertainment of the throng.

When Mr. North's coffin was carried from the church with Shoffer, Duke of Trolenfield leading on the right side, Mr. North's brother-in-law to be, a simple secretary, in the middle, and a farmer come hot foot all the way from Wales to fulfill this honor following, the other side staffed by officers in full regimentals, one wag was moved to comment that all that was required was an Indian chief to make the funeral complete.

It was agreed by those who claimed to know him well that Mr. North would have found the whole parade amusing.

Time being what it tended to be, the day of the funeral was also the day for Mildred's long planned afternoon tea. In the days preceding the funeral, Mildred sent around notes to all those invited informing them that she intended to follow the Scots tradition and give the party as planned, as a wake in Mr. North's honor. Mr. North, being such a miserly skinflint, she wrote, would have mourned the waste of food more than his own life if the event was canceled. Therefore, when the men left to follow the coffin to the graveyard, the ladies repaired to the rented garden, a cluster of glittering crows in the midst of spring flowers. Tea was drunk and stories told of the odd little fellow who had won the hearts of the Ton, then died, tragically, before he became unfashionable.

Most of the gentlemen, once they had seen Mr. North's body safely into the ground, came late to the tea. Later, the news sheets commented that the gathering was the most enjoyable funeral ever attended. Mildred Boarder's reputation as a society hostess would have been established by the event, except that she was marrying beneath her, and was unlikely to host another. Since it was a love match no one was moved to complain – beyond the bride's mother.

Shoffer, Duke of Trolenfield, was late to the wake to no one's particular surprise. It was well known that he was harassing the authorities, demanding the Duc of Attelweir be run to ground and brought to justice for the heinous crime of murdering his friend.

No one was certain about the exact circumstances of the crime. Despite that, rumors abounded. It was generally said that North discovered Attelweir in the act of forcing himself upon some well-bred young lady and acted to save the girl. Attelweir foully struck him down and alas, North died of his wounds before he could claim the girl's hand as his reward. Fortunately, the ever present Shoffer witnessed the attack and gave testimony of Attelweir's degenerate and murderous nature, saving some other poor girl from the burden of marrying Attelweir. The girl's name was a complete mystery – which also served to preserve her reputation – so no one inquired closely.

There was talk of a memorial of some kind for Mr. North, but no one could agree of what type or where and eventually the subject was dropped.

There was even a contingent of actors and actresses at the gathering – invited, but not required, after all, to make the afternoon a success. One well-endowed singer claimed publicly and repeatedly to have been Mr. North's mistress. As soon as Shoffer heard of this, he whisked the woman away – tucking a hundred quid into her glove as he assisted her into a hackney – but not before the story took root in the gossip pool. In death, Mr. North's name and reputation were cleared.

Mr. North laughed so hard when she heard all of this that she started her wound bleeding again.

The events of that traumatic evening had continued thusly:

Shoffer half crawled across the chamber to North's side. Tears were drying on his sister's cheeks as she held North's pale, unmoving head on her lap. When Shoffer touched her hand, North's eyes flickered and opened.

"Gone?" she whispered, smiling up at him.

Relief poured through him like an ocean wave.

"North! By the gods, do not scare me like that!"

"I do apologize," said North and winced when Shoffer's hand brushed over his bloody shirt.

"North told me what to say," said Beth. "And it worked. Attelweir has fled and he will not be back."

"Not with so many witnesses to his attempt to kill North," Shoffer agreed.

"Did you not hear me?" cried Lady Philomena. "Take him away to finish dying."

Shoffer gathered North into his arms and did not grant the dowager the slightest piece of his attention. Beth, however, gave a formal curtsy and smiled.

"Dear Grandmother, please remember, my dear brother and his friend have gifted me with enough guns for every day of the week. In future, I shall carry two. One for you and one for whomever you should find worthy of marrying me."

Then she turned and hurried after her brother. Lady Edith gave a half-hearted bob and trailed along behind.

"It is my fault," said Beth, touching North's cold hand. "I allowed him to take the gun from me. If I…"

"Never say so," said North. "I shall be so disappointed in you if you think you are responsible for the actions of another. Attelweir chose to steal your gun and it was Attelweir who fired it. Considering all his actions, will you take responsibility for his gambling, his womanizing?"

"No!"

"Exactly." North gasped and tightened her grip on Shoffer's shoulder.

Outside two carriages awaited them.

"Beth goes home with Lady Edith," whispered North. "Take me to your assignation house."

Shoffer paused, until that moment he had given no thought to what needed to be done beyond getting North to a physician, then he realized the consequences of that action.

"I must go with you," cried Beth. "I refuse to be left behind."

"Please, Beth, go home so my mind will be at rest," said Millicent. "Shoffer shall fetch my cousin Mildred. She is a sensible girl with experience in stillroom matters. When did you last tincture or compound?"

Beth's lips quivered, but she bit them to bring them under control.

"Promise me you will not die, dear Mr. North and I will stay behind."

"I shall do my best to obey," said North and with that, Beth had to be content and permitted the ducal footmen to assist her into her carriage and to bear her away.

Shoffer lifted North into the other carriage and directed it toward Maricourt Place. Once in the dimness of the carriage, Shoffer peeled the fabric back from Millicent's belly, exposing the wound. Powder burns marked one side of her stomach, near to a long, narrow, slowly oozing furrow.

"It went across, not in," gasped Shoffer and pressed his face into the curve of her neck. "Bless you for not being dying!"

"Run in, when we reach Maricourt Place and fetch Mildred out without letting anyone else know the events of the evening."

Shoffer obeyed – to a degree. Millicent bit her teeth when the carriage rocked and Mildred climbed in – followed by Mr. Johansen.

"What is he doing here?" demanded Millicent of Mildred.

"Mr. Johansen has just informed me, your brother Perceval has died!" said Mildred. "I thought you should know as soon as possible."

"Died?" Millicent gasped, clutching at her stomach.

"Indeed, Mr. North," said Mr. Johansen. "It would be most unwise of you to die at this moment as you have just inherited your brother's estate. A well maintained one, you know, worth near twenty thousand a year."

Millicent closed her eyes as Shoffer laughed.

At the assignation house, Millicent requested Mr. Johansen remain downstairs while Mildred and Shoffer saw to her needs upstairs. The housekeeper, with her energy divided tending to the gentleman lawyer downstairs –"tea, if you do not mind, ma'am" – and hot water and bandages for the upstairs – "no physician, thank you, Mrs. Foster, I wish for Mr. North to live!" – it accidentally came to pass that Mrs. Foster did not enter the bedchamber, leaving Mildred to care for the injured Mr. North, and was never given an opportunity to suspect his gender was anything other than male.

After her wound was gently washed and bandaged Millicent drew her blankets up to her chin and requested Mr. Johansen be brought to her.

"And lower the candles, Mildred, if you would."

"What are you about?" asked Shoffer.

Millicent did not look in his direction. It was a difficult decision to make and it was hers alone. She would never have a better opportunity.

When Johansen entered he found a pale, barely breathing Mr. North near buried under the weight of the coverlets. He raised a thin hand, which shook as he pointed at a table.

"There is paper there, Mr. Johansen. Sit down. I want you to take down my will."

"North, you are not so injured as that," cried Shoffer, even as Mildred caught her breath and began to sob.

"A precaution only, my dear friend," whispered North bravely. Returning her attention to the lawyer, North gave a tremulous smile. "His Grace, the Duke of Trolenfield has consented to be my executor and the will is simple to record. I give all I have inherited to be shared equally, outright, between my cousins."

Mr. Johansen wrote this out in legal terms, which took longer to write than to say. Before he finished, Mr. North added.

"And two hundred pounds to a Mr. Merit. As he is going to be butler to my cousin Felicity Boarder, I should like that he should have money put aside so that when she drives him crazy he may threaten to resign with confidence."

"The one who kept fainting?" inquired Mr. Johansen.

Mr. North rolled his eyes and laughed weakly. Once the will was written Mr. and Mrs. Foster were fetched up to sign as witnesses and a hackney was fetched to take Mr. Johansen home.

Shoffer waited until the front door shut behind him, then turned to Millicent.

"So, Mr. North will die of his wounds?"

"Apparently," said Millicent. "As you kept reminding me, the deception cannot continue forever. Besides, if North survives, Attelweir will return. If North dies, Attelweir must flee to the continent, a suspected murderer with his neck as forfeit, never to return and plague us again."

"I thank you for your sacrifice in care of my sister, Mr. North," Shoffer pressed her hand to his chest. "I shall honor your memory."

Millicent nodded, then accepted the laudanum wine Mildred had prepared, settled down in the bed, and slept.

Indeed, Millicent was vastly amused by everything to do with her alter ego's funeral. She sent Shoffer out to buy the most elaborate and gilt decorated coffin that could be found, demanded that it be lined with the finest white silk and even directed the type, number, and arrangement of the floral tributes.

"For a skinflint you have expensive tastes in afterlife furniture," grumbled Shoffer, who was paying for the event.

"I want a good send off," shot back Millicent. "What else is money good for at the end of your life?"

"Since you have bequeathed it all to your cousins, I should, as your executor, practice economy on their behalf." Shoffer wrote another few words on his note. "Besides, it seems a lot to pay to bury some criminal from the East End."

"We are all equal in the sight of God," joked Millicent. "Besides, it is becoming something of a family tradition."

"Mrs. Harvey was most efficient in finding a body," continued Shoffer. "Should I inquire how you came to find Mrs. Harvey?"

"No." Millicent snickered. "How you managed to have the magistrates accept the body of a stevedore who died in a knife fight as mine, I do not know."

"I simply reminded them that rumor cannot be trusted. I am the only witness to the crime, since Attelweir is fled to the continent. So, if I declared that Attelweir stabbed instead of shot you, how could they prove otherwise? Lady Philomena will not speak to the subject without damaging her own and Beth's reputation. They went away quite content. Since they never met you, my identification was considered enough."

"Of course, I forgot the power of the ducal stare." Millicent's voice faded away and she glanced over toward the window. Despite the early hour, the blinds were shut tight. She had no idea if it was a fine day or foul.

On the fourth evening after the shooting, Shoffer posted a notice to all the most popular papers announcing the sad demise of Mr. North. While Millicent lay recovering from her wound, Shoffer recruited Mildred's assistance in staffing Millicent's rented house. There the servants were informed that their new employer was a lady dying of consumption.

After Mr. North's death was announced, Millicent was transported to her own rented house where she was introduced to her staff as Mrs. Winthrop.

As Mildred supervised her sister's recovery in person, the servants rarely were required to enter the sick room, so did not discover the true nature of Mrs. Winthrop's illness.

Thus ended the life and career of Mr. Anthony North. Gentleman and fool.

"How many times must Mr. North be buried before he stays put?" inquired Millicent on the day of the funeral.

"This must be the last time," said Shoffer, frowning. "Be content. There is a will that states that your sisters are to receive a considerable inheritance. Their future is settled."

"Hardly legal, but that is nothing new." Millicent paused and stared at the duke. "I am sorry to have put you to so much trouble."

"You saved my sister from a life with that degenerate. I will be forever grateful."

"I know. You are an honorable man."

Shoffer stalked about the room in a state of some agitation. Millicent folded her hands on the comforter. It was getting harder and harder to hold back tears. She put most of her confusion and distress, hidden behind a wall of jokes and light-hearted banter, down to the pain of recovery. Given the circumstances, it was impossible to arrange for a physician to attend her so she had not been physicked and had to hope that her natural strength would pull her through.

The other part of her distress was the pain of losing Mr. North.

Her independent life was done. Now she was to return to the rules governing the behavior of women and to the places society assigned them. No longer Shoffer's friend, she was his mistress. Should she survive she would live in that little house with two servants, be unable to appear in public with her sisters or mother, lest she damage their reputations, and see very, very little of Shoffer.

Despite his declaration at Vauxhall, there was no way he could marry her and very few men took their London mistresses with them into the country. It simply was not done. The years stretched before her empty and dull.

"I have procured a special license, my dear," said Shoffer coming to stand before her. "Do you want your mother and sisters to be present for the ceremony?"

Millicent came upright in the bed, gasped and clutched at her wounded side. "You cannot be serious!"

"Oh? I thought you were fond of them," said Shoffer, mildly.

"I love them dearly, but I cannot marry you. It is too ridiculous to consider."

Shoffer raised an eyebrow at her. "Then you should be quite comfortable with the idea."

"Shoffer, you cannot say so. It is impossible. What would you say to anyone? Marrying your mistress would be bad enough, but what happens when they question my antecedents? Who shall you say I am? I have none. The true Helene Winthrop died a widow at the age of sixty-three. Millicent Boarder has been dead and buried for a year. If you marry me with anything other than my true name, then any child I bear you will be illegitimate. Your sons could not inherit your title or lands!" Her heart was pounding, as was her head, as she sank down on the pillows and turned her head away. "It cannot happen. I would not do that to you. To them."

Shoffer smirked at her. "Truly, when you are a woman you are given to the strangest fits and starts. Who shall question the legitimacy of the marriage? Who would bother to research your past?"

"Lady Philomena?"

"She is angry, I admit, but suspicion of this type is beyond her."

"No. I cannot do this."

"Do not be sillier than you must, North. Write illegibly in the marriage lines, no one will be the wiser."

"And what name will the vicar use when he prays to God to bless our union?"

This Shoffer had to think about.

"If he uses all your names and addresses you as Helene Millicent Winthrop nee Boarder, who shall say that the late Millicent was not named in honor of her cousin, Helene? Come," he said, when Millicent continued to twist her coverlet, "I shall not be put aside. Do you not love me?"

Millicent smiled, "You know I do. Enough to want what is best for you."

"That would be marriage to you. I had not enjoyed my life until you came into it. I have no doubt that as a lady you would be as interesting and entertaining as you were a man, now that you are wealthy..."

"Your money," muttered Millicent.

"Not so. Remember, you left your money equally shared between your 'cousins.' As executor of your will, I have directed that a quarter be given to Helene Winthrop. Ten thousand a year in rents, my dear. You are an heiress."

"And will you permit me to supervise my estates?"

"I would not dare to do otherwise."

"And may I accompany you when you go to visit yours?"

"Of course, else I would spend my time worrying that you would do something ridiculous in my absence."

She smiled at him. "Spending a season dressed as a man, and marrying a duke under a false name is quite ridiculous enough for one lifetime. I shall probably come over all dull and proper now."

Shoffer pulled her into his arms, careful of her wound, and kissed her.

"Oh, my dearest North. That I very much doubt."

Millicent took his hand and pressed it to her cheek even as her eyes closed.

"Shall we ever tell our children how we met?"

"No one would ever believe us. It is too ridiculous."

~end~

<u>And now, an excerpt from The Use of Changing Magic</u>

Chapter One

Norfarland paused on the edge of the windowsill. Deep within the shadowed bedroom, he could hear gentle breathing and the soft slither of bed curtains shifting in the night breeze. He descended from his perch, his battered boots making not a sound as he crossed the chamber. A delicate scent filled the room hinting of feminine fragility and innocence.

Norfarland frowned and sniffed. The scent of the room did not match that which was doused on the note currently tucked within his tunic. He had no idea how the young lady had slipped into his chamber and left this invitation for a night of love on his pillow, but it was no less welcome for being touched with mystery. He brought the note forth and inhaled. The note's perfume was bolder, with a hint of knowledge and strength. This room's scent was gentle by comparison. Soft. Teasing the senses. He was uncertain which he preferred. The room's scent was younger, fresher, the note's, more passionate.

Actually, he was certain. Passion was always his favorite scent.

Norfarland caressed the rich carvings of the bedpost and soft bedding. Thick and smooth and luxurious, truly the chamber was designed for romance. Norfarland smiled down upon the sleeping figure curled in the bed. The dainty miss of this morning's flirtation had fallen asleep awaiting her lusty admirer. He brushed his fingertips along the side of her face and she shifted in her sleep, turning away from the touch. Her blankets slipped and slid down her torso exposing naked generous breasts. Norfarland was amazed. Nothing in the girl's figure this morning had hinted to such endowment. He dragged his attention from that bounty to the face resting on the pillows.

Not, he realized, stepping back in shock, the girl of his fantasy, but the girl's mother!

"Well, lad, get yourself in," said Richatha, opening her eyes and drawing aside the blanket to expose her pearl pale body and long, strong legs. "What? You thought I didn't see you panting around my girl? I am not so much a fool as to grant you access to her. I have warned her about such men as you and we have an agreement, she and I. She tells me which young men she thinks will please me and I reward her for the news with such things as please her." The lady gathered herself and sat up in the bed. "Know this: I am not likely to let the chance of having a well-favored youth in my bed get away. Come in and do your best work, boy..." She ran her long-fingered hands down her torso and over her smooth belly. "If you please me, I shall see that you receive your full reward. If you do not..."

She left the threat unsaid.
The Adventures of Norfarland the Bastard ~ Book 27

High Lord Eioth put the familiar volume of Norfarland's adventures back on the shelf and ran one gloved finger along the edge of the bookcase. He regarded the dusty filos, aged scrolls, and heavy bound books without enthusiasm. Although there might not be any works of great note or dignity within this neglected library, nor rare or precious examples of the book binder's skill or the story teller's art, the papers that resided within these walls did not deserve the neglect they had suffered.

And suffered they had.

Eioth stomped hard on the floor and watched as well-fed mice scurried down the cases and fled across the floor.

The new owner of the books, a lesser cousin of a once noble house, was entirely unprepared for his inheritance. Eioth's visit to the newly inducted Lord Kelth was to educate him in his Ritual duties, his financial reality, and a myriad collection of other commitments. Three minutes after their first introduction, Eioth knew Kelth would be barely adequate in any of his roles. No one had bothered to prepare him; until recently, no one had thought he would be the one to inherit. Clan Kelth members with more money, more education, more... *style* applying for the title had all had been passed over in favor of an Elf whose only responsibility until a month ago had been an apple orchard near the Anonor Hills. Granted, it had been a well-managed apple orchard, but that was not the point.

The Clan lawyers had voted, overriding Eioth's reservations, and now Eioth was left to deal with the result.

Eioth knew better than to let his host perceive any negative opinion. As High Lord of North West Demesne, Eioth needed to maintain good relationships with all who answered to him. Unfortunately, the House of Kelth had fallen into the hands of this very distant branch after many years of bitter legal wrangling.

All knew the only reason Lord Kelth had been voted into his rank over all other applicants; he had a son who had a daughter.

Eioth selected another slender volume from the shelf and ran his fingers over the fine-tooled, yellowed leather cover, admiring the delicate embossing of the title, the evenness and depth of the flaring formal script. Unfortunately, all that effort had been expended on what was really a poor volume of poetry. He put the book back on the shelf and continued browsing.

It was sad to realize that fertility had become the deciding factor in bestowing titles and high responsibility. Eioth met Lord, son, and granddaughter when they'd taken possession of the house and lands and while he would grant that they were all dignified persons of good, ancient, pure Elvan blood, sadly; none of them had anything significant in the way of magical abilities. All three were bonded to the Element of Fire, but none could so much as complete the apprentice tasks, although Kelth assured him they practiced regularly. When they'd conducted the Hearth Fire Ritual the previous day, of the three, only the granddaughter had proven able to ignite the requisite fire – and that after three – *embarrassing* – attempts.

The reality of Kelth's promotion was that Eioth could not count on this family to maintain their share of the magical commitments for North West Demesne, thus adding to the weight of Eioth's existing magical responsibilities. A solution would have to be found. Eioth would have to visit this corner of his demesne every quarter (an unthinkable waste of time and effort), include this area in magics cast from his home (both unthinkable and difficult), or grant an exemption and permit Kelth to employ a Ritual Magician.

Sighing, Eioth opened another book. He took the long view in all things. He couldn't expend any additional magics and maintain the quality of his workings. His abilities were great, but he had other uses for his time and energies.

It was inevitable. Someone had to undertake the Kelth family's Ritual obligations if, and that was a great if, an unemployed elf of Master rank with the correct combination of Elemental bondings could be found. It would be best if Eioth himself located an adequate magician. And, because he knew how to plan, he should choose an unmarried male of a fairly good house. In due time, the daughter would be encouraged to consider a match, perhaps introducing a little magical ability back into the Kelth family line if – Eioth frowned at the book in his hand – if they were lucky enough to have children.

So many ifs.

So few of true talent and ability.

So few children.

Eioth closed his eyes against that remembered pain; so very few children were born to the High Court families and none at all to him.

The library door opened and the new Lord Kelth entered accompanied by Eioth's personal secretary, Mitash. Both males had the porcelain pale skin, silver eyes, and ashen hair of pure blood Elves. Both were tall, slender, and long fingered but only one had much in the way of sense in Eioth's opinion.

Mitash, his secretary, was as well-educated as it was possible to be, but had magical ability only in service to the Element of Earth. His magic was useful for some Rituals, but not diverse enough in power to be the solution to the Kelth problem. Not that Eioth was in any hurry to deprive himself of his secretary's service, but it would have been such a satisfying solution.

Kelth hurried across the stone floor. His shoes squeaked as he slipped a little on the thick layer of dust. The other sad thing about the Kelth family situation was that the lawyers had delayed the decision about inheritance until all of the ready cash in the estate coffers had been used. Money was another problem that Kelth was expecting his High Lord to solve. Eioth turned his attention to the next book on the shelf in order to avoid looking into the hopeful eyes of Lord Kelth. This cover was common thick brown leather, the edges stained with pale green swirls with no gilding, anywhere. Within, the age-yellowed pages were covered in spiky line after line of high, formal Elvish, handwritten in ordinary black ink. Eioth flipped idly through the pages. A private journal of some kind? Odd. What were someone's private musings doing in a somewhat public library?

Eioth was about to toss it back when he saw the title inscribed across the first page.

The Use and Complexity of Sex Magic
An Advisory Essay by an Adherent.

His eyebrows winged up. Sex Magic? He hadn't heard that phrase since he was a child, too young yet to experience any sexual urges. His Elemental magic tutor mentioned sex as a power source once only, sneering at those drawn by base lust to waste their time and abilities in that pursuit, that perversion of *true* magic. Of course, considering the spare, esthetic nature of his tutor, Eioth supposed that the tutor had never experienced sexual *anything* in his entire life. Eioth reviewed his memory for a moment and frowned. That one line, that single dismissal, was the extent of Eioth's knowledge of the subject of Sex Magic.

That was unacceptable.

Eioth knew himself well enough. He was unbearably, unendingly curious. It was the reason he was known to buy up whole libraries in his endless search for one more kernel of knowledge. Reading ancient and decaying books might be a waste of time, but it was his time and he would waste it as he chose. Therefore, he would study this *Essay* for whatever knowledge it might contain. If there was nothing to be gained, at least he would know he had made a seeker's sincere effort. Satisfied with his rationalization, even as the thought amused him, he tucked the book into his sash belt before he turned and inclined his head toward Lord Kelth.

"Is it possible High Lord Eioth that you might consider purchasing my library?" asked Lord Kelth eagerly, his gaze on Eioth's hand as it rested on his sash.

Eioth nodded, his fingertips tapping the now hidden book. Kelth was unlikely to have made visiting the neglected library a priority when exploring his new home. Eioth scanned the rest of the shelf and then turned, measuring the size of the library. Who knew what other oddities might be hidden in these shelves? What else had the "Adherent" written?

He smiled to himself. It was the same thought that caused him to buy, over and over again, piles of moldy, dusty old books.

"I believe I am interested, Kelth, if you would agree to sell them uncatalogued."

Kelth paused, obviously weighing the work involved in examining the masses of books in the hope of finding some rare and valuable volume against the gain of immediate payment. There was cost of hiring a librarian to be considered against the risk that all the books would be revealed as commonplace and valueless. He folded his hands and bowed.

"Of course, High Lord, I will accept what you consider a reasonable offer."

"Yes, you will." Eioth did not roll his eyes, although his secretary did. "My offer will be more than this library deserves based on my preliminary assessment, and will serve to provide you with some income in the short term. Should I discover something significant within these volumes, I shall render you additional payment."

Kelth began stammering his thanks and Eioth waited until the Elf ran out of words since he had already learned the futility of trying to interrupt him.

"Mitash," said Eioth. "Order the packaging of these books and send them on today in advance of our departure. No doubt we shall catch up with them on the road. Kelth, come with me. We have matters yet to discuss concerning the High Summer and Harvest Weather magics, those being your immediate magical needs. I can spare you three or four days more, Kelth, then I must leave in order to return home for my own High Summer Ritual and the gathering of the Synod."

"I am in your debt for any aid you can offer me, High Lord." Kelth glanced around the dusty room. "I believe the east courtyard is in better state than this chamber, if you would honor me? Shall we take some wine?"

"I do not drink wine, but I would prefer our discussion to be in less dusty air."

Eioth laid one hand over where the slim volume rested in his sash. Perhaps he should ask Mitash to watch for any other books on this subject as he packed.

No, it was better simply to ask him to put handwritten books in a marked box and go through them himself rather that reveal the subject of his interest. Bowing, Eioth gestured Kelth to precede him from the room, then took a few moments to give Mitash his orders before following.

***

Halidan tor Ephram ran one finger under the band of her headscarf, then tugged the damned thing off and tucked it into her sash. She didn't mind complying with the House rule requiring head coverings for mortal women – most of the time. The exception was during those few weeks of high and muggy summer, like today. Today her head felt as if it were melting from the inside.

Now it was approaching midday and the ancient schoolroom was filling with both light and heat. The old, dark wooden walls reflected the sunlight back toward the tall windows and the highly polished floors were almost too bright to look at.

A brief gesture from Halidan was enough to send two servants scurrying – soft footed – across the room to crank down the heavy outside awnings, effectively cutting the light in the room by half. However, the awnings – when combined with the linen window screens – cut off all stray breezes. By mid-afternoon this room would be insufferably hot, but there was no choice except to suffer. Elements prevented the daughters of the House from having any touch of the sun mar their alabaster skin.

I   f they actually had alabaster skin, it would have been more of a concern.

Silently, Halidan reprimanded herself for her unkind thoughts.

Calisa, the elder – her pale, rose-tinged complexion darkening as she concentrated – was currently standing in the center of the room, her hands curved across her chest as if cupping the breasts she did not yet have, as she assumed the Maiden Goddess posture. Halidan concentrated on keeping her expression blank as the Elvan girl slurred and stuttered her way through the graceful phrases of High Elvish Ritual Poetry.

Calisa shifted into the second posture – Invocation of Fertile Blessings–raised her hands above her head, drew in a deep breath, and began again, murdering ancient and profound words with poor cadence and worse pronunciation. Calisa managed Common and Low Court speech without difficulty, but the elegant and stately phrasing of High Court was beyond her, even after years of patient training, and the poor girl knew it. Worse, every time she made a mistake her face would redden and there was nothing, no cosmetic, no cream, that would keep her face the icy pale of the Traditional Beauty.

The youngest sister, Joian, snickered when Calisa stumbled for the third time, replacing the High Elvish word for *turning* with the Low Court word for *baby duck*.

"Joian. Silence," commanded Halidan. "Remember, it's your turn next and I am particularly interested in hearing your version of the Spring Awakening Ritual."

"But, it's summer," protested Joian.

"Spring will come again," said Halidan in her mildest voice.

It didn't help to become frustrated or angry with her students. They knew their value, their rank, and their mother's ambition. Being raged at by their mortal tutor wouldn't bother them at all. Particularly a tutor the mother despised.

It was Calisa's turn to snicker at her sister. Before a full-fledged fight could break out, Halidan clapped her hands.

"Enough, ladies. Your mother expects reports of your progress and a demonstration of skill at the end of this week. I cannot guarantee that she will ask for this season's Rituals. You must be expert with all."

Both girls fell silent with matching panicked expressions.

"Or," continued Halidan in a softer tone, "if you make a good effort I will hint to your mother that you demonstrate grace and beauty with one particular ritual–each. I will permit you to choose, but only after we have rehearsed them all. Remember, you must be perfect in the one you choose."

"Will that work?" asked Joian.

"We can only hope," muttered Halidan with a twist of her lips as she selected a small hand drum from a nearby table. She tapped out the rhythm of the Maiden Goddess Invocation – at less than half the proper speed. "Now, Calisa, say it with me."

Slowly, painstakingly, painfully, Halidan led the Elvan girl through the ritual. At half speed, and with another voice carrying the tune, Calisa managed to get through the first part of the Invocation without stumbling.

It was unlikely, in Halidan's opinion that either of the daughters of the Merchant House Pitchuri would ever be asked to perform the Rituals they were learning. The merchant family was Low Court Elvan by descent and the whole family together didn't have enough magic to light a prewarmed candle wick, let alone perform one of the major Rites. Nevertheless, the Matriarch demanded the girls learn the greater and lesser Rituals as well as all the graces and skills required of a Lady of a High Court House.

Halidan didn't mind the Matriarch's ambitions since it kept herself and her father well employed. Her father, as tutor to the boys of the House, and Halidan as tutor, companion, and good example to the young ladies.

Halidan's own knowledge of what was required from High Court families came from her unending reading of any book that came her way, and her father's guidance. Before she was born, her father had been employed for many years by a High Court family and it was he who taught her by his own example those little mannerisms that would never be found in a text. He also provided books on High Court protocols and the lineage and responsibilities of each High Court family.

Every time Halidan appeared before the Matriarch to report on the girls' progress it was clear to the ambitious Elf that Halidan possessed a higher level of the graces, language, and skills than her daughters could ever aspire to. Halidan's ash-white hair was an additional aggravation. To keep the peace her father decreed that Halidan's hair should be kept cut a bare half inch from her skull and she should wear the headscarves so fashionable amongst mortal women. Halidan obediently read to and taught, and felt more than a little sorry for the daughters of the House.

They were not particularly pretty, especially considering Calisa's unfortunate tendency to blush, nor were they talented to any extreme degree. They did have one virtue that gave their mother cause to hope and plan. They both had been born of an Elvan woman of provable fertility. Netha, wife of Pitchuri, had given her husband a total of five children. Five! And when there were High Court Houses who counted themselves lucky to produce one child in the current generation – and some Houses having difficulty producing that single one–Netha was certain her girls would find some House desperate enough for children to overlook Low birth and lack of magic and welcome a match.

Hadn't Merchant Pitchuri been voted head of his local guild mostly as an acknowledgment of his wife's fertility? Of that one skill envied by many–achievable by so very, very few. Impregnating his wife!

Several of the local Low Court Houses had already approached Pitchuri about alliances even though the girls were far from marriageable age, but Netha would not consider any of them. She was seeking nothing less than a High Court match. That alone explained her obsession about the girls' appearances.

Joian's hair was not sufficiently ash white for her mother's liking, being more a dull silver grey. Consequently, it was washed twice daily in a succession of mixtures all promising to bleach any pigment from the strands. Despite everything they did the girl's hair grew back in that same distressing color and she went through the day wrapped in a cloud of bleach, her hair brittle and stiff. Calisa was subjected to hour-long insult sessions delivered by her own mother, intended to train her out of her regrettable tendency to blush. The poor girl would become flustered as the hour for her abuse approached and she ended each day red faced and in tears. Halidan could not persuade the Matriarch that her plan was flawed and could only wait with cool cloths and soothing teas to settle the girl each evening.

In the center of the room Calisa waved her hands in what was supposed to be a gesture evoking clouds and uttered a phrase that, if she possessed the appropriate magic, would summon a rain of thin mud.

"Stop. Stop," cried Halidan, "Calisa. Please listen to the drum; it helps you. Let the rhythm shape the words in your mouth." Halidan gave a triple tap with the drum to warn her of the change in rhythm and started the second phase of the Invocation when the thunder of feet in the hallway outside distracted her student.

"Mother will have their heads if that's my brothers again," said Calisa, turning to face the door.

Before Halidan could respond the classroom door was flung open. She rose to reprimand whoever was disturbing the serenity of the House when the Matriarch Netha herself entered, her face stiff and stern. Three servants charged into the room on her heels and before Halidan could speak, two of them had seized Calisa and Joian and dragged them from the room. The third one approached Halidan, but did not touch her.

"Halidan tor Ephram, you are dismissed," said Netha. "Rise and leave at once."

By the Same Author

<u>BIO</u>:

D.L. Carter was decanted from her incubation pod in the outback of Australia many decades ago. This terrifying event was closely followed by shrieks of "There, there it goes, under the chair. Hit it with a brick!"

These valiant attempts to correct the existence of D.L. were, unfortunately, unsuccessful and she now resides in New Jersey, U.S., in a box with her toys, two human beings, and a variable number of cats.

Acknowledgments

I would like to acknowledge the hard work done by the staff of Corvallis Press. Wow, three grammatical errors per paragraph and you're still talking to me.

Copyright

RIDICULOUS

Copyright @ 2012 by D.L. Carter

Cover Design by Amber Scott
ebook: ISBN- 9781794241183

D.L. Carter LLC

East Brunswick NJ 08816

Made in the USA
Middletown, DE
31 May 2019